Suddenly the vines were shoved aside as three large golden fliers glided in, close enough for Varian to smell the aroma of fish and spice they exuded. Their long, pointed beaks had raised slightly, and she was being regarded by very keen and hostile eyes.

Very slowly, she extended her hand for the wing claw, its three digits lying loose. She took one between her thumb and forefinger and pressed very gently. Then, tentatively, the claw lightly closed about her fingers. . . .

THE MYSTERY OF IRETA

Dinosaur Planet

Dinosaur Planet Survivors

ANNE McCAFFREY

DEL REY

BALLANTINE BOOKS • NEW YORK

This novel is a work of fiction. Names, characters, and incidents either are products of the author's imagination or are used fictitiously.

A Del Rey® Book
Published by The Random House Publishing Group

Dinosaur Planet copyright © 1978 by Anne McCaffrey. First published in Great Britain by Futura Publications Limited in 1978.
Dinosaur Planet Survivors copyright © 1984 by Anne McCaffrey. First published in Great Britain by Futura Publications Limited in 1984.

THE DRAGONRIDERS OF PERN is a trademark of Anne McCaffrey. Reg. U.S. Pat. & Tm. Off.

All rights reserved under International and Pan-American Copyright Conventions. Published in the United States by The Random House Publishing Group, a division of Random House, Inc., New York, and simultaneously in Canada by Random House of Canada Limited, Toronto.

Del Rey is a registered trademark and the Del Rey colophon is a trademark of Random House, Inc.

www.delreydigital.com

ISBN 0-345-46721-3

Manufactured in the United States of America

First Edition: January 2004

OPM 10 9 8 7 6 5 4 3 2 1

DINOSAUR
PLANET

1

Kai heard Varian's light step echoing in the empty passenger section of the shuttlecraft just as he switched off the communications unit and tripped the tape into storage.

"Sorry, Kai, did I miss the contact?" Varian came in out of breath, her suit dripping wet, and bringing with her the pervasive stench of Ireta's "fresh" air, which tainted the filtered air of the shuttle's pilot cabin. She glanced from the unlit communications panel to his face to see if he was annoyed by her tardiness, but a triumphant grin cut through her feigned penitence. "We finally captured one of those herbivores!"

Kai had to grin in response to her elation. Varian would spend long hours tracking a creature in Ireta's damp, steaming, stinking jungles—hours of patient searching which all too often proved unproductive. Nevertheless, short of resorting to Discipline, Varian found it nauseatingly irksome to sit still in a comfortable chair through a Thek relay. Kai had wagered with himself that she would manage to avoid the tedious interchange with some reasonable excuse. Her news was good and her excuse valid.

"How'd you manage to capture one? Those traps you've been rigging?" he asked with genuine interest, though those same traps had taken his best mechanic and kept him from completing the seismic grid his geologists needed.

"No, not the traps." There was a hint of chagrin in Varian's tone. "No, the damned fool creature was wounded and couldn't run away with the rest of the herd." She paused to give her next statement full emphasis. "And, Kai, it bleeds blood!"

Kai blinked at her announcement. "So?"

"Red blood!"

"Well?"

"Are you a biological idiot? Red blood means hemoglobin . . ."

"What's odd about that? Plenty of other species use an iron base . . ."

"*Not* on the same planet with those aquatic squirmers Trizein's been dissecting. *They* have a pale viscous fluid." Varian was fleetingly contemptuous of his failure to recognize the significance. "This planet's one mass of anomalies, biological as well as geological. No ore where we should be striking pay dirt by the hopper-load, and me finding creatures larger than anything mentioned in text tapes from any planet in all the systems we've explored in the last four hundred galactic-standard years. Of course, it may be all of a piece," she added thoughtfully, as she pushed back the springy dark curls that framed her face.

She was tall, as were so many types born on a normal-gravity planet like Earth, with a slender but muscularly fit body which the one-piece orange ship suit displayed admirably. Despite the articles dangling from her force-screen belt, her waist was trim, and the bulges in her thigh and calf pouches did not detract from the graceful appearance of her legs.

Kai had been elated when Varian was assigned as his co-leader. They'd been more than acquaintances on shipboard ever since she had joined the *ARCT-10* as a xenob vet, on a three-galactic-standard-year contract. The *ARCT-10*—like her sister ships in the Exploratory and Evaluation Corps—had basic administrative and operations personnel who were ship-born and ship-bred. But the complement of additional specialists, trainees and, occasionally, high-echelon travelers for the Federated Sentient Planets changed continually, giving those on board the stimulation of meeting members of other cultures, subgroups, minorities and persuasions.

Kai had been attracted to Varian first, because she was an extremely pretty girl and second, because she was the opposite of Geril. He had been trying to end an unsatisfactory relationship with Geril, who had been so insistent that he'd had to change his quarters from the ship-born to the visitors' area of Earth-normal section in order to avoid her. Varian happened to be his new next-door neighbor. She was gay, bubbling with humor and intensely interested in everything about the satellite-sized exploratory vessel. She quickly infected him with her enthusiasm as she chivvied him into taking her on a guided tour of the various special quarters which accommodated the more esoteric sentient races of the FSP in their own atmosphere or gravity. Varian told him she'd been planet-bound—on how many diverse planets did not signify—so that she felt it was high time she saw how the Explorers and Evaluators lived. Especially since, she added, as a xenob vet, she often had to correct some of EV's crazier judgments and mistakes.

Varian was a good narrator, and her tales of planetary adventures, both as a youngster trailing after xenob vet parents and as junior in the same specialty, had fascinated Kai. He'd had the usual planetary tours to combat ship-conditioned agoraphobia, and indeed had spent a whole galactic year with his mother's parents on her birthworld. But he felt his must have been dull worlds in comparison to those responsible for Varian's wild and amusing experiences.

Another way in which Varian surpassed Geril was in her ability to argue pleasantly and effectively without losing her temper or wit. Geril had always been oppressively serious and too eager to denigrate anything which did not meet with her unconditional approval unconditionally. In fact, long before Kai heard that Varian was to be his co-leader, he had realized that she must have had Discipline, young as she appeared to be. He'd gone as far as to tap for a printout of her public history from the EV's data banks. Her list of assignments had been impressive even if the public record did not give any assessment of her value on those expeditions. However, he noticed she had been promoted rapidly—this, combined with the number of assignments, indicated a young woman slated for increasing responsibility and more difficult assignments. Granted her addition to the Iretan expedition had been made almost at the last minute when life-form readings had registered on the preliminary probe, but with her background Ireta ought not to post too many problems. Yet the planet was, as she'd said, rampant with anomalies.

"I suppose," she was saying, "if one has a third-generation sun with planets, one must expect peculiarities; such as Ireta, whose poles are hotter than its equator, stinking of—I'll remember the name of that plant yet . . ."

"Plant?"

"Yes. There's a small plant, hardy enough to be grown practically anywhere on temperate Earth-type worlds, which is used in cooking. In judicious quantities, let me add," she said with a wry grin. "Too much of it tastes like this planet smells. Sorry, I digress. What did the Theks say?"

Kai frowned. "Only the first reports have been picked up by our wandering Exploratory Vessel."

Busy mopping off the worst of her wetness, Varian turned to stare at him, towel suspended. "Fardles!" She sat slowly down in the chair next to him. "That's unnerving! Just the first?"

"That's what the Theks said . . ."

"Did you allow time enough for them to manage a reply? Scrub that question." Varian slumped against the backrest as she added, "Of course, *you* did," giving him full credit for his ability to deal with the slowest moving and speaking species in the Federated planets. "That's unlike EV. They're usually so desperately greedy for initial reports, not just for the all-safe-down."

"*My* explanation is that spatial interference . . ."

"Of course." Varian's face cleared of anxiety. "That cosmic storm the next system over . . . the one the astronomers were so hairy anxious to get to . . ."

"That's what the Theks say."

"In how many words?" asked Varian, her wry humor reasserting itself.

The Theks were a silicate life form, much like rock and extremely durable, and though not immortal, certainly the closest a species had evolved toward that goal. The irreverent said that it was difficult to know a Thek elder from a rock until it spoke, but a human could perish of old age waiting for the word. Certainly the older a Thek grew and the more knowledge he acquired, the longer it took to elicit an answer from him. Fortunately for Kai, there were two young Theks on the team sent to the seventh planet of this system. One of them, Tor, Kai had known all his life. In fact, though Tor was considered young in relation to the lifespan of his species, he had been on the *ARCT-10* since the exploratory vessel had been commissioned one hundred and fifty galactic-standard years before. Tor constantly confused Kai with his great-great-grandfather, who had been an engineering officer on the *ARCT-10* and whom Kai was said to resemble. It gave Kai a feeling of curious satisfaction to be on the same mission as a planetary co-leader with Tor. His conversation with Tor, while lengthened by space distance and Thek speech habits, was comparatively brisk.

"Tor had one word, actually, Varian. Storm." Kai added his laughter to Varian's.

"Have they ever been wrong?"

"What, Theks in error? Not in recorded history."

"Theirs? Or ours?"

"Theirs, of course. Ours is too short. Now, about that *red* blood?"

"Well, it's not just the red blood, Kai. There are far too many other unlikely coincidences. Those herbivores we've been shadowing are not only vertebrates and bleed red blood, but now that I've got close enough to have a good look, the things are pentadactyl, too." She opened and closed her fingers at him in a clawing motion.

"Theks are pentadactyl . . . after a fashion." Kai was well pleased they had no visual contact during the interchanges, as the Theks had an unnerving habit of extruding pseudopods from their amorphous mass, which tended to distract the viewer, sometimes to the point of nausea.

"But not vertebrate or red-blooded. And not coexistent with another totally different life form, like Trizein's marine squares." Varian fumbled at the opening of her belt pouch and withdrew a flat object, well wrapped in plastic. "It'll be interesting," she spread the syllables out, "to see the analysis of this blood sample." With a graceful push, she rose from the swivel chair and strode out of the pilot cabin, Kai following her.

Their boot heels echoed in the emptiness of the denuded passenger section. Its furnishinings now equipped the plastic domes grouped below the shuttle in the force-screened encampment. But Trizein's work was better accomplished in the air-conditioned storage compartment which had been converted into his laboratory. A terminal to the ship's computer had been rigged up in the lab so that Trizein rarely stirred from his domain.

"So you've finally got an occupant for your corral," Kai said.

Varian nodded. "See, I was right to plan ahead. At least we've a place big enough to stash him/it/her."

"Don't you know which sex?"

"When you see our beast, you'll understand why we haven't taken a close enough look to know." She shuddered suddenly. "I don't know what got to it, but whole chunks have been torn from its flank . . . almost as if . . ." She swallowed hastily.

"As if what?"

"As if something had been feeding on it—alive."

"What?" Kai felt his gorge rise.

"Those predators look savage enough to have done it . . . but while the creature was still living?"

The appalling concept silenced them both for several strides. A civilized diet no longer included animal flesh.

"I wonder if Tanegli's having any luck with those fruiting trees," she said, quickly redirecting the conversation.

"D'you know if he did take the youngsters with him? I was setting up the interchange."

"Yes," said Varian, "Divisti went, too, so the kids are in good hands."

"Just as well," said Kai a little grimly, "someone can manage them. I wouldn't relish explaining to the EV's third officer if anything happened to her pride and joy."

Out of the corner of his eye, Kai saw Varian bite her lip, her eyes sparkling with suppressed amusement. It was an embarrassingly well-known fact that young Bonnard had a case of hero worship for the team's male co-leader.

"Bonnard's a good kid, Kai, and means well . . ."

"I know. I know."

"I wonder if food on this planet tastes the way most things smell," said Varian, again changing the subject. "If fruit tastes of hydrotelluride . . ."

"Are we food-low?"

"No," said Varian, who was charged by the expedition's charter to procure any additional food suppliers needed. "But Divisti is a cautious soul. The less we use of the basic subsistence supplies, the better. And fresh fruit . . . you ship-bred types may not miss it . . ."

"Land-born primates have no dietary discipline."

They were both grinning, Varian cocking her head to one side, her gray eyes sparkling. The first day they'd met, at a table in the humanoid dining area of the huge EEC ship, they'd teased each other about dietary idiosyncrasies.

Born and brought up on the ship, Kai was used to synthesized foods and to the limited textures provided. Even when he'd been grounded for brief periods, he had never quite adjusted to the infinite variety and consistencies of natural foods. Varian had boasted that she could eat anything vegetable or mineral and had found the ship's diet, even when augmented from the life-support dome with freshly grown produce, rather monotonous.

"I'd call it educated tastes, man. And if the fruit tastes at all decent, you may be perverted to an appreciation of *real* food."

Just as they reached the lab, the panel shushed open, and an excited man came charging toward them.

"Marvelous!" He halted mid-stride and, losing his balance, staggered against the panel wall. "Just the people I need to see. Varian, the cell formation on those marine specimens is a real innovation. There are filaments, four different kinds . . . just take a look . . ." Trizein began pulling her back into his laboratory and gesturing urgently for Kai to follow.

"I've something for you, too, my friend." Varian extended the slide. "We caught one of those heavy-duty herbivores, wounded, bleeding red blood . . ."

"But don't you understand, Varian," Trizein continued, apparently deaf to her announcement, "this is a completely *different* life form. Never in all my expeditionary experience have I come across such a cellular formation . . ."

"Nor have I come across such an anomaly as this, contrasting to your new life form." Varian closed her fingers about the slide. "Do be a love and run a spectro analysis on this?"

"Red blood, you said?" Trizein blinked, changing mental gears to deal with Varian's request. He held the slide up to the light, frowning at it. "Red blood? Isn't compatible with what I've just told you."

At that moment, the alarm wailed unnervingly through the shuttle and the outside encampment and tingled jarringly at the wrist units that Kai and Varian wore as team leaders.

"Foraging party in trouble, Kai, Varian." Paskutti's voice, his thick slurred speech unhurried, came over the intercom. "Aerial attack."

Kai depressed the two-way button on his wrist unit. "Assemble your group, Paskutti. Varian and I are coming."

"Aerial attack?" asked Varian as both moved quickly to the iris lock of the shuttlecraft. "From what?"

"Is the party airborne, Paskutti?" Kai asked.

"No, sir. I have coordinates. Shall I call in your teams?"

"No, they'd be too far out to be useful." To Varian he said, "What *can* they have got into?"

"On this crazy planet? Who knows?" Varian seemed to thrive on the various alarms Ireta produced, for which Kai was glad. On his second expedition, the co-leader had been such a confirmed pessimist that the morale of the entire party had deteriorated, causing needless disastrous incidents.

As usual, the first blast of Ireta's odorous atmosphere took Kai's breath away. He'd forgotten to replace the deodorizing plugs he'd removed while in the shuttle. The plugs helped but not when one was forced to breathe through his mouth, as he was while running to join Paskutti's rapidly forming squad.

Though the heavy-worlders under Paskutti's direction had had farther to come, they were the first to arrive at the assembly point as Kai and Varian belted down the slope from the shuttle to the force-screen veil lock. Paskutti shoved belts, masks and stunners at the two leaders, forgetting in the urgency of the moment that the casual thrust of his heavy hand rocked the light-framed people back on their heels.

Gaber, the cartographer who was emergency duty officer, came puffing down from his dome. As usual, he'd forgotten to wear his force-screen belt though there was a standing order for those belts to be worn at all times. Kai would tag Gaber for that when they got back.

"What's the emergency? I'll never get those maps drawn with all these interruptions."

"Forage party's in trouble. Don't wander off!" said Kai.

"Oh, never, Kai, never will I do anything so simple-witted. I assure you. I shan't move from the controls one centimeter, though how I'm ever to finish *my* work . . . Three days behind now and . . ."

"Gaber!"

"Yes, Kai. Yes, I understand. I really do." The man seated himself at the veil controls, glancing so anxiously from Paskutti to Varian that Kai had to nod at him reassuringly. Paskutti's heavy face remained expressionless, as did his dark eyes; but somehow the heavy-worlder's very silence could indicate disapproval or disgust more acutely than anything he might have growled.

Paskutti, a man in his middle years, had been in ship security for most of his five-year tour with EEC. He had volunteered for this assignment when the call had gone through the mother ship for secondaries to assist a xenob team. Heavy-worlders often took semi-skilled tours on other worlds on the EEC ships as the pay was extremely good. Two or three tours would mean that a semi-skilled individual could earn enough credit to live the rest of his or her life in relative comfort on one of the developing worlds. Heavy-worlders were preferred as secondaries, whatever their basic specialty might be, because of their muscular strength. They were paid to be the muscles of humanoid FSP, generally a comment made respectfully, since the heavy-worlders were not just muscle men but numbered as many high-ranking specialists as any other humanoid subgroup.

There was, however, no question that their sheer physical presence—the powerful legs, the compact torso, massive shoulders, weather-darkened skin—provided a visual deterrent that prompted many sentient groups to hire them as security forces, whether merely for display or as actual aggressive units. Contributing to the false notion that heavy-worlders were ill-equipped with mental abilities was the unfortunate genetic problem that, though their muscle and bone structure had adjusted to bear the heavy gravities, their heads had not. Consequently, at first glance they did look stupid. Away from the harsh gravity and climactic conditions that bred them, heavy-worlders also had to spend a good deal of their time in heavy-grav gyms to maintain their muscular strength and to enable them to make a satisfactory adjustment when they returned to their home worlds. Perversely enough, the heavy-worlders were intensely attached to their natal worlds, and most of them, having made their credit balance high enough to retire in comfort, happily returned to the cruel conditions that had developed their subgrouping.

Paskutti and Tardma had joined the expedition out of sheer boredom with their shipboard security duties. Berru and Bakkun as geologists had been Kai's own choices since it was always good to have a few heavy-worlders on any team for the advantage of their physical attributes. Both he and Varian had been pleased when Tanegli, as botanist, and Divisti, as biologist, had answered the request for such specialists. When they had made planetfall and Varian had seen the unexpectedly large type of animal life which populated Ireta, she had blessed the heavy-worlders on her team. Whatever emergency they were going to meet now would be approached with much more confidence in such company.

Paskutti nodded at Gaber as the cartographer's hands twitched above the veil controls. Slowly the veil lifted while Varian, by Kai's side, shuffled with impatience. One couldn't fuss Gaber by reminding him that this was an emergency and speed was essential.

Paskutti ducked under the lifting veil, charging out, the squad at his heels, before Gaber had completed the opening. It was, as usual, raining a thin mist, which except for the heavier drops, had been deflected by the main screen as had the insects small enough to be fried by contact.

They could hear Gaber muttering anxiously under his breath about people never waiting for anything as Paskutti gave the closed-fist upward gesture that meant sky-trailing. The rescuers activated their lift-belts and assumed the formation assigned them at Paskutti's original briefing on emergency procedures. Kai and Varian were in the protected positions of the flying *V* formation.

Aloft, Kai turned his combutton to home in on Tanegli's signal. Paskutti gestures westward, toward the swampy lowlands, and indicated speed increase as his other hand adjusted his mask.

They flew at treetop level, Kai remembering to keep his eyes horizontal, on Paskutti's back. Oddly enough his tinge of agoraphobia bothered him less in the air, as long as he didn't look directly down at the fast-moving ground. He was cushioned by the air-stream of his passage, an almost tactile support at this speed. The monotonous floor of conifers and gymnosperms which dotted this part of the continent waved briefly at their passage. High, high above, Kai caught a glimpse of circling winged monsters. Varian hadn't yet had a chance to identify or telltale any of the aerial life forms: the creatures warily made themselves scarce when the explorers were abroad in lift-belts or sleds.

They increased altitude to maneuver the first of the basaltic clines and then glided down the other side, skimming the endless primeval forest, its foliage in ever-varied patterns of blue-green, green and green-purple. They met the first of the thermal downdrafts and had to correct, buffeted by the air currents. Paskutti signaled descent as the best solution. For him, it was, with his bulk of heavy grav-trained muscles, flesh and bone, but Kai and Varian had to keep compensating with their lift-belts' auxiliary thrust jets.

As the buzz of the homer intensified, Kai began to berate himself. He ought not to have allowed any exploratory groups beyond a reasonable lift-belt radius of the compound. On the other hand, Tanegli was perfectly capable of combating most of the life forms so far seen here while dealing with the exuberant nature of the youngsters in his charge. So what aerial trouble could they have fallen into? And so quickly. Tanegli had left in the sled just prior to Kai's scheduled contact with the Theks. They could barely have made their destination before running afoul of whatever it was. Tanegli would surely have mentioned any casualty. Then Kai wondered if the sled had been damaged. They'd only the one big unit and the four two-man sleds for his seismic teams. The smaller sleds could, in a pinch, take four passengers, but no equipment.

The land dropped away again and they corrected their flight line. Far in the purple distance the first range of volcanoes could be seen on the edge of the inland sea—a lake that was doomed to be destroyed by the restless tectonic action of this very active world. That was the first area he'd had tested for its seismicity because he'd worried that perhaps their granite shelf might be too close to tectonic activity and would turn mobile. But the first print-out of the cores had been reassuring. The lake would subside, probably giving way to small hills pushed up from beneath, clad with sediment and eventually folded under, for this was the near edge of the stable continental shelf on which the encampment had been placed.

The steamy, noxiously scented heat of the swamp-lands began to rise to meet them; cloying humidity intensified the basic hydrotelluride stench. The homer's buzz grew louder and became continuous.

Kai was not the only member of the party scanning ahead. Far-sighted Paskutti saw the sled first, in a grove of angiosperms, parked on a sizable hummock that jutted into the swamp, away from the firmer mass of the jungle. The great purple-barked, many-rooted branches of the immense trees, well-scarred by herbivorous assaults, were untenanted by avian life, and Kai was beginning to feel the anger of relief overcome concern.

Paskutti's arm gesture caught his attention and he followed the line of the heavy-worlder's sweep toward the swamp, where several tan objects were slowly being dragged under the water by the pointed snouts of the swamp-dwellers. A minor battle began as two long-necked denizens contended for the possession of one corpse. The victor claimed the spoils by the simple expedient of sitting on the body and sinking with it into the muddy waters.

Tardma, the heavy-worlder directly in front of Kai, pointed in the other direction, toward firmer land, where a winged creature, obviously recovering from a stun blast, was swaying upright.

Paskutti fired a warning triplet and then motioned the group to land on the inland side of the grove. They came to a running stop, the heavy-worlders automatically deploying toward the swamp since the likelihood of attack was from that quarter. Kai, Varian and Paskutti jogged toward the sled from behind which the foragers now emerged.

Tanegli stood waiting, his squat solid bulk a bastion around which the smaller members of the party ranged. The three youngsters, Kai was relieved to see, appeared to be all right, as did the xenobotanist, Divisti. Then Kai noticed the small pile of assorted brilliant yellow objects in the storage cage of the sled: more of similar shape and color were strewn about the clear ground of the small grove.

"We called prematurely," said Tanegli by way of greeting. "The swamp creatures proved curious allies." He replaced his stunner in his belt and dusted his thick hands as if dismissing the incident.

"What was attacking you?" Varian asked, staring about her.

"These?" asked Paskutti as he dragged a limp, furred and winged creature from behind the trunk of a thick tree.

"Watch out!" said Tanegli, reaching to his belt before he saw the stunner in Paskutti's. "I set the gun on a light charge."

"It's one of those gliders. See, no socket for the wing to fold," Varian said, ignoring the protests of the heavy-worlders as she moved the limp wings out and back.

Kai eyed the pointed beak of the creature with apprehension, suppressing an irrational desire to step back.

"Carrion-eater by the size and shape of that jaw," remarked Paskutti, peering with considerable interest.

"Well and truly stunned," Varian said with a final twitch of arrangement to the wings. "What was dead enough to attract it here?"

"That!" Tanegli pointed to the edge of the clearing, to a mottled brown bundle, its belly swelling up out of the coarse vegetation.

"And I rescued this!" said Bonnard, stepping clear of his friends so that Kai and Varian saw the small replica of the dead animal in his arms. "But it didn't bring the gliders. They were already here. It's very young. And its mother is dead now."

"We found it over there, hiding in the roots of the tree," said Cleiti, loyally supporting her friend, Bonnard, against adult disapproval.

"The sled must have alarmed the gliders," said Tanegli, taking up the story, "driven them away from her. Once we had landed and started collecting the fruit, they returned." He shrugged his wide shoulders.

Varian was examining the shivering little creature, peering into its mouth, checking its feet. She gave a little laugh. "Anomaly time again. Perissodactyl feet and herbivorous teeth. There's a good fellow. Nice to have something your own size, isn't it, Bonnard?"

"Is it all right? It just shivers." Bonnard's face was solemn with worry.

"I'd shiver too if I got picked up by huge things that didn't smell right."

"Then perisso . . . whatever it is, isn't dangerous?"

Varian laughed and ruffled Bonnard's short-cropped hair. "No, just a way of classifying it. Perissodactyl means uneven-numbered toes. I want a look at its mother." Careful of the nearby sword plants with their deceptively decorative purple stripe leaves, she made her way toward the dead creature. A long low whistle broke from her lips. "I suppose it's possible," she said in a sympathetic tone of voice. "Well, her leg's broken. That's what made her fair game to the scavengers."

A loud noise attracted everyone's attention: an ominous sucking sound. From the swamp a huge head and neck broke the slimy surface and wavered in their direction.

"We could be considered fair game, too, by such as that," said Kai. "Let's get out of here."

Paskutti frowned at the great and evil-looking head, fingering his stunner onto the strongest setting. "That creature would require every charge we have to stop it."

"We came for fruit . . ." Divisti said, pointing to the litter in the clearing. "They *look* viable, and fresh food would do us all good," she added with as wistful a tone as Kai had ever heard from a heavy-worlder.

"I'd say we had a safety factor of about ten minutes before that swamp creature's brain can make the logical assumption that we're edible," said Tanegli, as unconcerned as ever by physical threat. He began to gather up the scattered thick-skinned fruits and toss them into the storage cage of the six-man sled.

In point of fact, those sleds had been known to lift twenty, a capability never mentioned in the designers' specifications. The exploratory sled was an all-purpose vehicle, its ultimate potential not yet realized. High-sided and slightly more than eight meters long, with a closed deck forward for storage, the compact engine and power pack sat under the rear loading space. The vessel could be fitted with comfortable seating for six as well as the pilot and copilot, with the storage cage, as it was now. When the seating was removed or lashed to the deck, a sled could carry enormous weight, on board or attached to the powerful winches fore, aft and midships on either side. The plascreen could be retracted into the sides or raised in sections. The sled had both retro and forward jets with a vertical life ability, which could be used in defense or emergency flight. The two-man sleds were smaller replicas of the big one and had the advantage of being easily dismantled and stored: in flight, usually in the larger vehicle.

Augmented by the rescue squad, the foragers accumulated enough fruit to fill the sled's storage cage in the time it took more carrion-eaters to begin spiraling above the grove. The swamp head seemed mesmerized by the comings and goings of the group, swinging slowly back and forth.

"Kai, we don't have to leave him here, do we?" asked Bonnard with an apprehensive Cleiti by his side. He had the orphan in his arms.

"Varian? Any use to you?"

"Certainly. I'd no intention of leaving it. It's a relief not to have to chase something over the continent to get a close look." She frowned at the suggestion of abandonment. "Into the sled with you, Bonnard. Keep a hold on it. Cleiti, you sit on his right, I'll sit left. There we are. Belt up."

The others stood back as Tanegli took off in the sled, gliding insolently over the ooze and the undecided beast that still regarded the grove with unblinking interest.

"Set for maximum stun," Paskutti told them, glancing overhead. "Those carrion-eaters are coming in again."

Even as the rescuers lifted from the ground, Kai saw the carrion fliers circling downward, their heads always on the dead creature in the grass below. Kai shuddered. The dangers of space, instant and absolute, were impersonal and the result of breaking immutable laws. The deadly intent of these things held a repulsively personal malevolence that disturbed him profoundly.

2

RAIN and headwinds buffeted the airborne V so steadily on their way back that the heavily powered sled had long since landed when Kai and the heavy-worlders finally set foot in the compound. Varian and the three children were busy constructing a small run for the orphan.

"Lunzie's trying to deduce a diet," Varian told Kai.

"Just what is its anomalous state?"

"Against every odd in the galaxy, we have succored a young mammal. At least its mother had teats. It's not very old, born rather mature, you see, able to walk and run almost at birth . . ."

"Did you . . ."

"Debug it? Externally yes. Had to or we'd all be hosting parasites. I've interrupted more of Trizein's carefully scheduled work to run a tissue sample on it so we can figure out what proteins it must have in its diet. It's got some growing to do to reach momma's size. Not that she was very large."

Kai looked down at the tiny creature's red-brown-furred body: a very unprepossessing creation, he thought, with no redeeming feature apart from wistful eyes to endear it to anyone other than its own mother. But, remembering the waving swamp-dweller's head, and the hungry malice in the circling scavengers' relentless approach, he was glad they'd brought the thing in. Besides, it might occupy Bonnard and keep the boy from following him everywhere.

Kai stripped off his belt and face mask, rubbing at the strap marks. He was tired after the return trip. The heavy-worlders had immense resources of stamina, but Kai's ship-trained muscles ached from the exertions of the morning.

"Say, don't we have to contact the Ryxi, too?" Varian asked, glancing at her wrist recorder and tapping the reddened 1300 that meant a special time.

Kai grinned his thanks for the reminder and made for the shuttlecraft with a fair display of energy. There was still a lot of busy day ahead of him. He'd get a pepper to pick his energy level up, and he'd get a bit of a breather while he made contact with the avians. Then he had to go see that complex of colored lakes Berru had documented yesterday in her sweep south. He found it damned odd there were no more than traces of the normal metals you'd think would be in abundance everywhere on this untouched planet. Colored waters indicated mineral deposits. He only hoped the concentrations were heavy enough to make them worthwhile. There ought to be something in old fold mountains, if only some tin or zinc and copper. They'd found ore minerals but no deposits worth the name.

Kai's orders from Exploratory and Evaluation Corps were to locate and assay the mineral and metallurgical potential of this planet. And Ireta, a satellite of a suspected third generation sun, ought to be rich in the heavier elements, rich in the transuranics and actinides, neptunium, plutonium and the more esoteric of the rare elements above uranium on the periodic table, so urgently and constantly required by the Federation of Sentient Populations, the search for which was one of the primary tasks of the EEC.

The diplomatic might say that EEC was exploring the galaxy, seeking to bring within its sphere of influence all rational sentient beings, augmenting the eighteen peace-loving species already incorporated in the FSP. But the search for energy was the fundamental drive. The diversity of its member species gave the Federation the ability to explore more types of planets, but colonization was incidental to exploitation.

The three useful planets of the sun Arrutan had long been marked on star charts as promising, but only recently had the Executive Council decided to mount the present three-part expedition. Kai had heard the rumor that it was because the Theks wished to be included. This rumor was partially substantiated during his private conference with the EEC chief officer on board the exploratory vessel *ARCT-10*. The CO had privately informed Kai that the Theks had superior control of the three teams, and he was to consider himself under their orders if they chose to supersede him. Vrl, the Ryxi team leader, had been given the same orders, but everyone knew the Ryxi. Furthermore, it was common knowledge that having a Thek on a team spelled ultimate success: Theks were dependable, Theks were thorough, the ultimate altruists. The cynics replied that altruism was easy when a creature calculated its life span in thousands of years. The Theks had elected to be placed on the seventh world of the primary, a heavy-metal, heavy-gravity planet, exactly suited to Theks.

The light-cored planet, fifth from the sun Arrutan, with a low gravity and temperate climate, was being evaluated by the Ryxi, an aerial species that was in critical need of new planets to relieve their population pressure, and give industry and opportunity to the restless young.

Kai's assignment, the fourth planet in the system, exhibited curious anomalies. Originally designated a second-generation sun, with elements up to transuranic, Arrutan patently did not conform to that classification. A probe sent out for a preliminary survey registered that the fourth planet was undeniably ovoid in shape; the poles were hotter than the equator: the seas registered warmer than the land mass which covered the northern pole. There was almost constant rainfall and an inshore wind of variable velocities up to full-gale force. An axial tilt of some fifteen degrees had been postulated. The readings indicated life forms in water and on land. A xenobiological team was added to the geological.

Kai had requested a remote sensor to locate the ore concentrations, but at that point the storm in the very next system had been sighted and he found his request very low on the priority list. He was told that the original probe tapes would give him ample information to locate metal and mineral, and to get the job done *in situ*. Right now *ARCT-10* had an unparalleled opportunity to observe free matter in action.

Kai took the official brush-off in good part. What he did object to was having the youngsters dumped on his hands at the last minute. To his complaint that this was a working expedition, not a training exercise, he was told that the ship-born must have sufficient planetary experiences early in their lives to overcome the danger of conditioned agoraphobia. The hazard was not to be dismissed lightly by the ship-born: useless to explain to the planet-bred. But Kai railed against the expediency that made his team the one to expand the horizons of three members who were only half into their second decades. This planet was exceedingly active, volcanically and tectonically, and dangerous for ship-bred juveniles. The two girls, Cleiti and Terilla, were biddable and no trouble until Bonnard, the son of the third officer of the EV, instigated all manner of hazard-strewn games.

The very first day, while Kai and his team were dropping cores around the landing site to be sure they had landed on the more stable continental shield, Bonnard had gone exploring and had lacerated a protective suit because he hadn't remembered to activate the force-field. He had stumbled into a sword plant, as pretty as the harmless decorative plants in the EV's conservatory but able to slice flesh and suit to ribbons with the most negligible of contacts. There had been other incidents in the nine days since the party had landed. While the other team members seemed to make light of the boy's escapades and were amused by his adoration of Kai, the team leader sincerely hoped the little orphaned beast would divert Bonnard.

Kai took a long sip of pepper, its tart freshness soothing his nerves as well as his palate. He glanced down at his recorder, switched on the comunit, arranged the recording equipment to the speed necessary to slow the Ryxi speech pattern into understandable tones for later review. He could generally keep up with their rippling voices but a tape helped to resolve any questions.

Kai had been designated the liaison officer between the two groups. He had the patience and tact required for dealing with the slow Thek, and the ear and wit to keep up with the quick aerial Ryxi, who could never have communicated with the Thek and with whom the Thek preferred not to bother.

Right on time the Ryxi leader, Vrl, made the contact, trilling out the courtesies. Kai relayed the information that only the first reports from each of the teams had been picked up by the EV and reported his belief that the spatial storm viewed before the exploratory groups had left the ship must be causing sufficient interference to prevent a pickup of other reports.

Vrl, politely slowing his speech to a rate which must have been frustrating to him, said that he wasn't worried; that was for the Slows to fret about. Vrl's first report was the important one for his people: it confirmed the initial probe analysis that this planet contained no indigenous intelligent life form and could adequately support his race. Vrl was forwarding by interplanetary drone a full report for Kai's interest. Vrl ended by saying that all were in good health and full feather. Then he asked what winged life had been observed on Ireta.

Kai told him, speaking as fast as he could get the words past his teeth, that they had observed several aerial life forms from a distance and would investigate further when possible. He refrained from naming one form as the scavengers they were but promised, at Vrl's liquidly trilled request, to forward a full tape when completed. The Ryxi as a species had one gross sin: they hated to think that another aerial life form might one day challenge their unique position in FSP. This prejudice was one reason why Ryxi were not often included in EV complements. The other valid reason was that Ryxi fretted in enclosed spaces to the point of suicide. Very few bothered to qualify for Exploratory Services since they were so psychologically ill-suited to the life. Necessity had forced them into this mission and most of the members had spent the journey time in cryonic suspension. Vrl had been awakened two ship weeks before touchdown to be apprised of the necessary routine of report and contact with the other two sections. While Vrl, like all his ilk, was an interesting creature, vital, flamboyant with his plumage and personality, Kai and Varian were relieved to have the Theks along as balance.

"Did Vrl remember to be there?" asked Varian, entering the control cabin.

"Yes, and all's well with him, though he's mighty curious about winged life here."

"They always are, those jealous feathers!" Varian made a face. "I remember a deputation from Ryxi at the University on Chelida. They wanted to vivisect those winged tree Rylidae from Eridani V."

Kai suppressed a sympathetic shudder. He wasn't surprised. The Ryxi were known to be bloody-minded. Look at their courtship dance—males armed with leg spurs and the victor usually *killing* his opponent. You couldn't quite excuse that on the grounds of survival of the fittest. You didn't have to kill to improve the genotype.

"Is there another pepper going? I've been *trying* to keep up with my teammates." She slid into the chair.

Kai snorted at that folly and handed her a container of stimulant, chuckling.

"I know we don't have to keep up with the heavy-worlders," Varian said with a groan, "and I know that they know that we can't, but *I* can't help *trying*!"

"It's frustrating. I know."

"So do I. Oh, Trizein says the little creature is indeed a mammal and will need a lactoprotein, heavy in calcium, glucose, salt and a good dollop of phosphates."

"Can Divisti and Lunzie whomp something up?"

"Have done. Bonnard is feeding . . . or should I say, attempting to feed Dandy."

"It's named already?"

"Why not? It certainly isn't programmed to answer a meal call—yet."

"Intelligent?"

"Of a restricted sort. It's already programmed to a certain number of instinctive responses, being born fairly mature."

"Is that herbivore of yours mammalian?"

"Nooooo . . ."

"What's the yes in that no for?"

"Granted the viviparous and oviparous types often coexist on a planet . . . and that you'd get some very odd gene specialization to cope with environment here, but I cannot rationalize that aquatic-life cell formation with Dandy or with that big herbivore.

"And speaking of that beast, Trizein says its cell structure is remarkably familiar: he's going to do an in-depth comparison. In the meantime, I've his okay to use a CHCL3 gas on it so we can dress those wounds before they turn septic. Can we rig a force-screen arc over that corral we erected so the wound can be kept free of blood-sucking organisms while it heals?" When Kai nodded, she continued. "And would you also ask your core teams to keep an eye out for any scavengers circling? Whatever wounded the herbivore probably attacks other animals. One, I'd like to know what kind of predator is that savage to its prey; and two, there's always a chance that we can find amenable specimens by saving their lives. They're so much easier to capture when they're too weak to struggle or run."

"Aren't we all? I'll give the word to my teams. Only don't make this compound a veterinary hospital, will you, Varian? We don't have the space."

"I know, I know. Those that are large enough to fend for themselves go into the corral anyhow."

They rose, both revived by the peppers. But their brief

respite in the conditioned air of the shuttle made that first step outside a gasper.

"Man is an adaptable creature," Kai told himself under his breath, "flexible, comprehending his universe, a high-survival type. But did we have to get a planet that reeks?"

"Can't win 'em all, Kai," said Varian with a laugh. "Besides, I find this place fascinating." She left him standing in the open lock.

The rain had stopped, Kai noticed, at least for the moment. The sun peered through the cloud cover, getting ready to steam bake them for a while. With the cessation of rain, Ireta's insect battalions once more flung themselves against the force-screen that arched above the compound. Blue sparks erupted as the smaller creatures were incinerated, glowing blue where larger organisms were stunned by the charge.

He gazed over the compound, experiencing a certain sense of accomplishment. Behind him, and above the compound itself, was the tough ceramic-hulled shuttlecraft, twenty-one meters long, with its nose cone blackened by the friction heat of entering Ireta's atmosphere. Its stubby glide wings were retracted now, leaving it slightly ovoid in shape, the central portion being larger than either end. From its top blossomed the communications spire and the homing device that would guide in its children-sleds. Unlike early models of the compound-ship-to-planet shuttle, most of the vessel was cargo and passenger space since the incredibly efficient Thek-designed power packs which utilized an established isotope were compact and no longer took up the bulk of the shuttle's interior. An additional benefit of the Thek power pack was that lighter-weight ships, which had the specially developed ceramic hulls, could deliver the same payload as the structurally reinforced titanium-hulled vessels which were needed for the antiquated fission and fusion drives. The shuttle rested on a shelf of granite which, spreading out and down, formed a shallow amphitheatre, roughly four hundred meters in diameter. Varian had pointed out that the shuttle's first touchdown had been smack in the middle of some animal route, to judge by the well-trampled dirt. Kai had not needed any urging to change site. Open vistas might give you a chance to assess visitors, but it was a bit much for his ship-trained eyes.

Force-screen posts surrounded the present encampment in which temporary living, sleeping and working domes had been erected. Water, tapped from an underground source, had to be softened and filtered. Even so, those like Varian, who were less used to recycled water, which always tasted faintly of chemicals, grumbled about its mineral flavor.

Divisti and Trizein had tested several forms of Iretan vegetation and succulents, finding them safe for human consumption. Divisti and Lunzie had collaborated and produced a pulp from the greenery that might be nutritionally correct but had such a nauseating taste and curious consistency that only the heavy-worlders would eat it. But they were known to eat anything. Even, it was rumored, animal flesh.

Nonetheless, for the short time they'd been on Ireta, Kai was pleased with their accomplishments. The camp was securely situated in a protected position, on a stable shield land mass composed of basement rock that tested out 3000MY. There was an ample water supply and an indigenous resource of synthesizable food at hand.

A faint uneasiness nagged at him suddenly. He wished that the EV had stripped more reports from the satellite beamer. It was probably nothing more than interference from that spatial storm. The EV, having established that all three expeditions were functioning might have no reason to strip the beamer for a while. It would be back this way in a hundred days or so. This was a routine expedition. So was EV's interest in the storm. Unless, of course, the EV had run into the Others.

Peppers made you hyperimaginative as well as energetic, Kai told himself firmly as he started down the incline to the floor of the compound. The Others were products of myth, made up to frighten bad children, or childlike adults. Nonetheless, EEC units occasionally found dead planets and passed likely systems interdicted on the charts for no ostensible reason though their planets would certainly have been suitable to one or another member of the Federation . . .

Kai became angry with himself and, forcing down such reflections, tramped through the alien dust to Gaber's dome.

The cartographer had returned to his patient translating of taped recordings to the master chart, over which the probe photos were superimposed. As Kai's teams brought more detailed readings, Gaber updated the appropriate grid and removed the photo. At the moment, the tri-d globe looked scabrous. In the other half of the dome was the seismic screen which Portegin was setting up. Glancing quickly past it, Kai thought Portegin was losing his knack—the screen was on and registering far too many core-points, some barely visible.

"I'm days behind myself. I told you that, Kai," said Gaber, his aggrieved tone somewhat counterbalanced by a rueful smile. He straightened, twisting his neck to relieve taut muscles. "And I'm glad you've come because I cannot work with Portegin's screen. He says it's finished, but you can see it's not functioning correctly."

Gaber swung his gimbaled chair about and pointed his inking pen at the core monitor screen.

Kai gave a closer look and then began to fiddle with the manual adjustments.

"You see what I mean? Echoes! And then faint responses where I know perfectly well your teams have not had a chance to lay cores. Here in the south and the southeast . . ." Gaber was tapping the screen with his pen. "Unless, of course, your teams are duplicating efforts . . . but the readings would be clearer. So I have to assume that the machine itself is malfunctioning."

Kai barely attended to Gaber's complaints. In his belly a coldness formed, a coldness that came from thinking about the Others. But, if it had been the Others who laid the faintly responding cores, then surely this planet would have been interdicted. One thing was positive in Kai's mind: his teams had not set those other lights, nor duplicated work.

"Most interesting, Gaber," he replied with a show of an indifference he was far from feeling. "Obviously from an older survey. This planet's been in EEC library for a long time, you know. And cores are virtually indestructible. See here, in the north, where the fainter cores leave off? That's where the plate action has deformed the landmass into those new fold mountains."

"Why didn't we have those old records. Of course, a prior survey would account for why we haven't found anything more than traces of metal and mineral deposits here." Gaber meant the continental shield. "But why, under a logical regime, no mention is made of a previous seismic history, I simply cannot understand."

"Oh, it is old, and probably got erased for modern programs. A computer does not have an infinite capacity for data storage."

Gaber snorted. "Scorching odd, I call it, to send down an expedition without the full facts at their disposal."

"Perhaps, but it'll cut down on our time here; some of our work's already done."

"Cut down on our time here?" Gaber gave a derisive laugh. "Not likely."

Kai turned slowly to stare at the man. "What maggot's in your mind now, Gaber?"

Gaber leaned forward, despite the fact the two men were alone in the dome. "We could have been . . ." he hesitated, "planted!"

"Planted?" Kai let out a shout. "Planted? Just because the seismic shows old cores here?"

"Wouldn't be the first time the victims weren't told."

"Gaber, we've got the third officer's beloved and only offspring with us. We'll be picked up."

Gaber remained obdurate.

"There'd be no point in planting us. Besides, what about the Ryxi and the Theks."

Gaber snorted scornfully. "The Theks don't care how long they stay anywhere. They live practically forever, and the Ryxi were to plant anyhow, weren't they? And it isn't *just* those cores that convince me. I've thought so a long time— ever since I knew we had a xenobiologist and heavy-worlders with us."

"Gaber!" Kai spoke sharply enough to startle the older man, "you will not mention planting to me again, nor to anyone else in this expedition. That is an order!"

"Yes, sir. I'm sure it is, sir."

"Further, if I find you without your belt one more time . . ."

"Sir, it pokes me in the gut when I'm bending over the board," Gaber said as he hurriedly began fastening on the force-screen belt.

"Leave the belt slack, then, and turn the buckle to one side, but wear it! Now, bring your recorder and some fresh tapes. I want to recon those lakes Berru charted . . ."

"That was only yesterday, and as I told you I am three days behind . . ."

"All the more reason for us to check those lakes out personally. I've got to show some progress in my next report to EV on deposits. And . . ." Kai tapped out a code, waiting impatiently at the terminal for the print-out on the mysterious core sites, "we'll do a ground check on a couple of these."

"Well, now, it'll be good to get away from the board. I haven't done any field work yet on this expedition," said Gaber, pressing closed his jumpsuit fastenings. He reached for the recording unit and tape blanks which he distributed in leg pouches.

His tone was so much brighter and less foreboding that Kai wondered if he'd been unfair to keep the man continually in the dome. Could that be why Gaber had come up with the astounding notion that they'd been planted? Too little action narrowed perceptions.

But Gaber, as witness his laxity over the belt, was so nard-ing absent-minded that he was more of a liability than the youngest youngster in the landing party. As Kai recalled, Gaber's credentials rated him as ship-bred, having made only four expeditions in his six decades. This would likely be the last if Kai made an honest report of his efficiency. Unless, the insidious thought plagued Kai, they had indeed been planted. Better than most leaders, Kai knew how undermining such a rumor could be. Yes, it would be better to keep Gaber so fully occupied that he had no time for reflection.

Kai did, however, have to remind Gaber to strap himself into the sled seat, which the cartographer did with profuse apologies, while Kai checked the sled's controls and energy levels.

"I do wish I'd been born a Thek," Gaber said. "To live long enough to watch the evolution of a world. Ah, what an opportunity!"

Kai chuckled. "If they're not too involved with thinking to look around in time."

"They never forget a thing they've seen or heard."

"How could one tell? It takes a year to carry on any sort of a dialogue with an Elder."

"You young people can only think of quick returns. Not end results. It's the end result that counts. Over the course of my years on *ARCT-10*, I've had many meaningful chats with Theks. The older ones, of course."

"Chats? How long a lag between sentences?"

"Oh, not long. We'd scheduled replies on a once-a-ship-week basis. I found it extremely stimulating to formulate the most information in the fewest phrases."

"Oh, I'll grant the Theks are past masters at the telling phrase."

"Why, even a single word can have unusual significance when uttered by a Thek," Gaber went on with unexpected volubility, "When you can appreciate fully that each Thek holds within its brain the total knowledge of its own forebears, and can distill this infinite wisdom in single succinct words or phrases . . ."

"No perspective . . ." Kai was concentrating on lifting the sled out of the compound.

"I beg your pardon?" Gaber's apology was more of a reprimand.

"Their wisdom is Thek wisdom and is not readily applicable to our human conditions."

"I never implied that it was. Or should be." Gaber was distinctly annoyed with Kai.

"No, but wisdom should be relevant. Knowledge is something else, but not necessarily distilled from wisdom."

"My dear Kai, *they* understand reality, not just the illusion of a very brief and transitory lifespan such as ours."

The telltale, as sensitive to thermal readings as to movement of any object larger than a man's fist, rattled, informing the two men that they were passing over living creatures, at that moment hidden from their eyes by the thick vegetation. The rattle turned into a purr as the sensitive recorder indicated that the life form had already been tagged with the telltale indelible paint with which the various scouting teams marked any beast they observed.

"Life form . . . no telltale," exclaimed Gaber as the rattle occurred after a short interval of silence.

Kai altered his course in the direction of the cartographer's finger. "And moving from us at a fast rate." Gaber leaned across to the windboard to check the telltagger, nodding to Kai to indicate it was ready and set.

"Maybe it's one of those predators Varian's been trying to catch," Kai said. "Herbivores go about in groups. Hang on, there's a break in the jungle ahead of us. It can't possibly swerve."

"You're directly over it," Gaber said, his voice rough with excitement.

Both beast and airborne sled reached the small clearing simultaneously. But, as if it recognized the danger of an open space with an unknown enemy above it, the beast was a bare flash, a stretched and running, mottled body, ending in a stiffly held long tail—all the retinal afterimage Kai retained.

"Got it!" Gaber's triumphant yell meant the creature had been telltagged. "I've film on it, too. The speed of the thing!"

"I think it's one of Varian's predators."

"I don't believe herbivores are capable of such bursts of speed. Why, it outdistanced this sled." Gaber sounded amazed. "Are we following it?"

"Not today. But it's tagged. Enter the grid coordinates, will you, Gaber? Varian's sure to want to come look-see. That's one of the first predators we've been able to telltag. Luck, sheer luck, coming over that clearing."

Kai veered back to his original course, slightly north, toward the first body of water that Berru had sighted.

It ought to be near the inland sea which was shown on the satellite pictures. Reality, thought Kai echoing Gaber. The original satellite photos had been theoretical, in one sense, since they'd had to be shot through the ever-present cloud cover; while Kai, by flying over the depicted terrain, encountered reality, the direct experience. Kai could appreciate the essence of Gaber's comment: what an incredible experience it would be to watch this planet evolve, to see the land masses tortured and rent by quake, shift, fault, deformation and fold. He sighed. In his mind, he speeded up the process like the quickly flipped frames of single-exposure prints. It was hard for short-lived man to comprehend the millions of years, the billions of days that it took to form continents, mountains, rivers, valleys. And clever as a geophysicist might be in predicting change, such realities as geophysics had been able to observe in its not so lengthy history always exceeded projections.

Gaber's life instrument beeped constantly now, and with no counter-burr from the telltale they diverted again, this time to tag a large herd of tree-eaters.

"Don't recall pics of monsters like that before," Kai told

Gaber as they circled round the creatures, now partially visible through the sparse forest cover. "I want to get a good look. Set the camera and the telltale, Gaber. I'm coming around. Hang on."

Kai turned the air sled, braking speed as he matched the forward motion of the lumbering beasts. "Scorch it, but they're the biggest things I've seen yet!"

"Keep up," Gaber cried in nervous excitement, for Kai was skimming very low. "Those necks are powerful." The beasts had very long necks, mounted on massive shoulders which were supported by legs the size of tree stumps.

"Necks may be powerful but the brains aren't," said Kai. "And their reaction time is double slow." The beasts were looking back toward the direction from which Kai had first approached them. Several had not even registered the aliens' appearance at all but continued to strip trees as they passed. "Gigantic herbivores, foraging even as they move. They must account for half a forest a day."

One of the long-necked creatures neatly bit off the crown of a cycad and continued its slumbering progress with huge fronds dripping from its not too capacious mouth. A smaller member of the herd obligingly took up one trailing frond and munched on that.

"Heading toward the water?" Kai asked, impressed as well as appalled by the dimensions of the animals. He heard the tagger spit.

"There does seem to be a well-traveled lane through the vegetation. I tagged most of them." Gaber patted the muzzle of the tag gun.

Kai tilted the sled so he could observe the beasts. Ahead, and down a long incline, lay the shimmering waters of one of Berru's lakes. Kai took the transparency of the probe print and laid it over the replica of the scale map which Gaber had been patiently drawing from the data of Kai's teams.

"We should have the precipice on our right, Gaber. Adjust your face mask to distance vision and see if you can spot it."

Gaber peered steadily across the distance. "Cloudy, but you ought to change course by about five degrees."

They flew over terrain that gradually became more and more swamplike until water replaced land entirely. At this point a definite shoreline appeared, rising first into small cliffs of well-weathered gray stone which gave way to sheer cliffs rising several hundred meters in an ancient transform fault. Kai ascended and the passage of the sled alarmed cliff dwellers into flight, bringing an exclamation of surprised delight from Gaber.

"Why, they're golden! And furred!"

Kai, remembering the vicious heads of the scavengers, veered hastily from their flight path.

"They're following us," noted Gaber, unperturbed.

Kai glanced over his shoulder. As far as he knew, scavengers attacked only the dying or dead. Judiciously he applied more airspeed. The sled could easily outdistance them.

"They're still following us."

Kai shot a glance over his shoulder. No question of it, the golden avians were following but maintaining a discreet distance, and different levels. Even as Kai watched, the fliers changed positions, as if each wanted to see various aspects of the intruder. Again Kai loaded on more speed. So did the fliers, without apparently expending much effort.

"I wonder how fast they do fly?"

"Are they dangerous, do you suppose?" asked Gaber.

"Possibly, but I'd say that this sled is too big for them to attack, singly or with the numbers they have behind us now. I must bring Varian to see them. And tell the Ryxi."

"Why ever tell them? They couldn't fly in this heavy atmosphere."

"No, but Vrl asked me about Ireta's aerial life. I'd hate to tell him there were only scavengers."

"Oh, yes, quite. I agree. Merciful gods, look below to your left."

They were well over the water now, stained red by the mineral content of the rocks which bordered it and its watershed. Clearly visible was the plant-strewn bottom which shelved off slightly into murky brownness and considerable depth, according to Kai's instrumentation. From out of that depth a great body torpedoed, responding to a shadow cast by the sled. Kai had a startled impression of a blunt head, gray-blue shining skin, and too many rows of sharp yellow-white teeth, needle sharp. He heard Gaber's startled cry of horror. Instinctively he slammed on the emergency drive. And corrected hurriedly as they sped uncomfortably close to the curving cliffs.

Looking back, Kai saw only the rippling circles of the monster's exit and entry on the surface, circles converging together over the twenty-five meters of its jump. He gulped and swallowed against a dryness in his throat. As if that attack had been a signal, more aquatic denizens leapt and dove, and other battles began under and on the surface of the water.

"I think," Gaber's stammer was pronounced, "that we started something."

"Well, they can finish it," said Kai as he turned the blunt nose of the sled.

"The golden fliers are still following us," Gaber said after a few moments. "They're closing."

Kai spared a backward glance and saw the first rank of fliers moving steadily abreast of the sled, their heads turned toward him and Gaber.

"Go away," Gaber said, standing up and waving both arms at the birds. "Go away. Don't get too close. You'll get hurt!"

Half-amused, half-concerned, Kai watched the creatures swing away from Gaber's flapping. They also maintained their forward speed and their inspection.

"We're surrounded by them, Kai." Gaber's tone took on a worried note.

"If they were dangerous, they've had plenty of time to attack, I think. But let's just lose the escort. Sit down, Gaber, and hang on!" Kai hit the jet accelerator again, and abruptly left the fliers in the heat haze as the sled flung itself forward. There couldn't have been any expression on the golden faces, but Kai had the distinct impression that they'd been astonished by the sudden speed.

He must ask Varian what degree of intelligence was possible in these apparently primitive life forms. The Ryxi were not the only winged species in the galaxy but very few avian species were highly intelligent. Capability seemed to have a direct ratio to the amount of time spent on the ground.

Whatever life form would eventually dominate on this planet was still thousands of years away from emerging. That didn't keep Kai from wishful thinking and speculation. It would be nice to see the Ryxi superseded.

"Did you get some good tapes of them?" Kai asked Gaber as he reduced speed to cruising. No use wasting more power than necessary.

"Oh yes, indeed I did," Gaber said, patting the recorder. "You know, Kai, I think they showed considerable intelligence." He sounded astonished.

"We'll get Varian to give an opinion. She's the expert." Kai turned the sled to the coordinates of the nearest echo core. Varian might have some biological puzzles but he now had another geological one.

Despite what he said so nonchalantly to Gaber, the unexpected materialization of those cores unnerved him. True, this planet and the system had been in the computer bank, but surely there would have been some indication if it had already been surveyed. A previous survey, however, would account for the lack of ore deposit on these old mountains. The first party would certainly have mined the shield area, and quite likely whatever other likely land mass, or seas, had been workable; land which had long since been rolled under in subsequent plate activity. Why, though, had there been no such notation in the computer banks?

To set them down on a totally unexplored planet was unlike any previous knowledge Kai had of EEC. So Gaber's theory of planting the expedition returned to haunt his thoughts. EV had waited for their all-safe-down and conveniently disappeared in search of that storm. But what about the youngsters—more of an afterthought as members of the expedition than planned personnel. Above all else was the urgent need of the transuranics. Between the kids and the energy, Kai was certain he could discount Gaber's gloomy presentiment.

Even with the ability to pinpoint the exact location of the faintly signaling core, it took Gaber and Kai some hard slogging through dense and dangerous sword plants and some heavy digging to pull it from its site.

"Why, why, it looks like the ones we have," said Gaber in surprise that was almost outrage.

"No," said Kai, turning the device thoughtfully in his hand, "the case is fatter, the crystal dimmer, and it feels old."

"How can a core feel old? Why, the casing isn't so much as scratched, or dull!"

"Heft it yourself. It feels old," said Kai with a touch of impatience, and he was somewhat amused to see Gaber hesitantly examine the old core, and quickly hand it back.

"The Theks manufacture them, don't they?" the cartographer said, giving Kai a sideways look.

"They have done so, but I think . . . Gaber, it won't wash."

"But don't you see, Kai? The Theks know this planet has been surveyed. They're back for some reason of their own. You know how they like to watchdog a likely colony . . ."

"Gaber!" Kai wanted to shake the older man, shake him out of his asinine and dangerous notion that the expedition had been planted. But, as he stared at the man's eager, intense face, Kai realized how pathetic the cartographer was. Gaber must surely know this would be his last mission and was vainly hoping to extend it. "Gaber!" Kai gave the man a little shake, smiling kindly. "Now, I do appreciate your confiding your theory to me. You've done just as you should. And I appreciate the facts on which you base the notion, but please don't go telling anyone else. I'd hate giving the heavy-worlders any excuse to ridicule one of my team."

"Ridicule?" Gaber was startled and indignant.

"I'm afraid so, Gaber. The purpose of this expedition was too clearly set out in the original program. This is just an ordinary energy-resource expedition, with a bit of xenobiology thrown in as practice for Varian, and to keep the heavy-worlders fit and the youngsters occupied while the EV chases that cosmic storm. Just to reassure you, though, I'll query EV about your theory in my next report. If, by some remote chance, you're correct, they'd tell us. Now we're down. In the meantime, I really do advise you to keep your theory between us, huh, Gaber? I value you as our cartographer too highly to want you mocked by the heavy-worlders."

"Mocked?"

"They do like their little jokes on us light-gravs. I don't want them to have one on you. We've a laugh for them, all right—on the Theks—with this!" Kai held up the core. "Our rocky friends are not so infallible after all. Not that I blame them for forgetting all about this planet, considering how it smells."

"The heavy-worlders would make me a joke?" Gaber was having difficulty in accepting the possibility, but Kai was certain he'd found the proper deterrent to keep the man from spreading that insidious rumor.

"Under the present circumstances, yes, if you came out with that notion. As I mentioned, we have the youngsters with us. You don't really think the third officer of EV is planting her son?"

"No, no, she wouldn't do that." Gaber's expression changed from distressed to irritated. "You're right. She'd've opposed it." Gaber straightened his shoulders. "You've eased my mind, Kai. I hadn't really *liked* the idea of being planted: I've left research unfinished and I only accepted this assignment to try and get a fresh perspective on it . . ."

"Good man." Kai clapped the cartographer on the shoulder and turned him back toward the sled.

It occurred to Kai that he'd have all the arguments to press again once Gaber, and the others, learned that the EV had not picked up the secondary reports. He'd worry about that when the time came. Right now he had more to ponder in the ancient core in his hand. He didn't think they had any apparatus in the shuttle for dating the device. He couldn't remember if it had ever come up in discussions how long one of these cores could function. Portegin was the man to ask. And wouldn't he be amazed at what his malfunctioning screen was recording?

In fact, Portegin was already puzzling over the print-out when Kai and Gaber strode into the chart dome.

"Kai, we've got some crazy echo on the seismic . . . what's this?"

"One of those echoes."

Portegin, his lean face settling into lines of dismay, weighed the device in his hand, peered at it, turning it round and round, end for end, before he looked with intense accusation at Kai.

"Where'd you get this?"

"Approximately here," said Kai, pointing to the gap in the line of old echoes on the screen.

"We haven't cored that area yet, boss."

"I know."

"But, boss, this is Thek manufacture. I'd swear it."

Margit, who'd been filling in her report, came over to the two men. She took the core from Portegin's unresisting hand.

"It feels heavier. And this crystal looks almost dead." She regarded Kai for an explanation.

He shrugged. "Gaber saw the echoes on the recorder, thought you'd mucked it up, Portegin . . ." He grinned as the mechanic growled at the cartographer. "But I decided we'd better check. This was what we found."

Margit made a guttural noise, deep in her throat, of disgust and irritation. "You mean, we've spent hours doing what has been *done*! You wit-heads could have saved us time and use-less energy by rigging that screen right off."

"According to our computer banks, this planet had never been surveyed," Kai said in a soothing drawl.

"Well, obviously it has been." Margit glowered at the screen. "And you know, we've paralleled their line almost perfectly. Not bad for a first working expedition, is it," she added, talk-ing herself into a better frame of mind. "Hey," she said in a much louder, less happy tone of voice, "no wonder we couldn't find anything worth the looking. It'd been got already. How far does the old survey coring go?"

"Stops at the edge of the shield, my dear girl," said Porte-gin, "and now that we know from the old cores where the shield ends, we can start hitting some pay dirt for a change. I don't think we've done too much duplication—except per-haps in the north and northeast."

Kai thanked the compassionate computer that had put those two on this team with him—they might complain a bit, but they'd already talked themselves into a positive frame over the duplicated effort.

"I feel a lot better now, knowing there was a good reason we couldn't find any pay dirt at all!" Margit studied the screen and then pointed at several areas. "There's nothing here and here. Should be!"   •

"Signals are very faint," Portegin said. "Some may have just given up the ghost. If everything else there is worked out, is there any point in setting new cores, Kai?"

"None."

Aulia and Dimenon entered the cartography dome, closely followed by the other four geologists.

"Guess what Kai and Gaber found?" Margit asked. Ex-pressions of surprise and displeasure greeted her question. "They found out why we couldn't find anything . . . yet!"

So Kai and Gaber repeated the account of their afternoon's activities, and the relief that spread throughout the room was reassuring to the team leader. Everyone had a turn at examining the old device, comparing it with those they were setting, joking about ghosts and echoes.

"We can set up secondary camps right on the edges of the shield," Triv was saying excitedly. "Can we start tomorrow, Kai?"

"Surely, I'll reassign everyone to more profitable areas hopefully. Let me work it out. And Bakkun, I'll be out with you tomorrow."

The meal gong sounded, reverberating under the force-screen, so he dismissed them all, staying behind briefly to reschedule flights for the next day. They would have to set up secondary camps, as Triv suggested, but Kai wasn't all that keen to dissipate their complement. Varian hadn't yet had a chance to catalogue the worst of the predators and, despite the personal force-screens, a team could be caught too far away for help to arrive in time. That predator he'd seen today wouldn't be stopped by a puny personal force-screen. He also couldn't hold the teams back from finding deposits; they got credit bonuses based on the assays of their individual discoveries. That was one reason why the lack of finds so far had had such a serious effect on their morale. He couldn't risk a further check to their spirits and ambitions. He also couldn't risk sending them out against predators like those he'd seen today. So he must have a chat with Varian.

He emerged into an insect-noisy night. The force-screen, arcing over the encampment, was aglow with blue spits of light as nocturnal creatures tried to reach the tantalizing floodlights which illuminated the compound.

Had that other survey party, millennia ago, camped here? Would another group, millennia hence, return when his cores emitted shallow ghost blips on another screen?

Had they really been planted? The disturbing thought bobbed to the surface of his reflections, much as the aquatic monsters had been triggered by the shadow of the sled over the water. He tried to push down the notion. Had one of the others been tipped off secretly? Varian? No, as co-leader she was the least likely to have been informed. Tanegli? And was that why he was so willing to search out edible fruits? No, Tanegli was a sound man, but not the sort to be given private instructions while the team leaders were keyed out.

Not quite reassured within his own mind, Kai decided that congenial company would disrupt the uneasy tenor of his thoughts and he strode more purposefully toward the largest dome and his meal.

3

VARIAN was diverted by Kai's reception of the fruit when it was served as the evening meal. Divisti and Lungie had collaborated, and the table was spread with the fruit in its natural form, sliced into green juicy portions; fruit synthesized as a paste, reinforced with nutrients and vitamins; fruit added to the subsistence proteins; stewed fruit, dried fruit. Kai fastidiously tasted a minute piece of the fresh sliced fruit, smiled, made polite noises and finished his meal with the paste. Then he complained of a metallic aftertaste.

"That's the additives. There's no aftertaste with the fresh fruit," Varian told him, suppressing a mixture of annoyance at his conservative tastes and amusement at his reaction. The ship-bred were wary of anything in its natural form.

"Why cultivate a taste for something I can't indulge?" Kai asked when she tried to get him to eat more of the fresh fruit.

"Why not indulge yourself a little, while you have the chance? Besides," she added, "once you have the taste, you can program it into any synthesizer and duplicate it on shipboard to your heart's content."

"A point."

Varian had decided some time ago that it was just these little ship-evolved differences that fascinated her about Kai. He wasn't physically that much different from the attractive young men she'd known on the various planets of her childhood and during early specialist's training. If anything, Kai had kept himself more physically fit in the EV's various humanoid sports facilities than his planet-based contemporaries. He had a lean, wiry frame, slightly taller than average, taller than herself, and she was not rated short on any normal Earth-type planet, being 1.75 meters tall. More important to her in Kai than mere handsomeness, which he had, was the strength in his face, the sparkle of humor in his brown eyes and the inner serenity that had commended him when they'd met in the EV's humanoid dining area. She'd quickly recognized the aura of Discipline about him and had been overwhelmingly relieved that he was a Disciple and amused that his having passed the Training mattered to her on such short acquaintance. She'd accepted Discipline not that long ago herself, proud of her achievement and determined to suppress that pride, however much it meant that she could continue to advance in FSP service. A leader had to have Discipline since it was the only personal defense against other humanoids permitted by FSP and EEC, and of inestimable value in emergency situations.

Varian had been quite willing to develop a relationship with Kai and had privately done a good bit of crowing when she'd unexpectedly been tapped as a xenob on his geology expedition to Ireta.

"And what's this I hear? This planet's been raped before?"

"The shield land mass we're on has certainly been stripped," Kai replied, grinning a little at her blunt phrase. "Portegin only got the seismic screen rigged last night. Gaber thought it was malfunctioning because we got echoes where we'd cored, and faint impulses where we hadn't. So I did a deccod and found an old, old core."

Varian had already heard many of the details. "We were informed during our briefing on shipboard that the system had been in storage a long time."

"Well, there certainly was no mention made of a previous geological survey."

"True," and Varian looked thoughtfully at a vague middle distance as she drawled out the affirmative. There had been sort of a last minute rush to assemble this Iretan expedition, though the Theks and Ryxi had been scheduled for their respective planets for some months. "My team was sure added in a hurry. After they got print-outs of life forms from the probe scan."

"With all due respect, co-leader, the inclusion of your team doesn't puzzle me as much as no mention of a previous coring."

"I quite appreciate that. How old d'you think the cores are?"

"Too scorching old for my liking, Varian. The lines end with the stable shield area!"

Varian drew breath in a whistle. "Kai, that would mean millions of years. Could even a Thek-manufactured device last *that* long?"

"Who knows? C'mon, you can have a look at the device yourself. Then I've some tapes to play for you that I think you'll like."

"Those flying things Gaber was raving about?"

"Among others."

"Sure you won't have one more piece of fresh fruit?" She couldn't resist teasing him.

Kai gave her a fleetingly irritated look, then grinned. He had an engaging smile, she thought, and not for the first time. They'd seen a good deal of each other in the planning stages but far too little now that they had to deal with their separate responsibilities.

"I've had a sufficiency to eat, thank you, Varian."

"And I'm a glutton, huh?" But she snatched up one more slice from the platter. "What are these avians like? I don't trust Gaber's observations."

"They're golden-furred and I'd hazard that they're intelligent. Curiosity occurs only with intelligence, doesn't it?"

"Generally, yes. Intelligent fliers? Raking ramjets, this'll throw the Ryxi into loops." Varian crowed with delight. "Where'd you encounter them?"

"I went to see those colored lakes of Berru's and startled them out of the cliffs. By the way, the lakes harbor monsters every bit as big and dangerous as those swamp dwellers we saw this morning."

"This planet goes in for big things . . ."

"Big puzzles, too." They had entered the cartography dome now and Kai picked up the old core and handed it to her. "Here's my latest."

Varian hefted it in the palm of one hand. She saw another core on the table. "Is this one of yours?"

Kai looked up from the tape canisters he was sorting through and nodded.

Side by side, she could see the slight differences in circumference, length and weight.

"Does this previous coring explain why you've had so little luck in finding any ores?"

"Yes. The shield land has been stripped. My gang was relieved to know there was a good reason—this planet ought to be full of pay dirt. Now, however, we'll have to set up secondary camps in the new fold mountains . . ."

"Secondary camps? Kai, that isn't safe. Even if the worst you'd have to content with is fang-face . . ."

"Fang-face?"

"Well, that's what I call whatever chewed a piece off Mabel's flank."

"Mabel?"

"Must you keep repeating me? I find it a lot easier to name

'em than to keep calling 'em 'herbivore number one' or 'predator with teeth A.' "

"I didn't know you'd seen the predator?"

"I haven't. I can postulate from his tooth marks . . ."

"Would this be fang-face?" asked Kai as the tapes he and Gaber had made that afternoon began to appear on the viewing screen. He punched a hold on the one shot they'd had of the predator's head.

Varian let out a squeak as she got a good look at the toothy, snarling head, the angry little eyes upturned to the sled as the creature had flashed across the small clearing.

"Yes, that could be the villain. Six meters in the shoulder, too. You couldn't set up secondary camps that would keep him out. He could flatten you even with a couple of force-screen belts on you. No, I wouldn't advise secondary camps until we find out how far these sweethearts range."

"We could move the shuttle . . ."

"Not until Trizein has completed his current run of experiments. And why move? Are we low on power for travel?"

"No, but I was considering the commutation time. Cuts down effective time in the field."

"True. Frankly, Kai, I'd prefer to scout an area before you set up a secondary camp. Even those herbivores like Mabel, useless as they are, could be dangerous stampeding from a fang-face. However," she added, seeing he was adamant, "every animal in creation is afraid of something. I'll figure out what animals you'd have to contend with in an area and we can set up some safeguards around, say, one larger, suitably situated secondary camp and your field teams would be relatively safe . . ."

"You don't sound certain."

"I'm not certain about anything on this crazy planet, Kai. And your discovery today only makes my uncertainty more . . ." she grinned, "certain!"

He laughed.

She took one more long appraising look at the predator's

rows of needle-sharp teeth and then asked Kai to roll the tape. "Sure glad you were aloft when you met that fellow. Gaber managed to tag him? That'll help estimate his territorial sway. Oh, I say, aren't they lovely!"

The golden fliers were on the screen, and while it might have been the juxtaposition to the preceding predator, they seemed so benign and graceful.

"Oh, hold that frame, Kai, please!" Varian gestured for him to go back on the tape until she had the frame of the creature, suspended in its flight, its crested head slightly turned toward the camera so that both golden-colored eyes were visible.

"Yes, I'd agree that it's intelligent. Is that a pouch under its beak for storing fish? And it's a glider, I think. Roll it, Kai, I want to see if that wing can rotate. Yes, see, there! As it veers away. Yes, yes. Much more advanced than that carrion-eater this morning. Why is so much of our reaction dependent on the eye of a creature?" She looked up at Kai, whose brown eyes widened with surprise.

"Eye?"

"Yes. The eyes of that little mammal today . . . I couldn't have left it behind, Kai, short of mutiny, once I'd seen the frightened lost confusion in its eyes. Much less the entreaty in Bonnard's and Cleiti's. Those swamp horrors, they had tiny eyes, in comparison to their skull shape . . . wicked, beady, hungry eyes." Varian shuddered in recall. "And that new predator's eyes . . . fang-face has a wicked appetite. Of course, it isn't a hard and fast rule—the Galormis were a hideous example of camouflaged intent. . . ."

"You were on that expedition?"

Varian made a face. "Yes, I was a very junior member on the team at Aldebaran 4 when those monsters were encountered. My first assignment out of xenoveterinary college. They had soft eyes, mind you,"—eyes which occasionally still haunted her sleep—"mild-looking creatures, too, softish, perfectly amenable until full dark—then—whammie!"

"Nocturnal feeders—"

"Bleeders! Sucked the blood and then chewed the flesh . . . like what's been feeding on Mabel . . . no, it couldn't be Galormis. Teeth are too big."

"Why on earth call it Mabel?"

"Knew someone like her once, a walking appetite, hating the world around her, suspicious and constantly confused. Not much intelligence."

"What would you name the avian?"

"I don't know," she said after regarding the furry face. "It isn't easy until you've actually met the creature. But this species has intelligence and personality. I want to see more of them!"

"Thought you would. Although we couldn't tag them. They moved too fast. Kept up with the sled at cruising speed."

"Very good." A yawn caught her unawares. "All this fresh air, chasing wounded animals to doctor them what don't wish to be helped." She stroked his cheek and gave him a regretful smile of apology. "I'm going to bed. And you ought to, too, co-leader. Sleep on our puzzles. Maybe sleep'll solve 'em."

Kai could have wished it had, but he woke the next morning feeling refreshed, and the teams, when assembled, were in such good spirits that his rose, too.

"I've discussed secondary camps with Varian. Until she has catalogued the habits of the predators, she can't guarantee our safety," said Kai, "but she's going to set and search areas into which we can move, if we adhere to the safeguards she devises. Okay? Sorry, but you'll understand better if you see the marks on the herbivore's flank." He noticed by the grim expressions that everyone had looked at the creature.

"Boss, what about the gaps in the old cores, here, here and here?" Triv asked, pointing out the areas southwest and due south.

"Faults," said Gaber, slipping a scale transparency over the seismic map. "I read a massive overthrust here. Good area to search now but any seismimic would have been crushed. Or subsided too far below the surface to transmit."

"Triv, you and Aulia explore that overthrust today. Margit and Dimenon, your sector is here," and he gave them the co-ordinates in the southwest, and to Berru and Portegin, explaining that he and Bakkun would try to explore the Rift Valley since there were old cores leading up to it. He stressed that they maintain safety procedures, tag or telltale animals when possible, and note and report any scavengers circling over what could be injured livestock specimens for Varian.

As Kai and Bakkun lifted in their sled, Kai saw Varian on her way down to the corral. He saw the herbivore, Mabel, busily eating her way through what trees remained in the enclosure.

Bakkun, who preferred to pilot, brought the sled on its southeast heading.

"Why didn't our Theks know this planet'd been cored?" the heavy-worlder asked.

"I haven't asked our Theks if they know. But Ireta was not marked as surveyed."

"Theks have their reasons."

"Such as?"

"I do not presume to guess," replied Bakkun, "but they always have good reasons."

Kai liked Bakkun as a teammate; he was inexhaustible, cool-headed like all his race, thorough and dependable. But he had no imagination, no flexibility and once convinced of anything, refused to change his opinion in the face of the most telling facts. Theks were, to him as to many of the short-spanned species, infallible and godlike. Kai did not wish, however, to enter into any argument with Bakkun, particularly on such a heresy as Thek fallibility proven in the existence of seismic cores on this planet.

Fortunately the telltale bleeped. Bakkun automatically corrected course and Kai watched the remote-distance screen attentively. This time they found more herbivores running away from the sled's whine through the thick rain forest, occasionally caroming off trees so hard the top branches shuddered wildly.

"Come round again, Bakkun," Kai asked and flipped up the tape switch, hanging in against his seat strap as Bakkun acted promptly to his order. He swore under his breath because none of the creatures crossed any of the clearings, almost as if they expected an aerial attack and were crowding under whatever cover they could find.

"Never mind, Bakkun. Continue on course. I thought I saw another flank-damaged beast."

"We see them daily, Kai."

"Why didn't you mention that in your reports?"

"Didn't know it was important, Kai. Too much else to mention bearing on *our* job . . ."

"This is a joint effort . . ."

"Agreed, but I must know how to contribute. I didn't know the mere ecological balances were essential knowledge, too."

"My omission. But you would do well to report any unusual occurrence."

"It is my impression, Kai, that there is nothing usual about Ireta. I have been a geologist for many standard years now and I have never encountered a planet constantly in a Mesozoic age and unlikely to evolve beyond that stage." Bakkun gave Kai a sideways glance, sly and mysterious. "Who would expect to find old cores registering on such a planet?"

"Expect the unexpected! That's the unofficial motto of our profession, isn't it?"

The sun, having briefly appeared in the early morning to oversee the beginnings of day, now retired behind clouds. A local ground fog made flying momentarily difficult as conversation was discontinued. Kai busied himself with the seismic overlay, checking the old cores, which faintly glowed on the screen in response to his signal.

The cores advanced beyond the line of flight, right down into the Rift Valley, subsiding with the floor which composed the wide plateau. They were entering the valley now and

Bakkun needed all his attention on his flying as the thermals caught the light sled and bounced it around. Once past the line of ancient volcanoes, their plugged peaks gaunt fingers to the now lowering rainclouds, their slopes supporting marginal vegetation, Bakkun guided the sled toward the central Rift Valley. The face of the fault block exposed the various strata of the uplift that had formed the valley. As the little sled zipped past, saucily irreverent to the frozen geohistory, Kai was filled with a mixture of awe and amusement—in awe of the great forces still working which had formed the rift and might very well reform it many times imaginable in the existence of this planet; and amusement that Man dared to pinpoint one tiny moment of those inexorable courses and attempt to put his mark upon it.

"Scavengers, Kai," said Bakkun, breaking in on his thoughts. Bakkun gestured slightly starboard by the bow. Kai sighted the display on the scope.

"Must be the golden fliers, not scavengers."

"There is a difference?"

"Indeed there is, but what are they doing a couple of hundred kilometers from the nearest large body of water?"

"Are they dangerous?" Bakkun asked, with a show of interest.

"I don't think so. They are intelligent, showed curiosity in us yesterday, but what are they doing so far inland?"

"We shall soon know. We're closing fast."

Kai slanted the scope to take in the groups on the ground. The fliers were now alerted to the presence of an unfamiliar aerial object, and all the heads were turned upward. Kai saw threads of coarse grass hanging from several beaks. And, sure enough, as the sled circled, their elongated heads curiously followed its course. Some of the smaller fliers pecked again at the grass.

"Why would they have to come so far? For a grass?"

"I am not xenobiologically trained," said Bakkun in his stolid fashion. Then his voice took on a note of such unusual urgency that Kai swung round, scope and all, and instinctively recoiled against the seatback. "Look!"

"What the . . ."

The Rift Valley narrowed slightly where a horst protruded. Then, from the narrow defile one of the largest creatures that Kai had ever seen emerged, its stalky, awkward gait frightening in its inexorable progress. Sharpening the scope for the increased distance, Kai watched as the colossus strutted on its huge hind legs into the peaceful valley.

"Krim! That's one of those fang-faced predators."

"Observe the fliers, Kai!"

Loath to withdraw his wary observation of the menace, Kai glanced up toward the golden fliers. They had assumed a curiously defensive formation in the sky. Those still grounded now grazed, if that could be considered a proper description for the quick scooping jabs. Varian must be right about the bill pouches, Kai realized, for the fliers' beaks had an elongated appearance. They must be stuffing the grasses into the pouches.

"The predator has seen them! Those still on the ground cannot get airborne in time if he should charge." Bakkun's hand closed on the grip of the laser unit.

"Wait! Look at him!"

The heavy predatory head was now pointed in the direction of the fliers, as if the beast had just noticed their presence. The head tilted up, evidently registering the formation of the golden fliers. The creature's front legs, ludicrously small in comparison to the huge thighs and the length of the long leg bone, twitched. The thick, counterbalancing tail also lashed in reaction to the presence of the fliers. Almost greedily, Kai thought. The biped remained stationary for another long moment, then dropped awkwardly forward and began scooping up the grasses with its ridiculous forepaws, cramming great wads, roots, earth and all into its huge maw.

While the two geologists watched, the fliers began to run

along what Kai now distinguished as a low bluff. They dipped almost to the grasses below before becoming safely airborne.

"They are trailing more grass, Kai."

The leader focused the scope and saw the streamers trailing from hind- and wing-tip claws as the fliers beat steadily upward and away from the valley.

"Is that a seaward course they're on, Bakkun?"

"They are. And against a stiff headwind."

Kai turned back to the browsing predator who hadn't paused in his voracious consumption of the grass.

"Now why would both fliers and that monster need the grass?"

"It does seem an unusual additive," replied Bakkun, oblivious to the fact that Kai had been talking to himself.

"Would you set the sled down, Bakkun? At the other end of the valley from the beast. I want to get some samples of grass."

"For Varian? Or Divisti?"

"Maybe for both. Strange that the predator didn't attempt an attack, isn't it?"

"Perhaps it does not like flier meat. Or maybe they are formidable antagonists?"

"No. There was no hint of attack in the predator's manner, and only wary defense in the fliers. Almost as if . . . as if both recognized this as a place apart. That there was a truce here."

"A truce? Between animals?" Bakkun sounded skeptical.

"That's what it looked like. But the predator is certainly too primitive to operate on such a logical basis. I must ask Varian."

"Yes, she would be the proper person to query," said Bakkun, his composure restored. He brought the sled to a smooth landing on the low bluff the fliers had used to take off.

"We are not golden fliers," the heavy-worlder said in response to Kai's surprise at the landing spot. "That creature may decide to season its grass with us." He smoothly took over the scope. "You collect. I will watch."

The monster had not interrupted its feeding nor paid any attention to the sled. Kai dismounted with alacrity and, thumbing off his force-screen, began to gather grass. He was glad he had gloves because some of the blades had sharp edges—relatives to the sword plant, he decided. One clump came up, roots, earth and all, adding a new high to the malodorous air. Kai shook the earth free, remembering the birds had taken only the tops, not the root. Although the fliers had not gone in for the thicker-bladed vegetation, Kai took samples of everything in the vicinity. He stored what he garnered in a container and resumed his place on the sled.

"Look, he has not stopped eating grass, Kai," said Bakkun, returning the scope to him.

As Bakkun eased the sled off the bluff and into the air, Kai kept the scope on the predator. It continued eating, not even lifting its head as the two geologists passed over it.

Bakkun, having been given no orders to the contrary, navigated the sled through the narrow end of the valley. Beyond, the ground fell away again to a lower level without such luxuriant growth, the soil being sandier and supporting more of the tough shrub-type vegetation.

"The cores continue down this valley, Kai," said Bakkun, drawing his attention away from the monster and to the business at hand.

Kai looked at the seismic scanner. "Last one just beyond that far ridge."

"This Rift Valley is very old," said Bakkun. Kai was pleased to hear the half-question in the man's voice. "And the cores end beyond the ridge?"

"Indeed they do."

It was the first time Kai had ever heard uncertainty in a heavy-worlder's voice. He understood it and sympathized, for he felt much the same way himself.

The overthrust above which they now passed had occurred at least a million years before their arrival on this planet. Yet the manufacture of the core unit was undeniably Thek. Unless, and the stray thought amused Kai, the Theks had some-how copied an older civilization . . . the Others? The Theks as copyists restored Kai's sense of proportion. As he couldn't expect to compete with heavy-worlders on a physical basis, he ought not to compete with Theks on a longevity perfor-mance. The here and now were important, too: twice, trebly important to him considering how short a span he could an-ticipate, even with all the miracles of science. He and his team had a job to do *now* on Ireta. Never mind that it had been done before when Man was still at the single-cell stage swim-ming about at the beginning of a long evolutionary climb.

4

WITH the help of Paskutti and Tardma, Varian managed to dress Mabel's flank wound. The beast had somehow managed to loosen the edges of the filmseal, and, despite the force-screen over her corral, bloodsuckers had attached themselves to the suppuration. She had opened the wound further in her frenzy to free herself from the ropes the heavy-worlders used to restrain her. They had to lash her head to her uninjured hind leg before Varian could approach her.

Fortunately, once she dislodged the bloodsuckers, Varian thought the flesh looked healthy enough.

"I'm going to wash down and seal the entire leg," she told Paskutti, who was heaving with his exertions. "Just as well I'm vetting the bitten instead of the biter. Hate to run into him." She thought of the wicked head and the rows of vicious teeth glaring out of the frame Kai had taken.

"This creature couldn't put up much of a fight," said Paskutti.

The edge to his tone surprised Varian into looking at him. She didn't expect to see any emotion registered on the heavy-worlder's blank features, but there was an intensity in his pale eyes that gave her a momentary stab of fear. She got the distinct impression that the man was excited in some bizarre and revolting fashion, by the wound, by the concept of one animal eating another, alive. She turned back quickly to her task, loath to let Paskutti know she'd observed him.

They completed the veterinary work on Mabel without further struggle, but her tail, when she was released from the ropes, lashed out so viciously that they all retreated hastily beyond range. Without the proximity of her well-wishers, Mabel seemed unable to continue her aggressive behavior. She stopped mid-bellow and peered about her, as if puzzled by this unexpected respite. Her near-sighted eyes scanned so consistently above their heads that once they stood still, Varian realized that Mabel would never see them. Mabel's worst enemy then, Varian decided, was much larger than the herbivore's considerable bulk and was generally perceived by smell to judge by the rapid dilation of Mabel's nostrils.

"What now, Varian?" asked Paskutti as they left the corral.

In his very lack of tone color, Paskutti seemed to be impatient for her answer.

"Now, we check out what creatures inhabit the unknown land beyond the shield so that Kai and his teams can set up secondary camps. We've the sled today, Paskutti, so if you'd get tapes, we can do some prospecting."

"Weaponry?"

"The usual personnel defense. We're not hunting. We're observing."

She spoke more harshly than she intended because there was an avid intensity about Paskutti's innocent question that was off-putting. Tardma was as blank as ever, but then she never did anything, including smile, without glancing for permission from Paskutti.

As they reentered the encampment for their equipment, Varian saw the children grouped about Dandy's enclosure, watching Lunzie feed it. Its thick little tail whisked this way and that either in greed or in enjoyment.

"Is Dandy eating well?"

"Second bottle," said Bonnard with possessive pride.

"Lunzie says we can feed him when he gets to know us a bit better," Cleiti added, and Terilla nodded, her bright eyes big with such an incredible experience to anticipate.

Poor ship-bred wench, thought Varian, whose childhood had been spent among the animals of many worlds with her veterinarian parents. She couldn't remember the time when she hadn't had animals to cuddle and care for. Small creatures brought to her parents for healing or observation had always been her particular charges once her parents had decided she was a responsible youngster. The only creatures she had never liked were the Galormis. Her instinct for animals had warned her the moment those soft devils had been discovered on Aldebaran 4, but as a very junior xenob, she had had to keep her own counsel on her suspicions. At that she'd been lucky. She only had teeth marks on her arm where the Galormi that had attacked those in her dome had begun its nocturnal feeding. The creature had already killed its handler; its hollow incisors had proved to contain a paralytic with which it controlled its victims. Fortunately the night guard, alerted to trouble by the nonappearance of his relief, had roused her expedition, and the Galormis had been caught, contained and later exterminated. The planet was interdicted.

"We'll see how Dandy behaves himself first, Terilla," said Varian, firmly believing in an old adage, "once bitten, twice shy." The originator had not had the Galormis in mind, but the application was apt.

"How's Mabel?" asked Lunzie, sparing Varian a glance.

Varian told her. "We're scouting north today. Kai's teams

will have to set up secondary camps soon, but we don't want them encountering fang-faces, like the ones that ate Mabel. Also, the geology teams are supposed to report in if they sight any wounded beasts, so give us a toot right away, will you, Lunzie?"

The physician nodded again.

"Couldn't we come with you, Varian?" asked Bonnard. "If you've the big sled? Please, Varian?"

"Not today."

"You're on compound duty, and you know it, Bonnard," said Lunzie. "And lessons."

Bonnard looked so rebellious that Varian gave him a poke in the arm, and told him to shape up. Cleiti, more sensitive to adult disapproval, nudged him in the ribs.

"We got out yesterday, Bon. We'll go again when it's proper." Cleiti smiled up at Varian, though her expression was wistful.

A nice child, Cleiti, Varian thought as she and the heavy-worlders continued on to the storage shed for their equipment. Varian checked the big sled, despite the fact that Portegin had serviced it that morning.

They were airborne in good time, just after the morning's first downpour. As seemed to be the rule on Ireta, the clouds then reluctantly parted, allowing the yellow-white sunlight to beat down. Varian's face mask darkened in response to the change of light and she stopped squinting. Sometimes she found the curious yellow light of cloudy daytime more piercing than the full sun's rays.

They had to fly ten kilometers beyond the radius of the encampment before the telltale began to register life forms, most of them already tagged. The "dead" perimeter had been expanding ever since they landed as if knowledge of the intruders had been slowly disseminating among the indigenous animals. This was a slow-cop world, Varian thought, for on more . . . civilized, was that the word she needed? Advanced, yes, that was more accurate. On more advanced worlds, the news of strangers seemed to waft on the outgoing wind of their descent, and inhabitants made themselves scarce . . . Unless, of course, it was an intelligent, nonviolent world where everyone gathered around to see the new arrivals. Sometimes the welcome would be discreet, not defensive nor offensive, but distant. Varian thought of the defensive screen around the domes and snorted to herself. The thing wasn't needed—except to keep insects out. At least not under present circumstances, when the animals stayed far away. Maybe the solution to Kai's problem was simply to establish the physical secondary camp, complete with small force-screen, give the local wildlife a chance to drift away from the area and then let his teams move in.

Yet there was fang-face! The size of him! She recalled tree tops shivering at his passage in the tape Kai had made. The main force-screen would burn him, probably dissuade him . . . there hadn't been much animal life around those active volcanoes so creatures great and small on Ireta knew about fire and burn. The problem was that the smaller screens weren't powerful enough to stop a determined attempt by fang-face if he were hungry, or scared, and that was what she had to allow for—the appetite of such predators as fang-face.

Varian had taped a course for the northeast, the vast high plateau ringed by the tremendous "mountains of the moon," as Gaber had called them. Two subcontinents had ground into each other, Gaber had told her pedantically, to force high those great stone peaks. The plateau beneath them had once been ocean bed. Anyone returning to that area had been enjoined by Gaber and Trizein to look for fossils on the rock faces. It was here, at the foot of the new fold mountains, that Kai hoped to start finding pay dirt. This was well beyond the ancient corings. For some reason, the discovery of the old cores reassured Varian. Kai appeared worried about them and she couldn't imagine why. EEC wasn't likely to lose a planet they'd already twice explored. Besides, the Theks lived long enough to correct any mistakes they made—if they ever made any. Or maybe it was because they had time enough to correct any that it only appeared they were infallible.

Between the camp and the plateau they were heading for, with its coarse ground cover, not quite grass and not really shrub or thicket, was a wide band of rain forest through which Mabel's ilk passed and where a fang-face was liable to lurk. Far to the east were clouds, signs of volcanic activity. Occasional claps of thunder, not meteorological in origin, rumbled to the sensors of the sled.

They spotted one set of circling scavengers and landed to investigate, but the prey had long since been reduced to a bony structure. Any evidence of beast-gouging was long gone. The dead weren't carrion long on Ireta. Tenacious insects were riddling the skeleton with industrious pinchers so that even the bones would be gone in the next day. The tougher skull was intact, and Varian, first spraying with antiseptic, examined it.

"One like Mabel?" Paskutti asked as Varian turned the skull from side to side with her boot.

"Crested at any rate. See, the nasal passage extends . . . I'd say Mabel and her kind smell a lot better than they see. Remember her performance this morning?"

"Everything smells on this planet," replied Paskutti with enough vehemence to cause Varian to look up. She thought he was being humorous, but he was deadly serious.

"Yes, the place stinks, but if she's used to it, she'd catch the overlying odors and take appropriate action. Yes, it's her nose that's her first line of defense."

She took some three-dimension close-ups and with some effort broke off a piece of the nasal cartilage and a sliver of bone for later study. The skull was too cumbersome to transport.

The scavengers remained aloft, but as soon as Varian lifted the sled, they descended as if they hoped the intruders had discovered something they'd missed on the well-picked carcass.

"Waste not, want not," Varian muttered under her breath. Life and death on Ireta moved swiftly. Small wonder that Mabel, grievously wounded though she was, had struggled to stay on her feet. Once down, the wounded seldom rose. Had she done Mabel any favors, succoring her so? Or had they merely postponed her early death? No, the wound was healing; the gouging teeth had not incapacitated muscle or broken bone. She'd live and, in time, be completely whole again.

The sled was approaching the general grazing area where they'd found Mabel. Varian cut out the main engine, settling it to hover. The herd was there, all right. Varian caught sight of the mottled hides under the broad and dripping tree leaves, downwind of the creatures. They'd been too precipitous before and scared the herd off, with the exception of Mabel who hadn't been able to run fast enough.

Varian wondered at the intelligence level of the herbivores. You'd think this species would have learned to set out sentinels, the way animals on other inimical worlds did, to forewarn the main herd of the arrival of dangerous predators. No, the size of the brain in that bare skull had been small, too small, Varian realized, to guide the great beast. A tail brain, perhaps? Long ago, far away, she'd heard of that combination. Not uncommon to have a secondary motor control unit in so large a beast. And then the nasal passages had pushed the brain case back. More smell than sense, that was Mabel!

"I see one, flank-damaged," said Tardma, peering over the port side. "Recent attack!"

Varian sighted in on Tardma's beast and suppressed a shudder. She saw the bloodied mess of flank and wondered at the stoicism of the injured beast, chomping away at tree leaves. Hunger transcending pain, she thought. That's the dominant quest on this planet, the ease of hunger.

"There is another one. An older wound," Paskutti said, touching Varian's shoulder to direct her attention.

The wound on the second beast was scabbed over, but when she intensified the magnification she could see the squirming life was parasitic to the wound. Occasionally the herbivore interrupted its feeding to gnaw at its flank, and masses of parasites were dropping off, their hold on raw flesh loosened.

Slowly moving and staying downwind of the herd, they made their survey. With few exceptions, all the herbivore displayed the gruesome flank gouges. And the exceptions were the young, the small specimens.

"They can run faster?" asked Tardma.

"Not juicy enough, more likely," replied Varian.

"Protected by the adults?" asked Paskutti. "You remember that the smallest ones ran in the center of the herd when we first encountered this species."

"I'd still like to know why . . ."

"We may find out now," said Paskutti, pointing below.

At the farthest edge of the rain forest, one of the herbivores had stopped eating and had stretched itself up on its hind legs, its crested head pointing steadily north. It dropped suddenly, wheeling, emitting a snorting kind of whistle as it began to run due south. Another beast, not alarmed by the departure of the first, seemed to catch the same scent. It, too, whistled, dropped to all fours and began to trundle south. One by one, independently, the herbivores moved away, the smaller ones following the elders, and gradually overtaking them. The whistles grew more noisy, frightened.

"We wait?" asked Tardma, her blunt fingers twitching on the controls.

"Yes, we wait," said Varian, uncomfortably aware of the suppressed eagerness in Tardma's manner.

They didn't have long to wait. They heard the crashing approach some seconds before seeing it, a pacing creature, head low, short forepaws extended as it ran, its thick heavy tail counterbalancing the heavy body. The big-jawed mouth was open, saliva foaming through but not obscuring the rows of spiky teeth. As it ran past the hovering sled, Varian saw its eyes, the hungry little eyes, the vicious eyes of the predator.

"Are we following?" asked Tardma, her voice curiously breathy.

"Yes."

"To stop the ecological balance?" asked Paskutti.

"Balance? What that creature does is not balance, that's not killing for need: that's maiming for pleasure."

Varian felt herself inwardly shaking with the force of her words. She ought not to get so upset.

"Perhaps, perhaps not," said Paskutti and started the drive, to follow the predator.

Though it was not always in the scope, its course was easily followed by the broken or shaking trees, and sudden flurries of the avian life forms or the startled scampering of small ground creatures. Its speed was considerably more than the lumbering herbivores, and it was only a matter of time before it overcame the distance between them. If Varian found herself responding to the chase stimulus with quickened breath, dry throat and internal quivering, she was astounded by the metamorphosis of the heavy-worlders. For the first time since she had worked with them, they were displaying emotion: their faces contorted with an excitement, a lust, an avidity that had nothing to do with civilized reactions.

Varian was appalled, and had she been at the controls instead of Paskutti, she would have veered away from the finale of this chase. That, in itself, would have been an act to undermine her authority over the heavy-worlders. They were tolerant of light-gravity physical limitations, but they would have been contemptuous of moral cowardice. She had after all, Varian realized, organized this expedition to discover how dangerous the predator was to the herbivores and to secondary camps. She couldn't turn aside because of squeamishness. And she didn't understand her own reactions. She'd seen more hideous forms of death, worse battles of animal against animal.

The predator had caught up with the main herd. It singled out one beast, pursuing the terrified animal into a cul-de-sac

caused by fallen trees. Frantic, the herbivore tried to climb
the trunks, but it had ineffectual forefeet for such exercise
and too much bulk for the stumps to sustain. Bleating and
whistling, it slid into the predator's grasp. With one mighty
blow of a hindleg, the carnivore downed the fright-paralyzed
herbivore. The predator measured a distance on the quivering
flank; its front paws, far smaller than the massive hindlegs,
were almost obscene in this gesture. The herbivore screamed
as the predator's teeth sank into the flank and ripped off a
hideous mouthful. Varian wanted to retch.

"Frighten that horror away, Paskutti. Kill it!"

"You can't rescue all the herbivores on this world by killing
one predator," said Paskutti, his eyes on the scene below,
shining with what Varian recognized as a blood lust.

"I'm not rescuing all of them, just this one," she cried,
reaching for the controls.

Paskutti, his face once more settling into the more familiar,
emotionless lines, switched the sled to full power and dove at
the carnivore which was settling itself for a second rending
bite. As the sled's exhaust singed its head skin, it roared.
Rearing up, counterbalanced by the huge tail, it tried to grab
at the sled.

"Again, Paskutti."

"I know what I'm doing," said Paskutti in a flat, dangerous
voice.

Varian looked at Tardma, but she, too, had eyes for nothing
but this curious battle. Why, thought Varian, appalled, he's
playing with the predator!

This time Paskutti caught the predator off-balance. To
keep upright, it had to release the herbivore.

"Get up, you silly creature. Get up and run," cried Varian as
the whistling, bleating grass-eater remained where it had
fallen, blood oozing from the bitten flank.

"It hasn't wit enough to know it's free," replied Tardma, her
tone even but scornful.

"Drive the carnivore back, Paskutti."

Varian needn't have spoken, for that was what the heavy-worlder was doing. The predator, now recognizing an enemy above it, attempted to bat the menace from the sky with its forelegs and massive head. Instead, it was driven, back, back, away from the herbivore.

Paskutti played with the creature who impotently tried to defend itself. Before Varian realized what Paskutti intended, the man swung the sled and let a full blast of its jets into the predator's head. A bellow of pain assailed their ears as the sled accelerated violently forward, throwing Tardma and Varian against their straps. They were thrust in the other direction as Paskutti veered back to survey the effect of his chastisement.

The carnivore was trying to get its forepaws to its face, now blackened and bleeding from the jet blast. It rolled its head in agony as it lurched blindly about.

"Now let us see if it has learned a lesson," Paskutti said and drove the sled back toward the beast.

It heard the sled, roared and stumbled wildly in the opposite direction.

"There, Varian. It has learned that a sled means pain. That one won't bother any area where it hears sleds."

"That wasn't what I was trying to do, Paskutti."

"You xenobs get soft-headed. It's tough, that killer. It'll recover. You will want to tend the wounded herbivore?"

Controlling her sudden revulsion of Paskutti with a tremendous effort, Varian nodded and busied herself with her veterinary supplies. The herbivore was still on its side, too terrified to right itself and run. Its injured limb twitched and exposed muscles rippled, each time causing the herbivore to whistle and bleat in pain. Varian ordered Paskutti to hover the sled directly over the creature which was oblivious to anything except its terror and pain. It was simpler to sprinkle an antibiotic and spray the seal on from above. They continued to hover, at a higher altitude, until the beast realized that it was no longer in any danger and struggled to its feet. Then it sniffed about, and reassured, shook, bellowing as the reflex action caused discomfort in the leg. Abruptly it snatched at a hanging frond and munched. It looked for more food, turning about and then finally began to wander away from the trap, sniffing occasionally at the wind, bleating and whistling when it remembered it was wounded.

Varian felt Paskutti watching her. She didn't want to meet his eyes for fear he would see her revulsion of him.

"All right, let's extend our search in this area. We'll want to know what other life-forms live in these foothills before the geologists can safely work here."

Paskutti nodded and swung toward the northeast again. They encountered and tagged three more herding types. Varian, still numbed by the earlier incident, gradually woke up to the fact that each of the new species must have had some common ancestor before evoluntionary differences developed to put them into a subgrouping.

When they returned to the base camp as the evening drenching began, Varian noticed that Tardma and Paskutti were as glad to be released from the close quarters of the sled as she was. She told Paskutti to check the sled over, Tardma to give Gaber the tape files, and she went down to check on Mabel. The herbivore had reduced the trees of its enclosure to mere stumps. The full leg seal had held, and Mabel did not appear to favor the injured leg. Varian was both eager and reluctant to release her patient, but the logistics of supplying Mabel with sufficient fodder made her independence necessary. She decided to let Mabel go in the morning and follow it, at a discreet distance, in the sled. She would like to establish if it had any instinctive direction, if it had any communication with other members of its herd or species. Today the herbivores had responded to the dangerous approach of the predator on an individual basis. Too bad the silly fools couldn't gang up on their killer. By mass they could overpower it if they'd any courage at all. Or any leadership.

Could she stimulate Mabel's intelligence in any way, she wondered. And as quickly decided such a program would be impossible. It would take too long and the chances of success, with Mabel's brain space, were unlikely. Mabel needed some physical modifications to achieve any measure of intelligence. There wasn't room enough in its skull for more than essential locomotion. Unless it had spare brains in its tail! And they'd provide more motor control, too. Of course, she had encountered species with auxiliary nerve centers for controlling extremities while their intelligence, or main brain, was centrally located in the most protected part of their form. Man was, Varian reminded herself, not for the first time, rather badly designed. She understood the Theks held that opinion.

She was strolling thoughtfully back to the compound when she heard the whush of a returning sled and her name called. She caught sight of Kai's face. He looked happy about something. He was gesturing her to hurry up and join him. When she did, his usually composed face was brimming with excitement. Even Bakkun had an air of satisfaction about him.

"We've got some tapes you've got to see, Varian. We found one of your fang-faces . . ."

"Don't talk to me about *it*!"

"Huh? Had a rough day? Well, this will cheer you. I need your expert opinion."

"I will take our findings up to Gaber," said Bakkun, leaving the co-leaders together as he strode toward the cartographer's dome.

"You had a good day, then?" Varian put aside her negative mood. She had no right to depress Kai or spoil his achievement.

"Very good. Just wait till you see." He was guiding her toward the shuttle. "Oh, how was yours? Could you clear that northeast section of foothills for a secondary camp?"

"Let's see your tapes first," she said, and hurried him along to the pilot cabin.

"Admittedly, I don't know that much about animal behavior," he said as he slid the tape into the viewer and activated the playback, "but this just doesn't seem logical. You see, we found the golden fliers a good hundred and sixty kilometers from the sea . . ."

"What? Doesn't make sense . . ."

The tape was playing now and she watched as the fliers came on the screen, the threads of grass visible in their beaks."

"You didn't think to . . ."

"I got samples of all the greens, grass and bush . . ."

"And they *are* green, instead of half-purple or blue . . ."

"Now watch . . ."

"Fardles! What's that thing doing there?" The predator had entered the valley, a dwarf figure until the close-up lens magnified it to a comparative life-size. "That's the beast that ate Mabel and . . ."

"Can't be the same one . . ."

"I realize that, but they are double-dangerous. We had one today, took a hunk out of another herbivore until we intervened. Why, scorch the raker, he's eating grass!" Astonishment silenced Varian. "I wonder what's so essential in that grass. Damned curious. You'd think they'd have everything they need in their environment. Now, he might be local. But the fliers couldn't be . . ."

"My thinking, too. Now this is the part that really baffles . . ."

The viewer now came to the scene in which fliers were aware of predator and it of them, the defensive line of the golden creatures and their orderly evacuation.

"Kai! Kai! Where are you, man?" They heard the voice of Dimenon, Kai's senior geologist. "Kai!"

"Ho, Dimenon, we're up front," Kai replied, pressing the hold on the viewer.

"We're here for the transuranics, aren't we?" asked Dimenon at his most dramatic as he burst into the small cabin, an equally excited Margit beside him.

"You bet . . ."

"We found the mother's own end of a great whopping saddle of pitchblende . . . rich or I'll give you every credit in my account!"

"Where?"

"You know we were to follow the southeastern track of the old cores, pick it up where it faltered? Well, where it faltered was at the edge of a geosyncline, the orogenesis is much later than this area. It was Margit who noticed the vein, the brown luster in the one sunny interval we had. We planted seismimics on a rough triangulation, and this is the reading we got." Dimenon brandished the print-out tape as one proferred a treasure. "Rich—high up on the scale. Why, this one find alone justifies the entire expedition. And with all those new fold mountains, I'll bet this is the first of many. We struck it, Kai. We struck it!"

Kai was pummeling Dimenon and Varian was hugging Margit with complete lack of inhibition while the rest of the geological team began to crowd into the compartment to add their congratulations.

"I was beginning to wonder about this planet. There were traces, yes, but there ought to have been more ore deposits . . ." Triv was saying.

"You forget, Triv," Gaber said, inking smears on his face which was for once wreathed with genuine good humor, "we're on old continental shield, not likely to have been much anyway."

"All we had to do was get beyond the shield, and look what we've got already . . ." Dimenon again did his triumphant dance, waving the print-out tape like a streamer until it caught on Portegin's shoulder and began to tear. He ended his physical gyrations and carefully began to roll up the all-important tape, which he stowed in his chest pocket. "Over my heart forever!"

"I thought I was there," Margit teased him.

"This would seem to call for a celebration," Lunzie said, putting her head round the door.

"Don't tell me you've got some joy juice hidden away

somewhere?" cried Dimenon, waggling an accusatory finger at her.

"There's no end of ways to serve that fruit, you know," she replied, her manner so blandly innocent that Varian whooped.

"Wouldn't you know Lunzie would come through?"

"Three cheers for Lunzie! The distilling dietician!"

"And how would you know it was distilled?" asked Lunzie suspiciously.

"Why else was Trizein rigging up a fractional distillation column?"

That warranted more laughter and congratulations, which was why Varian noticed the solemn heavy-worlders were absent. She said nothing about it, though she wondered. Surely Dimenon had made no secret of the find on his way up from the sled park. Where were the heavy-worlders that they wouldn't join in the expedition's first real triumph?

Lunzie was saying that she wasn't certain how good the brew would be. The product had had no time to settle or age, but surely, Dimenon said in a wheedling tone, there'd be something to take the edge off the taste of it. The group began to file out of the shuttle, moving toward the general-purpose dome. Varian saw no sign of the heavy-worlders but there was light in the quarters they shared. Passing the central standard, she rang the alarm bell in alert sequence. The iris opening of the heavy-worlders' quarters widened slightly and massive shoulders and a head appeared, outlined by the light.

"Yes?" It was Paskutti.

"Didn't you hear, Paskutti? A massive find of pitchblende. Lunzie's distilled a beverage from the fruit. We're going to sample it by way of celebration."

A huge hand waved and the iris closed.

"They being aloof again?" asked Kai, pausing in his progress to the large dome.

"They do have different enthusiasms, it's true . . ." And abruptly Varian remembered the glimpse she'd had of Paskutti's intense reaction to the predator's attack on the herbivore.

"All work, no play ... c'mon, Paskutti," roared Kai. "Tardma, Tanegli, Bakkun ... you lot ..."

The iris opened again and the heavy-worlders sedately crossed the compound to join the celebrants.

5

By the time he had finished the first beaker of Lunzie's brew, Kai had considerably more respect for the versatility of the fruit and for Lunzie's resourcefulness, which was already legend in the expedition. He might almost become a fruit freak. His taste ran to a tart flavor in beverages, and this had a jolt that was satisfying as well as to his liking.

He was startled to see Lunzie gravely pouring small beakers for the three youngsters, but when he half-rose in protest, she gave him a placid nod. Kai watched as Bonnard sipped warily and then made a disappointed grimace.

"Aw, Lunzie, it's just juice."

"Certainly. What else did you expect to get from me at your age?"

"You've added something, though, haven't you, Lunzie?" said Cleiti, smiling to make up for Bonnard's complaint.

"Yes, I have. See if you can determine what it is."

"Probably something *good* for us," said Bonnard in a mumble which Lunzie might not have heard, for she was turning away.

Kai, thoroughly amused by the incident, moved to the dinner table and began to fill a plate. There was a mixture of synthesized and natural products, including a patty made of the algae Trizein had been cultivating. It tasted faintly of the hydro-telluride that permeated everything on this planet. Kai thought again that were it not for that stink, Ireta would be a wonderful assignment.

He stood a little apart as he ate, watching the other members of his teams to gauge the general reaction to Dimenon's and Margit's find. A strike automatically increased that team's expeditionary earnings and there could be some resentment. Of course, now that they knew the shield lands were stripped, they'd go right into the nearest orogenic zones. Finds would be the rule instead of the exception from now on.

And that would mean Kai would have to report the finds to EV. How long would he and Varian be able to suppress the fact that the expedition was no longer in contact with EEC? The teams would be expecting some sort of acknowledgment of their endeavors from the mother ship. Well, Kai thought, he was within standard procedural methods to wait until they'd done a thorough survey of the site and assayed the yield. That would give him a few days' grace. Then it was entirely within the realm of operations that EV might not strip the message from the beamer for another eight to ten days. After that, he and Varian might be forced to admit to the lack of communication. Of course, by that time, maybe the vessel would have passed beyond the interference of the storm and have picked up the backlog of reports. Kai decided not to worry about that problem right now and took a good swig of Lunzie's brew. It did go down smoothly, with only the faintest trace of hydrotelluride.

Glancing around the room, Kai noticed that Varian was intently watching the heavy-worlders, her brows contracted in an expression of mild bewilderment. Paskutti was laughing, which was unusual enough, at something Tanegli had said. Could Lunzie's brew be having a loosening effect on the heavy-worlders? That shouldn't puzzle Varian. He went over to her.

"Never seen Paskutti laughing before?"

"Oh, you startled me, Kai."

"Sorry, but they're ... they're not drunk on the stuff, certainly ..."

She held her own beaker out, peering at it quizzically. "They've had just as much as I have, but they're ... they're different."

"I don't see any difference, Varian. Except this is only the second time I've ever seen Paskutti laugh, and I've worked three standard years with the man. That's nothing to get upset about ... or," and he stared at her intently a moment, "did something happen today?"

"Yes, and no. Oh, just a rather brutal incident ... a predator attacking one of Mabel's type. Nasty piece of work." She gave herself a shake and then smiled with resolute good humor at him. "I'm too used to domesticated animals, I guess."

"Like the Galormis?"

She shuddered. "You do know how to cheer me up." She stuck her tongue out at him and then laughed when he did. "No, the Galormis were clever, in their own way. They had the wit to act appealing, like the beasts we have all come to know and love through the medium of the 3-D tapes. My old practical vet instructor always warned us never to trust any animal, no matter how well we knew, liked or trusted it. But ... oh, well. I have been with that dour bunch a lot, and I guess I'm imagining things. This is a happy occasion. So let's make it one. Tomorrow's going to be very busy. And," she added, turning her body to shield her words from anyone nearby, "what are we going to do about a message to EV?"

"Thought about that myself," and Kai told her how he proposed they handle the problem.

"That's okay by me, Kai, and eminently sensible. Only I sure do hope we hear within that period. Say, you might ask the Theks in your next contact if they do remember anything about a previous expedition here."

"Do I convey curiosity or disapproval because we were landed without any knowledge of a previous expedition?"

"Do the Theks appreciate either emotional prod?"

"I doubt it, but the trick is to get them actively thinking about everything."

"By the time they've had their think, we could well be gone from here." She paused and then, sort of surprised at her own words, added, "You don't suppose that Elder Thek is from the original group?"

"Varian, it takes a million years to produce the tectonic changes that buried the other cores. Not even a Thek is that long-lived."

"Its son, maybe? Direct memory transfer? I know they practice that between generations."

"That could be it!"

"What?"

"How all knowledge of Ireta got lost. Inaccurate memory transfer."

"There you go again, Kai, accusing the Theks of fallibility. And here they've done half your work for you!"

Kai gave her a quick worried look, but she was teasing him.

"Not the dangerous half . . . just sketched in the shields. Which reminds me, if you can spare them, I'd like to borrow the heavy-worlders tomorrow. We've got to move a lot of equipment, and Dimenon says the terrain is wicked. Gaber will have to be on the spot for detailed mapping."

"Who does that leave in camp on duty?"

"Lunzie prefers to stay in, on call. Divisti wants to do some tests, and Trizein won't stir out of his lab. Oh, fardles, the younger contingent . . ."

"Don't worry about them. I'll take 'em. I'd like to see the pay dirt myself. It'd do them good. We can spin off and leave you to work in peace. I think Bonnard could manage the tell-tagger, even if you don't—"

"It's not that I don't, Varian . . ."

"I'm teasing you, Kai. But the kids'll be quite as useful for me to check the vicinity for the deposition of wildlife as the heavy-worlders. So long as we stay in the sled," she added as she noticed Kai about to caution her.

Lunzie joined them at that point and Kai complimented her on the drink.

Lunzie frowned as she regarded the pitcher of liquid dubiously.

"It's not right yet. I shall distill it again, to see if I can't filter out that hint of hydrotelluride."

"By all means keep at it, Lunzie," said Kai and held out his beaker for her to fill, complaining when she did not.

"You don't need a big head for tomorrow. This fruit is potent." Lunzie nodded toward the heavy-worlders, whose deep laughs were rolling through the dome with increased frequency. "They feel its effect and their metabolism can tolerate more alcohol than ours."

"They do look drunk, don't they, Varian?"

"Drunk? Perhaps." It could, Varian thought, account for the way they were handling each other. Alcohol was a mild aphrodisiac for some species. She'd never heard that it affected the heavy-worlders that way. She was wondering if she ought to speak to them when suddenly, as if moved by a spontaneous signal, the heavy-worlders left the dome.

"It's good to see some can recognize their limitations," said Lunzie. "I will take their tacit advice and remove temptation."

Varian protested that she'd only had one serving: Kai had had two. Lunzie gave her a splash more and then strode out of the dome. Gaber half followed her, but a curt remark stopped him at the door. Scowling, the cartographer came back to Varian and Kai.

"The evening's only started," he said in an aggrieved tone. "Why did she have to remove the drink?"

"She's worried about its potency." Varian studied the pale greenish liquid in her beaker with marked suspicion. "It sure made an impression on the heavy-worlders."

Gaber snorted. "No need to deprive us because they have soft heads in spite of their heavy muscles."

Kai and Varian exchanged glances because Gaber was slurring some of his words, whether he was oblivious to the fact or not. He took a careful sip, closing his eyes to concentrate on an appreciation of the taste. "First decent thing on this planet," he said. "Only thing that doesn't smell. And Lunzie makes off with it. Not fair. Just not fair."

"We've a heavy day tomorrow, Gaber."

"Did *you* tell her to ration us?" Gaber was quite willing to transfer his irritation from Lunzie to Kai and Varian.

"No. She's the dietician and the physician, Gaber. This stuff is apparently not up to standard. There could be adverse reactions to it and tomorrow . . ."

"I know, I know," and Gaber waved his hand irritably to cut off Kai's sentence. "We've a big day tomorrow. Just as well we have something like this to sustain us when we're . . ." Now he abruptly broke off his sentence, glancing apprehensively at Kai who affected not to notice. "It does have a funny taste to it." He hurried off.

"Sustain us when . . . what, Kai?" asked Varian, concerned.

"Gaber came up with the ass-headed notion that we've been planted."

"Planted?" Varian suppressed the word behind her hand and then let her laughter loose. "I doubt it. Not on a planet as rich in the transuranics as this one. No way. Those ores are too badly needed. And it isn't as if they'd landed heavy equipment for us to do any sort of mining. Certainly not transuranic refining. Gaber's the original gloom guy. He can't ever look on the bright side of things."

"I laughed at him, too, Varian, only . . ."

"Co-leader Kai," Varian glowered at him sternly, "of course you did. It's stupid, silly, and I only wish that the other reports had been picked up from the satellite so I didn't have any doubts." She gave Kai a frantic look, then shook her head. "No, it won't wash. We're not planted. But, if we don't hear from EV, I wouldn't trust Gaber not to spread that rumor." She looked at her empty beaker. "Damn Lunzie! Just when I need a drop more."

"I thought we'd decided not to worry about EV."

"I'm not. Just grousing. I like that junk! It's got a certain curious jolt to it."

"Probably a nutritional additive," said Kai, remembering Bonnard's complaint.

Varian burst out laughing. "Trust Lunzie for that. Our health is her first concern."

Dimenon, his arm possessively about Margit, came strolling over to them. He couldn't have had more to drink than anyone else, since Lunzie had kept control of the pitcher, but his face was flushed and he was decidedly merry. He insisted to Kai that the pitchblende mine be named after Margit. She was equally insistent that they share the triumph, as was customary, and the two fell to good-natured bickering, each calling for support from special friends in the team until everyone was involved in discussion.

Gaber was not the only one annoyed by Lunzie's precipitous departure with the drink, and Kai was surprised to hear a good deal of veiled complaints about the heavy-worlders. It caught him unawares as he'd been more sensitive to friction between the geological teams.

The next morning, he had additional cause for thought about the heavy-worlders, for they were not operating in their usual stolid dependable fashion; they moved sluggishly, awkwardly, looked tired and were almost sullenly quiet.

"They couldn't have got hungover on two half-beakers," Varian murmured to Kai as she, too, noticed the glum manner of her team. "And their quarters were dark early. They ought to have got enough sleep."

"If they got to sleep . . ." Kai replied, grinning.

Varian dropped her jaw in surprise and then she giggled. "I tend to forget they must have a sex drive. It's a weird cycle, compulsive in the rut, so to speak, on their own planet. Generally, they don't when they're on a mission."

"There isn't a law against it for them, is there?"

"No, it's just they don't . . ." She seemed to find it mystifying. "Well, they'll sweat it out on those slopes this morning," she added, looking at the foothills that folded higher and higher until the overthrust mountains dominated the skyline. They were standing at the base of the saddle ridge of pitchblende, looking down the fold limb. The brown lustrous vein was visible where dirt had been blown clear. "This is a fantastic deposit, Kai. And so is its location. Why, one of the big mining ships can just squat right down and crunch up all of it without moving again." She had emphasized her words by rolling her *r*'s and gesturing graphically with her fingers in clawlike attitudes.

"I didn't realize you'd worked with a geology team before."

"Galorm was explored for its minerals, not its wildlife, Kai. Admittedly the wildlife made the beamlines, but we xenobs were just along to catalogue another variation of life."

"Do you ever mind?"

"What? Being second?" She shrugged and smiled to reassure him. "No, Kai. Energy is a lot more important than wildlife."

"Life," and he paused to stress the inclusiveness of the word, "is far more important than any inanimate object . . ." he gestured to the pitchblende.

"Which just happens to be essential to sustain *life*—on other planets, and in space. We have to sustain, protect and investigate. I'm here to inspect the life that exists on Ireta, and you're here to insure that life elsewhere can continue on its grand and glorious scale. Don't fret on my account, Kai. The experience I gain here may just one day put me where I really want to be . . ."

"Which is . . ." Kai was also trying to see what Paskutti and Tardma were doing with a seismograph.

"Planetary preserver. Now," she went on, noticing his diverted attention, "I'd better enhance the reputation needed to be one by studying those fliers of yours. I can survey this area first."

They both caught in their breaths as Tardma faltered, struggled to regain her balance and the backpack of delicate instrumentation which she was bringing up the far slope.

"What the fardles did Lunzie put in that joy juice of hers to queer them up so?"

"It's Ireta that's doing it to them! The drink didn't affect us that way. I'm off now, Kai. I've only to gather the youngsters."

"I'll need the big sled back here, you know."

"Yes, by sundown! Shout if you need it sooner," she said, gesturing to her wrist comunit.

Bonnard was disappointed to be dragged away before the first seismic shot, but when Dimenon told him it would take several hours to set up, he went willingly with Varian.

Terilla had been enchanted by unusual flowering vines and, carefully wearing her thick gloves, had gathered different types, which she had placed in the bags Divisti had given her for the purpose. Cleiti, who tended to be Bonnard's aide and assistant, regarded the younger girl's activity with supercilious disdain. Varian shooed them all toward the big sled and told them to settle in and belt up. She was checking the flight board when she was struck by the sled's elapsed hours of use. Surely she hadn't put twelve hours flight time on it yesterday? Even subtracting the two hours to reach these foothills, she couldn't have racked up more than six hours the day before. That left a huge whack unaccounted for—and made the sled due for a recharging and servicing.

She'd ask Kai about it when she returned. Maybe she simply hadn't recorded accurately, or the sled had been used here when she'd been busy elsewhere.

She showed Bonnard how to operate the tagger, Cleiti how to read the life-form telltale, and Terilla how to be sure the recorder was functioning as they'd be passing over relatively undetailed terrain. The youngsters were delighted to have some responsibility and listened attentively as Varian explained the quartering pattern she would follow as they surveyed the general vicinity for dangerous life forms. Although Varian was skeptical about the duration of their enthusiasm once the tasks had settled into routine, their exuberance made a nice change from the sober company of the heavy-worlders.

The three young people hadn't had that much occasion to see the raw life of a virgin planet, having had only the one trip since they'd landed on Ireta. They chattered happily as Varian lifted the sled and circled the geological site.

At first there wasn't much to telltale or tag. Most of the animal life was small and kept hidden from sight. Bonnard was jubilant when he tagged some tree-dwellers which Varian thought must be nocturnal since they didn't so much as move from their tree boles when the sled passed over them. Terilla periodically reported the recorder functioning but the ground over which they passed would make details of the area difficult to read. In the low foothills, as they quartered back toward the pitchblende saddle, the sled's noise flushed a group of fleet little animals which Bonnard gleefully tagged and Terilla triumphantly taped. Slightly put out by the success of the others, Cleiti's turn came when she read telltales of a cave-dwelling life form. They did not show themselves but the readings were low enough on the scale to suggest small creatures, burrowers or timid night beasts that would be unlikely to cause problems for any secondary camp.

In fact, Varian had to conclude that nothing of any potentially dangerous size could be found in the foothills surrounding the pitchblende discovery. Nonetheless, size did not, as she pointed out to the children, relate to the potential danger of a creature. Some of the smallest were the most deadly. The one you could hear coming was the safest: you could take evasive action. Bonnard snorted at the notion of running away.

"I like plants better than animals," said Terilla.

"Plants can be just as dangerous," replied Bonnard in a repressive tone.

"Like that sword plant?" asked Terilla with such innocence that Varian, who was suppressing her laughter at the girl's apt query, could not consider the child guilty of malice.

Bonnard growled at the reminder of his painful encounter with that particular plant and was patently trying to think of a put-down for Terilla.

"Your instruments are transmitting," said Varian, to forestall a quarrel.

The sled was passing over an area of squat trees and thick undergrowth which triggered the telltale at a large enough scale and sufficient concentration to warrant some investigation. The terrain was rocky and steep, which suggested the inhabitants were not ruminants. However, after circling without flushing the creatures, Varian decided that the area was far enough from the ore deposit to be a negligible danger. She marked the coordinates for later study when a ground expedition could be mounted. Despite the generally high level of violent life and death on Ireta, one could be too cautious. If Kai sited the secondary camp high enough up in the foothills to avoid the worst predatory life, the force-screen would be sufficient to deter poisonous insects and dangerous smaller animals. It wasn't as if a herd of Mabels was likely to come rampaging up the slopes and stampeding through the force-screen.

She finished her survey, cautioned the youngsters to check the seat belts they had loosened to attend to their instruments, and, tapping in the coordinates for the inland sea, she gave the sled full power.

Even so it took a good hour and a half to reach their destination. She wished that Divisti had had a chance to run an analysis of the grasses which Kai and Bakkun had collected at the Rift Valley. The report might have given Varian some insight into the habits of the fliers, but perhaps it was wiser to observe these fascinating creatures without preconceived notions.

Varian was pleased with the behavior of the youngsters on

the flight: they asked more intelligent questions than she'd been led to expect from them, sometimes straying in areas of which she had little knowledge. They seemed annoyed that she was not a portable data retrieval unit.

Cleiti was the first to spot the fliers, and preened herself for that feat later on. The creatures were not, as Varian had unconsciously expected, perched on the cliffs and rocks of their natural habitat, nor singly fishing. A large group—not a flock, for that was a loose collection of a similar species, and the fliers gave the appearance of organization—was gathered above the broad ends of the inland water, at its deepest part, where the cliffs narrowed to form the narrow isthmus through which the parent sea pushed the tide waters to flush the vast inland basin; a tide which seldom had force enough to crawl more than a few inches up the verge on the farthest shore, fifty kilometers away.

"I've never seen birds doing that," Bonnard exclaimed.

"When did you ever see free birds in flight?" asked Varian, a bit chagrined that her tone emerged sharper than she'd intended.

"I have landed, you know," said Bonnard with mild reproach. "And there are such things as training tapes. I watch a lot of those. So, those aren't acting like any other species I've ever seen."

"Qualification accepted, Bonnard, I haven't either."

The golden fliers were sweeping low in what had to be considered a planned formation. The sled was a bit too far for unaided vision of the observers to perceive exactly what happened to jerk the line of fliers to half their previous forward speed. Some of the fliers were dragged downward briefly, but as they beat their wings violently to compensate, they recovered their positions in the line and slowly, the whole mass began to lift up, away from the water's surface.

"Hey, they've got something in their claws," said Bonnard who had appropriated the screen from Cleiti and had adjusted it to the distance factor. "I'd swear it's a net. It is! And they're dragging fish from the water. Scorch it! And look what's happening below!"

Varian had had time to adjust her mask's magnification and the girls had crowded over the small viewer plate with Bonnard. They could all see clearly the roiling water, and the frenzied thrusts and jumps of the aquatic life which unsuccessfully tried to penetrate the nets and the captured prey.

"Nets! How in the raking rates do fliers achieve nets?" Varian's comment was more for herself than the children.

"I see claws half down their wings, there, where it goes triangular. Can't see clearly enough but, Varian, if they've an opposing digit, they could *make* nets."

"They could and they must have, because we haven't seen anything else bright enough on Ireta to make 'em for 'em."

Cleiti giggled, smothering the sound in her hand. "The Ryxi won't like this."

"Why not?" Bonnard demanded, regarding his friend with a frown. "Intelligent avian life is very rare, my xenob says."

"The Ryxi like being the only smart ones," said Cleiti. "You know how Vrl used to be . . ." Somehow the child lengthened her neck, hunched her shoulders forward, swept her hands and arms back like folded wings and assumed such a haughty expression by pulling her mouth and chin down that she exactly resembled the arrogant Vrl.

"Don't ever let him see that," Varian said, tears of laughter in her eyes. "But it's a terrific mime, Cleiti. Terrific."

Cleiti grinned at her success as Bonnard and Terilla regarded her with expressions akin to awe.

"Who else can you do?" asked Bonnard.

Cleiti shrugged. "Who did you want?"

"Not now, kids. Later. I want tape on this phenomenon."

The three youngsters immediately took their assigned stations as the sled followed the burdened fliers toward the distant cliffs. Varian had time to dwell on the subtler implications of the fliers' fishing. The creatures were quite obviously the most intelligent species she had encountered on Ireta. Nor had she come across another cooperative avian race: at least, at this level. Bonnard's xenob was not accurate in saying that intelligent avian life was rare: *dominant* intelligent avian life was, however. So often winged life was in such desperate competition with ground-based life for the same foods that all their energies had to be directed to the procurement of food, or the preservation of the home nest, and the succor of the young. When a life form specialized, dropping the fore-arm with manipulative skill for the wing of retreat, they lost a tremendous advantage in the battle of survival.

The golden fliers of Ireta seemed to have managed to retain the vestigial hand without expense to the wing, and thus used their flight advantage beautifully.

Occasionally smaller fish fell from the nets, back into the sea, to cause more frothing as the submarine denizens strug-gled to secure the prizes. Twice, immense heads rolled avidly up from the depths as the fliers passed with their tempting loads.

Now the four observers saw additional fliers materializing from the cloudy skies, swooping down to take positions along the edges of the nets, supporting the load and relieving the first fishers. Thus assisted, the formation picked up speed.

"How fast are they going now, Varian?" asked Bonnard, for the xenob had been carefully matching the forward motion, staying behind but above the fliers.

"With this tailwind, I make it twenty kph, but I think they'll gain air speed with all this reinforcement."

"They're so beautiful," said Terilla softly. "Even hard at work they're graceful, and see how they gleam."

"They look as if they were traveling in their own personal sunlight," said Cleiti, "but there's no sun."

"Yeah, what's with this crazy planet?" said Bonnard. "It stinks and there's never any sun. I did want to see a sun when I got a chance."

"Well, here's your moment," said Terilla, crowing with delight as the unpredictable happened and the clouds parted to a glimpse of the green sky and the white-hot yellow sun.

Varian laughed with the others and almost wished that the face masks didn't adjust instantly for the change in light. The only way she knew that there was sun at the moment was the shadows on the sea.

"We're being followed!" Bonnard's amused tone held a note of awe.

Huge bodies now broke the surface and slammed down on the shadow which the air sled cast on the waters behind it.

"I'm glad we're ahead of them," Cleiti said in a small voice.

"There's the biggest crazy I've ever seen!" Bonnard sounded so startled that Varian turned around.

"What was it, Bonnard?"

"I couldn't tell you. I've never seen anything like it in all my born days, Varian."

"Was the taper on it?"

"Not on *that*," said Terilla, apologetically. "Forward, on the fliers."

"Here, let me have it, Ter, I know where to point." Bonnard assumed control and Terilla moved aside.

"It's like a flat piece of fabric, Varian," Bonnard was saying as he sighted across the stern of the sled. "The edges flutter and then . . . it sort of turns over on itself! Here comes another!"

The girls gave small squeals of revulsion and delighted fear. Varian slewed round in the pilot seat and caught a glimpse of something gray-blue which did, as Bonnard said, flutter like a fabric caught in a strong breeze. She caught sight of two points halfway up one side (like claws?), then the creature flipped over, end for end, and entered the water, with more of a swish than a splash, as Cleiti put it.

"How big would you say it was, Bonnard?"

"I'd judge about a meter on each side but it kept switching.

I've got good tapes of that last leap. I set the speed half again higher so you can play back for more detail."

"That's using your head, Bonnard."

"Here comes another! Rakers! Look at the speed on that thing!"

"I'd rather not," said Terilla. "How does it know we're here? I don't see any sort of eyes or antenna or anything. It can't see the shadows."

"The fringes?" asked Bonnard. "Sonar?"

"Not for leaping *out* of water," replied Varian. "We'll possibly find out how it perceives us when we can replay. Rather interesting. And were those claws I saw? Two of them?"

"That's bad?" Bonnard had caught the puzzled note in her voice.

"Not bad, Bonnard, but damned unusual. The fliers, the herbivores and the predators are pentadactyl, which isn't an unlikely evolution, but two digits on a side flange?"

"I saw flying longies once," said Cleiti in a bright helpful voice. "They were a meter long and they undulated. No feet at all, but they could ripple along in the air for kilometers."

"Light-gravity planet?"

"Yes, Varian, and dry!"

The sun had slunk behind the clouds again and the thin noonday drizzle settled in so that the others laughed at her sour comment.

"Digits are important in evolution, aren't they, Varian?" asked Bonnard.

"Very. You can have intelligent life, like those avians, but until a species becomes a tool-user, they don't have much chance of rising above their environment."

"The fliers have, haven't they?" asked Bonnard with a broad grin for his play on words.

"Yes, Bonnard, they have," she replied with a laugh.

"I heard about them being in the Rift Valley, with grasses," Bonnard went on. "Is this why they got that type of grass? To make the nets?"

"There was a lot of thick, tough grass around the place where we saved Dandy, and that was a lot closer for them," said Cleiti.

"You're right there, Cleiti. I've thought the fliers might need the Rift Valley grass for some dietary requirement."

"I have some of the vegetation from the grove of fruit trees, Varian," said Terilla.

"You do? That's great. We can do some real investigation. How clever of you, Terilla."

"Not clever, you know me and plants," said the girl, but her cheeks were flushed with reaction to the praise.

"I take back what I said about your stupid plants," said Bonnard with unusual magnanimity.

"I'll be very keen to see how mature their young are," Varian said, having quietly considered the curious habits of the golden creatures for a few minutes.

"How mature? Their young? Isn't that a contradiction?" asked Bonnard.

"Not really. You are born very young . . ."

Cleiti giggled. "Everyone is, or you wouldn't *be* young . . ."

"I don't mean age, I mean ability, Cleiti. Now, let's see what comparisons I can draw for you ship-bred . . ."

"I lived my first four years on a planet," said Terilla.

"Did you? Which one?"

"Arthos in the Aurigae section. I've touched down on two more and stayed for months."

"And what animals did you see on Arthos?" Varian knew but Terilla so seldom volunteered any information, or had a chance to with such aggressive personalities as Cleiti and Bonnard.

"We had milk cows, and four-legged dogs, and horses. Then there were six-legged dogs, offoxes, cantileps and spurges."

"Seen any tape on cows, dogs, and horses, Cleiti? Bonnard?"

"Sure!"

"All right, cows and horses bear live young who are able to

rise to their feet about a half-hour after birth and, if necessary, run with their dams. They are therefore born mature and already programmed for certain instinctive actions and responses. You and I were born quite small and physically immature. We had to be taught by our parents or guardians how to eat, walk, run and talk and take care of ourselves."

"So?" Bonnard regarded Varian steadily, waiting for the point of her digression.

"So, the horse and cow don't learn a lot from their parents: not much versatility or adaptability is required of them. Whereas human babies . . ."

"Have to learn too much too soon too well and all the time," said Cleiti with such an exaggerated sigh of resignation that Varian chuckled.

"And change half of what you learn when the info gets updated," she added, sympathetically. "The main advantage humans have is that they do learn, are flexible and can adapt. Adapt to some pretty weird conditions . . ."

"Like the stink here," put in Bonnard.

"So that's why I'm curious about the maturity of the fliers at birth."

"They'd be oviparous, wouldn't they?" asked Bonnard.

"More than likely. I don't see that they'd be ovoviviparous . . . too much weight for the mother if she had to carry her young for any length of time. No, I'd say they'd have to be oviparous, and then the eggs would hatch fledglings, unable to fly for quite some time. That might account, too, for the fishing. Easier to supply the hungry young if everyone cooperates."

"Hey, look, Varian," cried Bonnard who had not left off watching through the screen, "there's a changeover on the net carriers. Bells! but they're organized. As neat a changeover as I've ever seen. I'll bet the fliers are the most intelligent species on Ireta."

"Quite likely, but don't jump to any conclusion. We've barely begun to explore this planet."

"Are we going to have to go over all of it?" Bonnard was briefly dismayed.

"Oh, as much as we can while we're here," she said in a casual tone. What if they had been planted? "Apart from its odor, Ireta isn't too bad a place. I've been in a lot worse."

"I don't really mind the smell . . ." Bonnard began, half in apology, half in self-defense.

"I don't even notice it anymore," said Terilla.

"I do mind the rain . . ." Bonnard continued, ignoring Terilla's comment. "And the gloom."

At which point the sun emerged.

"Can you do that again whenever we feel the need of sunlight?" asked Varian as the girls giggled over the opportuneness.

"I sure wish I could!"

Once again the angle of the sun projected a distorted shadow of the sled on the water and the fish, large and small, shattered the surface in vain attempts to secure the reality of that shadow. Varian had Bonnard tape the attacks for later review. It was an easy way to catalogue the submarine life, she said.

"I sailed once on shore leave at Boston-Betelgeuse," said Bonnard after the sun and the predatory fish had deserted them.

"You wouldn't catch me sailing on that!" said Cleiti, pointing to the water.

"I wouldn't, but something else would, wouldn't it?"

"Huh?"

"Catch you, silly face!"

"Oh, you're so funny!"

Additional fliers emerged from the clouds to relieve the net carriers who sped up and away, as if pleased to be free of their chore. The convoy, strengthened by the reinforcements, picked up speed, veering slightly east toward the highest of the prominences. They were not, as Varian had assumed, going to have to cross the entire sea to reach a home base.

"Hey, that's where they're heading. I can see other fliers on the cliff top, and the front is all holey, with caves!" cried Bonnard, delighted.

"They live in caves to keep their fur dry and their fledglings safe from the sea creatures," said Terilla with unusual authority.

"Birds have feathers, stupid."

"Not always," Varian replied. "And those fliers appear to have fur, which is, sometimes, a variation of a feather in some beasts."

"Are we going to land and find out fur sure?" asked Bonnard in a ponderous tone of voice so everyone caught his pun. Cleiti swatted at him and Varian groaned, shaking her head.

"No, we're not landing now. It's dangerous to approach animals when they're feeding. We know where the fliers live now. That's enough for one day."

"Couldn't we just hover? That won't disturb them."

"Yes, we could."

More of the golden creatures emerged from crevices and caves in the cliff and gracefully swooped up to the summit, which Varian could see was relatively flat for about five hundred meters, where it dropped off into very rough and boulder-strewn slopes.

"What're they going to do now?" asked Bonnard. "That net's too big to get in any one of those cave entrances . . . Oh . . ." Bonnard's question was answered as the entire group of fliers now carried the net up over the edge of the cliff and suddenly dropped one side, spilling the fish onto the summit plateau.

From every direction fliers converged on the catch. Some landed, wings slightly spread, to waddle in an ungainly fashion toward the shimmering piles of fish. Others swooped, filled their throat pouches and disappeared into their cliff holes. For all the varied approaches, the dispersal of the catch occasioned no squabbling over choice of fish. As the four watched, there were periods when no fliers were picking over the fish. They did seem to be selective.

"Sharpen the focus on the viewer, Bonnard," said Varian. "Let's get some frames of what they didn't eat . . ."

"Those fringe things, the small ones."

"Maybe that's why the fringe fliers were after us. They'd taken their young . . ." said Terilla.

"Nah!" Bonnard was contemptuous. "The fringes hadn't eyes, much less brains, so how could they be sentimental about their young?"

"I dunno. But we don't know that they aren't. Fish could have emotions. I read somewhere that . . ."

"Oh you!" Bonnard gestured her peremptorily to silence.

Varian turned, worrying that his attitude might bother the child since his tone was unwarranted, but she seemed unperturbed. Varian promised herself a few choice words with Bonnard. And then vetoed the notion. The young of every species seemed to work things out among themselves fairly well.

She peered into the viewer herself, to see the rejects. "Some aquatic creatures are capable of loyalties and kindness to their own species, but I'd say that the fringe organism is too primitive yet. They probably spawn millions of eggs in order for a few to survive to adulthood—to spawn again. Our fliers don't include them in their diet, though. Nor those spiny types. Bonnard, you've been helping Trizein and Divisti: take a good look! Seen any of those in the marine samples we've given them?"

"No. New ones on me."

" 'Course, we sampled from the main oceans . . ." Most of the fliers had disappeared now and only the rejected specimens were left, to rot on the stone.

"Varian, look!" Bonnard, again at the screen, gestured urgently. "I've got it lined up . . . look!"

Varian pushed his hand aside as he was so excited he was obscuring the view. One of the small fringers was moving, in that strange fashion, collapsing on one side and flipping over. Then she saw what had excited Bonnard: unsupported by water, its natural element, the internal skeleton of the creature

was outlined through its covering. She could plainly see the
joints at each corner. It moved by a deformation of parallelograms. It moved once, twice more, and then lay still, its
fringes barely undulating, then not at all. How long had it survived without water, Varian wondered? Was it equipped with
a dual set of lungs to have lived so long away from what was
apparently its natural element? Was this creature on its way
out of its aquatic phase, moving onto land?

"You got all that on tape, didn't you?" Varian asked
Bonnard.

"Sure, the moment it started moving. Can it breath
oxygen?"

"I hope it can't," said Cleiti. "I wouldn't want to meet that
wet sheet in a dark dripping forest." She shuddered with her
eyes tightly shut.

"Neither would I," said Varian, and meant it.

"Couldn't it be friendly? If it wasn't hungry all the time?"
asked Terilla.

"Wet, slimy, wrapping its fringes around you and choking
you to death," said Bonnard, making movements like his hor-
rifying image.

"It couldn't wrap around me," Terilla said, unmoved. "It
can't bend in the middle. Only on the edges."

"It isn't moving at all now," Bonnard said, sounding disappointed and sad.

"Speaking of moving," said Varian, glancing toward the
one bright spot in the gray skies, "that sun is going down."

"How can you tell?" asked Bonnard sarcastically.

"I'm looking at the chrono."

Cleiti and Terilla giggled.

"Couldn't we land and see the fliers up close?" asked Bonnard, now wistful.

"Rule number one, never bother animals when feeding.
Rule number two, never approach strange animals without
first closely observing their habits. Just because the fliers

haven't attempted to take bites out of us doesn't mean they aren't as dangerous as those mindless predators."

"Aren't we ever going to observe them up close?" Bonnard was persistent.

"Sure, when I've applied rule number two, but not today. I'm to bring the sled back to the pitchblende site."

"Can I come with you when you do come back?"

"That's possible."

"Promise?"

"No. I just said it was possible, Bonnard, and that's what I mean."

"I'm never going to learn anything on this trip if I don't get out and do *some* field work, away from screens and . . ."

"If we brought you back to the ship with a part or parts missing, left in the maw of a fringe or a flier, your mother would give us the deep six. So be quiet." Varian used a sharper tone than she normally employed with Bonnard, but his insistence, his air that he had only to wheedle enough and his wish would be granted, annoyed her. She was sympathetic to his irritation with constant restrictions. To the ship-born, planets gave illusions of safety because one was insulated from ship-learned dangers by an atmosphere miles deep, whereas in space only thin metal shells prevented disaster, and any broaching of that shell was lethal. No shell, no danger, in simplistic terms.

"Would you run through that tape, Bonnard, and see if we have good takes on the fringes," she asked him after a long pause, mutinous on his part, firm on hers. "There's something I want to check out with Trizein when we get back to camp. Fardles, but I wish we had access to the EV's data banks."

After another long pause during which she heard the slight whir of rapidly spun tape, Bonnard spoke. "You know, those fliers remind me of something I've seen before. I can almost see the printed label on the tape sleeve . . ."

"What about this tape?"

"Oh, clear pictures, Varian."

"They've reminded me of something, too, Bonnard, but I can't drag it out of storage either."

"My mother always says that if you're worrying over something, go to sleep thinking about it and you'll remember in the morning," said Terilla.

"Good idea, Terilla. I'll do so and so can you, Bonnard. Meanwhile, we're over new territory again. Man the telltale."

They got some good tags on a stumpy-legged ruminant, spotted but couldn't tag more small mammals like Dandy and surprised several flocks of scavengers at their work. They returned to the mining site just as the "gloom thickened," as Terilla put it. Kai was waiting with Dimenon and Margit with the equipment which the sled must transport.

"It's a very rich find, Varian," said Dimenon. He looked very tired and immensely satisfied. He started to add more but stopped, turning to Kai.

"And the next valley over shows another saddle deposit as large and as rich," said Kai, a grin creasing his sweat and dirt-smeared face.

"And probably the next one beyond that," said Margit, sighing wearily. "Only, that can wait until tomorrow."

"EV should have given us at least one remote scanner, Kai," said Dimenon, as he helped load the instruments. This sounded to Varian like the continuation of an argument.

"I requisitioned one, standard. Supply said they'd no more in stock. If you'll remember, we passed quite a few promising systems in the last standard year."

"When I think of the slogging we'd be saved . . ."

"I dunno," said Margit, interrupting Dimenon. She placed a coil of wire on the sled deck. "We do so raking much by remote. I know I've done something today." She groaned. "I feel it in every bone and in muscles I didn't know I had. We're soft. No wonder the heavy-worlders sneer at us."

"Them!" A world of scorn was expressed in Dimenon's single word.

Kai and Varian exchanged quick glances.

"I know they were bloody hungover or something earlier on, but I was glad enough of Paskutti's muscle this afternoon," Margit went on, pulling herself into the sled and settling down beside Terilla. "Get in, Di, I'm dying for a wash, and I bloody hope that Portegin's deodorizer has fixed the water stink. Hydrotelluride does not enhance the body beautiful. So how did you pass the day, scamp?" she asked Terilla.

While the three young people kept a conversation going, Varian wondered, as she set the sled on its baseward course, just what happened to occasion Dimenon's captious attitude. Perhaps it was no more than irritation with the heavy-worlders' behavior in the morning, and reaction to the excitement of such a rich find. She must ask Kai later. She didn't want her team coming into contention with his, and she would be the first to admit the heavy-worlders had been less than efficient. Or was Dimenon still irked over last night's alcohol rationing?

There were dangers inherent in mixing planet- and ship-bred groups, and EV kept it down to a minimum whenever possible. The Iretan expedition had needed the brawn of the heavy-worlders and Varian and Kai would simply have to work out the problems.

Varian was a bit depressed. A computer could give you a probability index on any situation. This mission had had a good one. But a computer couldn't adjust its input with such unexpected details as a stink and constant gloom or drizzle, affecting tempers, or a cosmic storm cutting off communications with the mother ship: it certainly hadn't printed out the fact that a planet listed as unexplored was now giving immutable evidence of previous survey, not to mention anomalies like . . . But *if*, Varian thought, there had been the survey, maybe such things as pentadactyl development and aquatic collapsing parallelograms were entirely possible! Yet which was indigenous? Both couldn't be!

Fliers having to find grass so far from their natural habitat?

Varian's spirits lifted again with excitement. And if the golden fliers, who were pentadactyl, were *not* indigenous, then the herbivores and predators they'd so far encountered were not indigenous either! Not anomalies: conundrums. And how? By whom? The Others? No, not the ubiquitous Others. They destroyed all life, it there was any substance to the rumor that such sentient beings existed.

The Theks might know about the previous survey . . . if Kai could stimulate them into a serious attempt at recall. By Matter! She'd sit through an interchange herself to find out! Wait till she told Kai that!

6

KAI had as much to reflect upon as Varian as he sledded back to the encampment. For one thing, he was minus some irreplaceable equipment that Paskutti and Tardma had dropped down a crevice. EV had allowed him only the minimum of seismic spares, and the last group he'd expect to be careless with equipment was the heavy-worlders. They moved so deliberately they avoided most accidents. He couldn't restrict the heavy-worlders from drinking the distillation, but he'd have to ask Lunzie to dilute any given them from now on. He couldn't afford more losses.

An expeditionary force was permitted so many credits in loss of equipment due to unforeseeable accidents, but above that figure, the leaders found their personal accounts docked. The loss of the equipment was bothering Kai more than any possible credit subtraction: it was a loss caused by sheer negligence. That irritated him. And his irritation annoyed him more because this should have been a day of personal and team satisfaction: he had achieved what he had been sent to do. Ruthlessly now, he suppressed negative feelings.

Beside him Gaber was chattering away in the best spirits the cartographer had exhibited since landing. Berru and Triv were discussing the next day's work in terms of which of the colored lakes would be the richest in ore minerals. Triv was wishing for just one remote sensor, with a decent infrared eye to pierce the everlasting clouds. A week's filming in a polar orbit and the job would be done.

"We do have the probe's tapes," Berru said.

"That only sounded land mass and ocean depth. No definition, no infrared to penetrate that eternal cloud cover."

"I asked for a proper prelanding remote sensing," Gaber said, the note of petulance back in his voice.

"So did I," said Kai, "and was told there wasn't a suitable satellite in Stores. We have to do it the hard way, in person."

"That would seem to be the criterion for this expedition," said Gaber, giving Kai a sly glance. "Everything's done the hard way."

"You've gone soft, Gaber, that's all," said Triv. "Not enough time in the grav gym on shipboard. I enjoy the challenge, frankly. I've gone flabby. This trip's good for all of us. We're spoiled with a punch-a-button dial-a-comfort system. We need to get back to nature, test our sinews, circulate our blood and . . ."

"Breathe deeply of stinking air?" asked Gaber when Triv, carried away by his own eloquence, briefly faltered.

"What, Gaber? Lost your nose filters again?"

Gaber was easy to tease and Triv continued in a bantering way until Kai turned the sled through the gap in the hills to their encampment. Kai had affected not to acknowledge Gaber's glance although, tied in with Gaber's notion of planting, "doing everything the hard way" could well be a prelude to the abandonment that was euphemistically termed "planting." It could account for quite a number of deletions in Kai's original requisition list. Remote sensors were expensive equipment to leave behind with a planted colony. But, if the colony were supposed to be self-sufficient, surely some mining equipment would have been included so that they could refine needed metals for building and for replacement of worn-out parts, like sled members. There would have been . . . "Do it the hard way" rang ominously in Kai's mind. He'd better have a long chat with Varian as soon as he could.

However, *if* this expedition were genuine—the urgent need for the transuranics was a chronic condition in the FPS—then someone, if not their own *ARCT-10* EV, would strip the message from the beamer satellite and take the appropriate action of returning to Ireta to extract the all-important ores and minerals and, incidentally, rescue them. The positive thought encouraged Kai, and he employed the rest of the trip by formulating messages; first to the Thek and then for the long-distance capsule. No, he'd only the one capsule. Two large deposits did not really constitute cause for dispatching it. So, first he could frame a message for his next contact with the Thek about the old cores, and the uranium deposits. He would hold the ldc until he could justify its trip. He'd no genuine cause for alarm, apart from a vague suspicion of an aging cartographer.

To his surprise, the heavy-worlders, who had left the site considerably before him to return by lift-belt, had not arrived at the compound. The other sleds had all returned safely. The youngsters were cosseting Dandy while Lunzie watched. She used her overseeing as an excuse not to answer the importunities of Portegin and Aulia for more joy juice. He saw neither Varian nor Trizein and had decided she must be in the xenochemist's laboratory in the shuttle when the heavy-worlders, in their neat formation, came swooping in from the north. The north? He started toward the veil lock to ask Paskutti about such a detour when Varian hailed him from the shuttle.

She sounded excited so he hurried over, leaving Paskutti till another time.

"Kai, Trizein thinks he knows why the fliers must need the grasses," she said when he got near enough. "The stuff is full of carotene . . . vitamin A. They must need it for eyesight and pigmentation."

"Odd that they'd have to go such a distance for a basic requirement."

"But it substantiates my hunch that the pentadactyls are *not* indigenous to this world."

Kai was lifting his foot through the iris and stopped, grabbing at the sides to balance himself.

"Not indigenous? What in the name of raking . . . what do you mean? They have to be indigenous. They're here."

"They didn't originate here," and Varian gestured him to come into the shuttle. "Further, those parallelograms I saw today aren't even vaguely arthropods, which would fit in with the vertebrates we've discovered like the herbivores, predators and even the fliers."

"You're not making any sense."

"I am. This planet isn't. You don't find animals forced to go hundreds of kilometers from their proper environment to acquire a dietary necessity. What is essential to them is generally supplied right where they live!"

"Now, wait a minute, Varian. Think. If your pentadactyls are not indigenous, they were brought here. Who, why would anyone want to relocate animals as large as that predator or your Mabel?"

She regarded him steadily, as if she expected him to know the answer to his question.

"You should know. They've already tipped us off. The Theks, slow-top," she said with some asperity when he remained silent. "The inscrutable Theks. They've been here before. They left those seismic devices."

"That makes no sense, Varian."

"It makes a lot of sense."

"What reason could the Theks possibly have for such an action?"

"They've probably forgotten," Varian said, grinning mischievously. "Along with the fact that they'd surveyed this planet before."

They had reached Trizein's lab and he was contemplating the enlarged image of some fibers.

"Of course, we'd need to have one of those avians of yours, Varian, to discover if it requires carotene," Trizein was saying as if he didn't realize that Varian had left the lab.

"We've Mabel," said Varian, "and little Dandy."

"You've animals in this compound?" Trizein blinked with astonishment.

"I told you we had, Trizein. The slides you analyzed yesterday and the day before . . ."

"Ah, yes, I remember now," but it was obvious to his listeners that he didn't remember any such thing.

"Mabel and Dandy aren't fliers," Kai said. "They're completely different species."

"Indeed they are, but they are also pentadactyl. So is the fang-face, and *he* needed the grasses."

"Mabel and Dandy are herbivorous," said Kai, "and the predator and the fliers aren't."

Varian considered that qualification. "Yes, but generally speaking, carnivores absorb sufficient vitamin A from the animals they eat who do get it regularly in their diet." She shook her head over the quandary. "Then fang-face wouldn't need to go to the valley. He'd get enough from chewing Mabel's flank. I don't make any sense out of it—yet. Besides, the fliers may have another reason for gathering grass, as Terilla pointed out today."

"You've lost me," said Kai, and then directed Varian's attention to Trizein, who had gone back to his microscopic viewer and was oblivious to their presence again.

"You'll understand when you see the tapes we got today of

those fliers, Kai. C'mon, unless you've got something else to do?"

"Frame messages to the Theks, but let me see what you taped first."

"By the way, Kai," said Varian, following him out of the lab, "we didn't encounter any life forms in the vicinity of the pitchblende saddle that would cause a secondary camp there any trouble. If the camp's set up properly, preferably on a prominence, and the force-screen posted deep, your team should be safe enough."

"That's good news. Not that I think you'd've scared anyone off with tales of herds of fang-faces."

"Fang-faces, for the record, are solitary hunters."

They had reached the pilot cabin and Varian inserted the tape for playback, explaining her conclusions and her desire to investigate the golden-furred fliers' colony more closely at the earliest opportunity.

"How closely, Varian?" asked Kai. "They're not small, and as I remember, those wings are strong and could be dangerous. I'd hate to get attacked by that beak."

"So would I. So I'm not going to be. I'll go slowly, Kai, but if they're as intelligent as the evidence suggests, I may even be able to approach them on a personal basis." When Kai began to protest, she held up her hand. "The fliers are not stupid like Mabel, or scared like Dandy, or dangerous like fang-face. But I cannot give up the opportunity to investigate an aerial species that acts in such an organized manner."

"Fair enough, but do nothing on your own, co-leader. I want heavy-worlders with you at all times."

"You're a friend! Did they improve with the day?"

"I've never seen them so clumsy: slow, yes, but never plain raking grease-fingered. Paskutti and Tardma dropped one of the seismimics down a crevice. I don't have so many that I can spare one," said Kai, "not if I'm to complete my survey." He shook his head again over the loss. "I'm not blaming you, or them; but it is a nuisance. And what are we going to do about that fruit distillation? I don't understand why it should have affected them so adversely when we weaker types had no trouble?"

"It might not have been the drink."

"What do you mean?"

Varian shrugged. "Just a notion. Nothing specific."

"Then let us find a specific, and have Lunzie run a few tests. It might be a mutational allergy. Say, did you send the heavy-worlders on any errands today? In the north?"

"North? No. They were at your disposal today. Now, about the pitchblende site. You'll be working from there again tomorrow? Okay, then I'll send a team in for a ground check. There seem to be only smaller animals, not, as I've told the youngsters, that size is any indication of potential danger. What other area do you want us to check out xenobiologically as a possible secondary base?"

Kai tapped out of the computer the print of Gaber's chart, updated now with the pitchblende site and the old cores.

"The shield edge is only two hundred kilometers to the northwest from here, so we won't need a secondary camp there yet. But Portegin and Aulia want to examine these lakes and go farther into this flatland area. Berru and Triv are scheduled to go due west, where there appears to be a wide continental basin. Might have petroleum pools: not as rich an energy source, naturally, but crude oil has uses. We might be able to refine enough to use as an auxiliary fuel for the . . ."

"Kai, did anyone use the big sled for any length of time this morning?"

"Just to reach the site. Then it was turned over to you. Why?"

"Because its elapsed flight time is longer than it should have been. Damned thing's due now for a power charge."

"So?"

"I dunno. Just that I don't usually make errors in my figures."

"We've enough worries, Varian, without imagining more."

Varian grimaced. "Like no contact with EV. Your teams'll be expecting some acknowledgement . . ."

"We've got some leeway, and I'll use every day of it."

"Yes, we do have stall time, don't we. By the way, those youngsters were very useful to me. I think I'll opt them again when I don't need to land," she hastily added as she saw the objections forming in Kai's startled face. "You might even consider," and she grinned slyly, "taking Bonnard with you on a coring expedition."

"Now just a minute, Varian . . ."

"They do say that overexposure cures a lot of fancies."

"True. How about helping me with that message to the Theks?"

"Sorry, Kai, I've got to release Mabel, check with Lunzie and get a wash before eating." Varian quickly opened the iris. "But I'd be happy to look over what you plan to say."

He made as if to throw something at her but she scampered away, laughing.

An hour later, he was certain that Varian at her worst could have constructed a better message to the Theks. It covered the main points and requested the return information required.

He beamed the message, confirming a contact hour two days later. It didn't give Theks much time to meditate their answers, but he had specified only yes, no or deferred answers.

The next day went as scheduled, the heavy-worlders restored to operating efficiency. Tardma and Tanegli did a ground survey of the densely vegetated area where small life forms had been telltagged by Varian and the youngsters. The creatures had maintained their anonymity but skeletal remains not yet disintegrated by insects and carrion-eaters indicated that, while carnivorous, the creatures were probably nocturnal hunters and not large enough to constitute a real danger. Further, they were unlikely to be caught so far from their own territory as the secondary camp. Kai spent the afternoon with Dimenon and Margit choosing a site. It was decided that

Portegin and Aulia could also use the camp for their westerly investigations.

Lunzie told Kai and Varian confidentially that the heavy-worlders ought to have had a higher tolerance for the fruit drink than the light-grav or ship-bred. She couldn't understand their reactions. However, she did not recommend rationing or watering the potion. She could bring the heavy-worlders in for a routine physical, which, she allowed, was a good idea for every member of the expedition, to check on any allergic tendencies or subtle infections acquired since planet-fall.

That evening Lunzie supplied enough of the fruit drink to make the evening extremely convivial. The heavy-worlders drank no more than anyone else, laughed infrequently as was their habit and retired when everyone else did. The following day there was no impairment of their efficiency, which increased the mystery of their behavior that first evening.

The contact hour with the Theks was duly kept by Kai. Varian arrived halfway through the ponderous and slowly delivered reply.

"No" was the answer to his questions about messages being stripped from the satellite and contact with the EV. He received the expected deferred answer concerning any knowledge of a previous survey and the discovery of the old cores. "Excellent" was their response to news of the pitchblende deposit, with "continue" added. To his comment that he had heard from the Ryxi, he got an acknowledgment. The Theks were reputedly tolerant of all species in a benevolent, impartial way, but Kai was left with the feeling that the Theks couldn't care less if the Ryxi maintained contact.

He was of two minds about their deferred answer on a previous survey. On one hand, he'd half hoped they could find a previous reference, though how they could, out of contact with their own kind and EV's data banks, he didn't know. On the other hand, he would have been obscurely relieved if they had proved their fallibility. Yet, if this case did shatter their reputation, something stable and secure would be lost forever to him.

"So they don't know," said Varian, blatantly pleased.

"Not actively at any rate," he replied, quite willing to take the Thek part to offset his mental disloyalty. "Of course, there are only several million planets in the universe on which life of some sort has evolved . . ."

"So we're constantly informed, but our sphere of interest is currently limited to this one stinking ball of earth. By the way, in order to set up your secondary camp, we're going to have to formulate a few plans," said Varian. "According to the old core pattern, the shield runs about two thousand kilometers in a long point to the southeast. That makes commuting back here unfeasible. I want to take Tanegli, Paskutti, Tardma and Lunzie and check out that area." She unrolled area charts, some of the topographical features already marked out in Gaber's neat draftsmanship. Over these were wash colors, the key at the side. "I've keyed it here to territorialities of the beasts we've tagged. I think the guide is adequate, but there is so much animal life in this area," and she indicated the plateau and rain forest just beyond the dead perimeters of the camp, "that I've only bothered with the big and dangerous ones. Here's a spot frame of each type we've observed enough to identify as herbivorous, carnivorous or omnivorous. As you can see, we've a ways to go before we've done even the most superficial cataloguing." She tapped vast areas of the outlined land mass which were pristine. "Here there be dragons!" she added in a fruity voice.

"Dragons?"

"Well, that's what the antique cartographers would say when they didn't know a binary bit about the indigenous life."

"Any more news on which species is which here?" asked Kai.

She shook her head, handing him several copies of the maps. "That's not as urgent as your geological work, and you needed some sort of a guide."

"This map is terrific, Varian. I thought you'd been out with your teams . . ."

"No, I sent them to get me this information and fill in some of the nearby gaps in our survey. Terilla and I collaborated on the composite."

"Terilla did these with you?" Impressed, Kai was poring over the charts.

"Yes, indeed. I know the youngsters were sort of dumped on us at the last moment, but I wish someone had thought to give us their records. Terilla's been a real find, and she could have been apprenticed right off to Gaber and kept him from falling so far behind. He even approves of her work." Varian grinned saucily at Kai. "You'll be relieved to hear that Bonnard's interest has been transferred."

"To Dandy? Or Mabel? In either case I am flattered."

"Mabel's long gone. No, Bonnard is aiming to get on my expedition to the golden fliers."

"At least he picks something demonstrably intelligent."

"I never said he didn't have good taste."

"Varian!"

"When's the contact with the Ryxi?"

"This afternoon at 1530 hours. If they remember."

"We do have problems with memory this trip, don't we? The Ryxi remembering to speak to us, the Theks remembering to think and EV remembering to get in touch with us. Well, back to my hot drawing board . . ." She started out of the pilot cabin. "Oh, hello, Gaber . . ."

"Varian, did you take all my chart copies?"

"Only the one Terilla was working on. Why?"

"I didn't know. I just didn't know and I was . . ."

"I did tell you, Gaber, but I guess you were so deep in the tape you didn't hear me. Sorry about that. I've given Kai copies, and I'm on my way back to your lair with these right now."

"Oh, very well then. And, if I didn't hear you, I am sorry."

To Kai, Gaber did not sound the least bit sorry. Kai went

back to studying the patterns of animals. The biggest herbivores, like Mabel and three other large types, could be found all through the rain forests, with their probable passages through the mountain ranges neatly designated by tiny drawings of the beasts. The predators, like fang-face, hunted singly: only one pair had been discovered, and they had been involved in a ferocious battle, which had deteriorated, in Paskutti's words, into a mating. The scope of the charts was hampered by the large uncharted areas, over which had been laid a transparency, indicating the general topographical features as seen by the initial cursory probe.

They had been concentrating on the relatively cooler portion of the shield mass, since the polar region was much hotter than the equatorial due to the hotter thermal core of the planet. They would soon have to penetrate those steaming jungles, a task Kai did not relish. The proliferation and diversity of life forms would be incredible in such warmth, Varian had warned him during their shipboard briefing sessions. The lush tropical jungles nourished life, provided quantities of food, as well as immense competition for any and all edible substances. In cooler climates, though Ireta could not boast a very temperate zone, there tended to be fewer species, since the food supply was limited by the more severe conditions of life.

With understandable satisfaction, Kai took his own maps, and added the two pitchblende finds to those of the day before when Portegin and Aulia had sited two large copper deposits, and Berru and Triv had marked three mountains of iron ores. Whoever had been here before had denuded the shield areas, but plate action in the ensuing millennia had made the unstable areas doubly rich. This was actually Kai's first search expedition: his other assignments had been remedial, finding veins which had faulted out, or flooding controls and deep-sea manganese dredging—all valuable experience and designed to aid him in a full-scale planetary survey like this one.

He was so deep in his thoughts that the warning of his

chrono jerked him to attention and bewilderment as to why he had had the alarm set.

The Ryxi contact! Belatedly he realized that he should have prepared a message for them. It was easier to read a written message fast than gabble spontaneously at the speed required for the Ryxi. He jotted down some notes as the communication unit warmed to its task. Diplomatically he phrased Varian's comments about the golden fliers.

Vrl came on as scheduled, asking for confirmation of contact with EV. Kai replied in the negative, but Vrl did not seem too concerned. He said that they had sent their full report by long-distance capsule to their home world. He intimated that he didn't care how long it took to arrive, he and his group were well and pleasantly established. Kai had half a mind not to say anything about the golden fliers if Vrl didn't ask. But the avian did. Kai told him the little Varian and he had observed. Luckily he had the tape on, for Vrl's excited reply erupted in Kai's ears at an incomprehensible speed. Kai got the impression that he was a lying discontent, envious of the Ryxi and making the whole species up. Vrl signed off before Kai could vindicate himself or arrange another contact time.

He was staring, bemused and somewhat aggravated by Vrl's overreaction, when he heard the sound of a cleared throat. Gaber was standing in the iris lock.

"I'm sorry to intrude, Kai, but we are missing one of the area maps. Do you have two copies of one there?"

Kai fingered the tough but thin sheets. They did stick together occasionally when the copying solution dried. "No, I've only the one set."

"Well, then a set is missing," said Gaber in his customary aggrieved tone and left.

Kai could see him shaking his head as he made for the shuttle's lock. Kai set the communicator for a slow replay of the interchange with Vrl, vowing that Varian ought to do an intensive study of those fliers as soon as possible.

7

In the next seven days, the expedition was too busy setting up the secondary camps to indulge in any activity not strictly necessary to its primary aims. Varian found time to return to the fish rock and bring several small desiccated specimens of the fringes for Trizein to study. The man buried himself in his laboratory until Lunzie found him asleep at his work desk. She forced him to take a break, eat and sleep. He did so unwillingly and when he woke, he stumbled about the compound with unseeing eyes, though he did stop once to stare at Dandy with a puzzled expression.

The little creature was quite tame and permitted out of its run when Bonnard and Cleiti were on hand. Varian had decided not to release it as, orphaned, it had no natural protector. Kai had to accede to her arguments since it was obvious the little beast would never reach a great size and was therefore no strain on the expedition's time or resources. Dandy was, by nature, timid and content to follow the youngsters about, its large liquid eyes wistful or startled by turns. Kai would privately have preferred more of an extrovert personality in a tamed beast, but Dandy posed no problem of aggressive behavior. Kai still thought it a very nondescript affair.

The golden fliers were continually seen in the skies, almost as if, Varian said one evening, they were as interested in the new occupants of their skies as the expedition was in them. She had been gleefully enchanted by Vrl's reaction to their existence for, as the slow playback continued, the Ryxi had spluttered a repudiation of Varian's report, indicating that an intelligent avian species was unlikely to occur again on any planet, under any conditions: the Ryxi were unique and would remain so, and any attempt to supplant their preeminent position in the Federation would be met by severe measures. Vrl suggested that this was a hoax which the biped had better forget, retract and abandon or he would recommend that all contact between Ryxi and Human be forthwith severed.

Once Terilla's animal maps were circulated, Tanegli and Gaber vied with each other for her time and skill to the point where Varian and Kai had to intervene. Unconcerned by such competition for her assistance, Terilla made it quite plain that she much preferred plants to charts or animals. Chuckling, Varian showed Kai the map the girl had inscribed for Tanegli indicating the disposition of flora, grass and shrub on the plains and swamp areas. A work schedule was evolved in which Terilla spent three afternoons with each man while her morning hours were hers. With increased work loads, Kai assigned tasks to Bonnard and Cleiti as he would any other member of the expedition. Tanegli usually opted for Bonnard and Cleiti when Terilla was not available for his botanical excursions. Sometimes Bonnard acted as recorder for Bakkun when administration duties prevented Kai from field work beside the heavy-worlder geologist.

Lunzie annexed Cleiti on those days to help her test Ireta's soil and vegetation for any unusual medicinal properties.

Two secondary camps were sited and occupied, but it was obvious that a third camp to the far east would have to be established to continue exploration of the easterly land mass. Kai projected that over half their expeditionary time would be spent in the eastern hemisphere. He hoped that the fifteen-degree axial tilt would mean some cooler weather in the polar regions when the teams had to move to complete the survey in the western hemisphere.

On neither of his next two contacts with the Theks did they have any good news for him of the deferred query or of the

EV. Kai's leeway on the matter of a response from EV was fast running out. He was prepared and had Varian's support when Dimenon forced an admission of a contact lapse. Kai cited the cosmic storm in such an offhanded manner that Dimenon never thought to ask if the ores report was the only message uncollected.

"How long a grace period we have now, I couldn't estimate," Kai told Varian afterward.

"Keep 'em so busy counting their pay dirt bonuses that they'll forget to ask."

"This is a raking rich planet, Varian."

"So? It's up to EV to stay in touch with us, if they want the energy materials we've found. They know where we are." Varian held Kai's gaze and she jerked up one eyebrow. "You aren't considering Gaber's ludicrous notion, are you?"

"It does occur to me now and then," Kai said, rubbing the side of his nose, feeling silly but actually relieved to hear Varian air the matter.

"Hmmm, yes. It occurs to me now and then, too. Have the Ryxi reported in again?"

"No." Kai grinned at her. "Did you expect them to?"

"No." She laughed. "They are so . . . pompously paranoiac. As if another intelligent avian could possibly threaten them. I mean, the giffs," which was the nickname she'd given the golden fliers, "*are* intelligent but so far from the Ryxi position that it's asinine for them to take umbrage." Varian sighed. "I'd love to evaluate their intelligence."

"Why don't you?"

"With your lot agitating for that eastern camp?"

"What about next rest day? Make a small start. Go observe them, relax for the day."

"Could I?" Varian brightened at the prospect. "Could I take the big sled, sleep out in it? We've got their flight habits well documented now, we've caught the fishing act often enough to establish that drill, but I don't know much about their personal life, or their matutinal habits. And there's only the one place for those grasses they eat. They do use swamp grass for net-weaving, but I don't know exactly how they accomplish the feat." She gave him a sideways frown. "You need a break as much as I do. Let's both go, next rest day. Paskutti and Lunzie can sub for us."

"What if we arrive on the giff rest day?" asked Kai with a very bland expression.

"There's always the possibility, isn't there?" she replied, not taking his lure.

Kai was astonished at how eagerly he looked forward to the break in routine. That showed how right Varian had been in suggesting it. Lunzie approved wholeheartedly, telling Kai she'd been about to recommend a day off for them both. She wasn't so sure that observing the giffs at close range constituted a proper holiday, but the physician was equally keen to know more about the giffs.

"What is there about winged creatures that fascinates us all?" Lunzie asked as they sat about after the evening meal over beakers of distilled fruit juice.

"Their independence?" asked Kai.

" 'If we had been meant to fly, we'd've been given wings,' " quipped Varian in a thin nasal voice, then continued in a normal tone, "I suspect it is the freedom, or perhaps the view, the perspective, the feeling of infinite space about you. You ship-bred types can't appreciate open spaces the way the planet-bred can, but I do need vistas on which to feast my eyes, and soul."

"Confinement, voluntary or involuntary, can have adverse effects on temperament and psychology, resulting in serious maladjustments," Lunzie said. "One reason why we include the youngsters on planetfall assignments as often as possible."

Kai remained silent, acutely conscious of his own sometimes pressing agoraphobia.

"We have surrogate wings," Lunzie continued, "in the agency of sleds and lift-belts . . ."

"Which do not quite produce the same freedoms," said Kai

slowly, wondering what it would feel like to be independent of all artificial aids: to dip, dive, soar and glide without the unconscious restrictive considerations of fuel, stress, mental fatigue.

"Why, Kai," said Varian, regarding him with delighted astonishment, "you're the last one I'd expect to understand."

"Perhaps," he said with a wry smile, "you planet-bred types underestimate the ship-bred."

Dimenon, who'd been in an uproariously good mood that evening, since he and Margit had flown in to report finding not only a stream running with gold nuggets but the parent lode, had brought out his hand piano. He began to render a boisterous ballad with interminable verses and a silly syllabic chorus with such an infectious tune that everyone joined in. To Kai's surprise, so did the heavy-worlders, thumping the plasfloor with their heavy boots and clapping with unusual enthusiasm.

Margit wanted to dance and dragged Kai onto the floor, yelling at Dimenon to leave off the endless verses and play some decent music. Kai was never certain when the heavy-worlders disappeared, but the convivial gathering lasted well past the rise of the third moon.

He awoke suddenly the next morning, with an urgency that suggested danger. When he scrambled out of the sleeping sack to the window of his dome, the scene was quiet. Dandy was sprawled asleep in his pen. There was no movement. The day had started, the brighter patch of cloud which was the sun was well above the soft slope of the eastern hills. Whatever had alarmed his subconscious was not apparent.

He was roused and so keyed up by the abrupt triggering that he decided to remain up. He dragged on a clean ship suit, inserted fresh linings in his boots and fastened them. He had a small larder in his dome and broke open a wake-up beaker, reminding himself to check with Lunzie today on the state of the stores. He could not shake his sensation that something was amiss, so he did a tour of the encampment.

There wasn't a smell of smoke in the main dome. Gaber was fast asleep in his, the windows were opaqued in the other sleeping quarters so he did not intrude. Remembering Trizein's tendency to work through a night, he made his way quickly to the shuttle craft, waving open the iris lock. The conditioned air inside gave him pause. Suddenly he realized that he hadn't put his nose filters in: and he hadn't *smelled* Ireta!

"Muhlah! I'm getting used to it." His soft exclamation echoed in the bare main cabin of the shuttle. Kai walked quietly back to Trizein's lab, opening the iris and peering in. Some experiments were in progress, judging by the activity of dials and gauges in the built-in equipment, but Trizein's form on the ledge-bed was motionless.

As Kai turned from the lab, he noticed that the supply hold iris was open. He must caution Trizein about that. Lunzie kept her decanted fruit brew in there. Kai had noticed Dimenon's conspicuous consumption the night before and his aggressiveness when Margit suggested he'd had enough. Kai didn't quite put it past the man to appropriate a flask for evening use in the secondary camp. Not a habit he'd approve or condone in any of his team members.

Although his inspection satisfied him that nothing was demonstrably wrong, his uneasiness remained until, after returning to his dome, he became immersed in the restricted file in the ship's data bank. By the time the rest of the expedition was stirring, he had rid himself of the backlog of detail. The inadvertent early rising had been rewarding.

Dimenon, looking untouched by the previous evening's carousal, arrived in the main dome with Margit, both suited up and ready to return to their base. They ate quickly, wanting to make an early start back, but as they were leaving, Dimenon asked Kai when he expected to contact the Theks again. He did not seem disturbed when Kai gave a time three days later.

"Well, let us know how EV appreciates our labors on this

stinking planet. Although—" Dimenon frowned and felt his nostrils. "Rake it! I forgot to put 'em in again!"

"Smell anything?" asked Kai, amused.

Dimenon's eyes began to widen and his mouth dropped in exaggerated reaction.

"I've got used to the stench!" He roared the statement, full of aggrieved incredulity. "Kai, please, when you've got through to EV, have them pick us up before schedule? Please, I've got used to the stench of hydrotelluride." He clutched at his throat now, contorting his face as though in terminal agony, "I can't stand it. I can't stand it."

Lunzie, who was literal-minded, came rushing up, frowning with anxiety while Kai tried to gesture reassurance. Others were grinning at Dimenon's histrionics, but the heavy-worlders, after uninterested glances at the geologist, turned back to their own quiet-toned discussions. Lunzie still hadn't realized that Dimenon was acting. He grabbed at her shoulders now.

"Tell me, Lunzie, tell me I'm not a goner. My sense of smell'll come back, won't it? Once I'm in decent air? Oh, don't tell me I'll never be able to smell nothing in the air again . . ."

"If the acclimatization should be permanent, you could always get an Iretan air-conditioner for your shipboard quarters," Lunzie replied, apparently in earnest.

Dimenon looked horrified and, for a moment, didn't catch the brand of the physician's humor.

"C'mon, partner, you've been bested," said Margit, taking him by the arm. "Better to smell the sweet air of another find . . ."

"*Could* you get so used to Iretan stink you'd never smell normally again?" Bonnard asked Lunzie, a little worried as he watched the two geologists leave.

"No," said Lunzie with a dry chuckle. "The smell is powerful but I doubt there's any permanent desensitization. The temporary effect *is* somewhat of a blessing. Do you have it?"

Bonnard nodded uncertainly. "But I didn't know I couldn't smell it anymore until Dimenon mentioned it." This worried him.

"Since you are now used to the overbearing smell, see if you can now distinguish other, previously unsensed odors while you're out and about today."

"Worse ones?" Bonnard regarded Lunzie, appalled.

"I can smell a difference in the blossoms I've been cataloguing," said Terilla. "And some of the leaves have an odor if you crush 'em. Not too bad a smell, really," she added helpfully.

That morning Kai checked with Lunzie about stores. She was not the sort of person to give spot replies and together they went to the store hold.

"I'm not missing any of the fruit distillation, if that's what you're worried about, Kai," she said in her direct fashion. "We've not made too many inroads in the subsistence supplies, either. I've been gradually phasing them out entirely, in favor of local protein."

"You have," Kai was surprised.

"You hadn't noticed?" There was a slight emphasis on the pronoun. Lunzie smiled briefly with pleasure at the success of her program. "We are losing hard goods, though, at a rate which worries me."

"Hard goods?"

"Knives, film and sheet extruders, spare charges for lift-belts . . ."

"What did the secondary camps take?"

"Not enough to account for some of these items. Unless, of course, they haven't reported the losses and have merely helped themselves when I was busy elsewhere." That solution sounded plausible. "If I may, I'll appoint Cleiti as requisitions officer and have her on hand when anyone needs to visit the supply hold. We can keep a check that way without giving offense . . ."

Or warning, thought Kai, and then decided that his imagination was working overtime. He did need that day's respite.

Varian returned to the camp from one of her search-and-identify sweeps early on the afternoon before rest day. She cornered Kai in his dome, scornfully clacking the tape holders that were stacked in front of him, tugging at the seismic point-out on the volcanic action in the northwest which he had been studying. Pressures were mounting on a long transform fault and he was hoping they'd have enough warning to be able to observe the earthquake when the phenomenon occurred.

"Leave that, Kai. You can zip through report work a lot faster with a fresh mind."

"It's early yet . . ."

"Raking right it is. I got back especially so I could pry you out of here before the teams come in and dump such glowing reports on you that you feel obliged to listen." She went back to the iris lock. "Cleiti! Did you organize those supplies for us? And where's Bonnard?" The reply was inaudible to Kai but satisfactory to Varian, who nodded. "If he's sure he's got what he needs, tell him to pack it into the sled beside my things. Kai, where's your pack? Ha! Thought so. Okay, what do you need?"

Varian moved purposefully to his storage chest so that Kai pushed back his stool and waved her away. She stood, grinning but adamant, while he packed what he needed into his sleep sack, and gathered up his safety gear. With a courteous sweep of his hand, he indicated he was ready.

"I knew I'd have to haul you out of here." Varian sounded grimly smug.

"Then what are you dragging your feet for?" asked Kai with a smile and exited before her. As an afterthought, he thumblocked the iris control. He didn't really want anyone to happen across the message tapes with the Theks.

As Varian neatly swung the big sled over the encampment, sparkling with the blue demise of insects, she groaned. "We should have brought a small unit for tonight. We'll have to sleep in belt-screens!"

"Not if we sack out on the sled floor," said Bonnard, eyeing the space. "I think there's room enough if we stack our supplies on the front seating and remove the side benches. Shall I activate the telltale?"

"This once, we'll leave it silent," said Varian. "There wouldn't be anything untagged this close to camp anyway."

A companionable silence enveloped the three and lasted the entire trip to the inland sea, which they reached just as the last speck of gloom, as Bonnard phrased it, began to fade from the sullen skies. Varian had marked a good landing site, a shallow terrace beyond and below the main congregation of the giffs but with a fine view of the summit where the netted fish were deposited.

The first hour after sunset there was a brief surcease of daytime insect activity before the nocturnal creatures became a menace. During this interim, Varian heated their evening meal on the bare stone terrace. Then, to the amazement of Bonnard and the consternation of Kai, she removed dead branches from the storage section of the sled and lit a small fire.

"Campfire is very comforting even if you ship-bred types think it's atavistic. My father and I used to have one every night on our expeditions."

"It's very pretty," said Bonnard in a tentative tone, and looked toward Kai to see his reaction.

Kai smiled and told himself to relax. Fire on shipboard was a hazard: his instant reflex had been to grab something to smother the flames, but as he eyed the small fire, which posed no danger to him, the dancing spikes were pleasantly hypnotic. The small warmth it exuded gave them a circle of light and certainly kept the insects away.

"The oldest belt-screen in the world," Varian said, poking the fire to fresh vigor with a stick. "On Protheon, they were particular about their firewoods, choosing those which gave off pleasant aromas. They liked scent with their warmth and light. I wouldn't dare try that on Ireta."

"Why not?" asked Bonnard, his eyes fixed on a point deep in the flames. "Terilla said there're some that smell pretty good—by Iretan standards. You know, Varian, I haven't been able to smell anything but Ireta! D'you suppose Lunzie could be wrong and my nose has gone dead?"

Varian and Kai both laughed. "You'll know soon enough when we get back to the EV," Varian told him.

"Yeah!" Bonnard's reply lacked any enthusiasm for return.

"You'd be sorry to leave?"

"I sure will, Kai, and it's not because we'll have to leave Dandy. There's so much to do here. I mean, tapes are great, and better than nothing, but this trip I'm learning hundreds of things. Learning's got a point . . ."

"You have to have had the theoretical study before you can attempt the practical," Varian said, but Bonnard waved that consideration aside.

"I've studied basics till data comes out my pores, but it isn't the same thing at all as being here and doing it!" Bonnard was emphatically banging his knee. "Like that fire, and all. Rakers, on shipboard you see flames and dash for the foamer!"

Varian grinned at Kai and caught his rueful expression.

"Your point's taken, Bonnard," she said. "And I think it's safe to say that you'll be in demand for more expeditions once Kai and I have made our report. Bakkun thinks highly of your performance as his recorder."

"He does?" Bonnard's expression, which had soured at the contemplation of return to EV, brightened with such a future. "You're sure?" His gaze went from Varian to Kai.

"As far as you can be sure of a heavy-worlder."

"Are there more expeditions planned, Varian?" asked Bonnard urgently.

"More or less," she replied, catching Kai's gaze. "I was signed on this tour for three expeditions requiring a xenob over a period of four standard years. You'd be eligible as a junior member in that time. Of course, you might opt for geology rather than xenob."

"I like animals," said Bonnard, testing the words in his mouth so as not to give offense to either leader, "but I do like . . . sort of fancy the more scientific aspects of . . ."

"I'd think you'd be best as an all-round recorder, with as many specialties in that area as possible," said Varian, helping him.

"You do?"

His reaction made it obvious to Kai and Varian that it was the mechanics of recording that fascinated the boy, rather than any of the individual disciplines. They talked about specialization as the fire burned down, was replenished, and burned down again. By the time Kai suggested they sack out, the two leaders had assured Bonnard that they would give him as much opportunity at tape and recorders as possible to see if this was really where his interests lay.

Safe under the sled's protective screen, they slept deeply and without a bother from the night creatures of Ireta.

Varian was aroused the next morning by something prodding her shoulder. She was still sleepy, but again she was prodded, more emphatically this time, and her name was whispered urgently.

"Varian. Varian! Wake up. We got company."

That forced her to open her eyes which she instantly closed, not believing her first sight.

"Varian, you've got to wake up!" Bonnard's whisper was anxious.

"I am. I've seen."

"What do we do?"

"Have you moved yet?"

"Only to nudge you. Did I hurt you?"

"No." They were both speaking in low tones. "Can you prod Kai awake?"

"I don't know how he wakes up."

Bonnard had a point. It wouldn't do to rouse someone who erupted out of the sack like a torpedo. He'd known how to rouse her since he'd often done so when they'd first acquired Dandy.

"Kai's quiet if you do it as gently as you woke me."

Varian grinned to herself. She wasn't sorry she'd included Bonnard on this trip. Last night's discussion had proved how much he'd needed the encouragement as well as the opportunity to talk without reservations imposed on him by the presence of older team members or the two girls. It had been obvious last evening that Kai would have preferred to have made this a duet trip, and a complete break from the exigencies of leadership. Now she'd pried him away from his tape decks, she'd do it again, without a third party.

They had slept head to foot, so while Bonnard prodded Kai's shoulder with his foot, Varian whispered the warning to him.

"Kai, wake slowly, don't move. The observers are observed."

She had her eyes half-open now, because the giffs were so closely ringed about the sled that, in her first arousal, she had seen a series of bright black eyes on a level with hers.

She almost giggled when a sharp orangy beak point tapped at the plascreen surrounding the sled, tapping gently as if not wishing to startle the sleepers.

"Muhlah!" was Kai's soft curse and there was a ripple of laughter in his tone.

"Is it safe for me to have a look?" asked Bonnard in his hushed whisper.

"Don't know why not. They're looking at us."

"Can they get in?" was Bonnard's anxious question.

"I doubt it," said Varian, unperturbed. She wouldn't guarantee that the plascreen could stand a concerted attack of heavier adult beaks, but she didn't feel that aggression was the giff's intent.

"I thought you wanted to see their matutinal habits, Varian."

said Kai, slowly raising his head from the sleep sack to prop it on his hand. He wasn't looking at her, but beyond her to the golden-furred faces peering in.

"That was my intention."

"As I recall it, I asked you what if it was their rest day?"

Varian couldn't suppress her laughter and Bonnard joined in, never dropping his eyes from the giffs.

"You mean, they're taking the day off to watch us?"

"They're at least starting the day doing it," said Varian, raising herself slowly out of the sack.

The avians moved restlessly, wings awkwardly held up.

"Hey, they can rotate the wings at the wrist . . ."

"Yes, Bonnard, I'd noticed." Varian had also seen the flexing of the three digits with the yellowed claws at the tips. The function of thumb and little fingers had been incorporated into the wing so Varian couldn't see how they would be able to weave with the three wing digits.

"Hey, they're not all here," said Bonnard, pointing up in a judiciously controlled gesture.

None of the giffs were perched on top of the plascreen, so that the sky was clearly visible. Outlined against the clouds was a formation of giffs going in a southeasterly direction.

"I think we've got the youngsters here," said Varian.

"The babes at that," said Kai, pointing to the trail of brownish slime that drippled down the outside skirting of the sled.

Bonnard muffled a chortle. "So what do we do now? I'm hungry."

"Then we'll eat," said Varian and began to pull her legs out of the sack, slowly, to give the giffs no reason for alarm. "Yes, they're the young ones," she said as she slowly got to her feet and stared down at the small bodies pressing in about the sled.

Seen in proper perspective, she realized none of these giffs were adult-sized. The tip of the longest head crest came only to her waist. She'd estimated that a fully grown giff would be as tall as an average human with a wingspan of at least eight to ten meters.

"What do we do?" asked Bonnard.

"Sit up slowly. I'll bring you breakfast in the sack," she said, moving carefully to the supplies.

Kai had pulled himself into a sitting position now and gratefully accepted the steaming beaker.

"Breakfast with an audience," he said, sipping.

"I wish they'd move or talk or something," said Bonnard, glancing nervously about him as he blew to cool the liquid in his beaker. He almost dropped it when one of the giffs stretched and flapped its wings suddenly. "They're not even trying to get at us."

"Look but don't touch?" asked Kai. "Frankly, I'd just as soon they kept to themselves. Those beak points look sharp." He glanced at Varian, who had a small recorder in her hands now, and holding it at waist level was slowly turning a full circle, recording the faces of their audience.

With equal care against sudden movement, she placed the recorder on one shoulder and turning again, stood so still for a long moment at one point that Kai asked what was up.

"I've the recorder directed on the main summit. There's quite a bit of activity there right now. I can't see what it's all about . . . oh, yes, I can. It's the adults. I'd swear . . . yes . . . they're calling this lot."

As reluctantly as any curious young creature, the juvenile giffs began to lumber awkwardly away, disappearing so suddenly that Bonnard cried out in alarm.

"They're okay, Bonnard," said Varian who had a better view. "We're right on the cliff edge. They've just walked off it and if you'll glance over your shoulder, you'll see them soaring away, perfectly safe."

"Muhlah!" exclaimed Kai with utter disgust. "We had 'em close enough and didn't telltag 'em."

"What? And scare them into bringing momma and dad down on us? We don't really need to telltag giffs anyway, Kai.

We know where they live, and how far they range." She patted the recorder. "And I've got their faces all on tape."

"They sure had a good enough look at ours," said Bonnard. "I wonder if they'll remember us next time."

"All furless, crestless faces look the same," said Varian with a laugh.

She was moving about the sled now without restraint and handed each a bar of subsistence protein. She perched on the pilot chair to munch hers.

When they had finished eating, joking about the manner of their awakening, they made ready to leave the sled. Kai and Bonnard carried the recorders and additional tapes, Varian had her gift of the grasses. Kai also wore a stunner, hoping he wouldn't have to use it. Not, he thought privately, that he'd have much chance the way those giffs could move.

As they emerged, the sun came through the cloud cover, for its morning inspection, Bonnard said. From the caves in the cliffs came hundreds and hundreds of golden fliers, as if called inexorably by the thin thread of sunlight. Bonnard quickly aimed the recorder and caught the spectacle of hundreds of giffs, wings raised, beaks open, caroling a curious warble as they turned in the sparse sunlight.

"Ever seen anything like that before, Varian?" asked Kai in amazement.

"Not quite like that. Oh, they are beautiful creatures. Quick, Bonnard, on the third terrace to the left, get that lot!"

The giffs, one after the other, dropped off the ledge, wings spreading and lifting, soaring, turning over, as if letting each part of their bodies bathe in the sunlight. It was a slow aerial dance that held the observers spellbound.

"They've got their eyes closed," Bonnard said, peering through the focusing lens of the recorder. "Hope they know where they're going."

"They probably have some sort of radar perception," said Varian. She increased her face mask's magnification to observe more closely. "I wonder . . . are their eyes closed for some mystical reason? Or simply because the sun is strong?"

"Carotene is good for your eyes," said Bonnard.

Varian tried to recall if she'd ever seen a fang-face or one of the herbivores squint or close their eyes completely during sunshine. She couldn't remember. Full sunlight was a rare enough occasion so that all human eyes were invariably on the sun. She'd check the tapes out when she got back to the camp.

"Now, look Varian, only some of 'em are doing the flying act," said Bonnard. He had swung around, recorder still operating, and focused on the juvenile giffs scratching about on the fish summit.

One of them let out a squawk, tried to back away from something and, overbalancing, fell back. Its companions regarded it for a long moment as it lay, flapping helplessly.

Without thinking, Varian began to climb toward the summit to assist the creature. She had put her hand over the top, when an adult giff, with a cry shrill enough to be a command, landed on the summit, awkwardly turning toward Varian. When she judiciously halted her climbing, the giff deftly flipped the juvenile to its feet with the wing claws. The wing remained a protective envelope above the young giff.

"Okay, I get the message, loud and clear," said Varian.

A second grating sound issued from the adult giff whose eyes never left Varian.

"Varian!" Kai's call was warning and command.

"I'm all right. I've just been told to keep my distance."

"Make it more distance, Varian. I'm covering you."

"It would have attacked me if it was going to, Kai. Don't show the stunner."

"How would they know what a stunner is?" asked Bonnard.

"Point! I'm going to offer the grass." And slowly Varian took the rift grasses from her leg pouch and with great care held up the sheaf for the giff to see.

The creature's eyes did not leave hers, but Varian sensed

that the grass had been noticed. She moved her hand slowly, to place the sheaf on the top of the summit. The giff made another grating noise, softer, less aggressive in tone.

"You're very welcome," said Varian, and heard Bonnard's snort of disgust. "Courtesy is never wasted, Bonnard. Tone conveys its own message, so does gesture. This creature understands a certain amount from both what I'm doing and what I'm saying."

She had begun to descend to the sled's terrace level now, moving deliberately and never taking her eyes from the giff. As soon as she was back, standing with Kai and Bonnard, the adult giff waddled forward, took up the grass and then, returning to the sea edge, dropped off. Once it had sufficient wing room, it soared up again and out of sight among the other fliers.

"That was fascinating," said Kai on the end of a long-held sigh.

Bonnard was regarding Varian with open respect.

"Wow! One poke of that beak and you'd've been sent over the edge."

"There was no menace in the giff's action."

"Varian," said Kai, laying a hand on her arm, "do be careful."

"Kai, this isn't my first contact." Then she saw the worry in his eyes. "I am always careful. Or I wouldn't be here now. Making friends with alien creatures is my business. But how I'm ever to find out how mature their young are if they're this protective . . ." She stopped, whistled her surprise. "I know. The giff was protective because it's used to protecting the juveniles. So, they're not equipped to protect themselves at birth, or for some time thereafter. Still," and she sighed her disappointment, "I would have liked to get inside one of their caves . . ."

"Look, Varian," said Bonnard in a whisper and indicated the direction with the barest movement of his forefinger.

Slowly, Varian turned to see a row of juvenile giffs watching from the summit, wings in a closed position, tilted up beyond their backs, wing claws acting as additional supports to their sitting. Varian began to laugh, shaking her head and muttering about the observer observed.

"So we're fair peek," said Kai, leaning against the edge of the sled and folding his arms. "Now what do we do in your program? Be observed in our daily morning habits?"

"You can, if you wish. Be interesting to see how long their attention span is, but there's a great deal going on up there." She pointed skyward where the giffs were circling, but some groups spun off in various directions, with purposeful sweeps of their wings. "We don't seem to have hit a rest day," she said, flashing a smile at Kai. "Bonnard, if I give you a leg up on the sled's canopy, I think you can see the summit. Can you tell me what the juveniles were squawking about? Or what overbalanced the one I wanted to rescue?"

"Sure."

"Just don't dance about too much. Your boots'll scar the plascreen. And no, you can't take 'em off," Kai added as Bonnard began to speak.

They hoisted him up and, moving with great care, Bonnard positioned himself where he could see the summit.

"There's dead fringes up here, Varian, and some slimy looking seaweed. Aw, would you look at that?"

The juveniles, attracted by his new position, had abandoned that section of the summit and waddled over to stand directly in Bonnard's line of sight. Disgusted, he propped both hands against his hips and glared, actions which set them all to squawking and shifting away from the edge. Kai and Varian chuckled over the two sets of young.

"Hey, recorder man, you missed a dilly of a sequence!"

"Don't I just know it!"

"C'mon down," Varian told him, having learned what she needed to know.

She wandered over to the sea edge of the terrace, lay down, peering farther over the drop.

"I'm not allowed up. Am I allowed down? There appears to

be a cave over to the left, about twenty meters, Kai. If I use a belt-harness, you could probably swing me to it."

Kai was not completely in favor of such gymnastics, but the belt-harness, winched safely to the sled's exterior attachments, could hold a heavy-worlder securely. He was glad not to be at the end of the pendulum swing as she was to reach her objective.

"Are they watching, Bonnard?" Varian asked over the comunit.

"The young ones are, Varian, and yes, one of the airborne fliers is watching."

"Let's see if they have any prohibitive spots . . ."

"Varian . . ." Kai grew apprehensive as he, too, saw the adult giff fly in for a close look at Varian's swinging body.

"It's only looking, Kai. I expect that. One more swing now and . . . I got it." She had grabbed and caught a stony protrusion at the cave entrance and agilely scrambled in.

"Rakers! It's abandoned. It's gigantic. Goes so far back I can't see the end." Her voice over the comunit sounded rumbled and then hollow. "No, wait. Just what I wanted. An egg. An egg? And they let me in. Oh, it rattles. Dead egg. Small, too. Well, only circumstantial evidence that their young are born immature. Hmmm. There're grasses here, sort of forming a nest. Too scattered at this point to be sure. They can't have abandoned a cave because there's been an infertile egg? No fish bones, or scales. They must devour whole. Good digestions then."

Bonnard and Kai exchanged glances over her monologue and the assorted sounds of her investigations, broadcast from the comunit.

"The nest grasses are not the Rift Valley type, more like the tougher fibers of the swamp growths. I wonder . . . okay, Kai," and her broadcast voice was augmented by the clearer tones that indicated she had left the cave, "pull me up."

She had grasses sprouting from her leg pouches as she

came over the lip of the ledge, and the egg made an unusual bulge in the front of her ship suit.

"Any sign of alarm?" she asked.

Kai, securing the winch, shook his head as Bonnard leaped to assist her out of the harness.

"Hey, their eggs are small. Can I shake it?"

"Go ahead. What's in it is long dead."

"Why?"

Varian shrugged. "We'll let Trizein have a gawk and see if he can find out. I don't necessarily wish to fracture it. Let me have that plascovering, Kai," and she neatly stored the egg, surrounded by the dead grasses, and then brushed her gloved hands together to signify a task well completed. "That's thirsty work," she said and led the way back to the sled where she broke out more rations.

"You know," she said, halfway through the quick meal, "I think that each of those groups was out on various set tasks . . ."

"So we're staying around to see what they bring home?" asked Kai.

"If you don't mind."

"No." He inclined his head toward the juveniles, some of whom had indeed lost interest and were bumbling about the summit at the far side. "I'm enjoying the reversal of roles."

"I wish I could get into a cave currently in use . . ."

"All in one day?"

"Yes, you're right, Kai. That's asking too much. At least, we've experienced no aggressive action from them. The adult construed my action as helpful rather than dangerous. It did accept the grass . . ."

They all glanced upward as an unusual note penetrated the sled's roof, a high-pitched, sharp sustained note. The juveniles on the summit came rigidly to attention. Varian gestured to Bonnard to take the recorder but the boy was already reaching for it, doing a scan of the skies before he steadied the device on the alert young.

A mass of fliers fell from the caves, gained wing room and flew with an astonishing show of speed off into the misty southwest.

"That's the direction of the sea gap. The net fishers?"

"The juveniles are clearing away," said Bonnard. "Looks like fish for lunch to me."

Out of the mist now appeared wing-weary giffs, barely skimming the water, rising with obvious effort to ledges where they settled, wings unclosed and drooping. Varian was certain she'd seen grass trailing from the rear claws of one. They waited, and so did the juveniles, occasionally poking at each other. Bonnard, fretting with the interval, moved toward the sled exit but Varian stopped him, just as they saw an adult giff land on their terrace.

"Don't move a muscle, Bonnard."

The adult watched, its eyes never moving from the sled.

"Now move slowly back from the exit," Varian told him and when he had completed the maneuver, she let out a deep sigh of relief. "What did I tell you the other day? You don't bother animals with food. You sure as rakers don't bother creatures waiting for lunch, if you want to stay in good with them."

"I'm sorry, Varian."

"That's all right, Bonnard. You have to learn these things. Fortunately no harm's done—either to you or to our mission." She smiled at Bonnard's downcast face. "Cheer up. We've also learned something else. They haven't let up surveillance of *us* for one minute. And they've figured out where we enter and leave this sled. Pretty clever creatures, I'd say."

Never taking his eyes off their guard, the boy sank to the floor of the sled.

They waited another three-quarters of an hour before Kai, remembering to keep his gestures slow, alerted them to the returning giffs. Cries raised from every quarter, and so many giffs were airborne that Bonnard complained bitterly that his frames would show more furred bodies and wings than anything informative.

Bonnard and Varian saw a repetition of the previous performance as the shimmering piles of fish were spewed from the nets. The juveniles waddled in and one adult, spotting a youngster stocking up his throat pouch, tapped it smartly on the head and made it regurgitate. Kai observed another adult separating fringes from the mass, dexterously flipping them over the edge of the cliff with quick sweeps of his beak. When it had apparently completed that task on its side of the catch, it carefully scrubbed its beak against stone.

"I got that on tape, Varian," Bonnard assured her as Kai pointed out another curiosity, an adult giff whose beak was being stuffed by others. The giff then waddled off the cliff edge, gained wing room and disappeared into one of the larger caves. Another took his place, to be filled up before flying off, this time to another large aperture. The juveniles were allowed to eat one fish at a time. There was a repeat of juvenile terror over a fringe, two fell over and were intertwined until rescued by a watching adult. Bonnard fretted at having to remain inside the sled instead of on it where he could have got much better tapes of the incident.

Gradually the supply dwindled, the juveniles losing interest and disappearing from the summit. Soon after, Varian noticed that no giffs were to be seen. They waited patiently until Kai became so restless with inactivity that Varian could not ignore the fact that they were not furthering their study of the giff by remaining either in the sled or on the terrace.

It was well past midday now. She'd enough on tapes for hours of study. Her announcement that they'd better get back to the compound met with instant action on the part of the two males. Kai checked the sled's lock for flight, motioned Bonnard to strap himself in and did so himself. Both were ready while she, laughing, was barely seated.

As she took off, she circled once over the summit, noting that small fringes were left to bake and deteriorate on the summit. She'd answered a few of her questions, but more had been raised by the day's happenings. She was reasonably pleased with the excursion, if only because it had been something she'd wanted to do.

8

KAI noticed the absence of the sleds as they circled an encampment strangely motionless. Only Dandy was visible, half-asleep in his pen, one hind leg cocked at the ankle. For some reason, that reassured Kai. Dandy had shown a marked tendency to react to any tension or excitement in the compound by cowering against the fencing of his pen.

"Everyone is indeed resting," said Varian who was piloting the sled.

"My teams must have made an early return to their camps."

"Yes, but where are my heavy-worlders? Not all the sleds should be gone."

"Bakkun said something about going to his place," said Bonnard.

"His place?" Kai and Varian asked in chorus.

"Yes. North," said Bonnard, pointing. "Bakkun's special place is in the north."

"What sort of special place?" asked Varian, signalling Kai with a quick glance to let her do the questioning. "Have you been there?"

"Yes, last week when I was out with Bakkun. It's not what I'd call special, just a clear circular place among the trees, closed off at one end by a rock fall. There's a bunch of the big grass-eaters, like Mabel, and some other smaller types. They've all got hunks out of their sides, Varian. Bakkun told me Paskutti was interested in them. Didn't he mention it to you?"

"Probably hasn't had time," said Varian in such an off-handed manner that Kai knew Paskutti hadn't mentioned it to her.

"Time? That was a week ago."

"We've all been busy," said Varian, frowning as she slipped the sled into hold and landed it lightly on the ground.

Lunzie was at the veil lock now, waiting to open it for them.

"Successful trip?" she asked.

"Yes, indeed. Everyone enjoying a quiet restful day here, too?" asked Varian.

Lunzie gave her a long searching look.

"As far as I know," said Lunzie slowly, her eyes never leaving Varian's as she closed the veil lock. "Terilla's working on some drawings in Gaber's dome, and Cleiti's reading in the main dome."

"Could I show Cleiti the tapes, Varian?"

"By all means. Just don't erase 'em by mistake!"

"Varian! I've been handling tapes for weeks with no blanking."

Kai could sense that Varian wanted Bonnard out of earshot. He was also aware that somehow or other the two women had exchanged some tacit information and were impatient to talk uninhibitedly. Kai had a few questions to put to Varian, too, about Bakkun, Paskutti and trapped herbivores.

"My teams get off all right?" Kai asked Lunzie to cover the conspicuous silence as Bonnard made his way across the compound. He paused to pat Dandy.

"Yes, all except Bakkun, who went off with the heavy-worlders on some jaunt of their own." Lunzie gestured toward the shuttle and they moved that way. "Remember asking me about stores, Kai?" she said in a low voice. "Someone raided our hold of a selection of basic medical supplies. Also, the synthesizer has been used enough to drain a power pack.

Now, the synthesizer may be heavy on power, but I hadn't used it that much on the new pack. So I had Portegin check it out this morning before he went off, and there's no malfunction. Someone's been using it. What was synthesized I couldn't say."

"Where did the heavy-worlders go, Lunzie?" Varian asked.

"I don't know. I was in the stores by then, when I heard sled and belts going. Then Portegin came, told me the heavy-worlders had taken off . . ." Lunzie paused, frowning in concentration. "That's odd. I was in the store hold, and they didn't come to me for any rations."

"No!" Varian's low exclamation startled the doctor and Kai.

"What's wrong, Varian?"

She had turned very pale, looked suddenly quite sick and leaned against the bulkhead.

"No, I must be wrong."

"Wrong?" Lunzie prompted her.

"I must be. There'd be no reason for them to revert. Would there, Lunzie?"

"Revert?" Lunzie stared intently at Varian, who was still leaning weakly against the bulkhead. "You can't think . . ."

"Why else would Paskutti be interested in flank-wounded herbivores that I didn't know anything about? I never thought Bakkun was callous. But, to say such a thing in front of a boy . . ."

Lunzie gave a snort. "The heavy-worlders don't have a high opinion of adult light-gravs, less of the shipbred, and children on their worlds never speak until they've killed . . ."

"What are you two talking about?" asked Kai.

"I'm afraid I agree with Varian's hypothesis."

"Which is?" Kai spoke testily.

"That the heavy-worlders have taken to eating animal protein." Lunzie's calm, detached tone did not lessen the impact of such a revolting statement.

Kai thought he would be ill, the sudden nausea was so acute.

"They've . . ." He couldn't repeat the sentence and waved one hand in lieu of the words. "They're Federation members. They're civilized . . ."

"They do conform when in Federation company," said Varian in a low, colorless voice, indicating how deeply shocked she was. "But I've worked with them in expeditions before and they will . . . if they can. I just didn't think . . . I didn't want to think they'd do it here."

"They have been discreet," said Lunzie. "Not that I'm defending them. If it hadn't been for Bonnard's chance remark . . . No," and Lunzie frowned at the floor plates, "I've been skirting the edges of a theory ever since that night . . ."

"The night you served them the fruit distillation." Varian rounded on Lunzie, pointing at her. "They weren't drunk! They were high. And you know why?" Neither had time to answer her hypothetical question. "Because of the violence . . ."

"Yes, violence and alcohol would act as stimuli on the heavy-worlders," said Lunzie, nodding her head judiciously. "They have a naturally slow metabolism," she told Kai. "And a low sex drive which makes them an admirable mutation for EEC expeditions. Given the proper stimulants and . . ." Lunzie shrugged.

"That's my fault. I shouldn't have let them drink that night. I knew. You see," Varian rushed on in a spate of confession, "that was the day a fang-face savagely attacked a herbivore. I noticed Paskutti and Tardma reacting strongly although I *thought* at the time I was imagining things . . ."

"That was the violence needed, and I compounded the problem by offering the fruit distillation." Lunzie was willing to share the responsibility. "They must have made quite a night of it."

"And we thought they'd gone to bed early!" Varian clapped her palm on her forehead, admitting stupidity. "With too potent a brew . . ." She started to laugh and then drew in her breath sharply. "Oh, no. No!"

"Now what?" demanded Kai sharply.

"They went back."

"Went back?" Kai was confused.

"Remember my asking you about the big sled's flight time?" Varian asked Kai.

"They went back and slaughtered that herbivore for its flesh?" Lunzie asked Varian.

"I wish you didn't need to be so revoltingly vulgar," said Kai, angry at the doctor as well as himself and his churning stomach.

"Yes," Lunzie continued, ignoring Kai, "they would definitely need additional animal protein . . ."

"Lunzie!" Now Varian tried to stop her, but the physician continued in her detached clinical way.

"I do believe they eat, and enjoy, animal protein. On their own planet, they have to eat it, little vegetable matter grows on high-grav worlds that is digestible by human stock. Generally they will conform to the universal standards of vegetable and synthetic proteins. I have given them subsistence foods high in . . ." Lunzie stopped. "Could that be why the synthesizer was overworked?"

"Protein?" asked Kai, desperately hoping that members of his expedition had not abrogated all the tenets of acceptable dietary controls.

"No, the other daily requirements they couldn't get from a purely animal diet. One thing that isn't missing from our stores is our sort of protein."

Varian, looking green, held up a hand to divert Lunzie.

"Didn't think you were the squeamish type, Varian," Lunzie said. "Still, your sensitivity does credit to your upbringing. The temptation to eat animal flesh is still strong in the planet-bred . . ."

"Kai, what are we going to do?" asked Varian.

"Frankly," said Lunzie, "though you didn't ask me, I'd say there was nothing you can do. They have been discreet about their vile preference. However," and her tone altered, "this only supports my contention that you can never successfully condition away a basic urge. It requires generations in a new environment to be positive of your results. Oh!" Lunzie had begun in her usual confident, pedantic tone. Her exclamation was startled. "I say, Kai, Varian," she looked from one to the other at her most solemn, "EV *is* returning for us, isn't it?"

"We have every reason to believe so," said Kai firmly.

"Why do you ask, Lunzie?" Again Varian seemed to hear something in the woman's question that Kai had missed.

"Gaber doesn't believe so."

"As I told Dimenon," said Kai, feeling the need to show unconcerned authority, "we are out of contact, but if the Theks aren't worried, neither am I."

"The Theks never worry," said Lunzie. "Worry is for people pressed by time. How long have we been out of contact, Kai?"

He hesitated only long enough to catch Varian's eye and her approval. Lunzie was a good ally.

"Since the first reports were stripped from the satellite."

"That long?"

"We surmise, and the Theks confirm it, that the cosmic storm EV was going to investigate after leaving us has caused interference and EV can't reach the satellite."

Lunzie nodded, stroking the back of her neck as if her muscles were taut.

"I gather Gaber has been spouting that asinine theory of his, that we're planted?" Kai managed a laugh that sounded, to him, genuinely amused.

"I laughed at Gaber, too, but I don't think the heavy-worlders have the same sense of humor."

"That would account for their regressive behavior," said Varian. "They'd be very much at home on this planet, and strong enough to survive."

"This generation would be strong enough," said Lunzie in her pedantic tone, "but not the next."

"What are you talking like that for?" Kai demanded angrily. " 'Next generation.' We aren't planted!"

"No, I don't think *we* are," and Lunzie was calm. "We're much too small a group for a genetic pool and the wrong ages. But that wouldn't inhibit the heavy-worlders from striking out . . ."

"Staying on Ireta?" Kai was appalled.

"Oh, they've everything here they require," said Lunzie. "Alcohol, animal protein . . . The heavy-worlders are often laws unto themselves. You've heard the tales, Varian," and the girl nodded slowly. "I've heard of several groups just fading into the scenery. If you can imagine the bulk of a heavy-worlder fading . . ."

"They can't do that," Kai said, wrestling with dismay, anger and a sense of futility for he hadn't a notion how to prevent the heavy-worlders from carrying out such a plan. Physically they were superior, and both he and Varian had often felt that the heavy-worlders merely tolerated them as leaders because it suited.

"They could, and we had better admit it to ourselves, if to no one else," said Lunzie. "Unless, of course, you can figure out something so disastrous about this planet that they'd prefer to return with us." It was obvious she felt that there could be no such circumstances to deter the heavy-worlders.

"Now there's a constructive thought," said Varian.

"Retro, please," said Kai. "We have no indication that that is their intention! We may have just talked ourselves into a crisis without any substantiation. Muhlah! It's no business of ours to interfere with the sexual requirements of any group. If they have to have stimuli to satisfy their drive, fine. We've created the indiscretion by ascribing unsavory and unacceptable actions to them and we don't even know if our speculations are valid."

Lunzie looked a little chagrined, but Varian was not so easily mollified.

"I don't like it! Something's out of phase. I've felt it since the day we went to Mabel's assistance."

"Violence is a stimulus for the heavy-worlders," said Lunzie. "And despite our strides toward true civilized behavior, it can prove a stimulus for us as well: a primitive, disgusting but valid reaction." Lunzie shrugged her acceptance of such frailty. "We aren't that far removed from the slime of creation and instinctive response ourselves. From now on, I shall judiciously dilute the distillation for everyone." She walked toward the exit. "And no one will be the wiser."

"Look, Varian, we don't *know* yet," said Kai, seeing how dejected Varian was. "We've taken isolated facts—"

"*I've* taken isolated facts . . . but Kai, something *is* wrong."

"Too much already. We don't need more."

"Leaders are supposed to anticipate problems so that they don't arise."

"Like EV failing to contact us?" Kai gave her a long amused look.

"That's EV's problem, not ours. Kai, I've worked with heavy-worlders before. I even . . ." she gave a weak laugh, "survived two weeks of gravity on Thormeka to have some understanding of the conditions that bred them. And I *did* notice that Paskutti and Tardma overacted to fang-face's attack on the herbivore. As much as heavy-worlders do react."

"We cannot interfere with the discreet sexual practices of any group, Varian, can we?" He waited until she'd reluctantly agreed. "So, we've now anticipated that there might be a problem, right?"

"It's my first big expedition, Kai. It's got to turn out right."

"My dear coleader, you've been doing a superior job." Kai pulled her from the bulkhead and into his arms. He didn't like to see Varian so dejected and, he sincerely hoped, needlessly worried. "None of my geology teams has been trampled or flank-bitten . . . You've sorted out some new life forms, a bonus on *your* binary bit, my friend. And you know, it'd be nice if we practiced some sex ourselves?"

He had startled her and laughed at her reaction, took her silence as acquiescence and kissed her. He met with no resistance, and a few minutes later they retired discreetly to his dome for the remainder of the rest day.

9

A WORLD which stimulated last evening's occupation couldn't be all bad, Varian decided the next morning, rising totally refreshed. Perhaps Lunzie had been wrong to think that, just because the heavy-worlders hadn't taken along protein rations, they were going to . . . Well, there was no proof that their day hadn't been spent in gratifying their sex drive, and not an atavistic pleasure in dietary habits.

Kai was correct, too. As they had no proof of any misdemeanor, it did no good to harbor base suspicions.

Easier said than done, thought Varian later as she conferred with the heavy-worlders on the week's assignments. She could not put her finger on a specific change, but there was a marked difference in the attitude of her team. Varian had always felt relatively at ease with Paskutti and Tardma. Today, she was conscious of a restraint, stumbling for phrases and words, uncomfortable and feeling that Paskutti and Tardma were amused by her. They had an air of smug satisfaction that irritated her, though she'd been hard-pressed to say what gave her that idea, as the heavy-worlders betrayed no emotion. The xenob team was keeping just ahead of the areas the geologists must probe on the ground. Unknown life-forms lurked in the heavy vegetation, small but equally dangerous, and force-screen belts were no absolute protection.

As the two heavy-worlders strode beside her toward the sled park, she could have sworn that Paskutti was limping slightly. Varian and Kai had agreed to hold off questioning the heavy-worlders and Varian had no trouble controlling her curiosity that day. That indefinable change in the heavy-worlders' attitude toward her acted as a crucial check.

It was a distinct relief to her to call an end to the day's scouting when pelting, wind-lashed rain limited visibility and made telltagging impossible. That it was Paskutti who called the actual halt to the exercise gave Varian some measure of satisfaction.

When they entered the compound, Lunzie was crossing from the shuttle to her quarters and gave Varian an imperceptible signal to join her.

"Something occurred yesterday," the physician told Varian in the privacy. "Tanegli has a gash across one cheekbone. He said he got it from a sharp twig when leaning over to collect a specimen." Lunzie's expression discounted that explanation. "And I'm certain that Paskutti is masking a limp."

"Oho, and Bakkun is not making full use of his left arm."

"In some primitive societies, the males fight for the favor of the females," Varian said.

"That doesn't hold. Berru is wearing heal-seal on her left arm. I haven't seen Divisti or the others today, but I'd love to call a medical on all of 'em. Only I did that too recently for the alcohol reaction."

"Maybe Berru just didn't like the male who won her?" asked Varian whimsically. Lunzie snorted. "I'd say the air was blue with response yesterday. Anyway, how come you're in so early?"

"Violent storm, couldn't see, and certainly couldn't telltag what was on the ground. I rather thought though," she added in a drawl, "that Paskutti and Tardma were quite ready to quit early."

"I've put a new power pack in the synthesizer and I'll keep strict account of my usage. Tanegli says he found two more edible fruits, and one plant heart with a high nutritional content. At least he *says* he found them yesterday . . ."

"We could still be computing from the wrong data," suggested Varian wistfully.

"We could be." Lunzie was not convinced.

"I could ask Bonnard if he remembers the coordinates of Bakkun's so-called special place."

"You could, though I don't *like* involving the youngsters in any part of this."

"Nor do I. But they are part of the expedition and this could affect them as well as us adults. However, I could just be in the general vicinity of Bakkun's run that day, and . . ."

"Yes, that would not be a blatant abuse of the child's trust."

"I'll see what Kai says."

Kai had the same general objection to involving the youngster at all. On the other hand, it was important to find out exactly what had occurred, and if the heavy-worlders were reverting, he and Varian would have to know and take steps. He cautioned Varian to be discreet, both with Bonnard and the search.

Her opportunity came about quite naturally two mornings later. Kai and Bonnard took off north to do a depth assessment of a pitchblende strike discovered by Berru and Triv. Paskutti and Tardma followed by lift-belt to track and tag some shallow-water monsters observed, at a safe distance, by the two geologists. Varian wanted to penetrate the telltag farther to the northwest, so she asked Bonnard to be her team flyer.

She did a good deal of work with Bonnard and managed casually to veer to the proper heading. She had checked Bakkun's flight tapes.

"Say, isn't this near where Bakkun had those herbivores?"

Turning from the telltagger, Bonnard glanced around.

"A lot of Ireta looks the same, purple-green trees and no

sun. No, wait. That line of fold mountains, with the three higher overthrusts . . ."

"You have learned a thing or two," said Varian, teasingly.

Bonnard faltered, embarrassed. "Well, Bakkun's been giving me instruction, you know. We were headed straight for that central peak, I think. And we landed just above the first fold of those hills." Then he added, "We found some gold there, you know."

"Gold's the least of the riches this planet holds."

"Then we're not likely to be left, are we?"

Varian inadvertently swerved, sending Bonnard against his seat straps. She corrected her course, cursing Gaber's big mouth, and her own lack of self-control.

"Gaber's wishful thinking, huh?" she asked, hoping her chuckle sounded amused. "Those old fogies get like that, wanting to extend their last expeditionary assignment as long as they can."

"Oh." Bonnard had not considered that possibility. "Terilla told me he sounded awful certain."

"Wishful thinking often does sound like fact. Say, you don't want to stay on Ireta, too, do you? Thought you didn't like this stinking planet, Bonnard?"

"It's not so bad, once you get used to the smell."

"Just don't get too accustomed, pal. We've got to go back to the EV. Now, keep your eyes open, I want to check . . ."

They were flying over the first of the hills but Varian didn't need Bonnard to tell her when they cruised over Bakkun's special place. It was clearly identifiable: some of the heavier bones and five skulls still remained. Stunned and unwillingly committed now, Varian circled the sled to land and also saw the heavy, blackened stones, witness to a campfire which the intervening days' rain had not quite washed away.

She said nothing. She was grateful that Bonnard couldn't and wouldn't comment.

She put the sled down between the fire site and the first of the skulls. It was pierced between the eyes with a round hole:

too large to have been a stun bolt at close range, but whatever had driven it into the beast's head had had enough force behind it to send fracture lines along the skull bone. Two more skulls showed these holes, the fourth had been crushed by heavy blows on the thinner base of the neck. The fifth skull was undamaged, and it was not apparent how that creature had met its death.

The ground in the small rock-girded field was torn up and muddied with tracks, giving silent evidence to struggles.

"Varian," Bonnard's apologetic voice called her from chaotic speculations. He was holding up a thin scrap of fabric, stiff and darker than ship suits should be, a piece of sleeve fabric, for the seam ran to a bit of the tighter cuff: a big cuff, a left arm cuff. She winced with revulsion but shoved the offending evidence into her thigh pocket.

Resolutely she strode to the makeshift fire pit, staring at the blackened stones, at the groove chipped out of opposing stones where a spit must have been placed. She shuddered against rising nausea.

"We've seen enough, Bonnard," she said, gesturing him to follow her back to the sled. She had all she could do not to run from the place.

When they had belted into their seats, she turned to Bonnard, wondering if her face was as white as his.

"You will say nothing of this to anyone, Bonnard. Nothing."

Her fingers trembled as she made a note of the coordinates. When she lifted the sled, she shoved in a burst of propulsion, overwhelmingly eager to put as much space between her and that charnel spot as she could!

Neither she nor Kai could ignore such an abrogation of basic Federation tenets. For a fleeting moment, she wished she'd made this search alone, then she could have forgotten about it, or tried to. With Bonnard as witness, the matter could not be put aside as a nightmare. The heavy-worlders would have to be officially reprimanded, though she wasn't sure how efficacious words would be against their physical strength. They were contemptuous enough of their leadership already to have killed and eaten animal flesh.

Varian shook her head sharply, trying to clear her mind of the revulsion that inevitably accompanied that hideous thought.

"Life form, untagged," Bonnard said in a subdued tone.

Willing for any diversion from her morbid and sickening thoughts, Varian turned the sled, tracking the creature until it crossed a clearing.

"Got it," said Bonnard. "It's a fang-face, Varian. And Varian, it's wounded. Rakers!"

The predator whirled in the clearing, reaching up to beat futilely at the air with its short forefeet. A thick branch had apparently lodged in its ribs. Varian could see fresh blood flowing out of the gaping wound. Then she could no longer ignore the fact that the branch was a crude spear, obviously flung with great force into the beast's side.

"Aren't we going to try and help it, Varian?" asked Bonnard as she sent the sled careering away.

"We couldn't manage it alone, Bonnard."

"But it will die."

"Yes, and there's nothing we can do now. Not even get close enough to spray a seal on the wound and hope that it could dislodge that . . ." She didn't know why she stopped; she wasn't protecting the heavy-worlders, and Bonnard had seen the horror.

Hadn't the carnivores provided the heavy-worlders with enough violence? How many other wounded creatures would she and Bonnard encounter in this part of the world?

"By any chance, had you the taper on, Bonnard?"

"Yes, I did, Varian."

"Thank you. I'm turning back. I must speak to Kai as soon as possible." When she saw Bonnard looking at the comunit, she shook her head. "This is an executive matter, Bonnard. Again, I must ask you to say nothing to anyone and . . ." She wanted to add "stay away from the heavy-worlders," but from the tight, betrayed expression on the boy's face, she knew such advice would be superfluous.

They continued back to the compound in silence for a while.

"Varian?"

"Yes, Bonnard?" She hoped she had an answer for him.

"Why? Why did they do such a terrible thing?"

"I wish I knew, Bonnard. No incidence of violence stems from a *simple* cause, or a single motive. I've always been told that violence is generally the result of a series of frustrations and pressures that have no other possible outlet."

"An action has a reaction, Varian. That's the first thing you learn shipboard."

"Yes, because you're often in free fall or outer space, so the first thing *you'd* have to learn, ship-bred, is to control yourself, your actions."

"On a heavy world, though," Bonnard was trying to rationalize so hard, Varian could almost hear him casting about for a justification. "On a heavy world, you would have to struggle all the time, against the gravity."

"Until you became so used to it, you wouldn't consider it a struggle. You'd be conditioned to it."

"Can you be conditioned to violence?" Bonnard sounded appalled.

Varian gave a bark of bitter laughter. "Yes, Bonnard, you can be conditioned to violence. Millennia ago, it used to be the general human condition."

"I'm glad I'm alive now."

To that Varian made no reply, wondering if she was in accord. In an earlier time, when peoples were still struggling to a civilized level that spurned the eating of animal flesh; to a level that had learned not to impose its peculiar standards on any other species; to a level that accepted, as a matter of course, the friendships and associations with beings diverse and wonderful: a woman of only three hundred years ago would have had some occasion to cope with utter barbarianism. It was one matter entirely for beasts to fight and kill one another, following the dictates of an ecology (not that she was prevented from succoring the weaker when she could) but for one species, stronger, more flexible, basically more dangerous because of its versatility, to attack a stupid animal for the sporting pleasure was unspeakably savage.

What were she and Kai to do about such behavior? Again she wished she hadn't brought Bonnard. She'd been too clever, so she had, involving the boy. Perhaps scarring him with such evidence of wanton cruelty. But she hadn't expected anything like this when she thought of investigating Bakkun's special place. How could she? And once discovered, strong measures were indicated. Too late now to say that the heavy-worlders had been discreet in their vile pursuits. Too late to wish she'd never wanted to check into their activities.

On the other hand, such aberrant behavior was better uncovered on a world where no other sentient species was comprised. She also found some measure of relief that the heavy-worlders had picked on the stupid herbivores and predators, rather than the lovely golden giffs. If they'd harmed them . . . Pure rage, such as she had never experienced before in her life, consumed her with an incredible force.

Startled, Varian composed her thoughts. She must discipline herself if she wanted to control others.

They were almost to the compound now, sweeping down the broad plain that led to their granite height. Varian found herself hoping that, for some unknown reason, Kai had returned early. That was the trouble with bad news: it didn't keep. The intelligence was a sore weight in her mind, festering with speculation, such as what were the heavy-worlders doing right now?

She landed, reminding Bonnard to say nothing, even to Cleiti or Terilla, most certainly not to Gaber.

"You be not Gaber," said Bonnard with a smile. "He talks an awful lot but he says so little . . . unless he's talking about maps and beamed shots."

"Wait a minute, Bonnard." Varian motioned him back, wondering about the wisdom of involving him further. She glanced toward the shimmering force-screen, the dance of dying insects registering blue across the field. She tried to think, calmly, whether there was anyone else in the compound she could trust. Then she glanced back at the boy, standing easily, his head slightly cocked as he awaited her command. "Bonnard, I'm taking the power pack from this sled. When the other sleds come in, I want you to remove the packs—hide them in the underbrush if you can't bring them inside. If anyone questions you, say that your chore is checking them for lead drains. Yes, that's logical. Do you understand me?" She was unclamping their sled's pack as she issued her instructions. "You know where the packs are in the smaller sleds? And how to remove them?"

"Portegin showed us. Besides, I just saw you do it." He gave her the hand-lift which she attached to the heavy power pack and heaved it from the sled. "I'll just get another hand-lift."

She could see in his expression that he had more questions he was eager to ask as he followed her to the veil lock where Lunzie now stood to admit them. As they passed her, the woman looked at the power pack Varian was trailing.

"One of the leads is clogged," Varian said.

"Is that why you're back so early? Good thing," and Lunzie's usually solemn face broke into a wide grin. She gestured toward Dandy's pen. Trizein was leaning on the fencing, staring intently at the little creature who was, for a second marvel, peacefully munching at a pile of grasses, oblivious to the scrutiny.

"Trizein's out of his lab? What happened?"

"I'll let him tell you. It's his surprise, not mine."

"Surprise?"

"Here, Bonnard, take the power pack from Varian and put it where it belongs . . ."

Varian indicated the shuttle to Bonnard, a gesture which brought a surprised glance from Lunzie.

"Well, then," she said, "in the shuttle and come straight back. You'll want to hear about the probable ancestry of your pet, too."

"Huh?" Bonnard was startled.

"Quick, to the shuttle with the pack." Lunzie shooed him off with both hands. "The power pack leads, Varian? That's a bit lame, isn't it?"

"Varian! Has Lunzie told you?" Trizein had looked away from Dandy and seen her. "Why didn't anyone tell me? I mean, I can speculate possibilities from disembodied tissues, but this . . . this creature from our prehistoric past . . ."

His words were diversion enough, but the ringing tone in which he spoke made Varian move more quickly to him.

"Prehistoric past? What do you mean, Trizein?"

"Why, this little specimen is an excellent example of a primitive herbivore . . ."

"I know that . . ."

"No, no, my dear Varian, not just *a* primitive herbivore of this planet, but an Earth-type herbivore, of the group perissodactyl."

"Yes, I know it's perissodactyl. The axis of the foot is through the middle toe."

"Varian, are you being dense on purpose to tease me? *This,*" and Trizein gestured dramatically to Dandy, "*is* the first step in the genotype of the horse. He's a genuine hyracotherium, *Earth* type!"

The significance of Trizein's point gradually dawned on Varian. "You're trying to tell me that this is not *similar* to an Earth-type horse, it *is* the lineal ancestor of an Earth-type horse?"

"That's exactly what I'm telling you. Not trying. Telling!"

"It isn't possible." Varian said that flatly, and her expression accused Trizein of teasing her.

Trizein chuckled, preening himself by straightening his shoulders as he beamed at each member of his small audience.

"I may seem to be the original absent-minded analytical

chemist, but my conclusions are always provable: my experiments conducted efficiently and as expeditiously as equipment and circumstance allow. Lately I've been wondering if someone has been trying to fool me, to test my ability or my tendency to digress. I assure you that I do know when two totally different life forms are presented to me as coexisting on this planet. It is too bad of someone. And I inform you right now that I am aware of this subterfuge. All the tissues you and your teams have been giving me suggest a sufficient variety of creatures to populate several planets, not just one. Didn't the Ryxi bring their own technicians? Is there life on the Thek planet that I'm being given such diverse . . ."

"What about that animal tissue the Bakkun gave you about a week ago?" It was a chance, but she wasn't surprised when Trizein answered her.

"Oh, yes, the cellular level is remarkably comparable. A vertebrate, of course, which checks to ten decimal places, mitotic spindle, mitochondria all quite ordinary in a hemoglobin-based species. Like that fellow there!" And he jerked his thumb at Dandy. "Ah, Bonnard," he said as the boy approached them. "I understand from Lunzie that you rescued the little fellow?"

"Yes, sir, I did. But what is he?"

"A hyracotherium, or I miss my guess," said Trizein with the forced joviality an adult often displayed for the unknown quantity of a youngster.

"Does that make Dandy special?" asked Bonnard of Varian.

"If he is a genuine hyracotherium, unusually special," said Varian in a strangled voice.

"You doubt me," Trizein said, aggrieved. "You doubt me! But I can prove it." He grabbed Varian by the elbow and Lunzie by the shoulder and marched them toward the shuttle. "One is not allowed to bring much of a personal nature on a small short term expedition such as this, but I did bring my own data disks. You'll see."

As they were propelled into the shuttle, Varian knew what she would see. For all his erratic speech and mental mannerisms, Trizein was invariably accurate. She only wished his data disks would indicate how Dandy's species got to Ireta. It was no consolation either to realize that Trizein was likely to prove that the warm-blooded pentadactyls were aliens to this planet and the fringes, with their cell construction of filaments, were native. It was all part of the total confusion of this expedition: planted or mislaid, exploring a planet already once cored, out of contact with the mother ship and in danger of a mutiny.

Trizein had shoved them into his lab and was now rummaging in his carry-sack, which swung from a bolt in the ceiling, withdrawing a carefully wrapped bundle of data storage disks. He located the one he wanted and, with an air of righteous triumph, inserted it into the terminal's slot. There was no indecision about the keys he tapped and, as he pressed the print-out tab, he turned toward them with an expectant look.

Before their eyes was a replica, except for coloration, of Dandy. Neatly printed, the legend read HYRACOTHERIUM, TERRA-OLICOGENE AGE. EXTINCT. Where Bonnard's pet had mottled reddish-brown fur, the creature on the screen was more dun and stripe: the difference necessitated by camouflage requirements, Varian realized, from one environment to another. An indication, also, that the creature had evolved to some extent here on Ireta. His presence made no sense yet.

"I don't understand about Dandy being like this old Earth beast. He's extinct," said Bonnard, turning questioningly to Varian. "I thought you couldn't find duplicate life-forms developing independently on spatially distant planets. And Ireta isn't even the same sort of planet as Earth. The sun's third generation."

"We have observed several inconsistencies about Ireta," said Lunzie in her dry comforting voice.

"Is there any question in your mind about this creature's

similarity now?" asked Trizein, exceedingly pleased with his performance.

"None, Trizein. But you were out in the compound before, why didn't you notice Dandy's similarity then?"

"My dear, I was out in the compound?" Trizein affected dazed surprise.

"You were, but your mind was undoubtedly on more important matters," said Lunzie, a bit sharply.

"Quite likely," said Trizein with dignity. "My time has been heavily scheduled with analyses and tests and all kinds of interruptions. I've had little time to look around this world, though I have, you might say, examined it intimately."

"Do you have other extinct and ancient Earth-type animals on that disk as well as Dandy?"

"Dandy? Oh, the hyracotherium? Yes, this is my Earth paleontological disk, I have ancient species from . . ."

"We'd better stick to one set of puzzles at a time, Trizein," said Varian, not certain she could absorb more conundrums today. If the fringes should turn out to be a life-form from Beta Camaridae, she'd go twisted. "Bonnard, the tape on the giffs is in the main console, isn't it?"

"I put it on data-retrieval hold when I showed it to Cleiti and Terilla. Under the date, and giffs, Varian."

Varian tapped up the proper sequence on the terminal and also transferred Trizein's disk to the smaller screen and a hold. The terminal screen cleared to a vivid frame of a golden flier, its crested head tilted slightly, enhancing the impression of its intelligence.

"Great heavens above! And furred. Definitely furred," cried Trizein, bending to peer intently at the giff. "There has always been a great deal of controversy about that among my colleagues. No way to be certain, of course, but this is unquestionably a pteranodon!"

"Pteranodon?" Bonnard squirmed, uncomfortable to hear such a ponderous name attached to a creature he liked.

"Yes, a pteranodon, a form of dinosaur, misnamed, of course

since patently this creature is warm-blooded . . . inhabiting ancient Earth in Mesozoic times. Died out before the Tertiary period began. No one knows why, though there are as many speculations about the cause . . ." Trizein suddenly warded off the face that flashed on the screen for Varian had tapped in another sequence from the data banks. The heavy jawed head of a fang-face snarled up at them. "Varian! It's . . . it's Tyrannosaurus rex. My dear, what sort of a crude joke are you attempting to play on me?" He was furious.

"That is no joke," said Lunzie, nodding solemnly.

Trizein stared at her, his eyes protruding from his skull as his jaw dropped. He glanced back at the predatory countenance of the tyrant lizard, a name which Varian thought extremely well suited to its bearer.

"Those creatures are alive on this planet?"

"Very much so. Do you have this Tyrannosaurus rex on your data disk?"

Almost reluctantly, and with a finger that noticeably trembled, Trizein tapped out a sequence for his own disk. The mild features and small body of hyracotherium was replaced by the upright haughty and dangerous form of fang-face's prototype. Again there was a difference in coloration.

"The force-screen," said Trizein, "is it strong enough to keep *it* outside?"

Varian nodded. "It should be. Furthermore, there aren't any of his kind within a comfortable ten to fifteen kilometers of us. When we moved in, they moved out. They have other, more docile game than us." The shudder that rippled down her spine was not for fear of Tyrannosaurus rex.

"You're sure it will keep its distance?" asked Trizein, concerned. "That creature *ruled* its millennia on old Earth. Why, he was supreme. Nothing could defeat him."

Varian recalled all too vividly a tree-branch of a spear inextricably lodged in a tyrant lizard's rib cage.

"He doesn't like sleds, Trizein," said Bonnard, not noticing her silence. "He runs from them."

The chemist regarded the boy with considerable skepticism.

"He does," Bonnard repeated. "I've seen him. Only to-day . . ." Then he caught Varian's repressive glance but Trizein hadn't noticed.

The man sank slowly to the nearest lab bench.

"Varian might tease me, and so might the boy, but Lunzie . . ."

It was as if Trizein, too, wished to hear a negative that would reassure him, restore matters to a previous comfortable balance. Lunzie, shaking her head, confirmed that the creatures did exist, and others of considerable size and variety.

"Stegosaurus, too? And the thunder lizard, the original dinosaur? And . . ." Trizein was torn between perturbation and eager excitement at the thought of seeing live creatures he had long considered extinct. "Why was I never told about them? I should have been told! It's my specialty, my hobby, prehistoric life forms." Now Trizein sounded plaintive and accusatory.

"Believe me, my friend, it was not a conscious omission," said Lunzie, patting his hand.

"I'm the true xenob, Trizein," said Varian in apology. "It never occurred to me that these weren't unique specimens. I'd only started considering that an anomaly must exist when you analyzed the fringe types and found them to be on such a different cellular level. That and the grasses!"

"The grasses? The grasses! And tissue slides and blood plates, and all the time," now outrage stirred Trizein to his feet, "all the time these fantastic creatures are right . . . right outside the force-screen. It's too much! Too much, and no one would tell me!"

"You were outside the compound, Trizein, oh, you who look and do not see," said Lunzie.

"If you hadn't kept me so busy with work, each of you saying it was vital and important, and had top priority. Never have I had to deal so single-handedly with so many top priorities, animal, vegetable and mineral. How I've kept going . . ."

"Truly, we're sorry, Trizein. More than you know. I wish I had pried you out of the lab much earlier," said Varian so emphatically that Trizein was mollified. "On more counts than identifying the beasts."

Nevertheless, would that knowledge and identification have kept the heavy-worlders from their bestial game? Would it matter in the final outcome, Varian wondered.

"Well, well, make up for your omissions now. Surely this isn't all you have?"

Grateful for any legitimate excuse to delay the unpleasant, Varian gestured Trizein to be seated on something more comfortable than a bench and tapped out a sequence for her survey tapes, compiled when she and Terilla were doing the charts.

"It is patently obvious," said the chemist, when he had seen all the species she had so far taped and tagged, "that someone has played a joke. Not necessarily on me, or you, or us," he added, glancing about from under his heavy brows. "Those animals were planted here."

Bonnard gargled an exclamation, not as controlled in his reaction to that phrase as Lunzie or Varian.

"Planted?" Varian managed a wealth of amused disbelief in that laughed word.

"Well, certainly they didn't spring up in an independent evolution, my dear Varian. They must have been brought here . . ."

"Fang-face, and herbivores and the golden fliers? Oh, Trizein, it isn't possible. Besides which, the difference in pigmentation indicates that they *evolved* here . . ."

"Oh yes, but they *started* on Earth. I don't consider camouflage or pigmentation a real deterrent to my theory. All you'd need is one common ancestor. Climate, food, terrain would all bring about specialization over the millennia and the variety of types would evolve. The big herbivores, for instance, undoubtedly developed from Struthiomimus but so did Tyrannosaurus and quite possibly, your pteranodon. The possibilities are infinite from one mutual ancestor. Look at humans, for instance, in our infinite variations."

"I'll grant it's possible, Trizein, but why? Who would do such a crazy thing? For what purpose? Why perpetrate such monstrosities as fang-face? I could see the golden fliers . . ."

"My dear, variety is essential in an ecological balance. And the dinosaurs were marvelous creatures. They ruled old Earth for more millennia than we poor, badly engineered *Homo sapiens* have existed as a species. Who knows why they faded? What catastrophe occurred . . . More than likely a radical change in temperature following a magnetic shift—that's my theory at any rate, and I'll support it with the evidence we've found here. Oh, I do think this is a splendid development. A planet that has remained in the Mesozoic condition for untold millions of years, and likely to remain so for unknown millennia longer. That thermal core, of course, is the factor that . . ."

"Who, Trizein, rescued the dinosaurs from Earth and put them here to continue in all their savage splendor?" asked Varian.

"The Others?"

Bonnard gasped.

"Trizein, you're teasing. The Others destroy life, not save it." Varian spoke sternly.

Trizein looked unremorseful. "Everyone is entitled to a bit of a joke. The Theks planted them, of course."

"Have the Theks planted us, too?" asked Bonnard, scared.

"Good heavens!" Trizein stared at Bonnard, his expression turning from surprise at the idea to delight. "Do you really think we might be, Varian? When I consider all the investigatory work I must do . . ." Lunzie and Varian exchanged shocked glances. Trizein would welcome such a development. " . . . to prove my conclusions of warm-bloodedness. I wonder, Varian, you didn't show me any true saurians, that is to say, any cold-blooded species, because if they did develop here as well, as a specialization, of course, it would substantially improve my hypothesis. This world appears to remain consistently hotter than old Earth . . . Well, Varian, what's the matter?"

"We're not planted, Trizein."

Daunted and disappointed, he looked next to Lunzie, who also shook her head.

"Oh, what a pity." He was so dejected that Varian, despite the seriousness of the moment, had difficulty suppressing her amusement. "Well, I serve you all fair warning that I do not intend to keep my nose to the data disk and terminal keyboard any more. I shall take time off to investigate my theory. Why didn't anyone think to show me a frame of the animals whose flesh I've been analyzing so often? The time I've wasted . . ."

"Analyzing animal tissues?" Lunzie spoke first, her eyes catching Varian's in alarm.

"Quite. None of them were toxic, a conclusion now confirmed by our mutual planet of origin. I told Paskutti, so you don't need to be so particular about personal force-screens when in close contact. Where are you keeping the other specimens? Nearby?"

"No. Why do you ask?"

Trizein frowned. He'd started and abandoned any number of lines of thought, and was now being brought up sharp.

"Why? Because I got the distinct impression from Paskutti that he was worried about actual contact with these creatures. Of course, not much can penetrate a heavy-worlder's hide, but I could appreciate his worrying that you might get a toxic reaction, Varian. So I assumed that the beasts were nearby, or wounded like that herbivore when we first landed. Did you ever show me a frame of that one?"

"Yes," Varian replied, absently because her mind was revolving about more pressing identities, like the name of the game the heavy-worlders were playing. "One of the hadrasaurs. I think that's what you called it."

"There were, in fact, quite a variety of hadrasaur, the crested, the helmeted, the . . ."

"Mabel had a crest," said Bonnard.

"You know, Varian, I think that Kai would be interested in Trizein's identification of Dandy," said Lunzie.

"You're quite right, Lunzie," said Varian, moving woodenly toward the lab's comunit.

She was relieved when Kai answered instead of Bakkun, though she'd prepared herself to deal with the heavy-worlder, too. She was conscious of Bonnard holding his breath as he wondered what she was going to say, and of Lunzie's calm encouraging expression.

"Trizein has just identified our wild life, Kai, and explained the anomaly. I think you'd better come back to base right now."

"Varian . . ." Kai sounded irritated.

"Cores are not the only things planted on this stinking ball of mud, Kai, or likely to be planted!"

There was silence on the other end of the comunit. Then Kai spoke. "Very well then, if Trizein thinks it's that urgent. Bakkun can carry on here. The strike is twice the size of the first."

Varian congratulated him but wondered if he oughtn't to insist that Bakkun return with him. She'd a few questions she'd like to put to that heavy-worlder on the subject of special places and the uses thereof.

10

BAKKUN made no comment on Kai's recall. He was apparently too engrossed in the intricacies of setting the last core for the shot that would determine the actual size of the pitch-blende deposit.

"You'll come back to the base when you finish?" Kai asked as he placed the lift-belt for the heavy-worlder by the seismimic.

"If I don't, don't worry. I'll lift over to the secondary camp."

There was just the slightest trace of emphasis on the personal pronoun. Bakkun's behavior had been grating on Kai all day, nothing he could really point to and say Bakkun was being contemptuous or insolent, but the entire work week Kai had sensed a subtle change in the heavy-worlder geologist.

Varian's ambiguous remark about things planted or likely to be planted dominated his nebulous irritation with Bakkun. The coleader was unlikely to panic over trivia, and the fact that she had bothered him on a field trip indicated the seriousness of the matter. What on earth could she mean by that cryptic remark? And how could Trizein's identification of the life forms clear up anomalies?

Maybe there'd been a message from the Theks and Varian had not wanted anyone, patching in on his sled's code, to know. He recalled her exact phrasing. She'd separated Trizein's achievement from the request for him to return. So, it wasn't Trizein's discovery in itself.

Rather than worry needlessly, Kai occupied his mind with estimating the probable wealth of energy materials on this planet, as computed by sites already assessed and the probability of future finds based on the extended orogenic activity in the areas as yet unsurveyed.

By the time he reached the base, he decided that Ireta was undoubtedly one of the richest planets he had ever heard about. It quite cheered him to realize that sooner or later EV would find this out, too. He, Varian and the team members would be rich even by the inflated standards of the Federation. The supportive personnel, and that would have to include the three children if Kai had anything to say about it, should also get bonuses. All three of them had been useful to the expedition. There was Bonnard now, lugging the power pack from one of the parked sleds. In such small ways, the youngsters had helped contribute to the success of the landing party.

Lunzie was operating the veil and greeted Kai with the information that Varian was in the shuttle. Bonnard, excusing himself as he ducked past Kai to deposit the power pack, went out again, heading toward Kai's sled.

"What is Bonnard doing?"

"Checking all the power packs. Inconsistencies have developed."

"In the power packs? We have been running through them at a terrific rate. Is that why?"

"Probably. Varian's waiting."

It did not occur to Kai until he was stepping into the shuttle that it was very odd for Lunzie to concern herself with mechanical trivialities. Trizein was at the main view screen, so rapt in his contemplation of frames on browsing herbivores that he was unaware of Kai's entrance.

"Kai?" Varian poked her head around the open access to the pilot's compartment. She beckoned him urgently.

Kai indicated Trizein, silently gesturing whether he should rouse the man. Varian shook her head and motioned him urgently to come.

"What's this all about, Varian?" he said when he had waved the lock closed behind him.

"The heavy-worlders *have* reverted. They took their rest day in fun and games with herbivores. And a fang-face. The herbivores they evidently sported with before they killed . . . and ate them."

Kai's stomach churned in revulsion to her quick words.

"Gaber's rumor was well spread before he spoke to you, Kai. And the heavy-worlders believe him. Or they want to. Those supplies we've been missing, the hours of use I couldn't account for on the big sled, the odd power pack, medical supplies. We're lucky if it isn't mutiny."

"Go back to the beginning, Varian," said Kai, sitting heavily in the pilot's chair. He didn't contradict her premise, but he did want to see exactly what facts contributed to her startling conclusions.

Varian told him of the morning's hideous discovery, of her conversation with Lunzie and then Trizein's revelation about the planted Earth dinosaurs. She wound up by saying that the heavy-worlders, while not outright uncooperative or insubordinate, had subtly altered in their attitude toward her. Had he noticed anything? Kai nodded as she finished her summation and, leaning across the board, flipped open the communications unit.

"Is that why Bonnard was removing power packs?"

"Yes."

"Then you think a confrontation is imminent?"

"I think if we don't hear from EV tomorrow when you contact the Thek, something will happen. I think our grace period ended last rest day."

Kai regarded her for a long moment. "You've worked with them longer than I have. What do you think the heavy-worlders would do?"

"Take over." She spoke quietly but with calm resignation. "They are basically better equipped to survive here. We couldn't live off the . . . the land's bounty."

"That's the extreme view. But, if they have believed Gaber and think we've been planted, couldn't their reversion be a way of preparing themselves to be planted?"

"I'd credit that, Kai, if I hadn't seen what games they played last rest day. That frightens the life out of me, frankly. They deliberately . . . no, hear me out. It's revolting, I know, but it gives you a better idea of what we'd be up against if we can't stop them. They killed . . . *killed* with crude weapons . . . five herbivores. Bonnard and I saw another wounded beast, a fang-face, Tyrannosaurus rex, with a tree-size spear stuck in his ribs. Now, that creature once ruled old Earth. Nothing could stop him. A heavy-worlder did. For fun!" She took a deep breath. "Furthermore, by establishing those secondary camps, we have given them additional bases. Where are the heavy-worlders right now?"

"Bakkun's on his way back here, presumably. He'd a lift-belt. Paskutti and Tardma . . ."

They both heard Lunzie shouting Kai's name. It took them a bare second to realize that Lunzie never shouted unless it was an emergency. They heard the thud and stamp of heavy boots echoing in the outside compartment.

Varian pressed the lock mechanism on the iris just as they heard a heavy hand slap against the outside panel. Kai tapped out a quick sequence on the comunit, slapped it into send and cut the power. As he was doing this, Varian pulled the thin, almost undetectable switch that deactivated the main power supply of the ship. An imperceptible blink told them that the ship had switched to auxiliary power, a pack that had strength enough to continue the lighting and minor power drains for several hours.

"If you do not open that lock instantly, we will blast," said the hard unemotional voice of Paskutti.

"Don't!" Varian managed to get sufficient fear and anxiety in her voice even as she winked, grimaced and shrugged her impotence to Kai.

He nodded acceptance of her decision. It did no one any good for both leaders to be fried alive in the small pilot compartment. He never questioned Paskutti's intention was real. He only hoped that none of the heavy-worlders had noticed the infinitesimal drop in power as Varian had switched from one supply to the other. He and Varian were the only ones who knew of the fail-safe device that had rendered the shuttle inoperative. Paskutti did not enter the small cabin as the iris opened. After a moment's contemptuous scrutiny of the two leaders, he reached in, grabbed Varian by the front of her ship suit and lifted her bodily out. He let her go, with a negligent force that sent her staggering to crash against a bulkhead. He gave a bark of laughter at the cry she quickly suppressed. As she slowly stood upright, her eyes were flashing with suppressed anger. Her left arm hung at her side.

Kai started to emerge to avoid a similar humiliating display of the heavy-worlders' contempt for other breeds. But Tardma had been waiting her turn. She grabbed his left wrist and twisted it behind his back with such force that he felt the wrist bones splinter. How he managed to keep on his feet and conscious, he didn't know. His abrupt collision with the wall stunned him slightly. A hand supported him under the right arm. Beyond him a girl was sobbing in hopelessness.

Determinedly, Kai shook his head, clearing his mind, and initiated the mental discipline that would block the pain. He breathed deeply, from his guts, forcing down the hatred, the impotence, all irrational and emotionally clouding reactions.

The hand that had held him up released him. He was aware that it had been Lunzie, beside him. Her face was white and set, staring straight ahead. From the rate of her respiration, he knew she was practicing the same psychic controls. Beyond her, it was Terilla who was weeping in fear and shock.

Kai rapidly glanced about the compartment. Varian was on her feet, struggling to contain a defiance and fury that could only exacerbate their situation. Trizein was next to her, blinking and looking about in confusion as he struggled to absorb his occurrence. Cleiti and Gaber were unceremoniously herded into the shuttle, the cartographer babbling incoherently about this not being the way he had expected matters to proceed, and how dared they treat him with such disrespect.

"Tanegli? Do you have them?" asked Paskutti into his wrist comunit. The answer was evidently affirmative, for the man nodded at Tardma.

Tanegli? Whom would the heavy-world botanist have—

Portegin, Aulia, Dimenon and Margit? As his broken wrist became a numb appendage, Kai's mind became sharper, his perceptions clearer. He felt the beginning of that curious floating sensation that meant mind dominated body. The effect could last up to several hours, depending on how much he drew against the reservoir of strength. He hoped he had enough time. If all the heavy-worlders were assembling here, then Berru would arrive with Triv. When had Bakkun gone then? Or had he assisted Tanegli?

"None of the sleds have power packs," said Divisti, standing in the lock. "And that boy is missing."

Kai and Varian exchanged fleeting glances.

"How did he elude you?" Paskutti was surprised.

Divisti shrugged. "Confusion. Thought he'd cling to the others."

So they considered the boy, Bonnard, no threat. Kai looked at Cleiti, hoping she didn't know where Bonnard had gone, hoping the knowledge wasn't clear in her naïve face. But her mouth was closed in a firm, defiant line. Her eyes, too, showed suppressed anger; hatred every time she looked toward the heavy-worlders, and disgust for Gaber blubbering beside her.

Terilla had stopped crying but Kai could see the tremors shaking her frail body. A child who preferred plants would find this violence difficult to endure, and until Lunzie had achieved her control, she couldn't spare the girl any assistance.

"Start dismantling the lab, Divisti, Tardma."

The two women nodded and moved to the lab. As they crossed the threshold, Trizein came out of his confusion.

"Wait a minute. You can't go in there. I've experiments and analyses in progress. Divisti, don't touch that fractional equipment. Have you taken leave of your senses?"

"You'll take leave of yours," said Tardma, pausing at the doorway as the chemist strode toward her. With a cool smile of pleasure, she struck him in the face with a blow that lifted the man off his feet and sent him rolling down the hard deck to lie motionless at Lunzie's feet.

"Too hard, Tardma," said Paskutti. "I'd thought to take him. He'd be more useful than any of the other lightweights."

Tardma shrugged. "Why bother with him anyway? Tanegli knows as much as he does." She went into the lab with an insolent swing of her hips and shortly emerged with Divisti, each carrying as much equipment as they could with a total disregard for its fragility. Heavy-worlder contempt for lightweights evidently extended to their instrumentation. An acrid odor of spilled preservatives and solvents overlaid the air.

With ears now ultrasensitive, Kai heard the landing whine of a sled. From the west. Tanegli had returned. He heard voices. Bakkun was with Tanegli. Shortly the other lightweight geologists were led into the shuttle, Portegin, his head bloody, half-carrying a groggy Dimenon. Aulia and Margit were shoved forward by Bakkun. Triv all but measured his length of the deck, forcefully propelled by Berru who entered behind him, a half-smile of contempt on her face.

Triv reeled to Kai's side, shielding himself from the heavyworlders by his leader's body. Berru ought not to have been so derisive, for Triv now began the breathing exercises that led to the useful Discipline that Kai, Lunzie and Varian were practicing. That made four. Kai didn't think either Aulia or Margit had qualified in their training. He knew Portegin and Dimenon were not Disciples. Four wasn't enough to overpower the six heavy-worlders. With luck, though, they might still swing the grim balance back toward hope for the lightweights. Kai had no illusions about their situation: the heavyworlders had mutinied and intended to strip the camp of anything useful, leaving the ship-bred and lightweights to fend for themselves, unequipped and unprotected on a hostile, dangerous world.

"All right, Bakkun," said Paskutti, "you and Berru go after our allies. We want to make this look right. That comunit was still warm when I got here. They must have got a message through to the Theks." He turned bland eyes on Kai, raised his eyebrows slightly to see if his guess was accurate.

Kai returned the gaze calmly. The heavy-worlder had surprised no telltale expression from him. Paskutti shrugged.

"Tanegli, get the rest of the stores!"

Tanegli was back a second later. "There aren't any power packs left, Paskutti. I thought you said there were."

"So there aren't. We've enough in the sleds and the lift-belts for some time. Start loading."

Tanegli went back into the storehold and, after a noisy few moments, emerged, staggering under a plaspack full of jumbled supplies.

"That clears the storehold, Paskutti." Tanegli glanced around the staring faces of the captives and, laughing uproariously at some private joke, left.

"No protests, Leader Kai? Leader Varian?" Paskutti's tone and smile were taunting.

"Protests wouldn't do us any good, would they?" said Varian. She spoke so calmly that Paskutti frowned as he regarded her. The limp left arm had obviously been broken by his mishandling of her, but there was no sign of pain or anger in her voice, merely a bemused detachment.

"No, protests wouldn't, Leader Varian. We've had enough of you lightweights ordering us about, tolerating us because we're useful." He used a sneering tone. "Where would we have fit in your plantation? As beasts of burden? Muscles to be ordered here, there and everywhere, and subdued by pap?" He made a cutting gesture with one huge hand.

And then, before anyone realized what he intended, he swooped on Terilla, grabbed a handful of the child's hair and yanked her off her feet, letting her dangle at the end of his hand. At Terilla's single, terrified scream, Cleiti jumped up, beating her fists against Paskutti's thick muscular thigh, kicking at his shins. Amused and surprised by such defiance, Paskutti glanced down at Cleiti. Then he raised his fist and landed a casual blow on the top of Cleiti's head. She sank, unconscious, to the deck.

Gaber erupted and dashed at Paskutti who held the cartographer off with his other hand, all the while dangling Terilla by her hair, the girl's eyes stretched to slits by the tautness of his grasp.

"Tell me, Leader Varian, Leader Kai, did you send a message to the Theks? One second's delay and I'll break her back across my knee."

"We sent a message," replied Kai promptly. "Mutiny. Heavyworlders."

"Did you ask for help from our estimable supervisors?" asked Paskutti, giving Terilla a shake when he thought Kai deliberated too long in answering.

"Help? From Theks?" asked Varian, her eyes never leaving the helplessly swinging girl. "It would take them several days to ponder the message. By then, your . . . operation will be all over, won't it? No, we merely reported a condition."

"Only to the Theks?"

Now Kai saw what Paskutti needed to know: whether or not a message had also been beamed up to the satellite. If so, he would have to alter his "operation" in accordance.

"Only to the Theks," said Kai, the mind-dominated part of his emotions wanting to add, "now release the girl."

"You know what you need to know," screamed Gaber, still attempting to reach Paskutti and make him release Terilla. "You'll kill the child. Release her! Release her! You told her there'd be no violence. No one hurt! You've killed Trizein, and if you don't let go of that child . . ."

Paskutti casually swatted Gaber into silence. The cartographer hit the deck with a terrible thud and rolled to one side. Terilla was dropped in a heap by Cleiti. Kai couldn't tell if the girl had been killed by the mishandling. He glanced surreptitiously at Lunzie who was staring at the girls. Some relaxation about the woman's eyes reassured him: the girls were alive.

Beside him, Triv had completed the preliminaries to Discipline. Now he, too, would wait until his strength could be of use. The hardest part was the waiting until such time as this controlled inner strength would be channeled into escape. Kai breathed low in the diaphragm, willing himself to the patience required to endure this hideous display of brute strength and cruelty.

Dimenon was rousing but, although he moaned in pain, Lunzie did not attend him. Margit, Aulia and Portegin kept their eyes front, trying not to focus on scenes they could neither stop nor change.

Tanegli came storming up the ramp to the shuttle, his face contorted with anger, a man controlled by his emotions, no longer the calm rational botanist, interested in growing things.

"There isn't a power pack in any of the sleds," he told Paskutti but he strode right up to Varian, grabbing her by both arms and shaking her. Kai willed her to feign unconsciousness. Such handling might impair any chance of that broken shoulder healing properly.

"Where did you hide them, you tight-assed bitch?" he cried.

"Watch your strength, Tanegli. Don't break her neck yet," said Paskutti, stepping forward in his urgency to arrest the angry man.

Tanegli visibly pulled back some force of the blow he had leveled at Varian. Nevertheless, her head rolled sharply backward but as she righted herself, her eyes were still open. The mark of Tanegli's fingers were vivid wales on her cheek.

"Where did you hide the power packs?"

"She's broken her left shoulder. Use that as goad," said Paskutti. "Not too much . . . just enough. Can't have her passing out with pain. These lightweights can't take much."

"Where? Varian, where?" Tanegli accompanied each word with a twist to her left arm.

Varian cried out. To Kai's ears, the echo was false since, in the throes of Discipline, Varian wouldn't feel pain right now.

"I didn't hide them. Bonnard did."

Margit and Aulia gasped at this craven betrayal of the boy.

"Go get him, Tanegli. Find out where those power packs are or we'll be backing the supplies out of here. Bakkun and Berru will have started the drive. Nothing can stop it once it starts." Paskutti twitched with a sense of urgency now.

"She'd know where he is. Tell me, where? Varian?"

Varian suddenly hung limply in Tanegli's grip. He let her drop to the deck with a disgusted oath and strode to the open lock. Kai heard three more steps before the man stopped, shouting for Bonnard to come. Then Tanegli called for Divisti and Tardma to help him search for the boy.

Paskutti looked down at Varian's crumpled figure. Kai hoped that the man didn't suspect that she was only pretending. An expression close to the snarl of a fang-face crossed the heavy-worlder's face, but he was expressionless again when he turned to Kai.

"March!" Paskutti gestured peremptorily to the lock. He motioned to Lunzie and the others to move: with flicks of his forefinger he indicated that each was to carry one of the unconscious ones. "Into the main dome, all of you!" he ordered.

As they crossed the compound, Dandy was lying dead in his pen, back broken. Kai was glad neither Cleiti nor Terilla would see their pet. The ground was littered with scattered tapes, charts, exposed records and splintered disks. Inadvertently he trod on one of Terilla's careful drawings of a plant. Forcing deep breaths from his diaphragm, he controlled the fury he felt at such wanton destruction.

The main dome had been stripped of everything useful. The unconscious were laid on the floor, the others motioned to stand by the farthest arc from the iris lock.

Outside, the search for Bonnard continued. Paskutti was now glancing first at his wrist chrono and then at the plains beyond the force-screen.

Kai's heightened hearing caught the faint sound of his name. Carefully he turned his head and saw Lunzie staring at him, saw her imperceptibly indicate that he was to look outside. By shifting slightly he could see out, could see two dots in the sky, the black line beneath, a tossing black line, moving black line, and then he knew what the heavy-worlders had planned to do.

The force-screen was strong enough to keep out ordinary dangers but not the massed attack of stampeded creatures. The camp's advantage of height above the plain and forest would be canceled. The heavy-worlders were herding the animals right up where they wanted them to do their damage.

Then Theks, receiving Kai's message, might react to it . . . in a few days' time. They might, if the thinking spirit moved them, send one of the younger Theks to investigate. But Kai doubted it. The Theks would rightly consider that any intervention of theirs would arrive too late to affect the outcome of the mutiny.

The lightweights would have to effect their own salvation. The heavy-worlders would have to leave the compound soon. Would it be soon enough? And how would they leave their scorned captives? Could Bonnard stay out of their grasp?

Paskutti's fingers twitched. He glanced, almost apprehensively at the wrist chrono, squinted at the oncoming black line.

"Tanegli? Haven't you found that boy?" Paskutti's bellow deafened ears made sensitive by the Discipline.

"He's hidden. We can't find him, or the power packs!" Tanegli was raging with frustration.

"Come back, then. We're wasting time." Paskutti was not at all pleased with this unexpected check to his plans. The look he turned on the limp figure of Varian was ominous. "How did she know?" he asked Kai. "Bakkun thought something was up when she used such a trivial excuse to bring you back early."

"She found the place where you spent rest day. And the wounded fang-face you couldn't kill." Kai's instinct was to continue to protect Bonnard as long as he could from possible retaliation. If they all died, the boy couldn't last on his own on Ireta. He'd have to seek what refuge the heavy-worlders would offer him.

"Bonnard! I told Bakkun he took a risk letting the boy see the arena." Paskutti's face reflected many emotions now, contempt, supercilious disdain, satisfaction in past performances. His upper lip drew back from his teeth in a travesty of a smile. "You wouldn't have appreciated our rest day. No matter," Paskutti glanced down the valley. "The rehearsal has paid dividends . . . for us!"

The sun put in its brief evening appearance, lighting the plain so that Kai discerned the bobbing bodies of the herbivores inexorably moving toward the encampment. The other heavy-worlders now congregated about the lock, their faces for once flushed with exertion and shiny with sweat.

"He's gone to earth," said Tanegli in a savage tone, glaring at Kai. "And all the power packs."

"We've no more time to look. Move the sleds out of the direct line of the stampede. Be quick about it. Do you all have lift-belts? Good. Then keep up and out of trouble until the stampede has passed."

"What about the shuttle?"

"It should be all right," said Paskutti, glancing at the vessel perched above the encampment on its ledge. "Move!"

The others did, in great leaping strides toward the sled park.

Paskutti stood in the iris opening, hands on his belt, glancing with unconcealed pleasure at the docile captives. Kai knew that the moment of ultimate danger was *now*! Would Paskutti seal them into the dome, conscious and cruelly aware of their fate? Or would he stun them?

His essentially cruel nature won.

"I leave you now, to your fitting end. Trampled by creatures, stupid, foolish vegetarians like yourselves. The only one of you strong enough to stand up to us a mere boy."

He closed the iris lock, and the thud of his fist against the plaswall told Kai that he had shattered the controls.

Varian, suddenly mobile, was peering over the bottom of the far window, her left arm dangling uselessly.

"Varian?" said Lunzie, doing something to the still body of Trizein. The man groaned suddenly, shocked back to consciousness. Lunzie moved to Terilla and Cleiti, nodding to herself as she administered restorative sprays.

"He's at the veil," reported Varian in a low voice. "He's opened it. He's left it open. I can see two others sky-borne. Bakkun and Berru probably. We ought to have a few moments when the herd tops the last rise when they won't be able to see anything."

"Triv!" Kai gestured and the geologist followed him to the rear arc of the dome, motioning the others to one side.

Kai's sensitized fingers felt the fine seam of the plastic skin. Triv placed his fingertips farther up the seam. They both took the requisite deep breaths, called out and ripped the tough fabric apart.

Lunzie had the two girls on their feet, staggering but conscious enough to stand. She turned to help Trizein.

"Where could Bonnard have gone to, Kai?" asked Varian in a tight voice that betrayed an anxiety not even the Discipline could mask.

"Well hidden enough to elude the heavy-worlders. Safe enough from what's coming. Now," and he turned to his comrades, "we cannot panic, but we must wait until the sky-borne heavy-worlders cannot see us or they will merely stun us down. Margit, Aulia, Portegin, you're all able to run?" They nodded. "Lunzie, you'll take Terilla? Is Gaber dead? Well, Aulia, you and Portegin help Cleiti. Triv will carry Trizein. I'll help Dimenon. Varian, can you manage?"

"As well as you. I'll back us up."

"I will," said Kai, shaking his head and looking at her hanging arm.

"No, you've Dimenon. I'll manage." She glanced out the window again.

It did not take sensitive hearing now to hear the approaching stampede. It did take stern control to remain calm.

"There are four in the sky now," said Varian, "and the beasts have reached the narrow part of the approach. Get ready."

Aulia stifled a cry of fear.

"Everyone, breathe deeply from the diaphragm," said Lunzie, "and when we give you the word to go, yell and *run*! Keep yelling. It stirs the adrenalin."

"I don't need any more," said Margit in a tremulous but defiant voice.

The thunder was deafening, the very plastic shook under their feet. Aulia was trembling so noticeably, Kai wondered if she could stand the strain.

"Now!"

Their concerted yells would never reach the sky-borne heavy-worlders. Margit was right, there was no need of additional adrenalin. The sight of the bobbing heads of the crested dinosaurs, bearing down on them, was sufficient to have lent wings to anyone. Dimenon, yelling at the top of his lungs, wrestled from Kai's support and outdistanced others as he made for the shuttle. Kai slowed his pace until Varian was abreast of him. Then the two leaders matched strides in the wake of the others, across a compound shuddering with the vibrations of the stampede. They vaulted the first terrace of the incline, nearly running down Lunzie as she angled Trizein into the lock. Varian steadied the physician as Kai fumbled for the lock control. The first of the herbivores reached the force-screen.

A high-pitched scream pierced through the overlying thunder and bellowing as the screen burned, flashed blue fire and broke with a terrible whining. The bodies of herbivores flowed into the compound, and then the mass behind the forerunners surged up, over the fallen and onward. The iris closed on that scene. Only the noise and vibration did not seem to diminish inside the shuttle, telling of the chaos, death and destruction outside.

As one now, Kai and Varian moved through the panting, shocked members of the expedition, to the pilot cabin. Varian fumbled for the hidden switch to restore power to the shuttle. Kai started to sit at the console and stopped.

"Paskutti took no chances on another message," he told Varian, looking at the wreckage of the board.

"What about maneuvering?"

"That's still intact. He knew what circuits to break all right."

They felt the shuttle move, heard something banging dully against the outer hull.

"They outdid themselves with the stampede," said Varian with an amused chuckle. She heard the startled exclamations from the main compartment and put her head around the frame.

"It'll take more than herbivores to dent the shuttle ceramic. Don't worry. But I would sit down."

She slid into the other seat, moving her useless arm out of her way when it flopped against the backrest. "As soon as the stampede has stopped, we'd better make our move."

"Bonnard?" asked Kai.

"Bonnard!" Portegin echoed the name in a glad cry in the main cabin. "Bonnard! Kai, Varian. He got in!"

The leaders saw the boy emerging from the lab, his ship suit dusty and stained, his face drawn with a sudden maturity.

"I thought this was the safest place after I saw Paskutti moving you out. But I wasn't sure who had come back in. Am I glad it's you!"

Cleiti was embracing her friend, weeping with relief. Terilla, bedded down by Trizein, called his name over and over, not quite believing his appearance. Bonnard gently put Cleiti's clinging hands to one side and walked to the leaders.

"They'll never find those power packs, Varian. Never! But I thought you'd be killed when I saw Paskutti lock the dome.

He smashed the control so I didn't see how I could get you out in time. So . . . I hid!" The boy burst into tears of shame.

"You did exactly as you should, Bonnard. Even to hiding!" Another shift of the shuttle sent everyone rocking.

"It's going to fall," cried Aulia, hands over her ears.

"It could, but it won't crack," said Kai, feeling the same postcrisis elation that had made Varian chuckle. "Stay calm. We've succeeded so far. We'll survive. By all the things that men hold dear, we'll survive!"

11

ALTHOUGH Kai's wrist chrono showed that only twenty minutes had elapsed from the moment they had reached the pilot's cabin, it had seemed an age of repeated shocks and jolts until all external noise ceased.

After moments of silence, Kai opened the iris lock enough to peer out. And saw nothing but mottled coarse furred hide. He stepped back, gesturing for Varian to look out.

"Buried alive in hadrasaurs," she said, irrepressible. Her eyes were very bright, her face lined with the stain of maintaining Discipline over the agony of her crushed and broken shoulder. "Open wider. They're too big to fall in."

With a wider view, they achieved only the vision of more bodies, darkness beyond. Kai reluctantly decided that they'd have to send Bonnard, who was agile and small enough to assess the new position of the shuttle. Bonnard was warned to keep a low profile in case the heavy-worlders were about.

"You might remember that it is now full dark," Lunzie said. "They don't have good night vision. *If* they are out there."

"Where else would they be?" demanded Aulia, hysteria in her shaking voice. "Gloating! Delighted with themselves. I've never liked working with heavy-worlders. They always think they're abused and misused, and they're really not good for anything but heavy muscle work."

"Oh, do be quiet, Aulia," said Lunzie. "Go on with you, Bonnard, see if we have a clear passage for the shuttle. I'll be glad to put a lot of distance between myself and the heavy-worlders as anyone else in this shuttle." She handed him a night mask and gave him a reassuring and approving grin.

"Portegin, would you check the control panel's circuitry?" asked Kai. "Varian, let Lunzie see to that arm now we've a spare moment."

"If after that, Lunzie gets a crack at your hand, Leader Kai."

"No 'ifs' about it. I do you first, him next," said Lunzie and reached for her belt pouch. "At least they left me something to work with."

"Why bother patching any of us?" demanded Aulia, sinking to the deck, head in her arms. "*We* can't last long on this planet. Paskutti was right about that. And *they've* got everything we *need*!"

"Not everything. They left us the synthesizer," said Varian with a snort. "Couldn't take that, built into the shuttle as it is."

"There's no power to run it. You heard Tanegli."

"Bonnard hid the sleds' packs. They'll do for the synthesizer."

"That's only delaying the inevitable," cried Aulia. "We'll all die once the packs are drained. There's no way to recharge them."

"Kai got a message out to the Theks," said Varian, hoping to forestall Aulia's imminent hysterics.

"The Theks!" Aulia burst out laughing, a shrill, mirthless

sound. Portegin came striding out of the pilot's cabin and slapped her smartly across the face.

"That's enough of that, you silly girl. You always do give up too easily."

"She has brought up a few harsh truths," said Margit in a weary voice. "Once the synthesizer is useless, we're as good as . . ."

"We can always sleep it," said Kai.

"I didn't realize that this shuttle had cryogenics," said Margit, but hope brightened her expression.

"This may be a small expedition, but it has all the basics. Or had," replied Kai and, finding the proper space between the bulkheads, pressed the release and showed them the hidden recess with the cryogenic supplies.

"But if Portegin could fix the comunit, we wouldn't have to cold sleep," said Aulia, her face also showing relief, "we could just beam EV—"

"No, and I might as well tell you right now," said Portegin, his expression grim, "I can't fix that panel. Not without the spare parts, which *they've* removed."

"I knew it," said Aulia, beginning to weep in the silence that followed Portegin's announcement.

"You know nothing," said Portegin sharply, "so shut up."

"Sleep is what we all need, right now. Regular sleep," said Lunzie, sparing Kai a significant glance.

Once Discipline had worn off, the four of them would need a full day's rest before they could recover from the necessary abuse of their systems. With Aulia in such a state and the others certain to react in one way or another to the shock of their experiences, their escape from the heavy-worlders would be meaningless if Kai and Varian could not maintain control.

"Sleep?" demanded Margit. "Under what's up there?" She pointed to the ceiling of the shuttle and shuddered.

"Look at it this way, Margit," said Dimenon, "we're beautifully secure. Even heavy-worlders will have to sweat to clean that . . . how should I phrase it—carrion? debris—away."

"No, Dimenon. We're not staying here," said Kai. "Our escape is best made now, under cover of the dark, so that when the heavy-worlders return, as I'm sure they will, they will presume that the entire shuttle is still here, buried under the stampede."

"The carrion-eaters of Ireta work swiftly," Varian said, perspiration beading her face as Lunzie continued her repairs on the broken shoulder. "But they've enough out there for days . . ."

Someone retched.

"Which gives us a certain leeway before they discover the shuttle is gone. *If* we move tonight."

"Where do you suggest we move to?" asked Portegin in a dry tone.

"That's no problem," said Dimenon with a snort. "We've a whole bloody planet."

"Not really," said Kai. "And they want this shuttle. They need it—if only for the synthesizer and the main power unit. Once they've found it's gone, they're going to look for it. And look hard. They've tracers on the sleds, and while they don't have the power packs," here he favored Bonnard with an admiring grin, "they're strong enough to dismantle the units and use 'em while they belt-lift. And find us."

"Not if we're well hidden," said Varian, emphasizing the "well" in a voice that held a ripple of amusement. "No heavy-worlder would think of it. And there'd be a lot of other life-form readings to confuse them."

Kai regarded Varian, his mind rushing through the possible locations, unable to guess what she had thought of, although Varian looked at him as if he ought to know.

"Our rest day was a rehearsal, too, though we couldn't know it at the time."

"The giffs?"

"Yes, that cave where I found the dead egg. It was enormous inside, and dry. Why it was abandoned, I can't figure. But it should do us."

Kai wanted to grab her in his arms, kiss and hug her for that suggestion, but it was neither the time nor the place.

"That's exactly the right place, Varian. We'd even register the same as the adult giffs. And the kids as juveniles! Varian, that's . . . that's . . ."

"The best idea we've heard all day," said Lunzie finishing when words failed Kai. There was as much relief in her voice as in Kai's. Varian beamed at the reception of her solution.

"Fine. We'll hole up there . . ." and he ducked as Lunzie swung at him for his pun, "get a good night's sleep and then do some heavy evaluation. I did, and don't forget this, my friends, get that message off to the Theks . . ." He held up his hand as Aulia opened her mouth to renew her arguments to aid from that source, "and as one of them is an old friend of my family on *ARCT-10*, I think I can promise that the message will not be ignored."

Aulia may not have been convinced, but Kai saw that others were willing to rest some confidence in that fact.

"Where has Bonnard got to?" asked Varian, shuddering as Lunzie finished her manipulation on her shoulder. "He ought to have been long back."

"I'll go," said Triv and was out of the lock before either leader could protest.

"Now, Leader Kai," said Lunzie, indicating it was his turn at her hands.

"Margit, would you break out some peppers for us all?" said Kai, surrendering his broken wrist to Lunzie and diverting his thoughts. "I don't think they got what was in the locker in the pilot's compartment."

"A pepper?" Margit moved with alacrity to the forward compartment, Aulia right behind her. "That's the second best idea I've heard today. Pray Krim they didn't get the peppers! Ah, the locker's untouched! Leave off, Aulia, pass them out to the others, first!" Her voice had turned hard.

"You know, this is the first time I've ever seen leaders required to use Discipline," said Dimenon, cracking the seal on the can Aulia had handed him. She was drinking hers as she passed others the restoratives. "I'm aware that a leader has to have the Training to lead, but I'd never seen it working. I couldn't figure out what had got into you, Varian, when you let them beat admissions out of you."

"I had to play the coward," said Varian, taking a long swig at her pepper. "Dead Disciples are no use to anyone. I'd guessed that Bonnard would be smart enough to hide. I do wish he'd get back now, though."

They all heard the noises at the lock. Kai slipped his half-sealed wrist from Lunzie's grasp and moved quickly to the lock, good hand poised in a clenched fist. Portegin and Dimenon joined him, their bare hands cocked back.

"I found him," Triv said, poking his head through the half-opened iris. "He'd been stacking all the power packs at the edge of . . . the dead beasts. He's gone for the others now." He handed three power packs through the lock to Portegin. "He says the heavy-worlders have started a fire on the ridge beyond us. We'll be able to slide the shuttle to our left, up the hill and they shouldn't see us. Dead and dying herbivores are hill-high in the compound. It's going to take some time before *they* realize neither we nor the shuttle are buried here."

"Good," said Kai and motioned Triv to return to help Bonnard. "We can be gone without a trace left for them to follow or find, bless this ceramic hull."

Once the resourceful boy and Triv had swung the power packs safely into the shuttle, they closed the lock. Kai and Varian took Bonnard into the pilot's compartment where he could diagram the shuttle's position, and the clearest way up the hill.

Paskutti's fist had wrecked the outside view screens as well as the communication unit so maneuvers would be blind. Not, Varian pointed out, that they could have seen all that much even with night masks, and they couldn't, under the circumstances, use the shuttle's exterior spotbeams. Both Kai and Varian could recall the coordinates for the inland sea without the tapes now spread across the compound's littered floor.

Triv and Dimenon synthesized enough padding to cushion the wounded on the bare plastic deck, and had set Margit and Aulia to clear up the worst of the spillage in Trizein's laboratory. He was unconscious again, the strain having been excessive for a man of his years. Lunzie thought he might have suffered a heart seizure as a result of the brutal treatment.

Maneuvering on the bare minimum of power, Kai and Varian, each with one good hand, eased the shuttle out from under its burden of hadrasaur corpses, up the hill and onto a course for the inland sea.

During the trip, Lunzie synthesized a hypersaturated tonic to reduce the effects of delayed shock and made certain every single person took their dose, either as a drink or a spray. With Triv and Dimenon's assistance, Portegin began to raid all unnecessary circuits to see if he could jerry-rig even an outgoing signal.

When they reached the inland sea, Kai hovered the shuttle while Varian, the lock iris partly open, shouted verbal instructions to the terrace they had happily occupied that rest day, which seemed so long ago. When the lock was a half-meter above the terrace, Varian and Triv jumped down. They would have to guide the shuttle into the cage, feeding Kai directions over their wrist comunits. Since the heavy-worlders were sure of their deaths in the dome, it was unlikely any of them would be listening on their own units.

The mouth of the cave was not large enough to accept the central bulge of the shuttle, but, by steadily pressing in against the rock, they forced a way through, ignoring the score marks on the ceramic skin of the shuttle.

Varian, standing in the darkness of the terrace, couldn't understand why the grating noise and vibration hadn't aroused the entire population of the cliff, but no crested head emerged to investigate.

Triv lowered Varian down to the cave by belt-line. Then, having secured one end on a rocky spur on the terrace, he joined her. The shuttle was far enough inside the cave not to be immediately visible. But Triv and Varian gathered up masses of dried vegetation and threw them in camouflage over the stern of the shuttle. Dimenon, Margit and Portegin came out to help, spattering the top and sides with moistened cave dung.

It didn't take long, but everyone was relieved to be inside the shuttle, with the iris closed behind them. Then the others settled themselves with what comfort they could find.

"You are going to rest, aren't you, Lunzie," asked Kai, hunkering down by her as she tended Trizein.

She gave a snort. "I'll have no option as soon as Discipline releases. But Trizein should be all right. It's natural for his system to seek repair in rest. And there won't be anything to disturb him. How're you?" she asked bluntly, glancing at his sealed wrist and then more intently at his eyes.

"I'm still under Discipline, but not for much longer."

She filled her spray gun. "I'll give everyone else slightly more sedation than necessary. That'll give us a chance for enough rest."

She moved about the cabin then, administering the spray.

Varian tapped Kai on the shoulder.

"We've accommodation forward, Kai."

He glanced round the recumbent forms and then followed her, gratefully lowering himself to the padding on the deck. Thin but thermal-lined sheets had been fashioned and ought, he thought, to suffice. The ship would keep the interior temperature at a comfortable level for sleepers. Lunzie and Triv joined them and settled down, too.

"It could be worse, Kai," said the physician, as if she read his thoughts as he stared down the bare cabin at the other sleepers. "We only lost Gaber, and that fool asked for it with his tardy heroics."

"Terilla and Cleiti?" asked Varian.

"Were mauled about, but no more. Worse for the psyche than the body. One doesn't wish that sort of treatment for anyone . . ." Lunzie grimaced.

"I'm more concerned about their reaction toward Kai and me when we seemed not to defend or protect them . . ."

Lunzie smiled. "They understand that. I know Cleiti's parents are Disciples, and I suspect Terilla's mother is. What they can't understand is the heavy-worlders' metamorphosis into brutal, cruel temperaments." Lunzie sighed. "All in all, I think we comported ourselves rather well, considering the odds against us and the unexpectedness of that mutiny."

Suddenly her body sagged and she sighed again with relief.

"I'm off," she said, fumbling with shaking hands for the sedative gun. "Are you two ready for it?"

"Leave it," said Kai. "We can do ourselves."

Triv offered his arm to the physician. "I'm off it, too, Lunzie." The release of Discipline was obvious in the gray that seeped into his complexion. He was nearly asleep before Lunzie had fully administered the drug. "I'll wake first," he mumbled, and his head dropped to one side.

Lunzie snorted as she turned the spray on herself. "Not if I beat you to it, my friend. That's the marvel of Discipline, or is it the bane, working even when you don't want it to." She exhaled raggedly and closed her eyes. "You've done well, leaders! You can rest easy on that score. Never met a . . . bet . . . ter . . ."

Varian chuckled. "You might know Lunzie would leave a compliment unfinished." She kept her voice low, though not even a repeat stampede would have wakened the physician or the other sleepers. "Kai? Will Tor respond?"

"He's more likely to than any other Thek."

"When?"

Discipline must be leaving her, Kai thought, hearing the anxiety in her roughened voice. He took her good hand in his and carried it to his lips. She smiled, despite her worry, at the caress.

"I'd say it will be a week before he could possibly arrive. I think we can hold them together that long, don't you?"

"After today, yes, I think we can. But Kai, they don't know we've no contact with EV. Thek help is grand but pretty poor consolation because it's debatable."

"I know. It is, however, contact." He felt Discipline leaving him, felt the massive fatigue, like an intolerable weight, press down on his abused body. Muhlah, but he'd be almighty stiff when he woke.

"Are you released, Kai? You look it."

He laughed softly, noting the drain of color from her face. He lifted the spray gun.

"Wait." She raised herself on her good elbow and kissed him on the lips, a gentle kiss but nonetheless an accolade. "I don't want to fall asleep kissing you."

"I appreciate that consideration," he said. And gave her a quick, affectionate kiss, pressing the spray against her arm, and then his own. He arranged his limbs and just had time to curl his fingers about hers before sleep overtook him.

·

12

KAI was not the only stiff one when they finally woke. And Lunzie had roused before Triv, which put her in a good mood. Trizein was improving, she told the leaders as she handed them each beakers of a steaming nutritious broth. Her own special recipe, she said, guaranteed to circulate blood through abused muscles and restore tissue to normal.

"You'll need to be limber. We've got to have more for the

synthesizer to masticate or I won't have enough of my brew to revive the others."

Kai sipped carefully of the hot liquid. Lunzie had not misrepresented its effectiveness. As the warmth descended to his stomach, he could almost feel the loosening of his stiff muscles. He did have to apply slight Disciplinary controls to reduce the ache in his wrist.

"How long did we sleep?"

"I'd say we made it around the chrono and half again," Lunzie said, glancing at her wrist bracelet.

"I *know* we didn't sleep a mere twelve hours or I've lost my knack at putting sedatives into a sprayer. Which I haven't."

"How long before the others rouse?" asked Triv, who was now awake.

"I'd say we have another clear hour or so before the dead arise."

"A little recon?" Triv asked the two leaders.

"Just remember," said Lunzie at her driest, "you've none of your force-belts anymore. Don't fall."

From reflex action, Kai found himself reaching for the stun locker door, and saw its open, empty shelves.

"Yes, indeed," said Varian with a wry laugh, "the cupboard is bare."

"And all we've got is bare hands . . ."

"One apiece," said Varian with a second laugh.

"Remember, you won't be able to use full Discipline today," Lunzie cautioned. "I trust the need will not arise."

"I doubt it. The giffs aren't aggressive," said Varian, setting her hand comfortably against her body before stepping through the iris. "Another reason why this is a perfect hideaway."

A scant few minutes later, as they peered past the mouth of their retreat, she revised her statement.

"Well, there are a few drawbacks." She squinted down at the waves beating against the foot of their twenty-meter-high cliff. To either side was an expanse of sheer rock. The line Triv had secured from the terrace flapped in the light breeze.

Looking up, Varian could see the giffs flying. "At least there's nothing but giffs airborne," she added with an exaggerated sigh of relief.

"And nothing for the synthesizer either," said Kai, trying to recall exactly what lay beyond the terrace and the rock-shelf on which the giffs dropped their catch.

Triv had gone to the rear of the cavern and came back now, a sheaf of dried grasses in each hand. "There's lots more of this, dried, but they'll provide some substance for the synthesizer."

"There's forest beyond the cliffs," said Varian, thoughtfully, frowning as she concentrated. "Blast, but we rely too much on tapes and not enough on our own recall."

"C'mon, don't fuss yourself, Varian. We'll collect grasses at least. Triv, how are you at climbing up ropes?"

"I'll learn, but I suspect it's the sort of thing Bonnard will do extremely well," he said with a grin, testing the rope and then peering up its length, his expression dubious.

Lunzie was not pleased with the grasses. Fresh, they'd have been perfect, but there was no telling how long they'd been lying about the cavern. Couldn't they get some fresh green—even treetops?

Treetops were about all they could reach, Triv informed the leaders when he and the youngsters had returned from their foraging. There was a tantalizing view of fruiting trees beyond a narrow but impassable canyon which separated the main cliffs from the forest beyond. At least on the terrace level which was, at the moment, all they could reach.

"The giffs watched us," Bonnard told Varian and Kai, "just like they did that rest day. Just watched."

"And I watched the skies for anything else," said Terilla, a curiously bitter note to her soft voice and an unsettling hardness to her face.

"Them?" Bonnard dismissed the heavy-worlders with a fine scorn. "They're still thinking we've all been smashed flat in the dome!"

There was, the two leaders noted with wry approval, a decided smugness about Bonnard to which he was, in fact, entitled. He, alone, had managed to evade and discommode the heavy-worlders despite their physical superiority.

"Let us devoutly hope that they continue in that delusion for a few more days," said Kai. "Until Tor has a chance to arrive. Can you manage another trip today?" he asked, eyeing the pile of fresh greens and estimating the finished, synthesized result.

Triv's answer was to turn back to the rope and begin the ascent, the others queuing to follow him.

"Morale's very good," Kai murmured to Varian.

"Now!" Varian's single bitter word reminded Kai that morale was fickle.

To bolster his own spirits, he sought Portegin, working in Trizein's looted laboratory on a pile of matrix slabs and the damaged console panel which he had removed from the piloting compartment.

"I don't know if I can fix the comunit, even if I pirate every matrix circuit we've got and do field links," the man said, running his fingers through his short hair. "They didn't leave us so much as a sealing unit and these connections are too fine to be done by hand."

"Could you rig a locator signal on the Theks' or even the *ARCT-10*'s frequencies?"

"Sure," and Portegin brightened to be able to give a positive response.

"Do so, then, preferably one the heavy-worlders can't tap."

"They've got to have power first, more power than they've got on their wrist units," said Portegin, grinning with a touch of malice.

Kai moved on, checking futilely in the storage compartments in the hope that something useful had been dropped by the heavy-worlders. He thanked providence for the ceramic hull of the shuttle which would not show up on the detectors the heavy-worlders possessed. The minor amounts of metal in the ship would easily be misread as ore in the cliffs. He tried again to remember if he and Varian had done much talking about the giffs in the hearing of any of the heavy-worlders. And remembered the tapes! Fighting the frantic pulse of fear, he also remembered the tangled, destroyed tape canisters strewn about the compound and now buried beneath megatons of dead beasts. Supercilious of the lightweights as the mutineers were, doubtless they had chucked tapes registered by either himself or Varian as being intrinsically useless. Kai forced himself to believe that possibility.

Everyone was busy at something, he noted. Triv and the youngsters were on the foraging party, Aulia was sweeping the main cabin with a broom made of short stiff grasses, Dimenon and Margit were hauling water up the cliff in an all too small improvised bucket.

"Try a piece," said Varian, offering him a brownish slab. "It's not bad," she added as he broke off a corner and began to chew it.

"Dead grass?"

"Hmmm."

"I've eaten worse. Very dry, isn't it."

"Dry grass, but it's bearable. There'll be plenty of this junk, so Lunzie is good enough to reassure us." Then her expression altered to one of distaste. "Trouble is, it uses a lot of power, and water, which uses power, too, to be purified."

Kai shrugged. Food they had to have, and water.

"We need at least a week for Tor to reply."

Varian regarded him for a long moment. "Exactly what good will Tor's appearance do us?"

"The heavy-worlders' mutiny, or I should say their success, depends on *our* silence. That's why they rigged our 'deaths' so carefully, in case we hadn't been planted. Why they'd believe Gaber is beyond me, but . . ." Kai shrugged. Then he grinned. "Heavy-worlders are big, but no one is bigger than a Thek. And no one in the galaxy deliberately provokes Thek retaliation. Their concept of discipline is a trifle . . . more permanent . . . than ours. Once we have Thek support, we can resume our interrupted work."

Varian considered this reassurance and, for some reason that irked Kai, did not appear as consoled as she ought.

"Well, Lunzie estimates we've got four weeks power at the current rate of use."

"That's good, but I'm not happy about four weeks stuck in this cavern."

"I know what you mean."

Their refuge was twice as long as the shuttle craft's twenty-one meters and half again as wide, but it ended in a rather daunting rock fall which may have been why the cave was abandoned by the giffs. There was not much space for privacy, and they couldn't risk lighting the innermost section, which would have lessened the cramping.

By the time the quick tropic night had darkened their refuge, Portegin had succeeded in rigging a locator, which he and Triv mounted in a crevice just outside the cliff mouth. After a final look to be sure that the stern of the shuttle was sufficiently camouflaged, Kai and Varian ordered everyone back into the shuttle. By the simple expedient of having Lunzie introduce a sedative into the evening ration of water, everyone was soon too sleepy to worry about confinement or boredom.

The next day Kai and Varian sent everyone but the convalescent Trizein out to gather greenery. They estimated that they had this second day secure from any search by the heavy-worlders: possibly a third, but they could take no chances.

The third day, apart from drawing water at dawn, was spent inside the cave. Portegin and Triv contrived a screen of branches and grass which could be used to secrete a sentinel at the cave entrance, to warn of any sign of either search from the heavy-worlders or, hopefully, the arrival of a Thek capsule. The angle of vision from the screen was limited but would have to suffice.

The fourth day passed uneventfully, but by the fifth, everyone was beginning to show the effects of the close quarters.

The sixth day Lunzie doctored the morning beverages so that everyone except herself, Triv and the two leaders were kept dozy. That meant that they had to maintain the watch themselves and draw the water at dawn and again at dusk.

By the end of the seventh day, Kai had to admit that Tor had not rushed to their assistance.

"What is our alternative?" Triv asked calmly at the informal conference the four Disciples held.

"There's cold sleep," said Lunzie, looking rather relieved when Kai and Varian nodded.

"That's the sensible last resort," said Triv, fiddling with a square of grasses he'd been idly weaving. "The others're going to become more and more dissatisfied with seclusion in this cave. Of course, once there aren't any messages for EV, they'll be bound to investigate." Something in their manner, in their very silence alerted Triv, and he glanced about him, startled. "EV *is* coming back for us?"

"Despite Gaber's gossip, there's no reason to suppose not," said Kai, slowly. "Once EV strips the messages, they'll come rattling here. This planet is so rich in all . . ."

"Messages?" Triv caught Kai's inadvertent slip.

"Yes, messages," said Varian, a sour grimace on her face.

"How many?" The geologist couldn't suppress his anxiety.

"The all-safe-down is the only one they've stripped."

Triv absorbed that depressing admission with no hint of his inner reactions. "Then we'll have to sleep." He frowned and asked, as an afterthought, "Only the all-safe? What happened? They wouldn't have planted us, Kai, there isn't a large enough gene pool."

"That, and the fact that we've the youngsters, is what reassures us," said Kai. "I feel that the EV is much too involved in that cosmic storm and the Thek were of the same opinion."

"Ah, yes, I'd forgot about that storm." Triv's relief was visible. "Then we sleep. No question of it! Doesn't matter if we're roused in a week or a year."

"Good, then we'll sleep tomorrow, once the others have been told," said Kai.

Lunzie shook her head. "Why tell them? Aulia'll go into hysterics, Protegin will insist we try to rig an emergency call, you'll get blasted for withholding information about EV's silence . . ."

"They're halfway there now," said Varian, gesturing toward the sleeping forms. "And we'll save ourselves some futile arguments."

"And any chances of being found by the heavy-worlders," said Triv, "until either EV comes back for us, or the Theks arrive as reinforcement. There's no way the heavy-worlders could find a trace of us in cold sleep. And there's a real danger if we remain awake."

Such a major decision should be democratically decided, Kai knew, in spite of the fact that he and Varian as leaders could arbitrarily act in the best interests of the expedition. Lunzie's assessment of reaction was valid. Kai spread his arms wide accepting the inevitable. He'd given Tor a week which, if the Thek had been going to respond, would have been more than adequate for the creature to make the journey from the other planet. If Tor himself had received the message. It could have been taken by one of the other two who would not necessarily pass it to Tor or bother about responding.

"I'd rather meet those heavy-worlders again with a healed shoulder," remarked Varian. "I hope they waste all their remaining power trying to find a trace of us."

Triv gave a mirthless laugh and rose, looking expectantly at Lunzie.

"I'm not usually spiteful," said the physician, getting to her feet, "but I'm of the same mind."

Lunzie prepared a preservative which she then administered to the sleeping. Triv, Varian and Kai checked each one until their skins cooled and their respirations slowed to the imperceptible. Kai toyed briefly with the notion of staying awake, of asking Varian to join him in the vigil until either Tor and EV arrived. But that would mean they'd have to stay outside, as the sleep vapor would permeate the shuttle. He'd no wish to remain away from his team, and less to inadvertently disclose their hideaway to the searching heavy-worlders. Soon the others were in the thrall of cold sleep.

"You know," announced Varian in a startled tone of voice as she was settling herself, "poor old Gaber was right. We are planted. At least temporarily!"

Lunzie stared at her, then made an amused grimace. "That's not the comfort I want to take with me into cold sleep."

"Does one dream in cryogenic sleep, Lunzie?"

"I never have."

"Seems a waste of time not to do something."

Lunzie handed round the potion she'd made for them to take in lieu of the spray.

"The whole concept of cold sleep is to suspend the sense of subjective time," she said. "You sleep, you wake."

"And centuries could pass," added Triv.

"You're less help than Varian is," muttered Lunzie and drank her potion, arranging herself.

"It won't be centuries," said Kai emphatically. "Not once EV has the assays on the uranium."

"That is a comfort," said Triv and drank his dose.

Tacitly Kai and Varian waited until the other two had quietened into the thrall of cold sleep.

"Kai," Varian said softly, "it is my fault. I had all the clues that pointed to a possible mutiny . . ."

"Varian," he said gently and stopped her words of apology with a kiss, "it was no one's fault, just a concatenation of forces. Content yourself that we are alive, so are they. Gaber brought his own end with an essential stupidity of temperament. And we had best suspend subjective time for a while."

"How long a while?"

He kissed her lightly again, smiling a reassurance he tried hard to make genuine. "EV will return for us. No matter how long it takes!" Not the most tactful remark to make. "Drink, Varian!" He raised his cup to her, waited until she followed suit and they drank together. "Nothing seems quite so bad when you've slept on it."

"I hope so. It's . . . jussss . . ."

Silence pervaded the shuttle. The mechanism that released a vapor to reinforce the sleep opened the proper valve. All life signs fell to an undetectable minimum.

Outside, golden-furred flying creatures roused with the advent of another gloomy, sultry Mesozoic morning.

DINOSAUR
PLANET
SURVIVORS

Affectionately dedicated to
Jeannie Cox
in memory of my first Pernese Dinner

1

KAI managed to part his eyelids to a narrow slit and saw the rock. He closed his eyes. There shouldn't *be* a rock. Especially a rock which could talk. For a sound, like his name, emanated from it. He seemed to be in physical control of only the area around his eyes. Otherwise he could not so much as twitch a finger. He tried to analyze his lack of sensation, reassured finally that he wouldn't have been able to think if he weren't in his body. And managed to open his eyes slightly wider.

"Kkkkk . . . aaaaah . . . eeee!"

The sounds corresponded to those in his name, but he hadn't heard them uttered in such a fashion in a long time. He struggled to think when and became aware that he possessed neck, shoulders, and chest. The paralysis was ebbing. Yes, he was aware that his chest was moving up and down normally, but the air that his lungs drew in seemed stale and left a curious taste in the back of his throat.

With the return of his olfactory sense, Kai knew that he hadn't been paralyzed. He'd been asleep.

"Kkkk . . . aaaa . . . eeee! Wuuuh . . . aaaakkhhhuh!"

He forced his eyelids wider apart. The damned rock dominated his vision; it was now canted dangerously over him. As he watched in unbelieving silence, the rock slowly extruded a rod which split into three tentacles. With these, the rock grasped his shoulder gently but firmly and administered a shaking.

"Tor?" Kai's tone was startlingly similar to the quality of sound the rock had issued. He cleared his throat of a thick phlegm before he repeated the name.

"Tor? You've come?"

Tor made a grinding noise which Kai took as affirmative though he sensed a reprimand that he would comment on the obvious. Kai groaned as memory returned. He hadn't been just asleep: he'd been in cold sleep. Tor had arrived in response to Kai's emergency call.

"Reeee . . . pppoooorrrtt."

Kai watched as Tor's rod placed on his chest a small gray oblong, its grill toward his mouth. He took a deep breath because his mind was not yet clear enough to find the words he'd need to account for disturbing the Thek at its own investigation of the system's outermost planet. His message had not been ambiguous: "Mutiny! Urgent! Assistance Imperative!" But it was possible that the entire sequence had not been transmitted before the heavy-worlders smashed the communications panel.

"Dee . . . taaa . . . illlll."

Kai felt the permaplas floor of the space shuttle sway as the rock that was named Tor settled beside him.

"Ffffuuuulllll." Tor added just as Kai opened his mouth.

Closing his mouth abruptly, Kai wished that Tor would give him a little more time to collect his thoughts. After all, time was on the Thek's side. But a full report in Thek terms still meant that his remarks must be succinct and limited but not the terse phrases which, in Kai's state of mental funk, would have been hard to edit. He could also speak at a normal speed. Tor would later adjust the replay to Thek convenience.

"Rumor permeated Exploratory Unit that plantation of group intended. Heavy-world personnel reverted to barbaric omnivory. Forcefully restricted all other members in one building. Drove large terrified herbivores toward building to effect our sudden deaths. Four Disciples effected timely release and sheltered in space shuttle which was buried under large corpses. Made nocturnal escape. Settled in natural cave unknown to the heavy-worlders, pending assistance. After seven days, cold sleep logical recourse. End report."

"Reeeeesssstt."

Kai felt a feather-light touch on his shoulder, heard a hiss, then felt the coolness of one sprayshot, an inch from a second. A curious warmth spread from his upper arm through his body with remarkable speed. Breathing became easier and, experimentally, he began to rotate his head and shoulders. His fingers tingled. He moved them with increasing ease.

"Reeee . . . essstt."

Kai complied, but the order was irksome. Granted, he had to assume that Tor knew more about the cold-sleep routine, but he felt clearheaded. Too clearheaded because he could remember in embarrassing detail everything that had led up to the necessity of cold sleep.

How long had that sleep been? He opened his mouth to ask, but he hadn't quite the brashness to inquire of a Thek how much time had elapsed between the sending of the emergency signal and Tor's response. One rarely asked Theks a question involving time since the long-lived silicon life-form counted in sidereal years of their planet of origin, which generally amounted to the centuries of more ephemeral species—such as Kai's.

His wrist! Tardma had taken such delight in breaking it when she and Paskutti burst into the pilot's compartment. Once they'd escaped from the mutineers, Lunzie had set the bones. Kai wriggled the fingers of his left hand experimentally. Wrist bones could take about six weeks to heal. He rotated his wrist. It was stiff but no more so than his right. Six weeks? Or more?

However long, it gave him some satisfaction to realize that the mutineers had not found the space shuttle. He smiled as he thought of the frustration that the loss would have caused

Paskutti! The mutineers would have searched as long as they had one operative lift-belt. The mutineers—Paskutti, Tardma, Tanegli, Divisti . . . Kai paused before adding Berru and Bakkun to that infamous roster. He couldn't understand their reason for participating in a mutiny; particularly one generated on the flimsiest of pretexts.

He rolled his head cautiously to the left, toward the row of sleeping figures: the remnants of his team of geologists and of Varian's xenobiologists. Varian had a lovely profile. Beyond his coleader was Lunzie, the medic, and Kai could just make out in the gloom the long sturdy figure of Triv. The four Disciples had been the last to go into cold sleep.

A series of curious deep mumbles made Kai turn his head to the right, toward the small pilot compartment of the space shuttle. Kai had seen one or two Thek extremities in evidence before, but Tor seemed to have lengths of itself draped in, under, behind, over, and through places in the shuttle's structure that Kai could not himself see. He blinked to relax his eyes. When he looked again, most of Tor was again within the creature.

That show of quick motion from a member of a species notorious for its imponderable silences, decades-long contemplations, and brevity of speech stunned Kai.

"Daaammaaggggggedddd."

In that one word the Thek managed to convey to Kai that not only was the damage extensive but also Tor could not effect repairs, a condition which annoyed the creature. Kai marveled then that Portegin's contrived beacon had managed to lead Tor to the shuttle.

"Exploration Vessel returned?" Kai asked after long consideration. It was a rather vain hope that the Exploration Vessel, which had deposited the three separate units in-system, was on its way to collect them.

"Nnnnoooo." Tor's response was neutral. Certainly the non-reappearance caused it no concern.

Kai sighed with resignation and found himself wondering if, out of all impossibilities, Gaber had been right: their little group had been planted. Gaber certainly was, since he'd been killed at the outset of mutiny. But the third group, the avian Ryxi who planned to colonize their planet, surely they must have wondered at the silence from the Iretan group? Immediately Kai was reminded that in his last contact with the Ryxi's temperamental leader, the creature had flown into a rage at Kai's innocent disclosure that Ireta had an intelligent winged species. But the Ryxi colony ship would have been piloted by another species, probably humanoid. Surely . . .

"Ryxi?" asked Kai hopefully.

A long silence ensued while Tor sent a single tentacle into the control console. Such a long silence that Kai was nerving himself to repeat the question, thinking Tor had not heard him.

"Nnnooo connntaaaact."

The inference was plain to Kai: the Thek did not care to keep in touch with the highly excitable, and by Thek standards, irresponsible winged sentients.

Kai was relieved. It was embarrassing enough to call the Thek for aid, but to have to apply to the Ryxi would result in considerably more humiliation. The Ryxi would thoroughly enjoy spreading such a grand joke throughout the universe at the expense of all wingless species.

Kai could move his head and neck easily now, and he checked the line of his sleeping companions. Varian's hand lay where it had fallen from his in the relaxation of sleep. Tor had placed a dim light somewhere in the shuttle, probably for Kai's reassurance since the Thek did not require light to see. Kai touched Varian's hand, still cold and rigid in the thrall of cryogenic sleep. He watched, holding his own breath, until he saw the slight rise and fall of her diaphragm in its much reduced life-rhythm. Then he relaxed, exhaling.

He turned back to Tor but sensed its complete withdrawal: it had become a large smooth rock, flattened on the bottom to conform to the deck, extruding not so much as a lump, bump, or pseudopod. This was the Thek contemplative state, and Kai knew better than to interrupt it.

He lay there until his nose began to itch. He stifled a sneeze with a finger under his nose, and then felt foolish. A sneeze couldn't rouse a Thek. Much less the sleepers. That desire to sneeze was the prelude to a growing twitchy restlessness in Kai which he recognized as the result of the stimulants Tor had injected. The Thek had not said that he couldn't move: it had only said to rest. Surely he had done enough of that.

Kai began the muscle-toning Discipline and, although he worked up a fine sweat, he soon realized that cold sleep had done him no discernible harm. Even the healed wrist responded perfectly. The plaskin Lunzie had used to set the break had long since flaked away. That meant they'd been asleep at least four or five months.

He looked at his wrist chronometer, but the device was blank. Even long-life battery tabs wear out. How long ago?

Exercise produced another effect and Kai, rising carefully, found his way through the cold-sleep mist that shrouded the shuttle to the toilet. Returning, he checked each of the sleepers, observing the curious transformation sleep worked on faces. Bonnard, for instance, in the middle of his second decade, looked more adult than Dimenon, twice the boy's age. Portegin looked as if he still worried about the effectiveness of the beacon he had contrived. Lunzie, the pragmatic medic, was smiling, a rare sight while she was awake, and her face had assumed a gentleness at odds with her ascerbic temperament. She'd admitted to having undergone sleep suspension before: her records had listed her chronological age but there had always been that detachment about Lunzie that struck Kai as bemused tolerance: as if she'd already seen most of what the universe had to offer and wouldn't spare the energy to be excited by anything anymore.

Triv, the other team member trained in Discipline, had a forbidding expression in sleep, a surprising strength in mouth, jawline and brow that had not been so apparent as the man went quietly about his normal duties.

Since Tor was still motionless, Kai sat down by Varian, feeling companionship even with her sleeping self. She was beautiful. Then he noticed that one side of her face slanted down, the other more or less up, leaving one eyebrow higher than the other, as if the cold sleep had surprised her. Suddenly he wanted very much to have the cheerfulness of her conscious company. Who knew how long Tor would remain an uncommunicative lump? He needed someone he could talk to, before his perspective was warped by self-accusative reflection in the gloomy silence. Varian was coleader: she should have been revived as a matter of course. Kai then realized that he ought to be relieved that Tor had been able to single him out. If the Thek had revived, say, Aulia, she would have gone into hysterics just being close to a Thek—and then she'd have convulsions when she realized that she'd been put in cryogenic suspension without being consulted! As a geologist, Aulia was very good, but she failed in areas of personal adjustments.

Kai looked about the dimly lit area for the revival kit and saw it in the dust just beyond the clean outline where he had slept. Dust? The shuttle had not, of course, been sealed completely—cold sleepers still need air—but for dust of any depth to have settled . . .

The sprays in the box were clearly marked for precedence, color-coded as well. Calibrations on the cylinders listed dosages according to body weight. Instructions on the first cylinder advised Kai to wait until the sleeper had shown definite signs of revival before stimulants were injected.

Kai carefully released the appropriate dose into Varian's arm and waited, trying to remember his own progress from cold sleep to consciousness. Her sleeping face exhibited no reassuring change. Maybe he hadn't administered enough. He checked the dose and wondered if he'd been mistaken about her body weight. He was hesitating over a second small spray when he saw her eyelids flutter. Only then did he realize that she was respiring at a normal rate.

"Varian?" He leaned over, touching her shoulder and smiling at the effort she made to unglue her eyes. An old tale popped into his head and, so prompted, he kissed her cool lips gently.

"Kkkkaaaaaiiiiii?" Her eyes opened fully and then the lids drooped back but the left corner of her mouth lifted in appreciation.

"Just relax, Varian. You'll be in working order shortly."

"Hhhhooooowww?" The word trembled out as an aspirated whisper.

"Tor came. Don't ask more questions, dear heart. Give the reviver a chance to penetrate. I'm right here. Everything is unchanged!"

"Nnughhh!" The groan came from her belly and made Kai laugh at the disgust vibrant in her protest.

"Well, a Thek bestirred itself on our behalf. It's got a full report. I taped it," he explained quickly as he saw Varian's astonishment. "It is apparently thinking my words over." Kai gestured to the silent rock. "Don't move yet," he cautioned Varian as he saw her neck tendons strain against the long immobility. "I guess I can give you the stimulants now, but don't bounce. Oh, and your shoulder's healed," he added as he gave her the second set of shots. Paskutti had shattered Varian's left shoulder just before Tardma had snapped his wrist.

Varian's fully functional eyebrows registered pleased amazement, immediately followed by a frown of thoughtful concern.

"No, I don't know how long we've slept, Varian. Paskutti damaged the shuttle's chronometer. It's just above the comunit, remember."

Varian rolled her eyes in frustration and began to clear her throat.

"Make haste slowly," he cautioned her, hand on her shoulder. "Or should I revive Lunzie? . . ."

Varian shook her head, working her tongue around her mouth as the tissues began to moisten. "Leaders first . . . and last . . ." Her voice sounded as disused as his had, and he repressed a smile.

"If your fingers and toes are beginning to tingle, try the small-muscle exercises of Discipline. They'll help circulation and toning."

Varian took a deep breath and closed her eyes to concentrate.

"I don't know what Tor's contemplating, Varian," Kai went on, "but it can't repair the comunit. It doesn't indicate whether it received our message or realized we weren't communicating on schedule. The *ARCT-10* hasn't been in touch, but Tor doesn't appear concerned. I can't tell whether that's due to normal Thek indifference or not." Then Kai laughed. "There's been no contact with the Ryxi."

Varian's chuckle sounded completely normal, and he grinned down at her. Her eyes were twinkling with laughter.

"In old tapes," she said, chewing her words out of her mouth slowly, "on my planet, Sleeping Beauty is wakened by a noble's kiss after a hundred years. Sweet way to wake up."

She raised her hand and touched his mouth with her fingers.

"And I'd give anything to know if it was a hundred years!" Kai replied, taking her fingers in his hand and kissing them in what he considered an appropriate fashion. He continued to hold onto her hand as a thought came to him. "We might have one quick way of finding out. Step out of this cave and let the golden fliers have a good look at us. If the giffs react, we can't have slept that long."

"Don't know the life span of giffs."

Kai shot a glance at the quiescent Thek. "I experience an earnest desire to be recognized by something that remembers *me*," and he prodded his chest with a fist, "besides that rock!"

"Hundred years'd mean no mutineers on watch."

"Point well taken. Even the freshest of their power packs wouldn't last more than two years. I'd also guess they'd stay at that secondary camp since they'd already stocked it last rest day . . ."

"Last rest day?" Varian regarded him with an amusement tinged with disbelief. "How long ago *was* last rest day?"

"Subjective or objective time elapsed?" he asked in reply and grinned to take the sting out of the notion.

"Good question." Varian could enunciate more clearly now. She began to flex her arms and knees. "Hey, my shoulder knit perfectly!" She rose, muttering under her breath as her rebelling muscles made the effort graceless. "Things seem to be all in working order," she added as she headed for the toilet.

While she was gone, Kai stared at Tor. Then he walked around the Thek, looking for the recorder. Irreverently he wondered if the Thek was sitting on it, had ingested it, or perhaps created a heat-resistant pouch in which it could keep bits and pieces of fragile alien manufacture.

"It's going to stay like that for days," Varian said in disgust as she joined Kai. "C'mon. I want to see what's been happening outside. And I want something to drink to take the dust out of my mouth—and to put some unprocessed food in my poor shrunken stomach."

She gave him a malicious wink, knowing that the ship-bred Kai never noticed the aftertaste of processed food as she invariably did.

They opened the exit iris of the shuttle just enough to squeeze through without diluting the cold-sleep gas significantly. But the atmosphere outside the space shuttle was like a hot smack in the face with a moist stinking cloth.

Varian let out a surprised grunt, then began to inhale deeply to adjust to the shocking change of temperature. At first Kai thought they must have emerged during the planet's night but, as his eyes grew accustomed to the dimness, he realized that the opening of the cave was covered with thick green foliage. There was a break where the Thek had pushed its vehicle through. The cone-shaped carrier was resting a few meters from the shuttle's entrance.

"Where are the power units?" Varian called as the two were drawn to examine the strange craft. "It's the same shape Tor is, only larger." She gestured with her hands in surprise, then reached out to touch the dull metal of the rounded stern. She pulled her hand back. "Wow, heat's radiating from it."

Kai was at the bow of the Thek vehicle, inspecting the scored heavy plasshield which was half-open on its pivots. He looked inside, trying to deduce the purpose of various odd protuberances and cavities on the metallic rim of the nose section.

"Only a Thek could pilot the damned thing with a nearly blind shield!" She turned away, indifferent to the mysteries of Thek navigation. "Now these," she said, catching a vine and testing its strength by hanging her weight from it, feet off the floor, "are enough to feed us for weeks if that's all we want."

Before Kai could stop her, Varian took a running start and, holding tightly to the vine, swung out beyond the cave mouth.

"Wheeeee!"

"Varian!" Kai rushed forward, catching her on the swing back, holding tightly to her hips. He'd a moment's horrific vision of the vine's parting, dropping her into the sea, meters below, to certain death.

"Sorry, Kai," she said in a tone that wasn't apologetic. "I couldn't resist the urge. Used to do a lot of vine-swinging as a kid on Fomalhaut." Then she relented as she realized her exuberance had scared him. "Irresponsible behavior when I'm not quite fit but—" and she grinned at him mischievously "—there's something about contact with a Thek which makes me behave . . ."

"Childish?" Kai's panic had subsided, and he realized that he, too, had overreacted.

"Yes, childish. Say, have you ever seen a Thek child, young, cub, pup, fledgling . . . or maybe you'd call it a pebble?"

Varian's laughter was contagious at any time and, despite his frustrations and worries, Kai laughed too, hugging her to him in wordless appreciation of her ability to find any amusement in their circumstances.

"There! That's better, Kai," she said, rubbing her nose against his. "I equate Thek with gloom and doom." Abruptly she released herself and grabbed a vine. "You know, there's something odd about such vines' growing on a giff's cliff. You don't suppose our presence here . . ."

In another abrupt movement, Varian held onto the vine and leaned out of the cave mouth, peering up at the sky and to her right.

"No, there's still giffs above us," she said, swinging in again. She allowed the momentum of the vine to carry her back out, looking to the left this time. "But this is the only cliff covered in vines. I'm sure it was barren rock when we wedged the shuttle in here." She made a third excursion, grinning as she released the vine on its inward sway, and landed back at his side. "A fruit-bearing vine, too." She reached down to her boot and whistled in shrill triumph, removing the slim blade lodged there. "Too frail, like us, to pierce a heavy-worlder's hide, but, praise Krim, they left 'em for us. I'm going to cut us juicy, fresh fruit for breakfast. Or whatever meal it is."

Before Kai could protest, she had put the knife between her teeth and was pulling herself up a vine, out of sight. He was testing the strength of another thick tendril when her cheerful voice advised him to look up. Instinctively he caught the object launched at him.

"Here comes another. And it's dead ripe so don't squeeze hard."

"Varian—" His fingers did exert too much pressure on the melon and the succulent sweet odor made his mouth water.

"I could eat these all by myself, Kai, so here's another one for you." Varian dropped to the cave floor.

"We shouldn't eat too much at first," Kai said. He sank down beside her as she sliced a segment off and offered it to him on her knife point.

"Quite likely," she said, slicing a second piece, for herself. She murmured with delight as she bit the soft green fruit. "Go ahead. Eat!" she urged, juice dribbling from the corners of her mouth.

"The things I do for the EEC," Kai said, pretending horror at having to eat unprocessed food. As the first sweetness dissolved in his dry mouth, Kai was willing to admit, privately, that natural food was undeniably juicier than processed.

They both ate slowly, chewing thoroughly.

"I suspect root vegetables would have been wiser in terms of protein content, but fruit sugar raises blood levels," Varian remarked thoughtfully. "Oh, but this is good. What I don't understand," she went on gesturing with her half-eaten slice, "is how those vines grew here. Granted," and she raised the slice to forestall Kai, "we don't know how long we've slept, and growth on Ireta is explosive. But the other cliffs are still clear. The giffs' main diet is fish and Rift grass. These vines aren't from the Rift, and this section of cliff looks more like forest than palisade. The vines grow right down to the water."

"Strangely selective, I agree. Did you see much of the giffs on your swings?"

"Some, circling high. I don't think they saw me if that's what you're wondering. It's early morningish—hazy, overcast. Couldn't see their food place from this angle, but I'd guess that the morning fishers are about their labors."

"We will wait," said Kai with careful authority, "until they have fed before we put in an appearance."

"Ah, you remember my lecture about disturbing feeding animals!"

"Not that much subjective time has passed, Varian!"

He grinned as she automatically twisted her wrist to glance at her unregistering chronometer.

"Lifetime batteries, huh?" she said in disgust.

Varian's eyes flicked toward the dim bulk of the shuttle. "Should we wake Lunzie or Triv?"

"I see no reason to until Tor has come to some conclusions."

"Or favors us with an accurate reading of elapsed time. *That's* what I'd like to know!" Varian was almost angry. "Why, if it weren't for the vines over the cave and the dead batteries we could just have overslept." A shudder seized her shoulders and shook her slender frame.

"The notion is leveling, isn't it," Kai said, understanding her mood perfectly. "The universe has gone by without noticing that we have faltered."

Even to himself he sounded as pompous as Gaber, and he quickly took a bit of melon to hide his embarrassment.

"Yes, that grits at me," she said. "We have such a brief time"—she gestured to the shuttle, and the brooding Thek inside—"in which to make a mark of any sort, to achieve some merit. I know I want to leave some sign that I tried! Krim *erase* those misguided, misbegotten, mutineers."

"I'd hate to think we were the sign of their achievement!"

Varian jumped to her feet and launched the rind of melon past the vine screen. They heard a faint *plop* as it hit the water below. "No, by Krim! We'll have something of our own to report out of this mess, and I don't care how long we have to sleep to do it. Some EEC vessel is going to strip that beacon. And when it does, it'll come streaming into orbit to tap Ireta's wealth! And I'll be here!"

2

THEY did not wish to dilute the sleep mist by unnecessary trips into the shuttle or to disturb the Thek until it was ready to communicate. So they settled themselves near the entrance to the cave. One of the short hard showers which dominated Ireta's tropical weather sent the vines rattling and twisting into the cave.

"You know something, Kai?" said Varian after a long companionable silence. "I can smell that wind."

"Huh?"

"I mean, I don't smell Ireta any longer. I smell other things, like rotting fish and decaying fruit and something else that smells worse than Ireta used to when we first landed."

Kai inhaled tentatively. "You're right!"

Neither of them was enthusiastic since the basic odor of Ireta was hydrotelluride. They had once had nose filters to neutralize the smell.

"I suppose," Varian said resignedly, "that it's better to get accustomed to the overriding stench of a place so you can smell other things, but somehow . . ."

"I know. Anything but hydrotelluride. On the positive side, Lunzie did say that one's olfactory sense can be . . ." Kai hunted for the appropriate word.

"Reconditioned." Absentmindedly Varian suggested a word, but she was already bent forward, toward the cave opening, sniffing deeply. Then she turned, sniffed again toward the interior. "Part of the new stink comes from the Thek's craft. What does it use for power?"

"My father told me that for short distances the Thek uses its own energy."

"Short distances? Like intersystem travel?"

Kai chuckled. "All things are relative. Thek, so they tell us, are a form of granite with a nuclear core for energy. That's how they make pseudopods. They keep a reservoir of liquid silicon which they move hydraulically to form extremities. Thek can move with extraordinary speed if they're charged up. The astrophysics officer on the *ARCT* told me that he'd heard from a reliable source that Thek like to sit on radio-active granite—which we'll probably find on Ireta if we ever get equipment again—Thek absorb energy that way."

"Whatever they use, it leaves a stink in a class all by itself. Way above Iretan normal." Varian grimaced expressively. "How do *you* know more about Thek than I do? I'm the xeno-biologist. Come to think of it, we never *do* study the Thek, do we?"

"Wouldn't do, would it?" Kai said with a laugh. "Consider-ing their position in the Federated Sentient Planets."

"Hmmm. Yes. Got us all properly awed and respectful, don't they? With their long silences and infallibility." She'd got to her feet, restlessly wandering about the Thek vehicle, carefully rapping the metallic base with her knuckles. "No one's ever been able to analyze Thek metal, have they?"

"No."

She turned abruptly from the cone-shaped ship and walked briskly to the vine screen. "Not all the stench comes from the Thek. Some of it's from up there! It's not only nauseating, it makes me feel . . . it unnerves me."

"It's inactivity that unnerves you, Varian." Kai was com-fortable enough on the cave floor.

"How *long* does it take a Thek to come to a conclusion?" She glared irritably at the space shuttle.

"Depends on the conclusion, I suppose. Varian . . ."

She had launched herself at him in a side assault which nearly caught him, but he managed to parry her attack. Laughing, she came at him again, and he grappled her wrists. Neither managed to toss the other, for their skill, despite lack of practice, was equal. They stopped feinting after a few more passes and worked into the series of isometric exercises that had always been part of Disciples' physical fitness programs.

Both were sweaty as well as dusty when they had finished. They stood near the cave entrance for the fresher air that was breeze borne.

"Nice to know that neither our reflexes nor our muscles suffered much deterioration from the cold sleep." Kai wiped off his brow and face with his sleeve.

"You've only smeared the dirt, Kai. I'm hoping it means we've not been asleep very long." She grabbed a vine and swung herself out into the lashing rain.

"And that only cleaned your face."

"Well, it's better than nothing. What I wouldn't give for a real wash!" She looked at the vine in her hands. "Hey, we can! C'mon, Kai, we can climb to the top of the cliff and let the rains wash us clean. It's coming down hard enough!"

"Wash in rain?" Kai was appalled. How could anyone get clean in rainwater? Especially Ireta's rain, which smelled nearly as bad as its air.

"Yes, wash in rainwater. It's not as antiseptic as those dust showers you use on the *ARCT-10* but it's a lot better than standing around in dead body cells and dust. Besides, one of us has got to get more fruit. I'm hungry again from all that physical exercise."

Kai's back was itching from sweat and there were grits under his ship suit. "I am hungry."

"Hungry enough to eat *raw* food?" She grinned. "I'll convert you yet."

"Necessity is doing that. We'd better make this a proper foraging trip," he added. "You check on the vines."

Kai opened the shuttle iris just wide enough to squeeze through, closing it promptly behind him so that only a puff of the sleep gas escaped. Tor was still immobile. Kai removed the knives from Dimenon's and Portegin's boots, unclipped a hammer from Portegin's belt, rifled Lunzie's supplies for antiseptic splashes and a couple of pain sprays, rolled up two of the thin thermal blankets to transport any fruit they found, and left without another glance at Tor.

Varian had been busy, too, looping long thick vines tightly about the shuttle's stern docking bars.

"If we're anchored here, we're not apt to get blown about in that wind. Wish the rain would let up, but it looks about middayish. There're only two giffs, and I can't always make them out in this rain. Any movement from Tor?" She took the items Kai handed her and disposed of them in her pockets. She knotted the blanket about her shoulders. "Here's your vine. Remember, Kai, don't look down!"

She leaped for her first handhold, wrapping her legs about the thick stem of the vine and began to shinny up.

Kai discovered that he had an almost irresistible need to look down, especially when his vine started rolling along the upper edge of the cliff. Despite Varian's efforts to anchor the vines, the wind smacked him against the stone. Nevertheless, he reached the top just as Varian did. Thunder crashed and cracked across the sea behind them.

Varian pointed to the sheets of rain slanting across the open water. "We could get swept off if that squall's as heavy as it looks."

Kai needed no urging and followed her across the cliff top to the doubtful shelter of the vegetation.

Suddenly Varian began to strip, throwing her boots, pouch, and blanket under the thick leathery leaves.

"Wow! That rain's shower force!" she cried. Shedding her coverall, face upturned, she stepped into the pelting rain. Discarding his clothing, Kai ventured more warily into the heavy rain. Then Varian was scrubbing his back, using her coverall as a towel. She guided the fabric to just that point between the shoulderblades where sweat made his skin itch.

"Wow!" she cried again in triumph. "Sand we can use as an abrasive—just don't rub too hard," she shouted at him through torrent and thunder.

They scrubbed themselves and each other, occasionally half-choked by the water as it streamed out of the heavens and bathed them. Except for his lingering feeling that it was ridiculous to be jumping about in a rainstorm on a cliff to get clean, Kai would have thoroughly enjoyed the improvisation. There was some truth in Varian's accusation that he had been sheltered in ship life. Before the mutiny, he had not been so exposed to elemental Ireta. There'd always been the sled or the compound and the safety of the force-screen. Today he was naked before the onslaught of a violent phenomenon on a primitive planet.

"Unless we've slept through a magnetic field slip," Varian yelled at him, "the sun ought to be out soon. Our overalls will dry in zero elapsed! I hope before we fry in our bare skins."

She was giving her suit one last rinsing when the shower passed, and the sun streamed through the cloud cover. Wringing their suits, they flapped them out as they splashed back toward the thick forest verge. They laid the suits out on the vines, just beyond the shade.

"Oh, I feel much better, Kai, much better," Varian said. She squeezed water from her hair and stroked it from her body with her hands. Then she reached up to her hair again. "You know, I think it's longer. If we only knew the rate of growth of hair during cryogenic sleep," she said, examining a lock carefully. "Well . . ." She shook her head again, droplets falling on him as she turned, head back and eyes closed against the brilliant sunlight.

"We can't tolerate that sun long, girl," he said as he guided her into the shade.

She caught at his hand, her fingers moving to his wrist, prodding the site of the break.

"Even that fracture isn't telling any tales. If you'd been an animal patient, I'd say the break was old enough for the extra calcium to have been reabsorbed." Suddenly her face looked bleak in the filtered light of the sun Arretan. "Kai, haven't we got something to gauge time against?"

He put both arms about her and held her tightly against him, kissing her cheek and stroking the wet spikes of her hair.

"We're alive, Varian, and we survived a mutiny. Help, however uncommunicative, has arrived. Meanwhile . . ."

He gathered her against him, positioning his hips against her pelvic bones, making his hands gentle in caress. She responded with soft movements of encouragement. Her kisses were sweet, and Kai began to wonder why nothing was happening to certain reflexes. He wasn't surprised, or offended, when he felt her shoulders begin to shake with amusement.

"Bones have healed," Varian said in what was almost a wail against his cheek, "muscles are great, but why aren't we in complete working order? We're only ancient objectively, not subjectively!"

Her utter dismay announced in laughter made Kai hug her more tightly, half in apology, half to steady himself because he, too, had to laugh at their situation.

"If you only knew how often I've wanted you all alone to myself, young woman . . ."

"Oh, Kai, I do know. I've felt the same way. It's bloody frustrating . . . Ooooh, that wind is mean!" She reached hurriedly for her blanket to wrap around them. The vegetation had sharp edges which the wind lashed against their bare skins. "And we'd better turn our clothes over. I think they're done on that side."

She darted out, but instead of just turning the clothing, she gave each a quick snap and returned with them, handing Kai his.

"If we don't wear 'em, something else'll crawl inside," she said, giving a little shudder at the tiny insects she had just shaken out of their suits.

As Kai inserted a leg into a damp trouser, he muttered about the durability of the wrong things.

"Let's start foraging, Kai. And I'd like to secure our vines to the cliff top some way. Ah, what do I spy here?"

"That's not fruit," her coleader replied, frowning at the cluster of brownish oval objects growing just above their heads.

"True, but the hadrasaurs used to make for such clusters, and poor Dandy loved 'em. Ah, and right beyond are fruit trees."

It didn't take long to collect enough fruit and nuts to fill their blanket rolls, so they secured their burdens across their backs, out of the way of climbing, and started across the open vine-covered cliff top.

"Giffs are out for a wing stretch," Varian said, waving her hand. "I know it's silly to suppose . . . Hey, they see us. They've changed flight angle." She stopped and admired the sight. "You know, if they actually remember us, we can't have slept that long!"

"Varian . . ." Kai felt his mouth drying as he reached for her hand and began to pull her backward, toward shelter. "That doesn't look like a welcoming party!"

"Kai, don't be afraid. We never did them any harm. They couldn't . . ." Then she was backing right beside him, no longer able to deny the menace in the attitude of the golden fliers who dove straight at them, necks extended, beaks slightly parted.

Kai and Varian reached the safety of the thick foliage just as the giffs veered off.

"They sure can maneuver," Varian exclaimed, though her admiration was couched in a voice made shaky at the narrowness of their escape. "But why, Kai? Why? Oh, Krims! What would have made them aggressive at the sight of humans?" She slumped down against a convenient tree trunk.

"The answer to that has to be 'other humans,' doesn't it?" He spoke gently because he knew how much Varian had admired the beautiful, inquisitive golden fliers. It was plain that the attack distressed her.

"So we can take it as printed that Paskutti and his friends penetrated this far . . . and didn't find us!"

"And were aggressive enough toward the giffs that the memory hasn't faded."

"So it could be recent memory? Okay, but if the mutineers hurt the giffs, getting this far, *why* has the cave been hidden? And how long did it take these to grow?" She thumped the thick vine cable beside her. "After all, we had to go cryogenic because the impassable chasm at this edge of the cliff stood between us and the vegetable matter we needed for the processor." She scrambled to her feet and began following the vine growth away from the cliff. "Whoops!"

Varian had gone no more than a few feet before she struggled to maintain her balance. Kai reached out to steady her.

"The chasm hasn't gone anywhere." She knelt down, her hand and arm disappearing as she sought the gap. "The vines have bridged it. And that doesn't follow because the giffs have kept their own palisades clear of vine." She resumed her seat, elbows on her knees, slapping one fist into the other. "Attack one, protect one. Makes no sense at all."

"Just how intelligent are the giffs, Varian?"

"I can't gauge it, but the two attitudes are incompatible. Except that . . . the giffs *are* protective. Remember the one that got back-stranded? Instant adult assistance. But . . ." and she held her forefinger up as she paused dramatically, "no aggressive move toward us that day, and we were only a few meters from them. Today—*swap*!" Abruptly she sat up and stared at Kai so intently he was startled. "But there were only two giffs . . ." she pointed her finger at him, "high up when we climbed *out* of the cave. Then it rained. And we were under cover when the sun came out. So . . . we were not *seen* leaving the cave. They think we don't belong there!"

Kai peered at the cliffs through the screening leaves. The giffs were settling in to watch.

"So we wait until dark, when they've all gone to roost or whatever giffs do at night. Here, have another hadrasaur nut!"

"My, aren't we brave! Natural food!"

They had to break the tough shell of the nut between two stones before they got to an irregular pale brown kernel. Varian looked at it curiously, sniffed and broke off a fragment. She grimaced at its taste and chewed it thoughtfully before swallowing.

"Maybe you have to acquire a taste for 'em," she said, inspecting the remainder of the kernel. Then she flipped it over her shoulder and smiled reassuringly at Kai's anxious expression. "I'll opt for the melon. You can taste that."

They had finished the sweet and juicy melon when they heard a whistling, bugling commotion. Varian sprang to the break in the vegetation, Kai just behind her.

The fishers had returned and all the adult giffs were assisting the net carriers. Varian remarked that either the community hadn't expanded much or fishing and carrying were limited to certain giffs. The two humans watched as the heavy woven grass nets were lowered and emptied on the flat surface that served the giffs as central food dump. There was a great coming and going as giffs filled their food pouches and delivered the day's catch to the cave- or nest-bound. The greed of the younger giffs was supervised by their elders.

"If only . . ." Varian began through gritted teeth and, sighing with frustration, she sat back against the tree trunk. Resignedly, Kai joined her. Despite the confusion of feeding, they could not have returned to the cave unnoticed. Then she grinned at Kai with a resurgence of her usual wry humor. "I wonder what they'd make of the Thek if it appeared?"

As they waited, rain fell in torrents again. The sun shone to make the jungle a steaming bath which they had to endure. Eventually they dozed.

It was the silence that roused them, for the wind had briefly abated at sunset. Disoriented, they struggled to their feet, staring uncertainly at each other in the fading light.

"The watchers are still watching!" Varian commented after peering through the leaves.

Nine golden fliers perched at various levels of the adjoining cliffs, all heads turned in one direction.

"Can they *see* us here?" Kai asked in a muted voice. "Or smell us?"

"Not when we're downwind of them. I can't believe they'd be aware of us." Varian did not sound certain. "That's not within the capability of their species. Smell—that's debatable. I think they rely heavily on sight. And I don't think that extrasensory gifts are a likely development on this planet."

"Comparing them to the Ryxi?"

"No, to what Trizein said about the primeval Terran life-forms they resemble." She slapped her hand against her knee. "If only we hadn't kept that man walled up in his lab, we might have resolved at least one of this planet's anomalies. How could creatures that lived in Mesozoic Terra come to be here on Ireta? Every xenobiologist in the FSP *knows* identical life-forms cannot spontaneously develop on distant planets— no matter how similar the worlds and their primaries!"

"Does that observation offer any clue as to how *we* can get back to our cave and Tor? I don't fancy rappelling down a vine in the darkness."

"Nor do I." Varian straightened suddenly. "Wait a sec! Before we slept, Triv and the others were back and forth to the ravine collecting for the synthesizer. The giffs were only interested: they watched, as I remember, and were certainly not aggressive. But—" and she shook her forefinger, emphasizing the condition—"they are protective of their young. Extend that and it's just possible that they're protecting the cave because it's within their territory."

"You mean they got protective over *us* after a single meeting and a few furtive vegetable raids?"

"It's possible. If only we knew how long we had slept! However," and Varian pointed at him, "*if* the heavy-worlders got here, and were their usual aggressive selves while trying to find the space shuttle, the giffs would resent such an intrusion. Well, let's say they did. So it is the heavy-worlders who changed the giffs' passive curiosity into active aggression. Only . . . that doesn't really explain the vine screen! Protectiveness can be conditioned, learned. Giffs *are* the smartest creatures we've met on Ireta, but could they be *that* intelligent? I don't think they've progressed that far."

Kai could only shrug as her voice trailed off: he knew little xenopsychology.

"Isn't that a mist rising?" Varian asked, straining to see in the gathering gloom of Ireta's swift twilight. "That might give us cover."

They watched eagerly as mist swirled up from the sea and over the cliff edge, but they hadn't taken more than ten paces from cover before four winged objects hurtled toward them, beaks ajar, wing talons extended. Varian and Kai reached shelter as giff claws tore strips from the leaves over their heads.

"How did they know? They couldn't bloody see!" Kai demanded when he recovered his breath.

"Sound!" Varian regarded her boots in disgust. She stamped a boot contemptuously. "These broadcast our movements. To demonstrate . . ."

She located a handful of loose chippings and threw them out onto the cliff. Though they knew they were safe, they both ducked at the whirr of wings as the giffs responded to the sounds.

"So?" asked Kai.

"So, while we're waiting . . ."

"How long is that likely to be now?"

"Giffs are not nocturnal. Sooner or later, habit is going to be too strong for them and they'll want to get back to their nests. Particularly," she added at his skeptical expression, "if we give them reason to doubt our continued presence here. Like a small avalanche down the ravine . . ."

"Ah . . ."

"Then, with our boots off, we tiptoe quietly home . . ."

"*Sounds* simple enough."

"I know." Her tone admitted that simple plans can suddenly develop serious flaws.

Nevertheless, they began quietly searching the ravine edge for a suitable natural slide. They then dammed it with a fallen branch to which they attached a vine. It was difficult to find enough stones and rubble to place behind the branch. Once a small shower cascaded into the ravine, and they suspended all movement until the whirr of wings disappeared. They worked quickly for Ireta's night would soon complicate things. As it was, they finished the last of their arrangements in the dark. Removing their boots, they secured them to the blanket packs across their shoulders.

"I have a sudden negative thought," said Varian, her lips against Kai's ears. "I can't remember how far it is to the edge of the cliff. We won't be able to see until we're there—or over it."

Kai contemplated that hazard. "Well, it's not going to make any difference when we try to cross in the dark, is it? So, if they're diurnal, they might just fall asleep if we give 'em enough time. Then . . ." he paused as a sudden notion occurred to him, "why not lengthen this release vine and go as far as we can, and make our avalanche when and if we need a diversion?"

Varian gave his head a quick squeeze and then turned to cut more vine. In whispered consultation, they estimated that the edge of the cliff was about thirty meters away, so Varian knotted sufficient vine to approximate that length.

Waiting in darkness punctuated by the noises of night creatures which nibbled, squeaked, and scrabbled was most tedious. Kai practiced the Disciplined breathing that calmed nerves, and exerted the strength of patience on an overactive imagination. Tiny noises in infinite variety assumed a menacing quality despite the slightness of sound. He could feel Varian, beside him, practicing the same exercises and was subtly comforted.

Varian's sudden disappearance from his side startled him.

"No mist, and only three sleepy bird watchers," was her quiet murmur in his ear a moment later.

"We go?"

Her answer was a hand on his, then she stepped in front of him, slowly parting the vegetation as he followed, playing out the release line as she cleared the way.

Although the vines lay in thick profusion along the cliff top, there was sufficient space between tendrils to allow their bare feet a reassuring contact with the cooling stone. Bent in a semicrouch, Kai watched Varian's white feet as they moved forward, always angled back in the direction of the ravine. He kept the line as taut as he dared. Varian, one hand lightly touching his shoulder, kept her eyes on the curiously luminous forms of the giffs, whose crested heads were turned toward the ravine. Their wings were folded. Kai wondered if they kept from falling over by clutching the rock with their wing-joint talons. They were so motionless, they had to be asleep.

There are many aspects of time, Kai thought grimly as he and Varian continued their stealthy, seemingly infinite journey. There is the objective time lost in cold sleep, which might have been centuries or only a few years. But the variety of time he was now experiencing was definitely hard to endure subjectively. His leg muscles began to twitch with the cramp of controlled motion. His hands were starting to sweat with a fear that an inadvertent tug would break the vine or that he wouldn't be able to release the key log to provide the crucial diversion.

Abruptly Varian stopped, twisted her torso to put her mouth to his ear.

"Kai, we've got to find the vines we used this morning. They'll be to our right. I can't see, but I feel we should move that way."

Kai glanced nervously at the sleeping giffs, now slightly to the right and behind them. Varian plucked at his sleeve, and he followed her light guidance, sliding his feet carefully over vines to the stone interstices. He almost fell over Varian when she crouched suddenly, and it took all his control not to jerk on the release line. He was also startled by the realization that only two more loops remained in his hand. As he turned to warn her, they bumped noses.

"I'm almost out of vine."

"I've found ours. I think." Varian took his left hand and placed it on the thick stem. She moved beyond his reach, but he could see her nod that she'd found her vine and he should move on down.

Kai forced Discipline on himself, willing the tension out of his blood and tissue. Then there was only a short piece of vine left in his hand, the final edge tickling as it curled into his palm.

"Varian!"

The white blur of face turned to him. He knew she'd seen his upraised hand; she made a thumbs-up gesture and crouched to run, her hand along the vine that would take her over the cliff and into sanctuary.

He pulled as firm and hard as he could, felt something vibrate along the length of the line. Then he began to run, hands before him on the rough vine trunk, counting his steps. Wouldn't do to hurtle over the cliff.

The rumble of the stones cascading into the ravine startled

him so much that he nearly lost count of his strides. The giffs roused with a squawk. He looked back at them. To his relief, their heads were turned away and their motion was upward.

"I'm at the edge, Kai!" Varian's voice was low but intense.

He found it, too, just as his leading foot slipped into a crevice. Then he closed his hands about the fat vine and, in blind faith that it was the right one, began to scramble down it. He scraped his knuckles against the cliff wall and then swung into free air, as the vine curved inward, still secured to the shuttle docking brace.

"Krims! I grabbed the wrong one," Varian suddenly exclaimed.

"Swing near me, Varian. I'll catch you!"

"No!"

He heard that defiant negative above the screams of the giffs. Only the Discipline that had been instilled in them both, that one leader must survive, forced him to continue down his vine until he was inside the cave and knew it was safe to let go. He staggered to his feet, able to distinguish the cave mouth by the slightly brighter darkness.

"Varian!"

"I'm to your right. I got the wrong vine. It's too short. Can you see me?"

He couldn't. The curtain of vines hid her. "Can you grab the next vine? Shake it!"

Tracing the sound, he found the agitated vine and hauled it back into the cave, bracing it.

"Okay, switch and slide!"

When her feet touched him, he guided her legs to the ground. They clung together, trembling with a reaction neither bothered to Discipline.

Then, hand in hand, they moved to the curved bow of the shuttle, unslung their improvised packs, carefully removing the fruit and nuts. Then they curled up together in the blankets and were almost instantly asleep.

3

"KAAAIIII!" The rumble that awakened Kai was a nightmare sound because the noise not only issued from a source uncomfortably close to his ear but it also vibrated through the stone under him.

"Huh? Whaaat?" Varian lifted her head from its pillow on his upper arm. "Tor?" She blinked up at the rock which, from her perspective, towered above them.

As she moved, the recorder was firmly placed on Kai's diaphragm, forcing an exhalation from him.

"Location old core?" the recorder said in lugubrious tones.

"The old core?" Varian's voice echoed the astonishment which she and Kai felt for that totally unexpected query. "We've nearly been murdered, stripped of all survival equipment, out of touch with everyone . . ."

Kai tightened his arm to silence her. "Typical Thek logic, Varian. It chose the issue important to it, not us. I wonder if that old core is what stirred Tor to come."

"Huh?" Varian struggled to a sitting position, drawing her legs away from Tor's meter-high triangular lump of granite.

"Where do you remember last seeing that core?" Kai asked her.

"Frankly, I'd other things on my mind than ancient geological artifacts and yet . . ." She frowned as she searched her memory. "It must have been in Gaber's dome. Paskutti wouldn't have been interested in it. Would Bakkun have hung on to it for some obscure reason?"

"Bakkun?" Kai thought of the heavy-world geologist with whom he had often teamed on field trips. "No, he wouldn't value it. He already knew where the ore sites were." Kai looked up at the Thek. "Original compound!"

Tor rumbled, but Kai was diverted by Varian's urgent tug on his arm.

"If he's going to the compound, Kai, we could take a power pack and go with him. The heavy-worlders couldn't have used the sleds without power. They might still be where they were stashed. If we could have some form of transport . . ."

"Accompany for search, Tor!" Kai said in loud measured tones, repeating the request as the Thek's rumbling continued.

"I wonder where we'd fit," said Varian, thoughtfully staring at the Thek vehicle.

The fit, as Kai discovered, was exceedingly close for just one of them. The spare power pack could be secured neatly to one side of Tor's pointed top but one full-sized human had to cram his body against the curve of the shield canopy, arching over the Thek's mass. After taking a long look at his flight position, Kai turned to Varian.

"I think you'd better wake Lunzie and Triv. The others can stay in cold sleep until we need them but I'd rather have the two Disciples awake."

"You're not expecting trouble, are you? Here?" asked Varian, incredulously spreading her arms to include the dim vine-bedecked cave.

"No." Kai grinned. "Not here! But I don't know how long I'll be with Tor." He shrugged. "You'd be better off with someone to talk to. *And* they could be useful, if only for the experience they've gained on other expeditions."

Varian nodded agreement and returned Kai's grin, then Tor closed the canopy about them. The Thek was warmer than Kai had thought, so he spent most of the mercifully short trip to the original compound site clutching desperately to the grips which Tor had fashioned for him on the shield's interior. Kai remembered the trip as a series of incredible acrobatics on his part and a green blur, for the Thek sled was capable of considerably more speed than the ones designed for humanoids. Finally Tor braked its forward speed and began an abrupt circling movement.

"Here?" Tor rumbled. The word reverberated in the enclosed space like a claxon.

Dazedly Kai looked down and wondered how Tor could have recognized anything at the speed with which it was circling. Kai felt nauseous.

"Here!" To stop the dizzying motion, Kai would have confirmed any location, but he had recognized the ledge on which the space shuttle had once rested. Tor braked the cone in the same spot and Kai groggily disengaged himself, then waited until the shield had been lifted and he could step back onto solid ground. It would be a long time before he volunteered to go anywhere in a Thek vehicle.

He turned and stared, open-mouthed at the compound. All too vivid in his memory was his last sight of it, littered with what the heavy-worlders had ruthlessly discarded: the little hyracotherium's body, neck snapped in a totally unnecessary display of brutality; Terilla's lovely botanical sketches ground into the dust; discs and shards of records. He heard thunder rolling. His heart skipped as he whirled anxiously toward the slope where he had first seen the bobbing black line of stampeding hadrasaurs which the mutineers had unleashed on the compound. But now the thunder was atmospheric.

In the midst of the sudden Iretan downpour, Kai now stared at an amphitheater of sand and stone. The only signs that humans had once inhabited the site were two broken stumps where the force veil had formed an opening. How long had it taken the scavengers of Ireta to reduce the mountains of dead hadrosaurs and scour the site clean? Not so much as a horn was left. And the lack of vegetation gave him no clue as to the passage of time. The amphitheater had been only a sandy bowl when they occupied it.

Of their own anxious accord, his eyes strayed to register

the reassuring absence of menace stampeding from the plain. Kai hadn't realized how that event had branded itself into his subconscious. He would have to try Discipline in sleep that night. He couldn't have an inhibiting incident crop up, possibly to interfere later with situations on different planets at an awkward moment.

"Where?" Tor had emerged from the vehicle and trundled beside him.

Kai pointed to the site of Gaber's dome, bleakly remembering that they had had to leave Gaber's body. It, too, had been returned to dust. In space, he had always wondered at that archaic burial phrase. It was appropriate here.

"The core was there!"

Tor slid down the slope, the unevenness of the surface posing no problem, but Kai noticed that the Thek left a steaming trail. He followed and the stone was still hot enough for the heat to penetrate Kai's thick boot sole.

"Here?" The sound grated out of Tor as the Thek stopped in the designated site.

"This was the site of the geology dome, the main shelter was precisely here," and Kai walked to the position. "The individual accommodations were across that part of the compound."

Then he stared at Tor because that was the longest plain speech he had ever made to a Thek and he wondered if the creature absorbed statements not couched in the shortspeech they preferred. He opened his mouth to structure the explanation properly when a rumble from Tor stopped him.

Not for the first time, Kai wondered if the silicon life-form might have a hidden telepathic ability. Now that he thought of it, you always knew what a Thek wanted to find out despite its succinct speech. You could distinguish a command from a question that required a yes or no answer, yet there had only been the one or two cue words to elicit a response.

Tor was on the move again, this time in an obvious search pattern. An extremity in the shape of a broad flange was poised just above the surface of the dusty compound floor. The Thek progressed ten meters in one direction, abruptly turned and examined the adjacent strip.

Clearly any effort on Kai's part would be redundant, so he strode down the slight slope to where the veil opening had been. Only the stub of the heavy-duty plastic column remained, and gouges proved it had been subjected to treatment its designer had never envisaged.

Kai knew that the mutineers had moved the sleds from the original parking site. They would have had to do it manually since Bonnard had hidden the power packs. Kai stood, raking the surrounding area with calculating eyes. There was no telling now how wide a swathe the dead hadrasaurs had made. He was also certain that the mutineers had grossly underestimated the scope of the stampede. Still, the mass of animals would have had to funnel through the narrow rock gorge leading to the compound. The sleds would have been taken to a place reasonably secure, which suggested uphill but nearby. The sleds were weighty, even for the muscles of heavyworlders. And they'd been somewhat rushed, having hoped to fly the four craft out of the area.

Kai struck off to his left where the heavily vegetated land slanted upward. He looked back toward the compound and saw Tor moving steadily on its search pattern. He wouldn't be inconveniencing the Thek if he pressed his own search. He rather supposed that Tor would have a time locating the core no matter how efficiently it worked. There was always the possibility that the mutineers had retrieved the object.

He devoutly hoped that they hadn't also retrieved the sleds. Or spitefully damaged them beyond use. But Kai reasoned the sleds would have been too valuable for wanton destruction. The mutineers would have been positive that they'd catch up with the people they considered inferiors, whom they'd left without any survival equipment. Nor would Paskutti have been easily deterred from an exhaustive search for the missing power packs. Which might well explain the giffs' behavior yesterday.

Kai almost climbed past the sleds: they were so covered in vine that they looked like a natural rock formation. He tore at the vegetation, cursing as fine thorns ripped his hands. He used his knife then, and he broke a branch from a tree to pry and cut away the obscuring growths.

If only one sled was intact . . . Units were sealed: even a heavy-worlder would have had to grunt to bash the sturdy plasteel frame and body skin.

He was the one to grunt and sweat now, contending with Ireta's heavy morning rain, which penetrated the leafy cover so that mud added to his problems: mud and the colonies of insects that had taken refuge in the shelter of vine and sled.

He felt, rather than saw, that the instrument console was intact, and disregarding the myriad tiny life-forms wriggling from beneath his fingers, found that the sled floor was unbroached and the essential power connectors undamaged.

With a sigh of relief, he leaned warily against a tree trunk only to be brought upright as a spurt of flame angling upward into the misty rain told him that Tor had taken off.

Too stunned to react for a moment, Kai stared as the fog roiled and then covered completely the passage of the Thek vehicle. Half-blind with sweat and apprehension, Kai started to run back to the compound. Without that power pack . . .

Varian had had one glimpse of Kai, body arched over Tor's mass, clinging valiantly to the improvised handholds. She didn't envy him the journey. Then the Thek vehicle slowly turned in the cramped space of the cave, proving Tor's expertise as a pilot. Of course, Tor ought to be expert, considering it was intimate with its source of power and the vehicle no more than a surround. How convenient to be a Thek, she thought, impervious to all the minor ills that beset frail species like her own: long-lived, invulnerable to anything short of a nova. Someone had once told her that Thek created novas to tone up their inner cores. And there'd been that droll story she'd heard in advanced training, that the various planets claimed by the Thek as "homes" were dead worlds covered with immense pyramidal mountains, in conical ranges. Elder Thek never died, they became mountains, too vast to move or be moved. And the asteroid belts common to most Thek systems were actually fragmented Thek who had not withstood the final journey to their chosen resting place.

She peered out between the vines to follow their flight and saw the reaction of the giffs. Those in midair seemed to pause, while those who stood preening themselves on the cliffs erupted into sound, bugling and whistling in tones that seemed to Varian both joyous and startled. Although there was no way a golden flier could keep up with a Thek-powered craft, those in the air made a valiant effort and were followed by what must have been the entire adult population of the colony.

Varian gasped as a shaft of sunlight penetrated the morning mist and rain. The golden fur of the airborne giffs seemed a sheet of brilliant yellow suspended between cloudy sky and misted earth.

Only then did it occur to Varian that the shape of the Thek's vehicle with its transparent canopy was vaguely birdlike, with swept-back wings. A further moment's thought, and she glanced at the basically ovoid shape of the shuttle and came to an inescapable conclusion. The *giffs* had been protecting the cave! They had granted sanctuary to what they thought was an incubating egg.

Varian burst out laughing. The poor giffs! How long had the "egg" been incubating? However long, it must have confused the giffs. And yet . . . her respect for the creatures grew. Not only were they food-catchers, grass-weavers and protectors of their young, they could extend those skills to include another species. Very interesting! This would be one for the tapes when she got back to the *ARCT-10*. Or if.

Varian entered the shuttle, opening the iris just wide

enough for her to squeeze through. The one interior light made for an eerie atmosphere. Varian was only too glad to revive Lunzie and Triv. She didn't fancy a prolonged lonely stay in the shuttle or crouched in the cave. She needed occupation. And reading revival instructions was first on her list.

She gave Lunzie and Triv their initial shots and sat down to wait. She couldn't give the next dose until their body temperatures had risen closer to normal. She worried about Lunzie. Was there a limit to the number of times one body could undergo cold sleep? Or did it depend on the length of time asleep?

She shook her head and turned her mind to more productive channels. If Tor had actually bestirred itself to investigate their situation, even if only for the sake of that ancient core, they could eventually expect adequate assistance. Nor had they been planted. Had they been, Tor would not have intervened no matter how eager the Theks were to acquire the core. She hoped that the object gave the Theks a hard time: *ARCT-10*'s computer records, which supposedly included much of the stored knowledge of the incredibly ancient Thek communities, had indicated no previous exploration of Ireta. Yet once Portegin had assembled and activated the seismic screen to read the soil and rock analyses of the new cores laid by the three geological teams, faint signals had shown up along the entire continental shelf: signals indicating the presence of cores on a planet reportedly never before explored. Kai and Gaber had unearthed one. Though its signal was weak, it hadn't differed from the new cores the geologists were planting. It had felt *old* to Varian. And it was obviously of Thek manufacture. The presence of an ancient network on the continental shelf did explain the absence of mineral deposits; obviously the planet had already been worked. Once the geologists ventured beyond the shelf to the tectonically unstable areas, the cores did what they were designed to do: register massive deposits that the shifting plates of the heaving planet had thrown up from its very active thermal core.

At least, Varian consoled herself, Ireta was interesting to the Theks even if the situation of the humans involved did not appear to concern them. Still, if the stranded victims of the mutiny could find and power up the sleds, they could improve their condition until adequate assistance did arrive.

Varian checked Lunzie and Triv. Nothing seemed to be wrong, and their respirations were speeding up. Abruptly she decided that she'd better get out of the shuttle for a few moments: she was not constituted to sit still and do nothing.

She wandered out to the cave entrance. Hanging onto a vine, she let her body fall beyond the overhang. Giffs were swirling about. She wondered how far they had pursued the swift Thek. They seemed to be talking the event over for the crested heads turned from one flying mate to another.

How beautiful the golden fliers were! Their bodies touched occasionally, forming brilliant lances of yellow as Ireta's sun made its morning inspection. She was all admiration for their economy of movement as they backwinged to settle on the cliff. They were not graceful as they waddled to form a loose semicircle. She hung out on the vine, fascinated by what had to be a council of the great giffs. Others emerged from caves to join the nucleus until the top of the palisade was alive with motion, with high-held triangles of giff wings, claw-fingers wriggling in agitation. The noise had become a gabbling bugling sound, curiously harmonious, rather than dissonant. What were they saying to each other?

Varian was so entranced by the spectacle that she didn't realize how precarious her hold was on the vine until she had almost slipped beyond the reach of the ledge. She got safely back, rubbing hands stiffened by clutching the cumbersome thick vine, torn between a desire to get closer and the wisdom of remaining unseen.

She settled by making herself comfortable at the far left side of the cave mouth, where she had a good view of the sky and cliffs and could still hear the chorus even if she couldn't see the conclave.

She looked out apprehensively when the bugling ceased and saw a contingent of giffs, nets dangling from their clawed feet, speed off for the morning's fishing.

She was utterly astounded then, when three giffs broached the vine curtain and, neatly disentangling their wings from the trailing greenery, came to a stop in front of the space shuttle. Their attention was on the shuttle, so they didn't see her.

Krims! she thought to herself. Then Varian was torn between amusement and sympathy for the obvious consternation of the three giffs. Had they expected to find the space shuttle broken open? A birdlike object had certainly left the cave. But there it was, unblemished and certainly intact.

Then Varian noticed that the middle giff was taller, its wings a fraction larger, than its two fellows. The smaller ones turned to Middle Giff, their whole attitude querying. They emitted soft chirps and a sound more like a feline purr than a bird noise. Middle Giff aimed its beak tentatively at the shuttle and tapped it lightly. Varian could have sworn it sighed. It resumed its meditative pose while the other crested heads turned respectfully to it.

Varian was seized with an almost uncontrollable desire to stroll nonchalantly up to them and say, "Well, fellows, it's like this . . ."

Instead she savored the perplexed tableau and wished that there were some way in which she could explain to her puzzled hosts and protectors. They were noble creatures, elements of dignity were visible even in that moment of acute perplexity. Would they—could they—evolve further? Somehow she couldn't imagine the Ryxi in a protective role toward another species of avian life. Fortunately, there was no way in which the Ryxi could jeopardize the giffs' evolution! She smiled to herself, watching the giffs as they continued to debate the puzzle. Middle Giff turned from one sidekick to the other, gurgling softly under their more audible commentaries. Vrl would be furious, Varian thought. Another flying life-form capable of reasoning. Thank Krim that the Ryxi had refused to credit even the little Kai had reported of avian life on Ireta. Ryxi could hold lifelong grudges which, in this instance, suited Varian perfectly.

The examining committee waddled to the edge of the cave ledge and dropped off, spreading their wings to catch an updraft. She watched them from behind her screen as they circled and landed among those left on the council rocks. More harmonious noise. Could the musicality of a species' utterances be an indication of their basic temperament? An interesting notion—harmony equated with rational thought? Discord with basic survival reactions?

She glanced at the sky, squinting as she found the sun. Kai and Tor had been gone a while. At the rate of speed Tor had left the cliffs, the trip back to the old compound would have required a fraction of the time needed to make the journey by sled.

Time! She scurried back to the shuttle and hastily checked her patients. She ought not to have been gone so long, yet she'd no way of measuring time. Lunzie felt warmer and her respiratory rate was quicker. Triv was all right, too. She couldn't risk leaving them again. She settled down, drawing the thin thermal sheet about her.

Even if Kai found a sled in working order, it would take him some hours to return. To pass time, she carefully peeled and ate another of the fruits, chewing slowly to get the most of its taste and to draw out the task of eating. Mentally she rehearsed phrases of a report she'd make to the Xenobiological Survey on the cooperative tendencies of the golden fliers.

A long sigh nearly lifted Varian from the hard shuttle plasfloor. Lunzie! Yes, the medic's head had turned and her right hand jumped, her feet twitched. It was time for the restorative. As she prepared Lunzie's, she looked over at Triv. His head had fallen to one side, his lips parted and a groan issued from deep inside the man.

"Lunzie, it's Varian. Can you hear me?"

Lunzie blinked, trying to focus her eyes. Varian remembered her own attempts and resisted the impulse to smile. Lunzie wouldn't appreciate humor at the expense of her personal dignity.

"Hnnnnn?"

"It's Varian, Lunzie. You've been in cold sleep. I'm reviving you and Triv."

"Ohhhhh."

Varian gave her the second of the two required shots and then turned to give Triv his shot. She could appreciate their sensations as long-unused nerves and limbs began to respond to mental dictates. Once the second shots had taken effect, Lunzie and Triv were soon sitting up.

"I only hope you took it easy at first," Lunzie commented to Varian in her usual way.

"Oh yes," Varian assured her blithely, aware that "easy" in Lunzie's lexicon probably differed from her own interpretation. "I feel great."

"So what happened?"

"That Thek, Tor—the one Kai knows—came."

Lunzie's eyebrows arched in mild surprise. "Not to our rescue, certainly—it wanted the old core!"

Varian grinned at the medic, pleased that someone else shared her cynicism about Thek. "Right! The one Gaber and Kai disinterred."

"What would it want that for?" Triv asked, his words slurred in his first attempt at speech.

Varian shrugged. "A Thekian reason. But Kai went off with Tor to find it. I hope that wretched thing's buried nineteen meters down. No, I don't," she contradicted herself quickly, "for that would mean we've been asleep far too long. At any rate, Kai took along a power pack to unearth a sled for us."

"If the heavy-worlders didn't wreck 'em," Lunzie said sourly.

"They wouldn't do that," Triv said. "They'd be too sure that they'd locate us and the power packs."

"A sled would be a powerful encouragement." Lunzie looked down at the darker mounds of sleepers. Then she began to manipulate her arms and legs in a Discipline limbering exercise.

"Do I smell fruit?" Triv asked, running his tongue over his lips.

Varian instantly set to peel fruit for Lunzie and Triv. While they ate slowly and appreciatively, Varian related the adventures she and Kai had had, and their conclusion that the heavy-worlders had penetrated to the giffs' territory. With great relish she recounted the visitation of the Elder giffs after Tor had left the cave. Triv was amused, but Lunzie interpreted Varian's report differently, though she offered no comment.

"Can we use the main cave safely?" she asked Varian as she rose stiffly to her feet. "Or are those fliers of yours apt to recon frequently? No matter, I'd rather be out in Ireta's stink than sit in this morgue." She gathered up the thermal sheet and stalked to the entrance.

Triv and Varian followed. Once outside, Lunzie regarded the vines for a long moment, her expression betraying nothing of her thoughts. Suddenly she began to sniff, at first tentatively, and then with deeper breaths. "What . . . the . . ."

Varian grinned at her consternation. "Yes, I'd noticed, too. We've got accustomed to Ireta."

"Don't those vines give you any idea how long we've slept?" Lunzie demanded.

"I wish my botanical expertise was not limited to edibility and toxicity," Varian said, not wishing to add that the expedition's botanist had mutinied. "Tropical growth has a vitality unlike others. Why don't you limber up more? You could shower with the next rain . . ."

"Say, Tanegli broke your shoulder . . ." Lunzie's strong fingers found the break point in Varian's shoulder. Her expression was inscrutable. "Reabsorbed! How long ago did Kai leave?" she added in a quick shift of topic.

"Early morning. Before the net giffs left for fishing." Varian swung a vine beyond the lip of the cave and, squinting against the sun which was burning through the heat haze, decided it must be midafternoon. "He could be back any time now."

"We'll hope so. D'you have anything more than fruit? Any protein? I feel an urgent need for something substantial."

"Well," Varian began brightly, "we were lucky enough to find hadrasaur nuts . . ."

"Were you now?" Lunzie's dry humor had survived cold sleep.

While Varian tried to sell the two on the merits of the pithy nuts, she tried to hide her growing apprehension over Kai's delay. Kai might ascribe some loyalty to Tor but she couldn't. It would be just like the creature to find the bloody core and bounce off with its treasure, ignoring Kai's welfare. Still, Kai would have had to disinter the sleds and check over the console. It could have taken a long time to find the sleds. Her anxiety sharpened her hearing and the giffs' cries were audible. Without explanation to Triv and Lunzie, she made a sudden running leap to a vine, swinging out to see what alarmed them. The haze had thickened, but the muffled whine of a sled was music to her ears.

"He's back. He's back," she cried as she ran to the vines anchored to the shuttle and began shinnying up. She was just pulling herself onto the cliff when the blunt snout of the two-man vehicle emerged from the obscuring haze and wobbled erratically in her direction.

Krims! Was the thing damaged? "Lunzie! Triv! Get up here!"

What was Kai attempting? The sled angled down, not as if he was attempting to circle and land in the cave. The flight angle was wrong. What was he doing? Reminding the giffs of the first peaceful visit they'd had from humans? No, not with the sled swinging like that. Glare kept her from making out the pilot behind the canopy. The giffs were alarmed, too, taking to the air in flocks. Some began to circle to investigate. The bow of the sled dipped again and, as Varian watched from the cliff edge, her heart in her throat, its forward motion was braked so fast that the vehicle fell rather than descended, bumping along the vines until she was afraid that momentum would carry it over the cliff. She even put out her hand in an unconscious gesture. With a final *grind*, the nose of the sled caught on the vines and it slowed to a halt. Then she could see that Kai was slumped over the console.

Forgetting any caution for the circling giffs, she clambered over the edge and reached the sled just as the first of the giffs landed. She eyed the creature over the stained and scratched canopy. The giff reared back, its wings half extended, the wing talons spread but, as she caught her breath and braced herself for an assault, a long warbling note restrained the giff. The creature's talons closed and its wings relaxed slightly.

She had time, then, Varian thought, to get to Kai. She pressed the canopy release and, once the plasglas had cracked open, she pushed to speed the retraction.

"Kai! Kai!"

"Kaaaiiiii! Kaaaaiiiii!" The giffs mimicked her as more landed and ranged themselves on either side of the first one.

At that moment, Kai moaned. Ignoring the giffs, Varian bent into the sled to tend to his body slumped over the console. A putrid stench now rose from the opened cockpit. Shuddering in revulsion, she hauled Kai upright. And shuddered again, mastering the wave of nausea that swept her. Kai's face was a mass of blood. What was left of his overall was matted against his bloodied flesh. The whole front of him was a bloody mess.

"LUNZIE! TRIV! HELP!" She screeched over her shoulder.

"UNNNNZZZZI IVVVVELLLLL." The giffs picked up the sounds.

"Shut up! I don't need a chorus!" Varian yelled at them to relieve the horror that she experienced looking down at her coleader. He moaned again.

Her fingers hunted for the pulse against the carotid artery. Slow, strong and regular. Strange. No, he'd been exerting Discipline. How else could he have returned to the cliffs in his condition?

Had Lunzie heard her? She glanced warily up at the giffs and was astonished to see that every head was turned away and the bodies seemed to be withdrawing from the sled. They looked, for all the world, as if they were avoiding an unpleasant smell. And so they were, for the stench still rose from the sled, and mostly from Kai. Could she risk leaving him and going to the cliff edge to hurry help?

"We're coming!" Triv's shout finally encouraged her.

She bent to look more closely at Kai's wounds. He appeared to have been attacked by something or somethings that sucked blood for as she eased a shred of his coverall from his chest, she saw the pattern of pinpoint marks on his skin, each with its own jewellike teardrop of blood. And that awful stink! Worse than anything that Ireta had inflicted on her before except, she realized now, that she remembered that frightful odor. It was not easy to forget: oily, marine, and utterly disgusting!

"Is it safe to approach?" Triv asked, poking his head over the cliff edge.

"It hardly matters, does it?" Lunzie replied, heaving herself onto the vine-covered surface.

"They're not aggressive now," Varian said in a well-projected voice, keeping her tone sweet. "I'd just move slowly."

"My intention, I assure you. How bad is Kai?"

"He's unconscious now. Must have Disciplined himself to get back. He seems to have run into a bloodsucker."

"Faugh!" Lunzie's face wrinkled in distaste and she pinched her nostrils. "What's that smell?"

"Kai."

"Your fliers don't seem to like the smell any more than we do," Triv remarked.

"Let's get him out of the sled while they're snooting the

wind," Lunzie said. "I really can't see enough through the blood."

Triv and Varian slipped into the sled to hoist out the unconscious geologist. Triv grimaced at muscles slow to respond to his commands as they guided the limp body out to Lunzie.

"That stink would suffocate a man," Triv remarked, taking deep gulps of fresher air. "Oh ho, what's wrong here?" He bent back inside the sled. "Did he drop this thing? Every malfunction light on the control panel is lit!"

"Krims! I was hoping we could fly him down to the cave in the sled," Varian said.

"I wouldn't advise it until I can get behind the control panel." Triv flicked off the power and closed the canopy.

Lunzie deftly peeled away the tatters of the coverall to disclose the hundreds of tiny punctures that had pierced Kai's skin, each one filled with blood. Varian removed the trouser legs.

"Even his boots are perforated," she told Lunzie. "I don't remember telltagging anything that could do this."

"You think he'd smell it coming," was Lunzie's dour comment.

"Watch it, girls, we've got company. Hey. . . ."

At Triv's warning, Lunzie and Varian looked up and received a giff-borne shower in the face as a flight of giffs skimmed over them and each emptied its filled throat pouch on the little group. Most of the unexpected drenching fell on Kai's exposed body, laving it clean of blood momentarily.

"Well, what d'you make of that?" demanded Triv. "Ah, there's more coming! No, they've got leaves!"

As deftly as the shower had been delivered, the thick green leaves dropped about Kai.

"What are they trying to tell us, Varian?" Lunzie wanted to know.

"They know that stink, Lunzie. They could know what attacked him. They must be trying to help us."

"They'd attack with claw and wing," Triv said thoughtfully, "not water and leaves."

"But they did attack you and Kai . . ." Lunzie began.

"This time they saw us all come from the cave." Varian seized one of the leaves and held it up to the giffs remaining beyond the sled. "What do I do with it?"

Lunzie picked up a leaf, crushing the pulpy tip in her fingers, sniffing and sneezing at the odor of the sap.

"One thing sure, it smells a lot better than he does. A neutralizer?"

"Varian! That big one . . ." Triv pointed and they looked at the largest of the giffs, who could have been the Middle Giff of the cave inspection, crushing a leaf in its talon and smearing it on its chest.

"What might work on giffs, might not work on us, but I've nothing else . . ." Lunzie muttered and tentatively squeezed sap over the oozing punctures on Kai's shoulder. "Well, what d'you know? It's a styptic! Quick, both of you, get to work. Even if the leaves only stop the bleeding, it's *something*!" She tasted the sap then. "Oooo. Bitter, bitter. Alumlike. Good. Now if it could also neutralize—whatever bit Kai is toxic as all . . . Hell!"

As if taking due note of Kai's condition, Ireta's unpredictable rain started to fall in drops big enough to hurt.

"Wouldn't you just know?" Varian cried in disgust, trying to shelter Kai's legs with her body as Lunzie and Triv leaned across his torso.

In moments Kai's hair was afloat in a puddle and the sap was being washed from those portions of his body which the concerted efforts of his friends could not shield.

"We've got to get him out of this. Are you sure we can't risk the sled?" Lunzie asked urgently.

Triv splashed to the vehicle and the women could hear him cursing, heard him slamming the plasglas canopy shut.

"Every damned red light is on. Those sleds are supposed to be impervious . . . We got company again. . . ."

"What we don't need are spectators. C'mon, Varian, Triv. We've got to get him down to the cave before he drowns."

"I'll just hoist him . . ." Triv said, grabbing Kai by the arm and staggering as he attempted to haul the unconscious man to his shoulder. "What . . ."

Varian grabbed to support the staggering Triv while Lunzie caught Kai.

"You're both just out of cold sleep," Varian said with some disgust. "Neither of you has regained any useful strength yet."

In a joint effort they carried Kai to the edge of the cliff.

"I don't like this," Lunzie muttered to herself as Varian located an untethered vine and hauled it up. "None of us is up to this sort of effort." She bent to protect Kai from the rain.

"Varian," Triv's voice was taut with alarm. "The giffs are surrounding us. Are they trying to push us off the cliff?" His voice rose as he planted himself in front of Lunzie and Kai.

Varian turned, rising from her crouch. With a sense of relief she thought she recognized Middle Giff as it took a forward step. Then it inclined its head to her and gestured one wing in as courtly a motion as any she'd ever seen from the mincing Ryxi. The wing tip pointed over the edge of the cliff. It moved to indicate Kai. Then both wings were spread, undulating to suggest flight. The huge raindrops beat against the wing surface, beading as the oil of the fur kept the water from penetrating.

"Does the giff mean what I think it means?" Triv asked Varian.

"If it does, it's a miracle."

"Now, wait a minute, Varian," Lunzie interposed. "I'm not about to surrender Kai to them."

"What choice have we? Dropping him into the sea because we haven't the strength to lower him into the cave? They've already helped us with the water and the leaves. They are used to flying burdens with the fish nets, working as a team. If they're smart enough to see we've got a problem in getting

Kai into shelter, they've also got a solution. The rain's getting heavier and the wind's picking up." Varian had to brace herself. "We've no other option."

Lunzie brushed her soaking hair from her face, staring up at Varian. Then a gust of wind buffeted the trio of humans. Lunzie capitulated, throwing up one hand in acceptance of their desperate situation. "You and Triv go on down. Part the vines and guide the giffs in."

With a final fierce look at the xenobiologist, Lunzie surrendered Kai's limp body to Varian. She took the vine that Triv indicated and slid out of sight over the cliff edge. Triv followed her. Suddenly the wind ceased its assault on her body and Varian realized that she was surrounded by wet giff legs and water-beaded feathers. Giff claws wrapped gently about Kai's ankles and picked up his limp arms by the wrists. Varian stepped back, heart in her mouth.

Then Kai was hanging in the air and more giffs found holds on him. For one horrified moment, Varian wondered if they were going to fly him up to one of their caves. But they lifted him well above the cliff, then maneuvered slowly out over the water and slowly began to descend. Could she be hearing the creak of overloaded bones in the storm winds? She could certainly *see* the effort in the straining pinions. Varian shook herself out of her paralysis and, finding the vine which Lunzie had used, began to slide down it. She slipped a bit on the rain-slick vine and was forced to abandon her scrutiny of Kai's descent to insure her own. Then she saw Lunzie and Triv holding back the thick vines so that the giffs could enter. Before her feet touched the cave's floor, Kai was safely deposited. Having delivered their burden, the giffs awkwardly backed away. Lunzie and Triv busily anointed the myriad punctures on his body, which were once again oozing droplets of blood.

"He's all right?" Varian asked Lunzie.

"Took no harm at all. I don't think they so much as bruised him. And this sap is definitely styptic."

Reassured, Varian turned to the giffs. The two species regarded each other over the injured man. It wasn't as if she could flap her hand at them, like a flock of ordinary birds, and shoo them away, nor did Varian wish to treat them so peremptorily for they had saved Kai twice already. In working with alien species, Varian had discovered that the sincerity of her intentions could be communicated by voice, even if the words were unintelligible to the hearer. She spread her arms wide, palms up, and imitated the wing gesture of Middle Giff.

"I don't know how to express our thanks and appreciation for your assistance, golden fliers," she said, deepening her voice and imbuing it with the very genuine gratitude she felt. "We could not have borne him so safely nor so quickly to shelter. Thank you, too, for the leaves." Varian pointed to Lunzie and Triv as they smeared Kai's wounds. "Thank you for all your assistance. We hope to remain on such good terms with you. Thank you."

"From all of us to all of you," murmured Lunzie. Then she smiled up at the giffs nearest her, holding up the leaf she was crushing and smiling more broadly. Varian could almost forgive her her dark humor.

A hum rose from the giffs and their orange eyes blinked rapidly.

"While you're in rapport with 'em, ask for more leaves. Unless you know where we can find 'em."

A slightly surprised chirp and the agitation of the vine screen brought their attention to the cave entrance. A group of smaller giffs entered, their wing talons clutching bundles of the leaves.

"Ask and you shall receive, oh skeptic," Triv muttered as the smaller giffs hovered, venturing inside the cave only far enough to drop their burdens safely to the floor. Then Middle Giff made a peremptory sound, a call more than a chirp, and all the giffs lurched to the mouth of the cave. To Varian, they appeared to fall off the edge. Then she saw them, beating strongly upwards and out of sight.

"Lunzie . . ." she began, turning to deliver a few choice words to the medic but Kai moaned, his voice rising to the feverish mumble. He thrashed about until Triv grabbed him by the arms and held him down.

"Get that thermal blanket, Varian. Whatever Discipline he was exerting has lapsed. Yes," and Lunzie laid her hand on his forehead and then his cheeks, "fever's rising. At least fever indicates the body is fighting the toxemia." She rummaged in her pouch for a moment. "Muhlah! I don't have so much as an antibiotic. He's going to have to do it the hard way. Take off the other boot, Triv, will you? And Varian, you pull off what's left of his clothes while I hold him up. Hmmm . . ." Lunzie paused to inspect Kai's chest. "The sap is closing the punctures. If only I had *something* . . . That Thek didn't say anything about *ARCT-10*, did it?"

"Only that the beacon hadn't been stripped yet."

"I shouldn't have asked. Is there any more of that succulent fruit, Varian? I'm still dehydrated and, if we could dilute some juice with fresh water, Kai might take it. He's going to need all the liquid we can get down him to combat the toxin."

Triv collected rainwater by holding a pail outside the vines to catch the torrential downpour. Varian squeezed juice until she had exhausted the supply. They all ate the pulp. At regular intervals, the diluted juice was dripped down Kai's throat. It seemed to ease his restlessness. Often he would lick his lips and frown during the fever dreams, as if searching for soothing moisture.

"Not an uncommon fever pastime," Lunzie assured them. "It's when they won't swallow, you've got problems."

By sunset Kai's fever had reached a new high and their supply of leaves was almost gone. Thought most of the punctures had closed, the sap seemed to ease his feverishness, and Lunzie hoped they could get more to last through the night. So Varian climbed to the cliff top, hoping there would be a giff she could signal to. She sighed with relief when she found a large pile of leaves neatly anchored to the vines by a stout twist of grass. Fruit was windlocked in an intersection of thick vine tendrils.

"Not so stupid, our fine furry friends," she said, elated and reassured, as she proudly displayed the leaves and fruit to Lunzie and Triv.

"I've been on worlds where there were other interpretations to such overtures," Lunzie replied sardonically.

"Yes, I appreciate that, Lunzie. Propitiation of unknown gods, fattening for the kill, ceremonial poisonings . . ." Varian dismissed such considerations with a wave of her hand. "To an experienced hand like you, I must seem incredibly naïve, but then I've generally dealt with animals which are pretty straightforward in their reactions. I really feel sorry for you, having to cope with that devious and subtle predator—man." She spoke in an even tone, but she held Lunzie's gaze in a steady stare. "My experience tells me to trust the giff, for they've shown us no harm—"

"Once we emerged from this cave. Actually, I cannot help comparing your fliers with the Ryxi."

"There's no comparison—"

"There is if you are trying to suggest the golden fliers remembered *man—us*," and Lunzie dug a thumb into her chest bone, "when you don't even know their life span, and we don't know how long we were in cold sleep."

"The giffs did remember: that intruders from the gap were trouble and that those in the cave were to be protected. They do protect the young of their own species. I just count us very lucky indeed that that instinct was passed onto us."

"I'd hate to think that this was a tradition handed down from elder to hatchling," Triv remarked. "What sort of a life span would you project for the giffs, Varian?"

As Varian did not wish to argue with Lunzie, she seized on Triv's calm question gratefully.

"The Ryxi are the only comparable species of a similar size exhibiting the same intelligence," she ignored Lunzie's snort of disgust, "and their life span is tied up with their libido. The males tend to kill their opponents off in mating duels. Ryxi females live six or seven decades. Like the giffs they don't seem to have any predators. Of course, I don't know what parasites they might be susceptible to. Then, there's the leech thing. If the giffs knew what topical treatment to supply for those puncture wounds, they *must* be vulnerable to it. However, let's give the giffs a life span similar to the Ryxi's . . ."

"They don't like comparisons—" Lunzie remarked.

"Say, sixty to seventy years Standard."

"We could have slept sixty to seventy years, or six hundred. You'd have thought Kai would insist on knowing how long he'd slept."

"You know that Thek don't reckon time in our measurements. Even if Kai had asked, would he have received a comprehensible answer?"

Triv regarded Lunzie's sour expression with a bemused smile on his face. "You do dislike the Thek, don't you?"

"I would dislike any species that set itself up as an infallible authority on anything and everything." A sharp gesture of Lunzie's arm dismissed the noble Thek with no courtesy. "I don't trust 'em. And this," her hand lowered toward Kai, feverishly twisting his head and trying to free his arms from the restraint of the sheet, "is one immediate reason why."

"We've been taught to respect and revere them," Triv began.

Lunzie snorted. "Typical xenob training. You can't help it, but you can learn from mistakes!"

Kai began to thresh in earnest, loosening the cocoon they had wrapped about him.

"Sap time!" Lunzie said, reaching for the leaves. "This medication is effective for an hour and a half. I wish I knew if there were side effects to prolonged application. I wish I had something to work with . . ." Lunzie's tone was fierce but her hands were gentle in their ministrations.

"What do you need?" Varian asked quietly.

"The small microscope plus the metal medicine container that Tanegli made off with!"

"I know the console was blinking its red head off, but none of the warning lights was steady," Varian said. "I'll take a look tomorrow. Portegin had enough tools to make that homing beacon, and I'm a fair mechanic when pushed. A few matrices may just have loosened in that hard landing. I remember the coordinates of all the camps . . . as if it were yesterday. . . ." Varian caught Lunzie's eyes and laughed. Lunzie's gaze was cynical. "Well, the last thing the heavy-worlders would be expecting is a raid by one of us."

"Do the bastards good to get shaken out of their sagging skins," the physician said. "If any of the original ones are still alive."

"A bit daunting to think they might all be safely in their graves, or whatever they do," said Triv, "and us alive and kicking."

"You get used to it," Lunzie said sourly.

"What?" asked Varian. "The kicking or still being alive when everyone else you know has long since been dead?" With those words Varian faced that possibility for the first time since she had awakened.

"Both," was Lunzie's cryptic reply.

"I'll have a go at fixing the sled first light tomorrow."

"I'll give you a hand," Triv said.

"Then you," and Lunzie pointed at Triv, "can take first watch with Kai tonight." She was wringing out another cloth to place on Kai's forehead. "I'm tired."

Varian gave the physician a searching look. Yes, Lunzie was tired of many things. Tired, resigned, but not defeated.

"Wake me for the next watch, Triv." Varian hauled the thermal blanket over her shoulders and was asleep almost before she could pillow her head on her arm.

Varian woke Lunzie at first light when Kai's temperature began to rise.

"That's the way of fevers," Lunzie told her, checking her

patient. "Some of the punctures are completely closed. That's good." Lunzie offered Kai juice which he thirstily gulped. "That's good, too."

Varian went over to Triv and was about to wake him when Lunzie intervened.

"Can you manage without him? He needs more rest than he'll let on."

"I'll call if I need help, then." Varian equipped herself with Portegin's few tools and shinnied up the vine to the cliff top.

First she had to empty the sled of the rainwater that had accumulated even in the brief time the canopy had been opened. That gave her a chance to examine the undercarriage. Although there were a few scratches from Kai's rough landing, there were no fracture lines on the ceramic. As she righted the sled, she noticed several small feathers. She picked them up, smoothed them and held them out to the fresh dawn breeze to dry. They couldn't be from giffs, which were furred, and once dry enough to show color, they were a greenish blue. The downy portion fluffed while the top of the quills remained rigid, too thick with oil to have suffered damage from their immersion. Carefully putting them in a breast pocket, Varian turned to the business at hand.

She switched on the power, and the blinking lights reappeared. The fault might be just in the console panel, Varian thought, for despite her confident claim to Lunzie, she wasn't a trained mechanic. If the sled's malfunction involved circuit or matrix adjustments, she would be unable to cope. Then they would have to wake Portegin. But the units were built to withstand a good deal of rough usage as well as long periods of idleness, stored in the Exploratory Vessel, so they had been designed to survive under just the circumstances that then prevailed.

Fortunately the wind was blowing over her right shoulder as she broke the console seal. She had also lifted the panel upward so her face was shielded. Otherwise the mold that had penetrated and thrived in the console interior would have covered her face. Instinctively she had held her breath and ducked away at her first sight of the purple mass. She lowered the console cover only far enough to watch the wind blow away the top layers.

Using one collar flap as an improvised mask, she tilted the sled into the wind, letting it dislodge additional layers until, at last, the outlines of the matrix panels were visible though covered with a soft purple fuzz. Even the color looked dangerous to her.

Then she took heart because, if the mold had seeped through the console seals, it could also cause minute circuit breakage. If she could remove the remaining stuff . . . Varian laid aside the panel but kept the collar flap across her mouth and nose as she bent to examine the slotted matrices. She delicately ran one of Portegin's tools along the edge of the matrix frame, the fuzz gathering on the shaft of the instrument, leaving the frame edge clean. She flicked the mess off the blade and cleaned the next portion. When she had cleared the accessible portions of the panel, she shook out Portegin's kit to find something that could reach into crannies and corners. If she left any of that mold inside, it would undoubtedly proliferate again. She needed a long-handled, fine-bristled brush which was patently not among Portegin's effects.

Then she recalled the greenish-blue plumage. "Fine feathered friends as well as furry ones," she cried.

Nothing could have been more suitable and she set about dusting and cleaning, always careful not to inhale any of the particles she flicked away. The quill was in fact superior to a brush, bending to fit into crevices and corners which would have defeated a stiff-handled tool.

When Varian could see no more purple fuzz anywhere, she replaced the console cover and sealed it, for whatever that action was worth. Switching the power back on, she was delighted to see that all but one of the malfunction lights were off. She gave the console a solid *thump* with her fist and the last one blinked out.

She finished just as the first of the day's rain squalls thundered across the inland sea. As she hurriedly closed the canopy, she noticed that she'd had three spectators. Middle Giff was among them, towering above his sidekicks. They regarded her with an unwavering orange gaze.

"And good morning to you." She bowed solemnly. "I've cleaned the console and the sled appears to be operative again. I'm going down for a while but I'll be back." Varian held the firm opinion that all species liked to be noticed, whether or not the language could be understood. From the way the giffs cocked their heads attentively, they were certainly hearing the sounds she made. Keeping her tone cheerful, Varian went on. "I'm sure you couldn't care less, but these blue-green feathers are superior mold dusters. Friends of yours?" She held up one feather and was certain that Middle Giff leaned forward to peer at it. "Couldn't have fixed the sled without it." She tucked Portegin's tool kit into her belt and then walked to the edge of the cliff, to slide down the vine. "See you later."

"See who later?" demanded Lunzie.

"The giffs."

Lunzie eyed her skeptically. "And the sled?"

"Nothing but a case of purple mold."

"You didn't inhale any of it?"

"I've more sense than that. A feather, opportunely deposited in the sled," and Varian displayed it once again, "cleaned what the wind didn't. Sled's all systems green. How's Kai?"

"The same." Lunzie stretched and pulled at stiff shoulder muscles. "I'll wake Triv when I have to. We got another delivery while you were out." Lunzie indicated the pile of leaves and fruit. "Apparently they have decided we need these," and she pushed at the hadrasaurus nuts with a sour expression on her face.

"They don't taste like much—"

"Like so much bumwad—"

"But they are full of protein."

"I'll put them through the synthesizer. Anything would improve their taste—or, should I say, lack of it?"

"I'll have a look round the secondary campsites. Without sleds, I don't think the heavy-worlders would have had enough mobility to spread out—"

"But then, we don't know how long we've been asleep, or how inventive and resourceful they were."

"True." Varian had no great opinion of the abilities of the heavy-worlders to reshape the local environment. "But I just might get an indication of elapsed time."

"They might even all be dead!" Hope was evident in Lunzie's voice.

"See you later."

"Take care, Varian."

When Varian emerged on the cliff top, the morning winds had picked up. The Three had left their perch above the sled, but the sky was well populated by the graceful creatures, soaring on thermal updrafts or gliding in to land on their cave ledges during the respite from squall and rain. Varian was aware that her every action was being observed as she settled in the pilot's seat. She felt slightly self-conscious as she closed the canopy and took off directly into the prevailing wind. When she had circled back over the cliff, she realized that the opening to the cavern was totally obscured by the vines. Small wonder the heavy-worlders had not found them.

Despite the airing the sled had received, the taint of that nauseating odor remained. Varian switched the air circulator to high without much effect. The sled did handle properly, she was relieved to note, but she kept a close check on the panel lights and the readout, visually estimating her altitude and her direction against the sun.

Those concerns kept Varian from noticing her escort until she was some distance from the cliffs. At first she thought that the three giffs just happened to be flying in her general direction. Then she couldn't ignore the fact that they were discreetly pacing the sled: curiosity or protection? Either way, their action was further evidence of intelligence. Serve those arrogant Ryxi right, Varian thought, to have another winged sentient emerge in the same solar system as their new colony.

When she began to recognize the landmarks close to the landing site and the scene of the stampede, she wondered if any of the animals they had originally tagged were still alive. She flipped on the telltagger. Of course, since she'd not had time to estimate the life expectancy of the various species she had tagged, this could well be another exercise in futility, but it was worth a try. Immediately the sensitive instrument registered movement as well as significant animal warmth but no *blurp* indicating tagged life-forms. Just then Varian shot across the end of a long swath of cleared and trampled ground. She had a fleeting glimpse of blunt heads poking into treetops, long-neck herbivores on their ceaseless quest for forage sufficient to keep life in their ponderous bodies.

If the telltagger had purred even once to indicate the presence of the indelible paint that had been used to mark the beasts, she would have been tempted to turn back and identify the creatures.

Varian continued toward the original compound. Whatever had attacked Kai might still be in the vicinity, looking for more blood. She shuddered with revulsion. Although Lunzie's dour assessment of the Thek motive was disturbing, Varian preferred to believe that the Thek had left before Kai was attacked. Thek might not have to indulge in defensive tactics because no intelligent species would dare attack them. To primitive predators of limited sense, the Thek was just so much rock, with no scent, and such infrequent motion as to make it unlikely as prey. No one could accuse the Thek of being emotional or of becoming involved with any non-Thek individuals though they were devoted to their own Elders. On the other hand, Varian mused, Tor had known Kai's family for several generations. Surely some conscience would have prompted the Thek to assist Kai if it had observed him in difficulties.

She had to concede that Tor had only awakened Kai because it needed him to assist in recovering the old core. Even if that were its entire motive, the secondary benefit had been Kai's awakening, then hers, and the acquisition of a sled which at least gave the stranded explorers mobility. Varian wasn't certain how much of an advantage that would prove. When she arrived near the heavy-worlders, she'd have to take precautions to prevent their seizing the sled. Krims! If she and Kai had only had a little more warning before that mutiny had erupted, they could have Disciplined against it.

Or could they? She grinned to herself. Four Disciples in full control of their inner resources were still no match for six heavy-worlders, unless they had the advantage of surprise. The heavy-worlders had had that. Nor could the four Disciples have retreated strategically for that would have given the mutineers hostages of the most vulnerable members of the expedition.

Varian circled the old compound and quickly spotted the small cavity toward the rear of the compound, well away from the site of the old geological dome which had housed the core. The Thek had had a long search. The old cylinder of the core had probably been kicked about in the stampede before being buried beneath layers of dead beasts. Succeeding years would have seen it planted deeper in dust and sand. How much dust would accumulate in the amphitheater in a year? How many years? How many years!

Deliberately Varian censored her thoughts and swung the sled about. Immediately she saw the broken trees where Kai must have blasted skyward in the sled. She tightened her circle to land deftly in that opening, all the time listening to the telltagger for any evidence of life in the area. Silence. So she opened the canopy. The other vehicles were partially exposed by the removal of the one she was using and Kai's efforts to clear the overgrowth. With any luck, all could be retrieved and made useful again. With creatures abroad like the one that had attacked Kai, they had better travel by air whenever feasible. Oh, for the comforting presence of a stunner in her holster!

For the life of her, she couldn't imagine which of the life-forms she'd observed before the mutiny could have mangled Kai in that fashion. She gave the weed-covered sleds a kick which dislodged any number of insects and stepped nimbly out of their senseless flight. None of them looked like a leech.

She returned to the sled and took off, circling above the compound, gradually widening the spiral upward while the telltagger chortled. There seemed no point in remaining there. She turned her sled northeast, noting that her aerial guardians had resumed their discreet cover.

Oddly reassured, Varian smiled to herself, a smile that faded as she began to examine her direction. Yet she felt reasonably certain that the mutineers must have remained at the northeast camp. They had spent their "rest day" there, and it was also reasonable to assume that they had hidden the supplies they'd synthesized nearby. Bakkun had initiated the mutiny from the northeast, not the southwestern camp built for Dimenon and Margit. Furthermore, the hunting in the northeast was known to be good.

The camp so briefly occupied by Portegin and Aulia had been located on one of the sawn-off bluffs that volcanic forces had pushed up in the area, like immense footrests or steppingstones. A narrow trail to the summit prevented attack by all but small agile creatures. Because of the presence of Tyrannosaurus rex, originally named fang-face by Varian, and the voracious grazers, the small life-forms which had remained in the vast plains area were timid or nocturnal. The one would have stayed away from unknown scents and activities, the other would be warded off by the simplest of shock gates, even if the main force field had to be turned off to conserve power. As the force fields had a usable life of three to four Standard years, the presence or absence of them might give Varian some idea of time elapsed.

However, as the bluff stood prominently above grasslands, with no convenient clumps of vegetation or trees in which to hide either herself or the precious sled, gaining access to the summit, or flying close enough to be identified provided her with an additional hazard. Weaponless, she didn't fancy being on foot for long on the plains unless the heavy-worlders had driven both predator and grazer away.

If the mutineers were obviously in residence, she was loathe to announce their reemergence.

As she neared the location, she switched on the telltagger which had become an irritant with its constant buzz and its distressing inability to *purr* the presence of tagged specimens.

She saw the dusty cloud, subdued quickly the surge of remembered fear and reinforced the support of Discipline which would prevent the distraction of unnecessary emotional responses.

She also saw, but dispassionately now, the bobbing black line at the base of the dust which meant stampeding animals. She pulled her sled upward, gaining altitude to see beyond the dust, and activated the forward-screen magnification. As they passed over the cloud, the telltagger spat furiously, vibrating in its brackets. Suddenly its activity ceased and Varian could see beyond the obscuring dust the monumental hulk of the predator, fang-face, once termed Tyrannosaurus rex, thunder lizard. Thunderous it was, but not chasing the stupidly fleeing herbivores. Instead, a small insignificant creature was running before fang-face with a speed that startled Varian. She increased magnification, and, despite Discipline, gasped in astonishment.

A man, a young man with a superb physique, his long, heavily thewed legs pumping in an incredible stride, was outdistancing the awkward but tenacious fang-face. The man appeared to be heading toward one of the upthrust bluffs, but he had a long way to go to reach its safety. From the exertion

•

evident in straining cords of his neck, the sweat pouring from his face, and the visible laboring of his chest and ribs, he did not have the distance in him.

Varian took a second, longer look at fang-face, wondering why the creature had eschewed the more succulent herbivores for a mere mouthful of man—and saw why. A thick lance was lodged under the beast's right eye. Just short of a fatal thrust, it wobbled up and down, providing the wounded pursuer with a smarting reminder of revenge. Occasionally, snarling in pain, it batted at the lance but failed to move it. Varian wondered what sort of point the hunter had used, and marveled at the strength which must have been back of a thrust to have placed the point so deeply in the beast's eye socket.

The runner had to be a descendant of the mutineers: he'd the build, if not the overdeveloped musculature of someone raised on a heavy-gravity planet. He'd made a very clever throw. Varian might object, as a xenob, about causing injury to any creature, but clearly she had to rescue the young hunter. He was quite the most superb young man she had ever seen.

Unfortunately she had no equipment on the sled to effect an air rescue. Not even a vine. She could hover just above the surface and coax him into the craft, but the speed of the thunder lizard was daunting. If he demurred . . . Why should he? Surely his parents—grandparents? great-grandparents?—must have passed on some version of their origins. Airborne vehicles would not frighten him out of his wits. On the other hand, any man who would take on a fang-face single-handed would not easily be frightened, even of something of which he had no previous experience.

She wheeled the sled to come up behind him, matching its speed to his phenomenal running stride.

"Climb aboard. Quickly!" she shouted as she hit the canopy release.

His powerful stride faltered, and he nearly fell. But, instead of altering his course to come alongside, he spurted off at a tangent.

"Do you want to be eaten by that monster?" She didn't know if he failed to understand her or thought her some new menace. Surely the language couldn't have mutated in a few generations. Or was it more than a "few?" She tried again to bridge the distance and again he swerved.

"Leave me!" he managed to shout, the effort to speak and keep up his pace visibly slowing him.

Varian raised the sled above him and reduced speed, trying to understand his startling reluctance to be rescued.

The runner appeared mature, surely in his third decade, though the exertion in his face might just make him appear older. He'll never make it to the bloody bluff, Varian decided with the detachment of her Disciplined state. So, let him pursue his goal or, rather, be pursued to his own purpose. She could make a timely intervention if it was required.

The fang-face had obviously never seen an air sled, or its brain could not register more than one nuisance at a time, for as Varian swung in its direction, it paid her no heed. Passing over it, Varian took note that the lance near its eye was not its only injury. Blood was pumping from several wounds in such quantities that Varian wondered how much more it could lose before collapsing. She circled just as the wounded animal staggered for the first time, roaring loudly. There was no doubt in her mind that the creature was weakening. She set the sled above and slightly behind fang-face, ready to intervene if the man had overestimated his ability to outlast his victim.

She had time to notice details of the runner on the screen. He wore little, mainly what appeared to be scraped hide covering his loins. Stout hide footwear was lashed tightly up to the knee of each leg. He wore a broad belt that Varian would swear had been part of a lift-belt unit once, from which several large knives and a pouch hung, flapping against the runner's legs. A tube was secured across his back, but she couldn't guess its function. In one hand he clutched a small crossbow, certainly a good weapon for piercing the hide and bone of most of the monsters that walked Ireta.

Varian reminded herself that she was not there to cater to the foibles of a young man being chased by a well-provoked carnivore. It also struck her forcibly that if he was reduced to crossbow and lance, she might be wasting her time in trying to find the mutineers' base. The microscope and other items which Lunzie needed had probably perished from neglect if this young man represented the present level of the survivors' lifestyle.

Three things happened at the same time: she decided to swoop down and pick him up willy-nilly; the thunder lizard let out a gasping roar and fell forward, plowing a furrow with its muzzle and chest, tried to rise and collapsed limply. The young man looked back over his shoulder and began to circle, still at considerable speed as he made sure the creature was lifeless.

Maintaining Discipline for immediate use, Varian landed the sled at a discreet distance from the bulk of the dead predator. She was a sprinter and knew that she could reach her vehicle before the extraordinary young man could catch her.

When she reached him, he was tugging at the deeply lodged spear. Inhaling deeply, Varian casually laid one hand beyond his on the shaft and exerted her Disciplined resource. The spear came away so fast that the young man, unprepared for the quality of assistance, staggered backward, leaving Varian with the spear. She examined its tip, Discipline overriding her natural repugnance for bloody objects. She wiped the point on the beast's hide, dislodging some of the myriad parasites and examined the spearhead. The metal had been tempered and fashioned with a ring of barbs, one reason the monster had been unable to dislodge it. Varian was amazed that she had. Of course, flesh and bone had come away, too. Already swarms of insects descended on the corpse.

"Can you understand me if I speak slowly?" Varian asked,

turning to confront the young giant. He was staring from her to the spear she had removed so effortlessly. He extended his hand to reclaim the spear. "I assume you do not understand me."

"Yes, I do. I'd like my spear back." When she relinquished it, he examined the barbed tip carefully. Satisfied, he turned his attention to her. Varian found those proud clear eyes very disconcerting, and she was glad of the shield of Discipline. "These take time to forge, and you might have damaged the barbs. You don't look as if you had that much strength in you."

Varian shrugged diffidently. So Bakkun and the others had progressed beyond tree limbs as weapons.

"I'm not considered particularly strong," she said, knowing that such a first impression might be valuable. "Are you one of the survivors of the *ARCT-10*'s exploratory group? Frankly, after a quick pass over this world, we didn't expect to find anyone alive. Your appearance . . . and competence . . . are a surprise."

"So is yours!" There was a faint hint of wry amusement and a reticence in his voice. "I am called Aygar."

"And I, Rianav," she said, quickly scrambling her name. "Why didn't your group remain at the expedition's site of record?"

His look was definitely quizzical. "Why didn't you home in on *our* beacon?"

"Your beacon? Oh, you've erected one at the northeast camp?" Varian was both disappointed at this intelligence and surprised, though she kept her assumed role and pretended mild criticism.

"Camp?" He was overtly derisive, but his manner turned wary. "You are from a spaceship?"

"Of course. We picked up a distress call from the system's satellite beacon. Naturally we are obliged to answer and investigate. Are you one of the *ARCT-10*'s original exploratory group?"

"Hardly. They were abandoned without explanation and with insufficient supplies to defend themselves." Indignation and rancor flickered in his eyes. His body tensed.

So that was the story the mutineers had spread. At least it was partially based on fact.

"You seem to have adapted to this planet with commendable success," Varian remarked, wondering what else she could get him to reveal, and perhaps estimate how long they'd slept. Would he be the first generation?

"You are too kind," he replied.

"My benevolence has a limit, young man. I am on my way to the secondary camp mentioned in the final report recorded on the beacon. Are any of the original expedition still living?"

Varian was trying to guess whose son he might be. Or grandson, she added bleakly. She opted for Bakkun and Berru, since they were the only heavy-worlders with light eyes. Aygar's were a clear, bright, shrewd green. His features were finer than could be expected from either Tardma or Divisti.

"One has survived," he said in an insolent drawl.

"One of the children from the original landing party?" Could she goad him into revealing more about the mutineers' interpretation of abandonment?

"Children?" Aygar was surprised. "There were no children on the original expedition!"

"According to the beacon," she replied, sowing what she hoped would be fertile seeds of doubt, "three children were included; Bonnard was the boy, and the two girls are named as Terilla and Cleiti, all in their second decade."

"There were no children. Only six adults. Abandoned by the *ARCT-10*." He spoke with the ring of truth in his voice, a truth which she knew to be false no matter how keenly he believed it.

"Discrepancies are not generally committed to satellite beacons. The message clearly read nineteen in the landing party, not six," she said, permitting both irritation and surprise to tinge her voice. "What're your leaders' names?"

"Now? Or then?" He covered his chagrin with anger.

"Either."

"Paskutti and Bakkun who was my grandsire."

"Paskutti? Bakkun? Those are not the leaders of record. This is all very strange. You mentioned one survivor of the original group?"

"Tanegli, but he is failing," and that frailty was anathema to Aygar's youthful strength, "so his passing will occur in the near future."

"Tanegli? What of Kai, Varian? The physician, Lunzie, the chemist Trizein."

Aygar's face was closed. "I've never heard those names. Six survived the stampede which overran the original camp!"

"Stampede?"

Aygar gestured irritably toward the far distant herbivores. "They panic easily, and panicked on the day my grandsire and the other five nearly died." He grounded his spear and straightened in pride. "Had they not had the strength of three men, they would not have outrun the herd that day!"

"Stampede?" Varian looked at the peaceful grazers as if assessing their potential. "Yes, well, I can imagine that a mass of them in hysterical flight might short even a large force field. And that certainly explains why only stubs of the plastic supports remain at the original site. Where are you now located? At the secondary camp?"

"No," he said and took the largest of his two knives with which he proceeded to hack at the softer belly hide of the dead beast. He had to use both hands and great effort to penetrate the thick tissue. "Once the power for the force field was exhausted," he continued, spacing his words between grunts as he made incisions, "the night creatures attacked. We live in caves, near the iron workings. We live on the flesh of animals that we trap or kill in chase," he went on with cold vehemence. "We live and we die. This is our world now. You arrive too late to be any use to us. Go!"

"Keep a polite tongue in your head, young man, when

speaking to me," Varian said in a colder voice, summoning Discipline to every fiber of her body.

He rose, tossing down the bloody hunk of meat he had just carved. His eyes narrowed at the tone she had used, but she preferred to precipitate an incident while she was at full Discipline, and when he had just concluded a wearying run.

"We no longer recognize the authority of those who abandoned us to this savage world."

"This world, Ireta, belongs to the Federated Sentient Planets, young man and you cannot—"

He made his move, goaded, as she had hoped, by her insufferable attitude. As she had expected, he came for her in a frontal attack, secure in his advantage of height and strength; swinging one arm wide, hand open, aimed to connect with the side of her head and knock her senseless. Had she not had the training of Discipline, she would probably have been crushed against fang-face, possibly skewered on a finely sharp claw. As it was, she caught his hand, used his forward momentum against him and threw him heavily to the ground.

Skilled in rough-and-tumble fighting he was up in a moment, but it was clear that his confidence as well as his body had been badly shaken by that fall. She didn't want to humiliate him for he was an intelligent, extremely attractive man who believed what he said about abandonment. But, unless she could prove herself superior to him, she would jeopardize the scheme she had in mind. And she must remember that her effectiveness now would protect Kai, Lunzie, and the sleepers in the space shuttle.

She ignored his feint to the right, but she was surprised as he launched himself into the air in an attempt to tackle her about the legs. Her reflexes were far quicker than his. She was above him as he dove and came down on his back, digging her fingers to the necessary nerve point through almost impenetrably hard muscles while she locked her other arm under his chin, forcing his head back. He tried to roll with her, but she caught her legs under his, forcing them with Discipline strength so far apart that a gasp of pain was wrung from him. She heard his ill-used garment split.

"In most cultures which settle differences by physical combat," she said in an even voice that did not indicate the strain under which she labored, "two falls out of three—and I assure you there would be a third for you—generally result in victory for the quicker opponent. I use the term 'quicker' because that is basically one of the advantages I have over you: my training in hand-to-hand combat was conducted by masters of the martial arts. I will of course never mention this incident to anyone. I also cannot allow you to persist in your aggression toward me or any other member of my mission, which has been sent to discover the whereabouts of the previous expedition and/or its survivors. I can assure you that the policy of the FSP and EEC allows generous terms to people in your position. Will you accept release in good faith, or will I be forced to turn your head just that fraction more which will crack the first and second vertebrae?"

She felt him swallow in an agony not purely physical.

"Do you accept?"

"You win!" The reluctant admission came through gritted teeth.

"I don't *win* anything." She made due note of his phraseology—"you win" not "I accept," and respected him. Slowly she released her grip on his legs, before loosening the neck lock and the nerve pinch. A tiny, additional squeeze on the nerve as she released her fingers insured her time to rise and move a suitable distance from him in case combat honor was no longer a principle in his adaptation.

He rose slowly, swallowing against a dry and strained throat. He made no move to massage the nerve pinch although his arm hung limply and ought to be painful. He also ignored his damaged clothing. She kept her eyes on his face, now somewhat obscured by the swarms of blooding insects whizzing about them and the carcass. He drew in deep breaths, his face expressionless, and she could easily understand her perturbation. The man was muscled, not as a heavy-worlder against the constant pull of gravity, but there couldn't be a milligram of unnecessary flesh on him: he was truly one of the most beautiful men in form and face that she had ever seen. She regretted having had to best him with the unfair advantage of her Discipline. Raised by heavy-worlder notions, there would be no forgiveness in him, for her. Nor could she ever explain why she had been able to throw him.

"Your physical strength was unexpected, Rianav."

"I have often found it so, Aygar, although I dislike having to resort to such exhibitions. I am a reasonable person, for reason tends to secure a more lasting outcome than a show of physical force."

"Reason? And honor?" He gave a dry sour laugh. "To have abandoned a small geological group on a savage world."

Varian opened her hands in a gesture of regret. "It is a risk of the Service which we all—"

"I did not. I had no option."

"In justice, you have the right to be bitter. You are the innocent victim of circumstances beyond ordinary control. The *ARCT-10*, the vessel which landed the Iretan expedition, is still missing."

"Missing? For forty-three years?" His contempt was obvious. "Were you looking for it when you found this beacon of yours?"

"Not exactly, but our code requires that we respond to your distress call."

"Not mine. My grandparents—"

"The call was heard and our ship has responded, *whoever* made the original signal."

"I'm supposed to be grateful for that?" He resumed his slicing of meat from the ribs of the monster, discarding the initial hunk, which was already crawling with winged vermin. Despite Discipline, Varian found herself revolted by his activity. "Forty-three years to answer a distress call? Mighty efficient organization, yours. Well, we've survived and we'll continue to. We don't need your help—now."

"Possibly. How many are you after two generations?" With such a small gene pool, she wondered if they were already inbred.

He laughed, as if he sensed her thought. "We have bred carefully, Rianav, and have made the most of our—how would *you* term it, inadvertent plantation?"

"Ireta is not on the colonial list. We checked that immediately for we are under no compunction to aid a colony which can't fend for itself." Her Discipline must be dropping, Varian thought, from the sharpness with which she answered him. Gaber's rumormongering had lasted unto the second generation.

"To be sure," he said, angry sarcasm masking as courtesy. "So, what are your plans now, honorable Rianav!"

She gave him a long look, playing her role as rescuer to the hilt. "Instructions, rather. I shall return to our base with my report on your presence."

"No need to concern yourself with me."

"How can you possibly transport all that . . ."

"We've learned a trick or two," and Varian was certain that his smile was faintly superior.

"May I have the coordinates of your present location?"

His grin was more amused than insolent but the mockery was in his reply.

"Run at a good steady pace to your right, through the first hills, turn right up the ravine, but mind the river snakes. Continue along the river course to the first falls, take the easiest route up the cliff—it's pretty well marked by now, and follow the line of limestone—you do know limestone from granite, I assume? The valley widens. You'll know when you've reached us by the cultivated fields." There was pure malice in his grin now. "Yes, we find that vegetables, fruits, and grains are required to maintain a balanced diet, even if we can't process our food." He had been gouging past the ribs of the dead beast and now suddenly, his arms dripping with blood, he held up a huge dark brownish red lump. "And this, the liver of the thunder lizard, is the most nutritious meat available."

"Do you mean to tell me that you slaughtered that creature just for its liver?" Her xenob training broke through her elected role.

"We do not kill indiscriminately, Rianav: we kill to survive." Coldly he turned back to his task, leaning partly inside the ribs to reach more of the choice liver.

"The distinction is, of course, valid. However, we have no knowledge of the dangers of walking about this land of yours. Is the secondary camp of record far from your present location?"

"No." He had removed the curious tube from his back. From the tube he pulled a tight roll of what appeared to Varian to be synthesized fabric, light, waterproof, and durable enough to have lasted forty-three years. He spread the fabric with a practiced flip on the ground, piling the choice chunks of meat and covering them quickly, folding over the edges of the fabric to prevent insects from attaching themselves to the meat. "I'll meet you there in three days' time."

"Will it take that long to return to your base?" Varian could not keep the astonishment from her voice.

"Not at all," he said, severing more choice morsels. As he added these to the pack and covered them, he glanced skyward. Varian followed his gaze and saw that the carrion fliers were massing in their circles. She also noticed the three giffs to one side of the others and wondered if Aygar did. "We have to be quick after a kill. Or be mistaken for the corpse by those. No, I shall be in my home before nightfall, but my fellow exiles must be told of this happy reestablishment of contact with other worlds."

He had what Varian judged to be fifty or sixty kilos of meat. Lashing the tube to the base of the meat, he deftly added straps, padded where they would cross his shoulders, and made a portable package. One eye on the scavengers, he now rinsed his arms from a water bottle, then covered them with mud, scooped at a distance from the slaughtering ground. Then he swung the pack to his back, settling the pads properly. He stared at her so intently that a faint stirring of alarm prompted her next action.

From a pouch on her upper arm, she took out the dark plastic box in which she once carried stimtabs. He could see that she had something in her hand but not what. She pretended to depress a switch with her thumb, holding her hand close to her mouth.

"Unit Three to Base. Unit Three to Base." She made a disapproving noise. "Recorder's on. They've all left the encampment!" She gave Aygar an angry glance. "Base, I have made contact with survivors, coordinates 87.58 by 72.33. Returning to Base. Over." She operated a thumb switch again and then replaced the box in her pocket. "Leaving for base at once. They'll hear about this. In three days then, Aygar, and good luck!" She swung away from him, walking rapidly toward the sled.

From the corner of her eye, she saw him set off at a steady jog and sighed in relief. For a moment, it seemed to her as if he might do something. A glance at the sky showed her that Aygar's departure might have been a signal and she a negligible danger, for the scavengers were backwinging to land. Out of the grasses other creatures slunk toward the feast. She was relieved to be so close to the sled but only felt completely safe when she had fastened the canopy overhead.

She guided into the clouds to head southwest. She caught sight of him again and marveled that he could run so easily, burdened as he was and after the exhausting chase. There might be something to say for implantation after all if the process resulted in such superbly fit people.

She wished she had a working wrist unit to tell Lunzie about the survival of the mutineers as well as the slanted account passed down to their descendants. She wished she could have figured out a way to ask Aygar if his people had encountered the creature that had attacked Kai, and if they knew what could be used to cure him. On the other hand, she now knew that the second camp had been abandoned. She debated the wisdom of continuing to it since it would be unlikely she'd find anything of value to her. Certainly none of the equipment Lunzie needed. Of course, if Kai were not considerably improved, and Varian refused to consider the worst, she had a good reason for approaching Aygar again today. Surely his people must have encountered the leech-creatures and might even have developed an antidote for the toxemia. She could say that another member of her landing party had been attacked—which was true enough anyhow. She grimaced at the comunit on her console and suddenly realized that the device was operative, even if there was nowhere to communicate to. But, Varian told herself cheerfully, there were four other sleds with equally undamaged comunits. They could wake Portegin, have him utilize what matrix slabs were necessary from one or two of the sleds and repair the shuttle's smashed unit, at least for intership communications. That would give them two, maybe three sleds available for use. It might not be enough to reach a passing EEC ship outside the stellar system, but certainly they'd be able to reach the Thek again. Or the Ryxi.

Varian grimaced at the thought of having to appeal for help to the Ryxi: how they would flaunt that news about! More vital, she didn't want the Ryxi to know more about the giffs than they already did.

Kai *had* to recover. After the mutiny of the six heavy-worlders, their situation had been difficult at best, desperate at the worst. They had emerged from cold sleep in a very much improved position, despite Kai's injury. The mutineers had had their own problems on Ireta, and Varian felt that her initial contact with the younger generation had established a position of undeniable superiority. Or had she? Something about Aygar's manner toward the end of their encounter bothered her. That's why she had instinctively invented a "contact" with a "base."

She could feel the laxness of her muscles as Discipline eased. She ate the rest of the fruit, inadequate though it was to replenish her energies. Why hadn't she thought to take a pepper with her, she wondered peevishly. Probably, she amended her own forgetfulness, because the last peppers had been used to overcome delayed shock after escaping the stampede of the herbivores.

She smiled as she recalled Aygar's legend of that incident. Did he know how silly it was for *six* people to be deliberately abandoned to form a colony? He didn't know the first thing about genetics. Well, yes, he must if he'd mentioned breeding.

It was fatigue more than curiosity that made Varian decide to continue on to the old camp. She'd be safe there and able to snatch an hour's sleep before the return journey. She was so nearly there anyhow, she might just as well have a look.

4

THE rain, combined with a dismal heat mist, made the site more desolate than she remembered it. She'd spotted a stand of fruit trees on the final leg of her journey and, hovering the sled, had picked the upper branches free of succulent ripe yellow globes. Consequently she felt less weary when she glided the sled to land on the square of the old secondary camp. And it did look ancient.

The original dome, which would have been comfortable

for two people, was missing but the space it had occupied was an ovoid barren of all growth in the center of an octagon of long stone buildings. Tiny plants now grew in cavities where windblown dirt had accumulated. The buildings had been so well built that Varian wondered why the mutineers had moved. Of course, just then the rain kept the insects away, but there would be a superb panorama of the surrounding plains, not that she supposed the heavy-worlders had indulged themselves that way. Most of the visible buttes supported crowns of trees, heavily vined, but the area adjacent to the octagon had been cleared several meters on all sides and covered with a concrete which, to be sure, was now cracking as the more tenacious vines reclaimed their customary dominion. Beyond that apron was lush growth, but the buildings—she couldn't call them homes or houses because of their forbidding aspect—claimed her attention first.

As Varian approached the nearest, she saw that the windows had been glazed yet when she rubbed away grime, she could barely see through the dense and irregular glass. When her eyes had compensated for the gloom, she could see the interior had been stripped of everything but the stone shelving set into the corners of each room. The only door was made of stout wooden panels, coated with some glossy substance which obviously protected the wood against the depredations of Ireta's insect life. Set above the handle of the locked door were four metal tumblers, coded to some pattern, for the handle would not move at her touch although the tumblers rolled easily under her thumb. A cursory examination of the other seven buildings told her they were identical: four rooms, two on either side of an entry hall. The windows were too narrow for any but a young child to climb in or out of. With such stoutly built dwellings, why had they moved? There was plenty of room for expansion on the bluff top.

She went beyond the octagon and saw outbuildings, two with chimneys well blackened even after decades of scouring

rain. One proved to be a forge and marks on the concrete behind it indicated the complete removal of another installation,
as well as the squat thick form of a kiln. What power would
they have used for the forge? Water? Up here? No, but there
was no shortage of wind! She had become so accustomed to
the buffeting of the almost incessant breezes that blew from
moderate to gale force through the course of every Iretan day,
that she'd almost missed the most obvious and easiest power
source.

Paskutti had not been idly bragging when he'd said that he
and his band could survive nicely on Ireta. If Aygar was to be
believed, and the barbed steel tip of his lance gave fair evidence of metal craftsmanship, they didn't need the Federated
Sentient Planets. Maybe not the FSP, thought Varian, kicking
at the mud, but they'd need a larger gene pool or their community risked dangerous inbreeding that could wipe out all they
had achieved.

She should reserve her sympathy for her own problem—
Kai's restoration—and she wasn't getting any help on the bleak
butte. But she couldn't resist the urge to peer into the buildings set apart from the living quarters. They might provide
her with a measure of information on the quality of life
the mutineers had established for themselves. With metal-
working, glass manufacture, windpower, and pottery, they'd
achieved a commendable basic standard. One long building,
downslope and nearer the luxuriant growth, attracted her interest since it was so obviously set apart from the industrial
sites. The door faced the brush and Varian paused, puzzled. Despite the wild profusion of lush vegetation, something about
the area struck her as odd. Then she realized that the fruiting
trees were placed at regular intervals, and each row comprised
different types. Moving closer, she saw metal stakes holding
up another form of vine from which thick pods hung: a series
of thorny bushes bore huge red berries, then another stand of
trees and beyond the trees, against a low retaining wall were
smaller plants, weed vines choking them and, on the wall,

tucked into niches as if by design, a curious feathery purple moss.

Purple was not her favorite shade after the mold, Varian realized, even as she had to admit that she was looking at an overgrown garden. She turned then to the long hut and observed what she had failed to notice at first—it had no windows. A storehouse for the garden's produce? Yes, for now that she was closer, she could see the carved panels in the door. Vines, trees, and plants were each so carefully delineated on that door that even someone with little botanical knowledge would be able to identify the specimens once the carvings had been memorized.

What had Aygar said? They had learned a long time ago to balance their diet? Varian recognized the carotene-rich grass from the rift valley that the giffs as well as Tyrannosaurus rex had needed. Turning constantly to check against the door's carvings, Varian found each of the plants growing in rows in the neglected garden. Divisti, the expedition's botanist, must have been responsible for that catalog of Ireta's edible flora.

Varian pushed her way through the overgrowth, gathering fruits which she recognized, until she reached the vine with pods. One split with ripe readiness as she touched it, exposing large pale green beans. The bean had a wholesome smell. She bit, taking the smallest possible morsel to roll about in her mouth, tensing to spit out an unwelcome flavor. But the taste was mealy, the flesh of the bean crisp, but so satisfying that she consumed the contents of the entire pod greedily. She ate as she gathered the beans, as much as her arms could hold. Then she strode back to the sled, depositing her harvest. She had wheeled back toward the garden when she exclaimed in exasperation. Climbing into the sled, she guided it to the garden.

As she picked and plucked, she was careful to take samples from each row of Divisti's garden, including the leaves or tufts of the various wall plants. She wondered if Divisti had ever thought her garden would one day succor those the heavy-world botanist had once tried to kill. At the foot of the garden, held back by thick staves, Varian came at last to a fine stand of the thick-fuzzy leaves that the giffs had brought her for Kai's wounds.

"So, the bloodsucker got to you, too, huh?" Varian was subtly pleased that one denizen of this planet caused the heavy-worlders more pain than pleasure.

When the sled was as full as possible, she checked once more that she had a sample of each variety carved on the door of the storage barn. Elated by the unexpected dividend, she set a straight course for the giff palisades, cutting due south and speeded on her way by a smart tail wind.

She was astonished, then, no more than five minutes in the air, to see the recognizable figure of Aygar trotting along a twisting ravine.

Two thoughts occurred to her at once, and she diverted the sled to come up behind him.

"Aygar, I must speak with you," she said, and sighting a ledge beyond him, settled the air sled, waiting until he came up to her before she slid down to his level. "I've been trying to find you. Base reported to me. One of our party has been attacked by some—some—thing . . ."

"Which sucks blood?" he asked quickly.

"You know it?"

"We call them fringes."

"Fringes?" Varian masked her shock with an understandable curiosity. Surely those aquatic life-forms that Terilla had named "fringes" had not been amphibious. She shuddered with revulsion.

"They come in a variety of sizes," Aygar went on, "are warmth seekers and fasten onto their prey, preferably lying on it, otherwise enveloping it between their two halves—"

"Their what?"

"I don't know what your training is, Rianav, but surely you have seen strange life-forms before Ireta." Aygar knelt, taking one of his knives to draw a fringe in the dust. "They move by collapsing the parallelograms of the side: they have two digits here and here, and can use them to clasp their envelope tightly about the victim, if it is alive. If not, they settle on it, and eat away!" He shrugged with indifference. "One can usually smell them coming but, of course, you haven't been here long enough to know, have you?"

"Two days," Varian found herself answering far more casually than she felt because, again, that curious reticence held her: a reticence evidently not stemming from Discipline. "But, if you know about these fringe things, you know how to treat them?"

"The victim's still alive?" This gave Aygar some surprise.

"Yes, but unconscious and delirious, bleeding profusely from the worst of the . . . puncture wounds."

"I thought exploratory teams were equipped with belts to protect them from—"

"I don't know whether his belt was activated or not," said Varian severely in a tone that implied she intended to find out if any basic precaution had been neglected.

"If he doesn't die in the first few hours, then the punctures reached no vital areas and he'll survive. If you're near the original campsite, find a squat thick-trunked plant with leaves like this: they are covered with a soft down or fuzz." He neatly sketched the leaf with which the giffs had supplied them. "Gather the thickest ones, squeeze them directly over the punctures and keep repeating the treatment until the wounds seal."

"I'm told he's running a very high fever . . ."

"Use an antipyretic, of course. When that didn't reduce the fever, one of the original members of our group used a parasitic purple moss which usually grows on the north side of the green plum or yellow-juice melon trees. There ought to be some nearby. Boil the moss, let it steep, and get it down the man's throat. Tastes vile but it will reduce fever."

Aygar rose, shifted the burden of meat on his shoulders and started off.

"End of interview," Varian murmured to herself. She was too relieved by the information he'd given her to take offense at his curt departure or his lack of real surprise at seeing her again so soon the same day.

She scrambled up the side of the ravine and back into the safety of the sled as fast as if a fringe had been homing in on her blood warmth.

Terilla's fringes! The same aquatic life-form that the giffs took care to avoid when caught in their grass nets. And if the creature was basically amphibious, no wonder it had lasted a long time after the other water-breathers had died. But that had been a small creature, like an almost transparent kerchief. Yet Varian recalled all too vividly the voracity with which the sea fringes had flung themselves after the reflection of the sled on the water. She stared at her hand a moment as if she could imagine what that same fringe could do, folding itself into a sucking envelope . . .

She shook her head: she was suffering the depression and enervation of the post-Discipline state. She reached for more of the pods and munched slowly at the beans: they were even more satisfying than the sweet fruit.

Purple moss, huh? That same purple moss that had grown in Divisti's wall, no doubt. She wondered if she'd taken enough, but at least she knew what to harvest.

The trip was exceptionally profitable though one discovery displeased her a great deal: forty-three years was a long time for *ARCT-10* to have remained missing. And not long enough for a small sea creature to develop into something large enough to attack a man. To be sure, the larger species might have existed on Ireta when the expedition had first landed; they'd barely explored the continental basement shield area before the mutiny.

Varian shuddered again, reminding herself that one reason for her revulsion of the fringes must in part stem from her experience with the blood-sucking Galormis—by day so friendly, by night deadly.

The rain cleared and the omnipresent mists dispersed as the setting sun took a final look at the world it had spawned. The giffs were behind and above her, their golden selves glorious against the muted haze of the western twilight. She hadn't noticed them when she was on the compound bluff, nor when she had intercepted Aygar. Nonetheless she felt they'd made the entire journey discreetly within sight of her.

Krims! but she was tired. Now, if she could keep her wits about her, and the light held long enough to land inside the cave . . . Other giffs whirled up from their vantage points to escort her the last few kilometers, and she was touched by the courtesy, if that's what it was. Had the giffs, as well as Lunzie, worried over her long day's absence?

She made a good landing, considering she was aiming her sled into a dark hole, faintly illuminated on the left by a small campfire. She let the sled down at the far right, bumping just once as she misjudged the uneven stone floor.

"Is Kai improving?" she called as she flipped open the canopy.

"Yes, but we've run out of leaves again," Lunzie said, rising from her position beside Kai's bundled form.

"I've more and food besides. And a helluva lot to tell you."

"Any equipment?"

"No, but I have a specific remedy for that fever." Varian took the purple moss from the piles of food in the sled, offering it to the medic who accepted it skeptically.

"This?" Lunzie smelled it. "Why?"

"Highly recommended by a local resident." Varian grinned wearily at Lunzie's reaction. "Yes, I ran one down. Oh, it's all right. I made out that I was one of a relief team. He's Bakkun's grandson." She offered the information with a huge grin, as if it were the best joke in the galaxy.

Lunzie fingered the moss for a few more seconds before she searched Varian's face. "Grandson!"

"Yes, we cold-slept forty-three years."

"Well, it's not much longer than I'd estimated," Lunzie

said, and Varian was deflated by the medic's calm acceptance. "What else have you here?" Lunzie peered at the dark mounds in the sled.

"Everything's edible, and this sort of pod bean tastes better than the fruit. Just how *is* Kai?" she asked, struggling out of the sled and trying not to stagger too much as she crossed to Kai's supine body. "Has he recovered consciousness yet?" She all but collapsed beside him.

"No, but the fever is down a little. Hold still a moment," Lunzie said. Before Varian realized what the medic was doing, she felt the spray icily stinging her arm.

"You shouldn't waste it. I've so much . . ."

"It's no waste," Lunzie was saying, her voice getting farther away as consciousness left Varian. "You can't see yourself but you're drained white. Did you use Discipline all day long?"

5

VARIAN came awake by degrees: the first one being her awareness of voices in low earnest conversation, either too far from her for the individual words to be audible or too soft, to keep from rousing her. She thought to get up, but it proved difficult to assemble the energy. Could she have been in cold sleep again? No! She was resting, rather comfortably, on a bed of springy boughs, not the flat plasfloor of the space shuttle or the dust of the cave. She felt an occasional breeze waft across her face and exposed hands.

She didn't feel so much tired as disinterested. Yet, in the

back of her mind, a spark started with the observation: she had so much to tell Lunzie. Sneaky of her to knock Varian out like that.

She continued to listen and realized that two men were speaking. Then Kai was better! It was good to hear him. But he wouldn't be well enough in three days' time to join her against Aygar. They'd better wake Portegin and get the technician functioning. No way was she meeting Aygar, and whoever accompanied him, in three days' time without strong support. And if she was this tired after a day's use of Discipline, would she recover sufficiently in three to draw on that inner reserve again?

What was it about Aygar's manner that bothered her? The expression in his eyes had been wary, speculative, evaluating, not at all the reaction she might have expected from a man making first contact with off-world visitors! That was it! He had been expecting someone. Not her. And not someone who could best him in personal combat.

Varian became conscious of a rich, nutty smell. Her stomach began to rumble and her mouth to salivate. She stirred restlessly, keenly aware that she was very hungry.

"I told you that the stew would get to her," Lunzie said suddenly. Varian opened her eyes.

Lunzie, Triv, and Kai made a semicircle on one side of the crude hearth, complete now with a spit and crane from which a pail hung.

Varian propped herself up on one elbow. "Whatever it is, I'm starving."

"Lunzie mixed a bit of everything you brought in, and it turned out very tasty indeed," Triv said, filling a smoke-hardened fruit shell with the mixture. He presented this to Varian and, with a flourish, added a rudely carved wooden spoon.

"The amenities of home have improved." Varian made an appreciative chuckle. "How's Kai?" she asked in a quieter tone. Although Kai was propped up, he was far too passive for her liking.

"We started to revive Portegin," Triv said, squatting beside Varian so his body shielded her from those at the fire. "Kai's still feverish. Says some kind of giant fringe attacked him. He's not recovering as well as Lunzie would like," he said in a quick whisper, then raised his voice to a normal level. "Kai thinks that once we have the matrix slabs from the other sleds, we can rig communications, probably patch most of what Paskutti smashed."

"I was hoping that we could, Triv." Varian tasted the stew and then began to devour it as fast as she could. "This is delicious!" It was natural then for her to get up and join the two at the fire, and natural for her to pause by Kai before refilling her bowl. His color and the lassitude were alarming, and the smile he gave her was strained. "You look much better than when I last saw you."

Kai gave a derisive snort. "I can't have looked much worse than I feel now."

"Why?" Varian went for a light touch. "Didn't you like the purple moss Divisti grew just to cure your fever?"

Kai grimaced in such disgust that the others laughed.

"It makes a very effective antipyretic." Lunzie broke off with a wry grin. "I wonder what Divisti's reaction would be if she knew how much it was going to help *us*." Then she turned to Varian, with no humor in her gaze. "You did say, last night, that we'd cold-slept forty-three years?"

"I'd have told the rest of my news if I hadn't been so rudely interrupted," she said with a sour glance at Lunzie who only grinned back.

"You did fall asleep at a crucial point," the medic said. "*Are* any of the mutineers still alive?"

"Only one. Tanegli."

"You met him?" Kai asked.

"No. I met a sturdy young man named Aygar. An accomplished young fellow who was busy killing a fang-face with a barbed metal spear."

Kai made an expression of utter disgust. "Accomplished?"

"His strategy was good," said Varian, seeing no point in going into needlessly distressing detail.

"Do you know if they're in the secondary camp?"

"They abandoned that for a more suitable site."

"Where was Divisti's garden then?" Kai's tone was querulous.

"I'll start from the beginning—"

"When you've finished that second bowl," Lunzie said firmly.

Varian ate with indecorous haste and pleasure, glad of the opportunity to organize her thoughts. Feeling revitalized as she scraped up the last of the tasty stew, she began her account of the previous day's incidents with the unexpected escort of the giffs.

The listeners, and gradually Portegin became aware enough to listen, too, did not interrupt with questions, letting her narrative flow. Lunzie's eyes had a malicious sparkle as Varian gave a very brief account of overpowering the young Aygar, adding that he'd just finished a rather exhausting race to outdistance an enraged fang-face. Varian noticed that Kai frowned over that show of strength. Well, perhaps she should have restrained her actions there but she sincerely doubted she'd ever catch Aygar unawares again, or best him. All four listeners commended her for posing as a representative of a new expedition in search of the first. The only hazard to that blatant lie would be a confrontation with Tanegli.

"But he's reported to be frail and not expected to live much longer," Varian said.

"Let us devoutly hope he is not included in the party you meet then." Lunzie brought her brows together. "What I do not understand is why he, one of the oldest of the heavyworlders, has survived when the younger ones, like Bakkun and Berru, are dead."

"How long would their heavy-gravity advantage last on a light world?" Triv asked.

"Unless they found some way to simulate heavy-gravity conditions and exercise under them—"

"Well, they would have had to manhandle all the stone they built with up to the bluff," Varian said, "and there were eight large buildings plus six or seven smaller ones, with slate for roofs."

"That would have helped," but Lunzie's tone was hesitant with doubt.

"If they all indulged in 'chase-the-fang-face-till-it-bled-to-death,'" Varian said with considerable acrimony in her voice, "they didn't dare get fat."

"Obviously, their descendants have no such problem, and inherited physiques capable of considerable muscular development," Lunzie continued. "Since this Aygar depended on physical endurance to outrun an enraged predator while it was bleeding to death, and then tried to take you on, Varian, the strength factor is still on their side. I think we'd better attend that meeting in force and in Discipline. Right, Kai?"

"I'll be with you, Varian!"

Even as Varian nodded agreement, her eyes flicked to Lunzie's and registered the denial the medic would not voice.

"We must have communications, though." Varian glanced toward Portegin, who was looking more alert now.

"I'm sure I can rig something, especially if the sled units are operative. With that many matrices available, I might even fix what Paskutti smashed in the shuttle—at least for planetary use."

"I wish we had some kind of long-distance defensive tool," Varian said, scratching her ear. "There was something in Aygar's manner that worries me, but I can't figure what!"

"What sort of weapons did he carry?" asked Portegin.

Varian described the crossbow and Portegin laughed. "We can do better than that if Lunzie has any anesthetic left?"

"As a matter of fact, I do," Lunzie said, a trifle surprised.

"Not much," she cautioned, holding up her hand, "but enough to provide for a few medicated bolts."

"Good, then all I need is some hardwood and I can contrive a dart gun that would immobilize your crossbow user before he could cock it."

"So long as we get to shoot first," Varian said.

"You'd better!" Lunzie's expression was as uncompromising as her tone.

"I don't *want* to shoot anyone," Varian said. "Cold sleep didn't change my moral values."

"No, just drastically changed our circumstances. We're five . . ." and Lunzie's finger did an arc including them all, "against I haven't figured out how many progeny in two generations from six parents. We had few advantages over the heavy-worlders to begin with, and have fewer now that they're completely ensconced in terrain we haven't seen. They're very well adapted to the environment." She nodded at Kai. "You gained an advantage yesterday, Varian. We've got to maintain it, such as it is, no matter what we have to do to keep it. We can't keep in constant Discipline. Above all, we have to protect the sleepers!" Her arm swung back toward the shuttle.

"I'm consoled by the fact that the giffs take that on themselves," Kai said.

"A point, but only when none of us can assume that responsibility." Lunzie turned back to Varian. "Aygar gave you no indication how many people are in the new settlement, or why they left the old?"

"He was as wary of me as I was of him . . . once we agreed not to fight anymore. But there were eight buildings in the camp they had abandoned, and the dome had evidently gone with them, for there was a circle where it had stood in the center of the octagon the other buildings formed. Each house had four rooms. And except for built-in stone shelving, they were empty."

"Four times eight gives thirty-two which tells us nothing, really," said Lunzie. "Tardma might have been able to produce two, maybe three children; she was the oldest. Berru and Divisti could have born a child a year easily for twenty or so, if they were forced to. I hazard they alternated paternity and kept track of whose was whose, to have as wide a gene pool as possible—"

"They'd still be in trouble by the third or fourth generation when recessive—"

"As I recall their medical records," Lunzie gently interrupted Kai, "Bakkun, Berru, and Divisti came from different genetic stock than the other three, who were from Modrem in the Cluster. There's also a freak genetic twist that prevents recessives from surviving on heavy-world planets. The babies are either shipped offworld or . . ." Lunzie sighed, continuing briskly. "So that six are, were, the finest physical specimens, with nary a blurred chromosome for three or four generations back of adjustment to heavy-gravity worlds. Prime breeders."

"Aygar resembles Berru," Varian said for no reason at all except the long thoughtful pause had to be broken.

"Then I'd be more careful than ever with that young man. Neither Berru or Bakkun was short of brains."

"Which is why I never figured they'd join Paskutti," Triv remarked. "How could they have fallen for Gaber's rumor that we were planted."

"But we have been," Varian said, unable to contain laughter that bubbled up in spite of her realization of the incredible odds against them. "At least until *ARCT-10* remembers they left us here. Kai, did Tor say anything to you on your way to the compound?"

"I was far too busy hanging on to talk. And when we got to the compound, Tor began to search for the core so I went looking for the sleds. I'd just found them when I heard Tor blasting off." He shook his head as he remembered his unworthy thoughts at that moment. "When I got back to the compound, I saw it'd left the power pack with a lifter, and the cavity where it'd found the core."

"It never even waited to see if the sleds were operable?" Portegin asked.

"Well, those sleds are built to withstand tremendous pressures and adverse conditions," Kai replied, temporizing.

Lunzie snorted.

"Then Tor may be back?" asked Portegin.

"I wouldn't count on it, Portegin," Lunzie said. She had been busy at the hearth and now brought a filled shell to Kai. "I know it tastes vile but it brought your temperature down. Drink up."

"It smells vile, too," Kai said, regarding the purple liquid with distaste.

"Which means it does you more good," said Varian with a laugh.

Kai drank it all in one gulp. His violent shudder was no affectation and to take the taste away, he quickly sucked at the slice of fruit Lunzie handed him.

Varian covered her smile. Kai was becoming dependent on natural foods despite his aversion to them. She was a bit startled to realize that Lunzie was advancing on her with a stern air. The medic's fingers closed on the younger woman's wrist, timing pulse rate.

"I'd prefer it, Varian, if you could take a full day's rest after your exertions—"

"We both know I can't, Lunzie. Triv and I have got to retrieve the other sleds."

"I could go along and dismantle what we need," Portegin suggested.

"You're not ready for that sort of exertion yet, my friend," Lunzie said.

"I'd rest easier if we got all the sleds here."

"Don't see any problem in that, Kai." Triv rose to his feet and extending a hand pulled Varian to hers. "That four-man sled will easily take the other two, lashed into the cargo bed. All Varian'll have to do is watch out for the fringes."

"You can *smell* them coming," Kai said.

"That's why Varian has to come along," Triv said. "I can't smell anything but Ireta yet."

"From which direction did it attack you, Kai?" Varian asked.

"Behind." Kai grimaced. "I'd just locked the power pack into position and turned when it rushed me. I thought it was just a larger dose of Ireta's usual stink."

"Wait a minute," Lunzie called as Triv and Varian moved toward the sled. She rummaged under the stores and then held both hands high. From one hung a thick coil of rope, from the other what could only be a force-field unit and, more miraculous still, a wrist comunit.

"Where did you find those?" Varian leaped over the fire in her eagerness to examine the prizes.

Lunzie permitted herself a grin at the effect of her treasure trove.

"Bonnard had the unit and the forcebelt on. Remember the mutineers never caught him so he had all his gear. You wear the forcebelt, Varian. I doubt the fringe would suck electrical impulses for long. The rope," which she tossed to Triv, "I synthesized out of our very plentiful vine."

Varian buckled the forcebelt on and felt reassured by its weight about her waist. Lunzie strapped on the wrist unit.

"Now, you can keep me informed. Time's a'wasting." Lunzie gave Varian an encouraging grin.

"Just don't forget the odor, Varian," was Kai's parting advice.

Varian and Triv hauled the sled to the lip of the cave on the far left so the air cushion would not throw dust on the fire and the convalescents. Just as they dropped over the edge, a treacherous draught caught the sled and Varian had all she could do to correct the downward plunge of the craft. Immediately they were surrounded by giffs, heads anxiously pointing seaward, although what the creatures thought they could do to save the sled, Varian didn't know.

"How could they spot that we're in trouble?" Triv cried,

straining backward in his seat, his eyes glued on the water rushing to meet them.

Out of the corner of her eye, Varian caught a flash of thick, suckered tentacle, felt it bang against the sled's rear flange. Then the giffs attacked the appendage, their sharp beaks slicing into the flesh until it fell away.

"By the First Disciple, that was too ruddy close," Triv exclaimed as Varian fought for an upward air passage. They had skimmed the surface of the sea itself.

Circling up and back toward the cliffs at a safer height, they looked down. The tentacled monster, propelling itself after the vague shadow cast by the sled, writhed as the giffs continued to dive until it was forced to submerge.

"I think I better rig some sort of wind indicator at the mouth of the cave," Triv said, more to himself than to her. "If it hadn't been for those giffs . . ."

Varian, aware that she was trembling from reaction, heartily endorsed Triv's idea of a wind indicator. Then they were above the cliffs and suddenly drenched by the torrential rains that had accompanied the treacherous wind squall.

The rains had passed by the time they had reached the first compound. The sun was having its noontime look. Steam rose from drying foliage, which encouraged the myriad biting, sucking, buzzing insects to swarm about the sled as Varian made her landing. Triv was silent beside her, but it wasn't until they were down that she realized why.

"It seems only yesterday . . ." he said in a low voice, staring about the deserted natural amphitheater. His gaze went from the spot where the main dome had been, to Gaber's cartography unit, to where the mutineers' accommodations had been. Then his lips thinned and his eyes hardened.

"The here-and-now is more important, Triv," Varian said.

Because she had the belt, Varian insisted that Triv stay in the safety of the canopied sled while she attacked the vegetation that covered the remaining sleds. She found the stick Kai must have used, its point dug deep into the soft loam. She flailed away at colonies of slugs, worms, and multilegged insects which had made burrows between the sleds: a miniecology that at another time she would have enjoyed examining. When she had the worst of the vegetation cleared, Triv emerged. It took their combined efforts and much sweaty heaving to lift the sleds free of a dirt that had a consistency of hardened adhesive. But then, the sleds had been settled deeply on their edges for over four decades.

"I can't see any breaks in the substructure," Triv said, running knowledgable hands along the side panels.

"This model sled's come out operational from worse battering, not to mention the slime sand on Tenebris V," Varian said, settling herself at the control console of the four-man sled. "Now, for the tricky part." Turning off the forcebelt, she wet her finger to test the prevailing wind. "You stand well to my right and move when the wind shifts. The purple mold'll bubble up like Divisti's moss tea." She retrieved another feather from her breast pocket and saluted Triv with it before she reactivated her forcebelt. "Don't let this stuff touch you, even if it gets me," she added as she used Portegin's seal breaker along the line.

She strained her body away from the console as the mold boiled from its prison. Varian kept the panel in front of her face as the light winds dispersed the frothy fungi. She prodded with her feather at clumps momentarily caught on the lip of the unit. When she was sure that the worst had been blown away, she began to clear the delicate matrix panels, tickling the corners where fungi might hide, and slipping the tip of her feather in and under, back and forth into every part of the console. Then she dusted the control panel.

When she had refitted and sealed the unit, she motioned to Triv to install the power pack.

"I won't take time to dust the other panels now, Triv. Let's strap 'em in the cargo bed and get out of here." Varian felt uneasy. She could smell nothing unusual, even when she turned off the forcebelt to be sure it was not filtering the nauseating sea odor that would herald the arrival of a man-enveloping fringe.

The two sleds fit easily across the cargo section and Triv secured them deftly with stout twists and knots. After two hours of intensive labor, they had accomplished their task. How oddly comforting to know what time had passed again, Varian thought. She frequently consulted the console chrono during their labors. She asked Triv to take the four-man sled, since he was stronger and more rested than she. She maintained a position to his port so that she could see both his hand signals and watch the lashed sleds in case they should shift in adverse winds.

Varian caught Triv's first signal the moment they were fully airborne but she saw no shift in the sleds. Then she saw him pointing upward and noticed the three giffs veering in to take up their escort positions. She'd had such a fright with the marine beast that she hadn't even noticed their out-going escort. She chuckled to herself, wondering if these were the same three, or if they flew escort in rotation. Had their discreet surveillance somehow prevented a fringe attack? She must remember to ask Kai if the giffs had accompanied Tor's craft, though she doubted it at the rate of speed Tor could travel.

Their return journey was without incident. Varian took the small sled in first, reversing at the hover and getting as close to the space shuttle as possible to give Triv sufficient room to maneuver. He parked the four-man sled neatly against the left-hand side of the cave. Lunzie and Portegin, moving with some residual stiffness from his long sleep, helped to unload.

Portegin was for starting his project immediately but Varian cautioned him about the purple fungus. So they positioned a sled with its nose well over the cave edge, secured by rope to the heavier craft so that the wind, now sweeping down over the cliffs, would blow the fungus away from their living quarters.

"I see how to do it, Varian," Portegin told her a bit impatiently.

"Let *him* do it," Lunzie said, unbuckling Varian's forcebelt even as she protested.

"I feel fine."

"That's because you haven't seen yourself," Lunzie replied with a disparaging sniff. "You need as much restorative as I can pump into you."

"I'm tougher than I look," Varian said. She whirled around when she heard Kai laugh.

"If I have to listen to Lunzie, so do you, coleader. Now sit down here, take your medicine, and suffer with me." Kai motioned her to sit beside him.

Varian did so, thinking it was the first time she'd had a chance to look *at* him since his injury. He seemed better, but red blotches still marred his forehead and hands. Lunzie handed them each a shell bowl.

"More moss?" Varian asked, seeing the color of Kai's.

"I've fixed the taste," Lunzie said.

Varian sniffed at hers, expecting the rich smell of the morning's stew. "Krims! What'd you put in this?"

"What's good for you! Drink it." And she turned away to ladle portions for everyone else.

"She *has* fixed the taste," said Kai after a sip and pulled himself to a sitting position. "But only after I made her sample it." Kai grinned. "Whatever she added makes me hungrier than ever. I'd eat anything handed to me and ask for more." He drained his bowl and picked a small red fruit from the pile beside him.

"Kai! You're eating fruit! Fresh fruit!"

"I told you I was hungry enough to eat anything! Even this—this natural stuff!"

By the time the two sleds had been cleared of fungi, with Triv's assistance, Portegin had begun to reassemble the available communications matrices. While Triv and Varian had been away, Portegin had dismantled the damaged shuttle comunit. The slabs were laid out under more of Lunzie's plasfilm to protect them from the dust and debris that the wind blew about the cavern. Portegin shortly began muttering about doing delicate work with a hammer and tongs. He crouched like a troglodyte while Triv suggested that he transfer his operation into the big sled and the protection of the transparent canopy. Lunzie grudgingly surrendered one of her few medical probes to be heated to seal the connections.

"The joints won't last as long as they would if I had the proper equipment but they ought to hold well enough," Portegin announced after thanking Lunzie for her sacrifice.

Triv offered to assist Portegin as the man's small-muscle control showed the effects of long disuse. They rearranged the seats in the larger sled and came across unexpected riches. Tucked between the seat back and the curve of the hull were two stun guns, three forcebelts, and a lift unit for power packs, rolled tightly up in a spare coverall.

"Bonnard, that clever scamp. He must have hidden them, while the mutineers were mauling us in the shuttle," Varian cried, dancing about with the belts and guns held high in jubilation.

"D'you suppose he hid anything else in the other sleds?" Kai asked.

They searched thoroughly, but the food packs which Bonnard had secreted had been penetrated by insect or fungi and were empty.

"Disinfected, these tubes'll make good containers," Lunzie said.

Portegin was to make the last find, the most important one, and that only by chance, for the curve of the blunt sled had concealed it well. His hands found the real treasures: eight matrices, still in a film coating which even the purple fungus had been unable to penetrate, five tiny separators, several dozen stun-capsules, and another wrist unit. The items had been glued to the surface by some gummy substance that had long since hardened. Over the decades it had become brittle so that Portegin's touch had loosened the riches from their unlikely hidey-hole. The five surveyed their wealth in a silence broken when Varian laid tentative fingers on the stun gun.

"In forty-three years, they would have exhausted all their supplies. No matter how clever they are, they couldn't achieve the technology to produce more."

"Not if they hunt that thunder lizard of Trizein's with a crossbow and lance," Lunzie said. "Nice to have an advantage again."

Varian hated weapons but was exceedingly grateful to see them. The discovery also lifted from her mind the depression that had plagued her. She was far more tired than she cared to admit and not even Lunzie's nutrient soup had reduced that weariness. In her present state she'd never be able to use Discipline effectively for any long period, and any encounters with Aygar and his peers presumed full Discipline on her part. To have such accoutrements when she kept that appointment gave her the psychological advantage she needed.

"If they're metal-working and smart," Triv noted as he hefted a stunner in his hand, "they'll have found the ingredients for primitive explosive weapons. This stunner doesn't have the effective range of a projectile weapon, even of that crossbow."

"Strategy can make up for shortcomings—or short ranges," Varian noted in a light tone.

"Even if you have to crash and destroy them, those sleds aren't to fall into the mutineers' hands," Kai said forcefully, swearing again as his voice cracked.

"We don't necessarily have to bring the sleds into sight," said Varian, "not when we have lift-belts."

"Let's not talk of destroying the sleds," Portegin urged, holding up both hands in dismay at the notion. "I can bypass the start switch so that only we'd know how to start one."

"Can you patch a line from wrist unit to the shuttle or the sled?"

"You're not taking the four-man sled, are you, Varian?" Kai asked.

"Krims! no, but you'll want to hear what's going on, won't you?"

"If I only had some sort of a magnifier . . ." Portegin was muttering under his breath. "Lunzie, you *must* have something? . . ."

She handed him a loup, but warned Portegin of the dire consequences of chipping or breaking one of her precious few medical aids.

When Kai volunteered to help Triv and Portegin, Lunzie would have none of it. She forced him to alternate bathing his injured hands in the sap with wringing out cloths for his face wounds. Then she made Varian lie down for an hour's rest before having her go on a provisions hunt. With all the ravenous appetites she had to satisfy, Lunzie needed more raw vegetable matter for the synthesizer, and she also wanted to locate more of the edible fruits, pods, and herbs nearby.

Varian thought she'd be unable to sleep with Triv's and Portegin's murmuring and swearing, the sough and rustle of the wind through the vine screen, and the odd sounds made by Kai and Lunzie, but it seemed she'd only closed her eyes when Lunzie was shaking her awake again.

Since Triv seemed to have little to do while he watched Portegin assembling a matrix comb, Varian was a bit grumpy when Lunzie hustled *her* to the sled. Varian's temper was not much improved by the mizzling rain that made visibility poor, but Lunzie pointed curtly to the brighter skies to the southwest and told Varian to make for a spot where they could see what they picked without getting drenched in the process.

Immediately three giffs curved away from those few idly circling the caves. It was well past the return of the fishers, and most adult fliers were already inside their caves, sleeping off their meal, or whatever they did.

"Do they do any more than follow?" Lunzie asked after observing them for a time.

"Not when I'm airborne . . ."

"When they consider you safe?" Lunzie asked with a wry grin.

"Come to think of it, when the scavengers began to circle in on that dead beast, the giffs were picking up speed."

"That could be useful."

Something in her idle tone, that of a woman not much given to chitchat, warned Varian that Lunzie had several purposes in the flight.

"How seriously ill is Kai, Lunzie?"

"Hard to say with no way of testing. Feeling is returning to his hands and the skin of his face isn't as numb, or so he tells me. There's no question that he's suffered some motor impairment in his hands. I'm hoping that will pass once the last of the toxic fluid is flushed out of his system. I want to get more of that moss if we can find it, and I want a store of those succulent leaves around at all times." Lunzie showed Varian a long red weal on her hand. "The sap is analgesic. I'm not used to dealing with raw fire."

"How long, then, before Kai is well?"

"He's not going to be physically fit for several weeks. I'd prefer to keep him from any exertion at all for four or five days. Then a *slow* convalescence."

Varian digested that in silence.

"Triv can accompany you and Portegin if he's finished patching. But I must watch Kai."

"Yes, he's likely to try something stupid because he feels responsible for us all."

"What is it about this meeting that worries you, Varian?"

"I wish I could answer that. There was something about Aygar's attitude . . ."

Lunzie chuckled in high amusement. "I'll bet there was."

"Lunzie! You said yourself I'm not at my best—"

"At your very worst, you'd be a joy to a man deprived of a woman. And one hell of an acquisition to their gene pool."

Varian didn't dismiss that notion, but it was not, she was

certain, the entire answer to the enigma of Aygar's cryptic expression.

"Sexuality could have been part of it, Lunzie, but it's more as if . . . as if he had a surprise for me. And he did mention their beacon. Yes, the beacon had something to do with it and something that would, in his mind, neutralize my ability to throw him."

"Why do they have a beacon?" Lunzie asked. She thoughtfully pursed her lips as Varian shook her head. Abruptly the medic pointed ahead and to starboard.

"Isn't that moss down there?"

Varian banked sharply, noticing the small animals scurrying from the sound of the sled. She threw on the telltagger, but it only made noises appropriate to the small life-forms rapidly leaving the area. When they had landed, Varian kept one eye on the giffs. As long as they circled lazily, she felt safe.

"Not the right moss," Lunzie said disgustedly. She held a sample under Varian's nose.

"It stinks!"

"It's cryptogamous!"

"Really?"

"Propagates by spores. What we want is bryophytic. You didn't happen to notice how much of the stuff in Divisti's garden is also bryophytic?"

"If it's fungoid, I'm automatically prejudiced." Varian gave a small shudder. "But I didn't notice fungi in the garden. And the purple moss was the only one of its sort."

"Don't disparage fungi. Some of the oddest and most repellent are delicious and highly nutritious."

"And smelly?"

"You planet-bred types do worry about smell, don't you?" Lunzie grinned at Varian, and began to scrub her hands with dirt to remove the moss.

"I'd think smell would bother you shippers a lot more."

"Is it safe to explore a little here?" Lunzie asked, glancing around the small copse.

"I don't see why not," Varian replied, after a glance at the giffs. "I'll just turn up the volume on the telltagger."

They ventured farther among the huge, high-branching trees, noting the nail grooves where the long-neck herbivores had steadied themselves to reach the upper leaves and branches. Similar stands of trees were scattered about the vast plain. Distant hadrosaurs, distinguishable by their crests, were bending saplings down to reach the edible twigs.

After concluding that the area had been overgrazed, the two women took to the air again, moving southeast until the land fell away in a huge old fault of several hundred meters' height. The vegetation in the lower portion differed drastically from that of the plain. There were also more clearings in which to land the sled, but the telltagger buzzed so continually that Varian declined to take an unnecessary risk.

"We can try the swamps where we found the hyracotherium tomorrow," Varian suggested and Lunzie agreed that this might be a more profitable site for the purple moss.

They were turning back when Varian sighted pod-bearing trees, at the northern end of the fault. Although there was room enough to land a space cruiser, the land was occupied by large tusked animals that were either fighting or bashing headlong into slender trunked trees to dislodge pods for noisy consumption. The air sled frightened the creatures off, but Varian preferred to hover well above the tuskers while Lunzie picked, happily muttering about high protein content.

"Make a note of these coordinates, will you Varian? We'll want more of these. They're what give my special stew its flavor."

Taking another tangent back to the sea cliffs of the golden fliers, they made one more stop, in fruiting trees which Varian also noted for future reference.

The fragrance of the ripe fruit, picked from boughs grazing animals couldn't reach, filled the enclosed air sled with tantalizing sweetness.

"No more stops no matter what you see, Lunzie. It's getting dark, and I don't fancy night landings in that cave."

"I might just wake Bonnard," Lunzie said after they'd ridden on in silent appreciation for the sunset display of distant lightning that brightened clouds in the far west. "He can run this boat, can't he? He's smart, quick, and he thinks. Besides—"

"Look, if you're worried, Portegin can stay with you."

"My concern is for you, co-leader, not myself. Not that any of you are safe if it's new blood they're after."

"What exactly is bothering you, Lunzie? Tell me now. I've had enough surprises."

"It may just be my suspicious nature, Varian, but your Aygar did mention a beacon. It is forty-three years since the mutiny . . ."

"So?"

"What do you know of unrest among planetary minorities?"

"Huh?" It took Varian a moment to grapple with the sudden switch. "I'd heard rumors that choice planets usually end up managed by one of the FSP majors. Financing was the usual rationale. Krims!—You don't mean . . ." Varian shot a horrified glance at Lunzie, "you don't mean that the *ARCT-10* might have been taken over by another set of mutineers, do you?"

"A compound ship does not lend itself to mutiny." Lunzie gave Varian a tight grin. "*Too* many minorities involved, too many different atmospheres, too bloody strict a surveillance against a possible takeover. Command can, you know, close off, gas, or eject any section of a compound ship without affecting overall stability, life support, drive or control elements. And the *ARCT-10* had a large Thek group. *No* minority goes against Thek. What I had in mind were the rumors of expeditions on worlds such as this, where sizable teams simply disappeared. Not planted, but no sign of natural disasters or deaths accidental or otherwise. Just the rumor and no official acknowledgment of the problem. No official announcement about finding the lost units, either. Of course, the change-state problems of this immense Federation could account for the lack of news or official confirmation. Very little gets done quickly, especially when Thek are concerned. Forty-three years since our distress call?" Lunzie's expression was grimly thoughtful. "That, my dear coleader, is long enough for a homing capsule to arrive at its destination and to permit an expedition to reach the distressed party. In my opinion, that's why your Aygar was not much bothered by the gene balance in his settlement. And the reason he was surprised you hadn't homed in on *his* beacon."

Varian inhaled a long whistle. "That does put a frame around his attitude. But three days? Could he be that certain of a touchdown when they don't have any communications?" Varian followed again, mulling over Lunzie's theory. "When I crossed his line of march, he did get rid of me as fast as he could."

"Which might mean the newcomers have arrived or are ex-pected soon."

"He certainly expects to own Ireta!"

"Your space law's worse than your botany, Varian. If my theory has any substance, you were possessed with sheer ge-nius when you posed as a new FSP expedition."

"I was? Why?"

"One," and Lunzie ticked off her points on fingers, "the heavy-worlders don't suspect you are from the original team; they can still assume that we died of our own incompetence after the stampede or went into cold sleep. But if," and an-other finger emphasized that point, "an FSP relief party ar-rives before *their* reinforcements, summoned by that homing capsule, they will not have clear title to the planet."

"How could they think they'd have a clear title anyhow?" Varian demanded.

"There's a considerable code of space law dealing with

shipwrecked survivors who reach habitable planets and/or stranded expeditionary members who manage to achieve a certain level of civilization."

"What does that code of space law say about mutineers?"

"That's why it's safer for *us* to be a relief party."

"If at first you don't succeed, have another go?" Varian asked drolly.

"Precisely."

"But, Lunzie, when the reinforcements arrive, they'd know there aren't any other ships orbiting the planet."

"The reinforcements, my dear Varian, are probably illegal and would be most anxious not to be hailed by another vessel. They'll probably enter the atmosphere under radio silence and as quickly as possible to avoid detection. Since the obvious orbit of a rescue ship is synchronous with the site of original landing, even a large ship can escape detection if the captain has any intelligence.

"And then set about raping this rich world and indulging in their anachronistic behavior. It's easy now to understand why specialists of the caliber of Bakkun and Berru went along with that asinine rumor about our being planted. They had a world to gain."

Varian's expression was grim. "Too bad they didn't live to enjoy it. But, Lunzie, they did mutiny and they mustn't be allowed to profit by it."

"They haven't yet," Lunzie replied wryly. "And though their descendants cannot be held liable for the sins of their predecessors, we have to stay alive to prove that a mutiny did occur."

"Then how—" Varian began indignantly.

"The descendants would only get partial claims," Lunzie explained hurriedly. "Don't worry about that now. Consider this instead: once their relief ship arrives, it will almost certainly contain sleds and instrumentation. They'll be able to mount a full-scale search for our shuttle."

"That doesn't mean they'll find it."

"I suppose we won't *have* to produce a shuttle," Lunzie said.

"It's away mapping the continent," Varian announced airily. "Regulations don't specify how large a search party has to be, so five of us are all our ship could send. And Tor knows—" Varian let out a whoop of laughter that caused Lunzie to wince as the sound reverberated in the confines of the sled's canopy. "Those heavy-worlders have outsmarted themselves, Bakkun and Berru included. This planet's been Thek-claimed for millions of years, if that core Tor was so nardling eager to disinter was Thek-manufactured. And it has to be." .

"Whether it is or isn't, Varian, may not be germane, considering the span of time since its implantation. You can be certain that Bakkun included precise details of the rich transuranic potential of Ireta when that homing capsule was launched. An expedition will arrive equipped to strip this planet as thoroughly as the Others. And argue about who had the right to do so later."

A shudder ran through Varian's body. "Are there really any Others, Lunzie?"

"No one knows. I've stood on one of those barren worlds that must once have been as lush and lovely—and as rich—as this one."

"The mutineers mustn't rape this one."

"You've my complete support."

"The old *ARCT-10* may even reappear . . ."

"We'd best consider what resources *we* can muster," said Lunzie. She raised her hand when Varian began to protest. "I never count on luck. Tomorrow you, Triv, and Portegin will have lift-belts and stunners when you meet Aygar. You and Triv will have the advantage of full Discipline." The medic paused before she added solemnly, "And I'd better give you all barriers."

"Barriers?" Varian cast a startled look at the medic. That aspect of Discipline was entrusted to only a highly select few.

"Barriers are the only real protection you and our sleepers

would have if heavy-worlders have landed." Lunzie spoke quietly. Almost, Varian thought, as if she regretted the necessity of revealing this unexpected strength, rather than the need which dictated its use.

They flew on in silence until the looming white cliffs emerged from the shroud of evening mists and the black, beribboned opening that was their refuge yawned before them.

6

AFTER everyone had enjoyed the tasty stew Lunzie had concocted and as much of the ripe fruit as they could eat, Varian asked Lunzie to air her theory about the mutineers' plan for Ireta.

"That's just how the heavy-worlders acquired the S-192 system," Triv said with considerable indignation.

"S-192 was a two-g world," Lunzie pointed out.

"This one has wild animals for them to eat," Varian said grimly.

"Not to mention transuranic deposits that would make claim-holders extremely wealthy," said Kai, "if they could validate their claim."

"Which they can't because we're alive." Portegin's voice was angry.

"Hmm, but they don't know it," Varian reminded him.

"Keep two points in mind, my friends," Lunzie said. "The mutineers' descendants have survived and have maintained a good level of technology if they're forging metal and have constructed a beacon. That qualifies them—"

"We've survived, too," and Portegin sat straight up, incensed.

Lunzie regarded him humorlessly for a moment. "We," and her voice left the slightest emphasis on the pronoun, "must continue to do so. My second point is that the descendants of the original mutineers cannot be prosecuted for the felony of their grandparents."

"Tanegli's still alive." Varian was surprised at the edge in her voice.

"So I suspect that his first suggestion to the commander of the expected vessel will be to find us," Kai said. "When they didn't find the space shuttle under the dead beasts after the stampede, they knew that someone survived and went cryo."

"Aygar believes that they were deliberately abandoned," Varian said.

"Your little lie and what Aygar has been told are all that kept him from attacking you, Varian." Lunzie's tone betrayed her anger. "We have to keep you and them," the medic jabbed her finger at the shuttle, "alive until *ARCT-10* returns."

Portegin gave a snort of derision. "The *ARCT* probably blew up in that cosmic storm."

"Unlikely," Lunzie said. "I once slept seventy-eight years and still was collected by my original ship."

"You think the *ARCT-10 will* come back for us, Lunzie?" asked Portegin, amazed.

"Stranger things have happened. Whatever Aygar believes, Varian, Tanegli knows different, nor can he ignore the fact that some of us may have survived. He cannot take the risk that the *ARCT-10 will* return and with the information left in our beacon, recover the shuttle. Right now we must make plans that will safeguard not only us but the sleepers. Equally important, set ourselves up as scouts totally unrelated to the *ARCT-10*. If that ship did blow, its deadman's knell will be recorded and known to every space commander—including the mutineers' relief ship—so we can't pose as a relief unit from the *ARCT-10*."

"From what ship did we originate then, Lunzie?" Kai was slightly amused, but his husky voice betrayed his physical debility.

Varian looked at him quickly, wondering if he objected to Lunzie's dominance. His eyes were glittering, but not with fever. He seemed to be encouraging the medic's unexpected inventiveness.

"We can take our pick—freighter, passenger, another Exploratory Vessel . . ." Lunzie shrugged, suddenly reverting to her usual passivity. "Recall what you told Aygar, Varian."

"That I was part of a team sent in answer to the distress call."

"Any vessel has to investigate such a signal . . ." Portegin said.

"But only a Fleet ship could tap our beacon's messages," Triv reminded them.

"And *he'd* know how rich this planet is and send a party down if only for finders' fees." Portegin capped Triv's remark.

"That's what I implied," said Varian. "Then Aygar gave me his version of the facts."

"That his grandparents had been abandoned? . . ." Kai asked.

"Deliberately abandoned," Varian replied with a grimace, "after the tragic accident that demolished their original site. No mention of either of us as leaders, remember."

"Paskutti had that honor?" Kai was amused.

Varian shrugged. "I didn't ask. I did inquire about the children. I also said that the *ARCT-10* was still missing." Varian hesitated, dubious now about that admission.

"Why not?" Kai shrugged. "If the ship had returned within the Standard year, as planned, none of us would be where we are now. What puzzles me is the forty-three years. It doesn't take anywhere near that time for a homing capsule to reach its destination. And I know the mutineers had ours."

"They would have had to wait to be sure that the *ARCT-10* wasn't just delayed," Varian suggested.

"Could they have known that the *ARCT-10* never stripped the beacon of messages?" Lunzie asked.

"Only Kai and I knew that."

"Bakkun might have guessed," Kai said slowly.

"By what we didn't say rather than what we did?" Varian asked. Kai nodded.

"We ought," Kai went on, "to have invented a message from the *ARCT*."

Lunzie snorted. "I don't think that would have kept the heavy-worlders satisfied once they'd had their bloody rest day . . . and tasted animal protein. Brings out the worst in them every time."

A taut silence ensued, broken as Varian shuddered, then said, "But Divisti's garden produced sufficient vegetable protein to support twice as many heavy-worlder appetites."

"I'd say they waited," Lunzie began, picking at her lower lip for a moment before she continued. "They would have tried to locate the shuttle and the power packs which young Bonnard so cleverly concealed. They knew Kai'd sent out some sort of message, before Paskutti smashed the comunit? Well, then, they'd have had to wait to see if assistance arrived. They would have had to assume also that we'd rig some sort of distress beacon to attract rescue, even if it did take the Thek forty-three years to bother to investigate."

Varian broke in excitedly. "You don't suppose that they could have rigged an alert for a landing?"

"No way." Portegin shook his head violently. "Not with the equipment they had. Remember it was replacement parts they took with the stores, not full units."

"Yes, but Aygar spoke of iron mines, and they've been working a forge."

Portegin kept shaking his head. "Bakkun was a good all-round engineer, but even with all the matrices I've got, I couldn't make that sort of a scan system, not planetwide, and that's what they'd need."

"So," Kai said in summation, "they waited to be sure *ARCT* wasn't making the scheduled pick-up. They also waited until they could be reasonably certain our distress signal was unheard and then too weak. Then they sent the homing capsule to one of the heavy-world colonies inviting settlers and technicians."

"And if a colony ship, large enough to transport enough people and supplies, is to make the journey profitable, they'd have to build a landing grid," Triv exclaimed.

"Which explains why they left the very good settlement they had in the secondary camp," Varian cried.

"And why Aygar chooses to meet you there rather than at their new site," Lunzie finished with a sour grimace. "Such an undertaking also explains forty-three years."

"Even for heavy-worlders, it would take years to clear this sort of jungle and hold it back while they got a grid in place," said Portegin with some awe.

"Probably with a homing device built into the acknowledging capsule to confirm arrangements and approximate time of arrival," Triv added.

The group reflected on this solution with no joy.

Triv broke the silence. "I'd opt for us to come from a Fleet ship, a cruiser. They make periodic reports to a Sector HQ and no one in his right mind messes with a cruiser."

"Would Aygar know that?" Varian asked facetiously.

"No, but the captain of the incoming ship would," Triv replied. "And a search party could have been set down here to check on the distress call while the cruiser goes on to the Ryxi and the Thek planets."

"Now that our identity is established," Kai said with an attempt at heartiness, "I suggest we transfer to the campsite built for Dimenon and Margit. If it still exists."

"Don't see why it wouldn't," Triv said. "The heavy-worlders wouldn't have wasted belt power dismantling and transporting it."

"Wouldn't we go to the original site?" asked Portegin.

"We did," Varian replied, "but Kai got attacked there, didn't he? So we should move to the second auxiliary camp." She rose and stretched. "And we'd also better fill in the holes of the vine screen. Then the sleepers will be safe."

The next morning, Triv took one of the smaller sleds to investigate the secondary camp which had been sited for Dimenon and Margit to use as a base for their explorations of the southwestern part of Ireta's main continent. Assisted by Varian and Lunzie, Portegin gathered the matrices removed from the other two small sleds and the undamaged units in the shuttle. He was optimistic that with these components, he could rig working comunits in the two small sleds and the four-man sled, plus an ordinary homing beacon, consonant with their role as a rescue team from a Space Fleet cruiser.

Lunzie proved the deftest in making minute welds with the heated tip of a surgical probe, all the while muttering about the misuse of her precious medical equipment on inanimate objects.

Varian's usefulness to the project was shortlived. She was unable to limit herself to controlled dexterity for long, and announced that she was better suited to shifting vines than matrices. It was hard, sweaty labor, hampered by Ireta's sudden squalls and then steamy sunheat. The vines clung with tenacious webs of sticky fibers to the rock, so she hacked away, pried loose, and tugged at the tendrils to rig a full curtain across the entrance. At the same time, she rigged fiber ropes to pull the vines back to allow for the entry and exit of the sleds. She coaxed additional new vine tendrils across the chasm, setting them to fill in. At the rate vegetation grew on Ireta, the cave ought to be densely screened in a matter of weeks.

Triv returned with the welcome news that the other camp had survived, although it had become the residence of creatures large and small. However the fortified posts were functional so that, once cleared of intruders, the camp would be habitable.

Lunzie made good use of the vines left over from Varian's camouflage trimming and created emergency rations from the vegetable matter and more light blankets from the residual fibers. These were packed into the two smaller sleds while Kai was made comfortable in the larger. Lunzie made a last check on the sleepers and set the time release for additional sleep vapor. As Triv pulled back the vine curtain, using Varian's cords, the three sleds emerged just as the evening rain began to splash down. They landed briefly on the cliff, while Triv joined them and took over the controls of one sled from Lunzie who then joined Varian and Kai in the larger sled.

As Varian lifted, she searched the leaden skies. "No giffs!"

"They've sense enough to come in out of that rain," Lunzie said, drying her hands as she looked at the raindrops battering the sled's canopy.

"They followed me, you know."

"So you told me. Not superstitious, are you, Varian?" the medic asked with an ironic chuckle.

"Enough to prefer their company to their absence."

"They stood guard a long time," Kai said in his husky voice.

"You're both allowing them far more intelligence than they deserve."

Varian turned her head to give Kai a broad grin which he answered. Then the rain squall quickened and she had to keep her attention on flying for the rest of the journey.

Although Triv and Portegin had arrived in advance of the four-man sled, Kai was struck by the eeriness of landing in the gloom of Iretan twilight at a campsite which he knew had been uninhabited for over four decades. It seemed to have slept, unchanged, as they had.

Rationally, he knew that part of its lack of change was due to the rocky site, but the dome which Dimenon and Margit had set up was only slightly browned by wind and weather. A small fire burned on the hearth outside. Its light was cheering and its smoke a partial deterrent to insects until the force field could be powered up. The pack was quickly connected and crackled immediately with tiny spurts as insects were vaporized. Small bits of char drifted down as Kai stiffly made his way from the sled to the dome. He was heartily disgusted with his weakness and kept to himself the fact that he still had no feeling at all in the areas where the fringe had sucked deepest. He couldn't prevent furtive glances for fringes lurking beyond the veil. He worried briefly if the creatures could be stopped by the force field. Of course they could— Force fields had even held back the stampede of the herbivores . . . for a time.

He was trembling again, to his disgust. Only a short walk, and he was spent. Lunzie had cautioned him against using Discipline to overcome the weakness of convalescence, but surely a daily routine of basic Discipline exercise would be beneficial. Might even be essential if Varian's meeting with Aygar proved unlucky. Kai wasn't easy about that confrontation, even with all three armed. He'd spent some time trying to estimate how large the mutineers' group would be after two generations of breeding. And if a colony ship had arrived, there could be thousands to back the heavy-worlders' claim. Either way his team was at risk.

Where had the *ARCT-10* disappeared to? Why had Tor been so uncharacteristically keen to find the old core? Why had the Thek then departed? Kai reminded himself that a mere human did not demand explanations of a Thek. Out of sight, out of mind, yet Tor had awakened him to find the core.

And how had the Ryxi flourished on their new planet? Kai wondered, though he knew that Vrl, his contact with the volatile avians, probably wouldn't have worried about the geologist's silence. Certainly the Ryxi wouldn't have communicated with the Thek. Surely, though, Kai reasoned, the commander of the Ryxi colony vessel ought to have tried to raise the Iretan group, if only prompted by courtesy. Probably the silence of the Iretan expedition was thought to mean that the *ARCT-10* had collected the Iretan team as scheduled.

Which brought Kai back to the original question: What had happened to the *ARCT-10*? The great compound ships were constructed to withstand tremendous variations of temperature and stress. Short of a full nova, an EEC vessel could endure almost anything. Possibly, a black hole would consume a whole EEC ship, but no EEC ship would approach such a hazard. As no known species that was inimical to the Federated Sentient Planets was capable of space travel, nothing short of the Others could have attacked the *ARCT-10*. A real mystery. Kai exhaled deeply.

"Does supper not appeal to you? I'd thought you were resigned to eating natural foods by now," said Varian, breaking Kai's reverie.

"I'm hungry enough to eat anything." He grinned at her as he accepted a bowl.

Once they had finished eating, Lunzie rinsed out the bowls and filled them with fruit steeped in its own juices. By then Kai was more tired than hungry so he put the bowl to one side and slipped down under the light blanket, closing his eyes. As he drowsed, he heard Portegin yawning loudly, complaining that he hadn't done much to be so tired.

"You're not quite recovered from cold sleep yet, you know," Lunzie remarked. "You'll have a full day tomorrow. Sleep now. There's nothing more needs doing tonight."

Kai was aware that the others were seeking their blankets and, as he lay, waiting for sleep to overtake him, he grew envious of their ability to drop off so quickly. He was all the more surprised then to hear Lunzie's quiet voice.

"Portegin, Varian, Triv, you will listen to me. You will hear nothing but my voice. You will obey only my voice. You will follow my directions implicitly for you entrust your lives to me. Acknowledge."

Fascinated, Kai listened to the murmured assent of the three.

"Portegin, you will feel no pain, no matter what is done to the flesh of your body. From the first blow, your body will be nerveless, impervious to pain. You will not bleed. You will command your body to relax and your flesh to absorb injury without discomfort. You will be unable to reveal anything except your name, Portegin, your rank as helmsman first class of the FSP Cruiser *218-ZD-43*. You are part of a rescue mission. You know no more than that of your present. Your childhood years are open, your years of service as well, except that all service was with the Space Fleet. This is your first visit to Ireta. You will feel no pain, no matter what is done to the flesh of your body and the channels of your mind. You have a barrier against pain and mental intrusion. Your mind is locked to control. Your nerves and pain centers are under my control. I will allow nothing to cause you pain or distress."

Lunzie asked Portegin to repeat her instructions but the man's toneless murmur was inaudible to Kai.

The medic then began to instruct Varian, whom she called Rianav. Here the parameters were more complex. She drew on Varian's two years in her birth-planet's martial corps, building a detailed recent memory which seemed to include facts of personal history unexpectedly known to Lunzie but not to Kai. The hypnotic briefing would insure that Varian–Rianav acted and thought as a career Fleet officer. She also erected barriers to protect Varian–Rianav against any intrusion or pain above and beyond the control Varian could produce herself with the exercise of Discipline. The cover personality for Varian was tightly woven out of fact and half-truth and so logical that Kai wondered if Lunzie was using the life history of an actual person. Kai was awed for he realized that he was listening to an accomplished Adept, and there had been nothing in Lunzie's service profile to indicate such competence. Of course, there wouldn't be, beyond a mention of a term at Seripan, the center where Discipline was taught; a fact only other Disciples would recognize as significant.

As Lunzie quietly set barriers in the mind of Triv—Titrivell, Kai began to wonder if there was any covert reason why *ARCT*'s administrators had recommended her as medic. He decided that it was only chance: what else? Most medics were Disciples since hypnotic control to inhibit pain was more effective than anesthesia and the simplest method of curing mental trauma. The Iretan expedition had been considered a straightforward search for transuranics which was why, Kai was certain, two relatively young people were given the co-leadership. He thought grimly of the counts against himself and Varian: mutiny and a minority group all but established on what should have been an extraordinarily rich FSP planet. Exploration and Evaluation Corps wouldn't like that, much less the FSP, who preferred to keep all transuranics under their control, leasing them only to stable corporations.

He supposed they should have remained awake and done their utmost to thwart the heavy-worlders, though how they could have accomplished anything significant without equipment or weapons he was incapable of imagining. A leader's prime responsibility was to bring back the full complement of his expedition, preferably having completed his assignment. A resigned sigh escaped his lips.

"You were awake, Kai?" Lunzie's voice was soft and Kai realized that she had moved beside him with a bowl in her outstretched hand.

"So, you fixed some fruit?" he asked, opening his eyes and looking at her.

She nodded. Odd that he had never noticed before what beautiful and compelling eyes she had.

Kai lifted the neglected shell in gentle salute and drank the juice before he began to eat the fruit.

"I wasn't hungry. But I'm awfully glad you can give them more protection, Lunzie."

"Yes, it's always easier to lie if you think you're telling the truth."

"I won't worry so much about that meeting tomorrow."

"I'm sure you won't." The medic's low voice was tinged with amusement. She took the emptied shell from his hand.

Whatever Lunzie had added to the innocent fruit was potent. He swam down into darkness, completely aware that in the morning, he would not remember that Lunzie was an Adept.

7

RIANAV wished that they had a squad of troopers with them. Titrivell and Portegin were good men; she'd been in several tricky situations with them but, if her commander's suspicion should prove valid, three troops in a four-man sled, equipped with only forcebelts and stunners, were woefully insufficient.

Still, until a colony ship did somehow slip through the commander's surveillance, three veterans could cope. She doubted the survivors had any sophisticated weapons if that Aygar had been hunting with a crossbow and lance. Not that such a primitive weapon was ineffective: bolts from a crossbow could penetrate thick metal and, at close range, probably knock fragments from the ceramic hull of the sled. The original landing party's stunners would by now be inoperative. She'd match herself and Titrivell against any two or three of Aygar's size so she really had no reason to be apprehensive about the meeting. Except Aygar's insistence that it be held away from his current living area.

Once she had set the course for the secondary camp, she

gestured to Portegin to take the controls. She must be fresh for the conference. Titrivell took the starboard observation post while she settled herself to port. Not that there was much to see except huge trees festooned with climbers and swaths of damaged vegetation where large beasts had broken trails through the dense jungle. She didn't fancy any ground work there.

"Lieutenant?" Portegin interrupted her, and she followed the direction of his point.

"The size of the creatures! Recorder going, Portegin? I want the captain to believe this!"

"Aye, aye, ma'am."

Titrivell leaned amidships, to see past Portegin's shoulder. "They must weigh megatons. Glad we're up here instead of down there."

"Bet they give the heavy-worlders a tussle." Portegin glanced over his shoulder as they passed the herd of creatures, eating whatever was within the reach of their long sinuous necks.

"We'll have no jokes here, Portegin." Rianav's tone was stern. One couldn't permit even subtle hints about sentient carnivores. Any member of the Federation that defied the civilized edict forbidding consumption of living creatures did so at the peril of its FSP membership.

"Well, Lieutenant," said Portegin in a chastened tone, "I have heard from reliable sources that, on their own planets, the heavy-worlders don't adhere to Prohibition."

"All the more reason for our mission, then. Stupid as these creatures appear to be," and she waved at yet another herd of foraging beasts, "they deserve as much of a chance to evolve as any other species. And our protection while they do so."

"Lieutenant, fliers at eleven." Portegin was pointing at an airborne species.

There were three of them. Golden of either feather or fur, Rianav could not be sure at the distance, but their presence in the sky was oddly reassuring.

"Shall I take evasive action?" asked Portegin when it became obvious that the golden-winged creatures had altered their course to take up a position on the same level, and at the same speed, as the sled.

"I don't think that's necessary, helmsman. They do not appear aggressive. They're probably curious. We can outdistance them at any time should they turn hostile." Rianav took unusual pleasure in their exceptional escort, watching the graceful, powerful sweep of the huge pinions.

"They're watching us, ma'am," Titrivell called. "The heads of all three are turned in our direction."

"They're doing us no harm."

They paused once in their outward journey. Rianav spotted a huge stand of fruit trees, the top boughs sagging under ripe fruit, a pleasant change from service rations. It did not occur to any of the three that it was unlikely for them to know if the fruits were edible.

When they reached the vast plain dotted with buttes and meandering herds of grazing animals, Rianav ordered the helmsman to circle gradually in on the target area. She took the monitor to search for any sign of Aygar and his people.

"They're probably hidden in those hutments," Titrivell remarked.

"Full Discipline," she said, with a nod to indicate that she appreciated the possibility. "Helmsman, stand by the sled. If we are overpowered or I should signal you off, you are to report back to the commander. This sled must not fall into other hands. Keep your comunit open at all times and be on the lookout for any indication of a large craft landing in that direction." Rianav pointed toward the northeastern hills where she suspected the heavy-worlders were encamped.

At the speed with which Portegin was circling, she and Titrivell would have sufficient time to complete Discipline. But as she initiated the drill, she felt an unexpected energy, the most powerful surge of adrenalin she had ever experienced in Discipline. Glancing at Titrivell, she saw that he must have had a similar jolt. Of course, one expanded one's abilities with every use of Discipline, but this? Rianav must ask her commander when she returned to the cruiser.

Portegin neatly brought the sled to a landing on the bare circular mark left by a dome which must have occupied that area for a long time.

Titrivell opened the canopy and Rianav stepped out smartly. Titrivell followed, closed the canopy, and nodded to Portegin to secure it. Rianav caught the slight widening of Titrivell's eyes just as she heard a slight *crunch*, and turned slowly in the direction of the sound.

Six figures, three men and three women, ranged themselves in an almost insolent parody of the parade stance of troops. Each wore a standard-issue ship suit. Despite Discipline, the sight gave Rianav a flash of concern. Then she noticed that the ship suits were patched and that the six neither wore forcebelts nor carried stunners. The reinforcements had not, then, arrived. These were descendants of the original force, mocking her by appearing in their ancestors' garb.

Rianav was, however, grateful for the stunner at her side. Each of the six was taller, broader, heavier than she or Titrivell.

She hesitated only that brief moment for evaluation and then strode forward, not quite leisurely but not in formal martial pace. She glanced from one face to the next, almost as if she expected to recognize someone. Halting, exactly four meters from Aygar, she saluted.

"You are prompt, Aygar."

"And you!" The man curved his lips in a half-smile, as his eyes flicked toward Titrivell, correctly standing two paces behind his lieutenant, then toward the pilot at the controls of the closed sled.

"Did your injured man survive?"

"Yes, and sends his gratitude for the remedy."

"Any more trouble with fringes?"

"No." Rianav said. "But you would certainly be safe from that menace on this butte? . . ." Her comment trailed into a question.

"We outgrew its limited accommodations," Aygar said. That prompted some smiles from his five companions.

"You may be unaware of the provisions made by the Federated Sentient Planets to reimburse survivors—"

"We're not survivors, Lieutenant," said Aygar. "We were born on this planet. We *own* it."

"Really, Aygar," said Rianav in a conciliatory tone, gesturing at the others, "six people can only *own* as much as supplies their needs."

"We are more than six."

"No matter how much your original number has multiplied, it is clearly stated in FSP law—"

"*We* are the law here, Rianav! *We* accuse you of trespass."

The change of intensity in his voice alerted Rianav with her Disciplined sensitivity. She had her stun gun out and was firing at Aygar and the two on his right before they could complete their forward springs. Titrivell was not a millisecond later in stunning the other three.

With her gun in hand, for she had set for medium shock and she wasn't certain how long such superb bodies would be affected, she strode to the sprawled forms, motionless on the dusty ground. Aygar's eyes glittered with anger as she leaned down and, grabbing his right arm, hauled him onto his back. She nodded to Titrivell to perform the same courtesy to the others.

"You'll be unable to move for approximately fifty minutes. Doubtless your grandparents mentioned stunners? You and your companions will suffer no ill-effects from stunning. We will continue our mission. We prefer not to use weapons on other humanoids, but three to one are unfair odds. Nor are we trespassers, Aygar. Our cruiser heard the distress signal and responded. We are morally obliged to do so. No doubt your isolation is the reason for your failure to comprehend the common laws of the galaxy. I will be lenient in your instance and not report your aggressive reaction to my superiors. You cannot *own* a world which is still listed as unexplored in the Federated Register. Possession may be considered primary in law, but you possess," and she stressed the word with a slight pause, "very little of this jungle world no matter how many offspring were produced by the original party. But that's not a matter for me to decide. I report fact as I observe it."

The tendons in Aygar's neck stood out in his attempt to break paralysis by sheer willpower.

"You could do yourself injury, Aygar. Relax now and you'll suffer no harm."

Punctuating her advice, thunder cracked and lightning spewed blindingly out of the sky. The thin clouds which had begun to gather during the fracas had coalesced with a ferocity fitting the aerial display.

"There! Something to cool you down." Rianav clipped her stunner to her belt. Gesturing Titrivell to follow, she strode to the sled.

"Are there many more like that?" Titrivell asked as he settled himself in the sled.

"That's what I think we'd better find out." As she took the controls, Rianav motioned to Portegin to slide into the other front seat. "Aygar gave me directions by foot. Whether they're accurate or not, we can but follow and see. 'Run at a good steady pace,' he told me, 'to your right, through the first hills, turn right up the ravine, but mind the river snakes. Continue along the river course to the first falls, take the easiest route up the cliff, follow the line of limestone, until the valley widens.' We'll know their settlement by the cultivated fields." Rianav snorted derisively.

She guided the sled along the course she had taken on her first visit, then intersected the ravine where she had encountered Aygar. She continued along the ravine and soon came to a fast river, diverted from its old channel by the debris of a huge rockfall. They followed the river upstream for some distance to a beautiful curtain of wide falls roughly forty meters high.

"Useful, too," Portegin said, pointing to port. "They've set up a waterwheel and what looks like a generator station."

He glanced at Rianav to see if she intended to investigate, but she was already angling the sled above the falls, keeping one eye starboard for the well-marked path, so that Titrivell and Portegin saw the second, larger falls before she did.

"Have they a power source there, too?"

"Yes, Lieutenant, another one, larger," Portegin reported, homing in on the site with the camera eye.

"And there are the cultivated fields," Titrivell said as the sled rose above the falls, "and a discontinuity fold!"

"A what?" Rianav asked, keeping her eyes on the scene before her.

"Which would explain this raised valley," Titrivell went on. "Old sea bed probably. Look at the size of it!"

"And the reason why they abandoned the butte site," Rianav said. "This plateau is large enough to support the biggest colony ship they build. Can you see evidence of a grid?"

Rianav spiraled the sled, then set it to hover as the three took in the vast area. The foreground was clear despite the beginning of a misty rainfall. The river and the terraced fields that began at its banks disappeared into a haze. In the far distance orange red flashes at several different points suggested that volcanoes added smoke to the heat mists. Portside of the river was the inevitable lush and tangled jungle growth, slanting upward to crown the heights and edges of the broad valley.

"Lieutenant, look!" Titrivell directed Rianav's attention to the settlement to starboard. "Clever of them to use that stranded beach formation."

"The what?"

"And look, ma'am, if you can spot it in the haze, the rock . . . it's ore bearing! No mistaking that color." Titrivell whistled, his eyes wide with excitement. "Just look how that color continues. The whole narding cliff's packed with iron ore."

"A second reason for switching camps, then," she said in a dry tone, dampening the rising enthusiasm Titrivell was displaying.

"See, over there, chimneys!" Titrivell continued, undaunted. Rianav applied a half-turn. "A foundry, all right, and a big one. And blast it all, they've got rails . . . leading to . . . Lieutenant, would you—about thirty degrees and—"

"We're looking for a grid, Titrivell!" she said but corrected the helm.

"We don't need to *look*, Lieutenant," replied Titrivell, "if those rails lead to a mine or . . ."

She gave the sled a bit of power, and they glided along the edge of plateau wall. Abruptly the vegetation disappeared and a huge pit opened below them, glistening in the rain.

"Or an opencast mine like this one!"

"I didn't know you were so knowledgeable about mining, Titrivell," Rianav said with a shaky laugh. She hadn't expected such evidence of industry from Aygar's barbaric appearance and primitive weaponry.

"You don't need to know much not to miss that sort of operation, ma'am," Titrivell said. He looked now beyond the pit, and Rianav, following his gaze, turned the sled away from the mining area, down toward the immense flat plateau.

"They sure didn't have far to haul," Portegin remarked at his post. "Nor far to go home, either. There's a sizable settlement three degrees starboard, ma'am."

"I'm far more interested in whether the grid is finished or not." Rianav was also aware that she should render as full a report as possible to her commander, and that included the number of inhabitants. She diverted the sled to fly over the buildings that shortly became a geometrical arrangement, at the center of which was an expedition dome: its plastic had been scarred by wind and abrasive sands, darkened by sun, but it was still usable and, apparently, the focal point of the settlement.

Despite the rain, people seemed to be pursuing their normal tasks. The unexpected overflight of the sled was seen and soon people were pointing at them.

"There is a grid, ma'am," Portegin said, lifting his head from the camera scan. "I can't think why else so much of the undergrowth would be cleared from half the plateau. There's even a road leading to the area."

Rianav swung the sled about. "I'd like a headcount on this pass, Portegin, Titrivell." She nosed the sled down and slowed its forward speed.

"I make about forty-nine," Portegin said, "but the children keep moving about."

"I count fifty. No, fifty-one. A woman just came out of the dome and she's assisting someone, a man. That makes fifty-two."

"The old man must be the one survivor of the original group," Rianav said. She increased their speed and headed toward the road Portegin had mentioned.

No observer could miss the grid, despite the mud and windblown debris that covered its lattice design, for the soil was divided into squares as far as they could see in the rain.

"Got to give such people credit," Portegin said. "Heavyworld stock or no, that's quite a feat. Going from nothing to that in four decades."

She went far enough across the plateau to confirm that the project was probably finished, then circled widely, heading back toward the settlement.

"Are we going to land?" Portegin asked as they approached. They could see that a crowd waited at the edge of the settlement. "The old man's waving. He expects us to land." Portegin seemed nervous.

"It is our mission after all, Portegin," Rianav remarked dryly.

"And none of them have stunners or Aygar's group would have had 'em," Titrivell added.

"Aygar might not have mentioned our encounter to anyone in authority," Rianav said. "All his welcoming party were young."

"It's to their advantage, Lieutenant, to remain 'unrescued' until that colony ship arrives," Titrivell added.

Portegin snorted. "But we're here, aren't we?"

"It's not as if they won't do very well under the Shipwreck Contingencies," Titrivell said.

"Aygar has greater ambitions, as we heard," Rianav noted. "That's not our problem, fortunately. All we had to do was check out the distress call."

She landed the sled a hundred meters from the crowd, passing control over to Portegin with the same instructions she had given before. With Titrivell behind her, she proceeded up the slight incline. The old man, the woman assisting him, hobbled forward as rapidly as he could with a badly twisted leg.

They might, Rianav thought, have had the metallurgy requisite to make a grid, but they'd missed out on medical skill. There had been a medic included in the original expedition, hadn't there?

"You're from the colony ship?" the old man exclaimed excitedly. "You're orbiting? No need. See," and he gestured to the plateau behind Rianav, "we've got the grid laid. You've only to lead the ship in." He continued to move forward and Rianav realized that he was about to embrace her.

She backed off, saluting as a courteous way to avoid contact. "Your pardon, sir, Lieutenant Rianav of the Cruiser *218 Zaid-Dayan 43*. We picked up your distress signal from the beacon—"

"Distress signal?" The old man drew himself up to a pridefully arrogant stance, his expression contemptuous. "*We* set no distress beacon."

He'd been a powerful man at one time, Rianav thought objectively, but under his loose tunic, his muscles sagged, stretching the hide at its underseams. Pockets of flesh hung from his big bones.

"We were abandoned, yes. Most of our equipment smashed in a stampede. We could send no message. We'd lost all our sleds and the space shuttle. Those misbegotten, nardy high and mighty shippers never bothered their heads to come back. But we managed. We survived. We heavy-worlders do well on this planet. It's ours. And so you forget that distress beacon. We didn't set it. We don't need your sort of help— You can't rob us of what we've made."

From the corner of her eye, Rianav saw Titrivell draw his stunner. The woman at the old man's side noticed the movement and restrained him, murmuring something which cut through his angry renunciation.

"Huh? That?" He peered nearsightedly, and then his face took on a sneering look as he recognized the naked weapon. "That's right. Come among peaceful folk with a stunner. Blast your way through us! Take all we've worked for these long decades. I told the others we'd never be allowed to keep Ireta. You lot always keep the prizes for yourselves, don't you?"

"Sir, we answered a distress signal as we are required to do by space law. We will report your condition to Fleet Headquarters. In the meantime, may we offer you any medical supplies or—"

"Do you think we'd take anything from the likes of you!" The old man was spluttering with indignation. "Nothing is what we want from you! Leave us alone! We've survived! That's more than the others could have done! We've survived. This is our world. We've earned it. And when—"

The woman beside him covered his mouth with her hand.

"That's enough, Tanegli. They understand."

The old man subsided, but as the woman turned to Rianav and Titrivell, he continued to mumble under his breath, throwing angry glances at the two spacers.

"Forgive him, Lieutenant. We bear no malice. And as you see," her broad gesture took in the well-constructed buildings, the fields, the obviously healthy people behind her, "we do very nicely here. Thank you for coming, but there is no distress now." She took a half-step forward, her body shielding the old man as she added, "He has delusions at his age, about rescuers and about revenge. He is bitter, but we are not. Thank you for answering the signal."

"If you didn't send it, then who did?" Rianav asked.

The woman shrugged. "Tardma, one of the originals, used to say that a message was sent before the stampede. But no one came. She was often contradicted."

In her own way, the woman was as eager to be rid of them as Aygar had been. But it was also obvious to Rianav that Aygar had said nothing, at least to the woman and the old man, about the earlier encounter.

"Nothing you need from our stores? Medicine? Matrices? Do you have an operative comunit? We can request a trader to touchdown. They're always looking for new business and a young settlement . . ." Rianav looked past Tanegli. The woman must be his daughter, for she bore a resemblance to him. The others stood back quietly, but obviously were straining to hear every word. Some of the smaller children were working their way round to get a good look at the sled.

"We're self-sufficient, Lieutenant," was the adamant reply.

"No trouble with the indigenous life-forms? We've seen some huge—"

"This plateau is safe from the large herbivores and their predators."

"I shall make my report accordingly." Rianav saluted and, with a smart about-face, strode back to the sled with Titrivell.

She didn't like having her back to the group. She could feel the tension in Titrivell, but Discipline kept her pace controlled and suppressed her urge to look behind her.

Tension showed in Portegin's face and he shoved the canopy back hard enough for it to bounce forward again on its track. Rianav and Titrivell wasted no time climbing into the sled and were barely seated when Portegin executed a fast vertical lift and without spoken order, headed directly back over the falls.

"Every single one of those adults was bigger than we are by a third of a meter, Lieutenant," Portegin said. His lips were dry.

"As soon as we're out of sight behind that ridge, take a direct course to our camp, helmsman."

"They might not have had gravity to contend with," Titrivell remarked, "but that's a mighty fit bunch of people."

"They'd have to be to survive on this planet and keep their aim in mind."

"Their aim, Lieutenant?"

"Yes, helmsman. They want to own all of this planet, not just that plateau or whatever other rights they'd possess on a shipwreck claim."

"But they can't do that! Can they, Lieutenant?" Portegin shifted uneasily in the pilot's seat, clasping and reclasping the control bar with anxious, quick fingers.

"We'll know more after we've made our report to the proper authorities, helmsman."

Then it was Rianav's turn to fidget, rubbing her fingers across her forehead because what she said sounded somehow wrong, and she couldn't imagine why.

They were silent all the way back to the base; a silence partly imposed by the stormy weather, which made conversation in the sled difficult, partly due to the fatigue of Rianav and Titrivell as they came down from the height of Discipline.

Suddenly the sun, as if bored with meteorological displays,

melted through the clouds, and they were treated to vast panoramas of jungle, clear to the distant southern range of volcanoes, and on the east to the thrust of high jagged peaks, bare of the luxuriant purple and green vegetation that seemed indestructible. Glancing around, Rianav caught sight of the three winged fliers and her anxiety dissipated for a reason she was unable to fathom.

The three remained discreetly above and behind the sled until Portegin descended to the vertical landing point in front of the camp's veil screen. As Rianav climbed out of the sled, the golden fliers circled once, then disappeared to the northwest. As she had felt comforted by their curious escort, now she felt sad at their abrupt departure.

The veil screen opened, and a woman walked out to meet them.

"Report, Varian."

Blinking in confusion, Rianav gave her head a sharp shake. She did not recognize that person as part of her command.

"I promised you a barrier, Varian," the woman said with a droll smile. "Did I set it too deep?"

At that posthypnotic cue, the overlay of Rianav gave way to Varian. "Krims! Lunzie, how did you manage that sort of change?" Varian turned around, staring at Triv who had so recently been another person entirely, and Portegin.

Triv was shaking his head, too, while Portegin, emerging from the sled, nearly fell in his surprise.

"Hey, what happened? We're not from any cruiser!" As the realization of his day's adventure seeped into his true self, Portegin collapsed against the side of the sled. "You mean, we just went in among those heavy-worlders and . . . How?"

"Lunzie did it," Varian said, laughing with relief and nervousness as she absorbed the enormity of what they had done.

"He who thinks he's telling the truth is more convincing, Portegin," Lunzie remarked.

"And you made sure our truths matched?" Triv asked.

"I'm better pleased that they weren't needed. Come on in," Lunzie said, wagging her hand to indicate tiny insects flying through the veil opening. "Kai's fretted long enough."

"He's improving?" Varian asked.

"Slowly. That fringe toxemia is affecting his sense of touch. He burned his hand picking up a hot shell and wasn't aware of heat or pain. I smelled the seared flesh. We must all watch out for him."

Varian, entering the domed shelter, found herself viewing it with Rianav's values: neat, functional on a primitive level, but cramped. Rianav also looked over the slightly built man—the effects of the poisoning were evident in his posture as well as the pallor of his face. Aygar was more to Rianav's liking. Varian reasserted herself with an angry shake of her head. She was not Rianav, the lieutenant of a nonexistent cruiser; she was Varian, veterinary xenobiologist. It was obvious from the state of Kai's health, that she must assume the leadership of what remained of the expedition. Or was she leader? Lunzie had been acting far more decisively than she and along more constructive lines. Rianav lingered in Varian's perceptions. Varian wished fervently to be only herself again, without these disruptive second thoughts.

"I am glad you got back safely, Varian," Kai said, his face lighting with a wide smile. Odd blotches marred his face where the fringe punctures had healed but left bleached circles. Varian wondered if that flesh was desensitized as well. "Lunzie kept reassuring me you'd be safe, but I don't trust those heavy-worlders."

"They're not heavy-worlders anymore," Triv said with a derisive snort. "Not even Tanegli. He's just a crippled flabby old man with delusions."

"I'd question the use of 'delusion,'" Varian said, sounding like her alter ego again.

"Why don't you start at the beginning?" Lunzie suggested. But once they had seated themselves and Varian began speaking, she was Rianav, reporting dry fact. Triv added his observations while Portegin listened, occasionally shaking his head as if he could not reconcile his barriered experience with what he was hearing.

"Did Tanegli recognize you?" Kai asked.

"No. But then he hardly expected to see us," Varian said, aware of a vague sadness for Tanegli's disintegrating body and personality. Or was that Rianav thinking? "We presented ourselves as a rescue party, and while only a week of subjective time has passed for us, it was forty-three years for him."

"Rianav—I mean . . ." Triv corrected himself with a laugh and then a sly glance at her, "Varian makes a convincing lieutenant, Kai."

"Our appearance, even as a rescue team, upset Tanegli," Varian went on, determined to suppress one set of her reactions. "He expected to see heavy-worlder colonists emerge from that sled, reporting from their mother ship."

"Aygar didn't mention his encounter with you?"

"No—"

"And he handpicked his reception committee at the old compound," Triv said with a derisory grin. "Only they weren't fast enough for Disciplined troops." When Lunzie gave him a sideways glance of amusement, Triv's expression turned to one of chagrin. "Well, we were Disciplined and we thought we were troops."

"So you needed the stunners?" Lunzie's question was more statement.

"They made the difference all right," Varian said. "On medium, they'd only be immobilized about fifty minutes. It was raining."

"A thoroughly chastening experience for your friends, I've no doubt," Lunzie said. "It's also less likely they'll mention their abortive attempt when they return to the plateau. Not that that matters one way or another."

"You mean, our deception will be discovered when the colony ship lands?" Kai asked.

Lunzie blinked once as if he had taken her meaning entirely wrong, but he couldn't think how.

"First thing they'd do after landing is try to find us," Varian said, "once they have the equipment and personnel to mount a planet-wide search."

"Oh?" Lunzie was amused. "I thought you said you were a convincing rescue team."

"Yes, but . . ."

"That colony ship is not coming in with due authorization from FSP," said Lunzie, ticking off her points. "You said they had primitive hydroelectric plants? Then they've enough to send pulsed code signals to alert the colony ship. Which, because it is not authorized, will not wish to be challenged by any FSP cruisers in the system. Remember, colony-sized ships have got to start slowing once they enter a solar system. They'd come in on a polar entry, more than likely. Did you see a beacon during your sweep of the settlement?"

"No, too hazy, but I'd say it was on the far edge of the grid, on the ridge," Portegin said.

"Would it have a reciprocal facility?" Lunzie asked.

"They had all the spare matrices from the shuttle," Portegin said in a sour tone.

"Bakkun had the basic technical knowledge to improvise," Kai said, remembering the man's personnel record.

"It'll buy us more time if they have augmented their communications," said Lunzie, pleased.

"More time for what and how?" Varian asked. She was surprised to see a twinkle in the medic's eyes as Lunzie turned to her.

"To establish our own claims on Ireta. Believe me, with as grand a larceny as this, no colony ship commander is going to land unless he's very sure there *isn't* a cruiser lurking behind one of Ireta's moons or—" Lunzie turned to Portegin. "Do we have enough matrices to contact the Ryxi?"

"The Ryxi?" Varian was startled by the question. She glared

at Lunzie in sudden antagonism. The Ryxi mustn't learn about the giffs.

"I'd quite forgotten about them," Kai said.

"I'd rather we didn't," Varian said in a tight voice. "How could they help us?"

"*Why* would they?" Triv wanted to know.

"Vrl wasn't pleased with Kai's report about the giffs," Varian began urgently. "You must know what the Ryxi are like, Lunzie?"

"Oh, I do. As I recall it, Kai, you mentioned that the Ryxi had sent out a homing capsule directing their colony ship to start. They'd be well settled in by now—"

"Why would they help us?" Kai asked. He was as unhappy about contacting the Ryxi as Varian but for a less altruistic motive. "They probably assumed that the *ARCT-10* picked us up decades ago."

"The Ryxi generally employ human crew for their space-craft," Lunzie said, cutting through Kai's objections. "I'd be vastly surprised if they didn't have a supply ship calling in at intervals."

"You mean to ask them to pose as Varian's cruiser? What good would that do except delay the colony ship awhile?"

"Any delay helps our purpose." Lunzie was unruffled.

"And what is our purpose?" Varian asked, a little relieved that perhaps the Ryxi needn't personally be involved.

"Delay. Especially to delay that colony ship from landing and consolidating the heavy-worlders' gains."

"Their plans have worked out very well so far," Varian said. "They have established and maintained a settlement on a brutal, primitive world—"

"Whose side are you on?" Kai asked, startled by her comment.

"Ours, of course. But you can't deny that the survivors have done a thundering good job of being stranded—for whatever reason."

"They are, however," and Lunzie's cool tone rebuked Varian more pointedly than Kai's agitation, "about to commit grand theft against the Federated Sentient Planets."

"Grand theft?" Triv was torn between laughter and shock.

"What else do you call stealing a planet?" Lunzie asked, completely serious. "Which is what they'll achieve if that colony ship lands. Oh, FSP can still charge Tanegli with mutiny . . ." and Lunzie shrugged at that useless display of legality. "We, and the sleepers, will get sweet nothing for a lapse of forty-three years because we didn't produce any significant results in opening the planet."

"We were sent on an exploratory mission," Kai began defensively.

"Which remains incomplete." Lunzie made another eloquent shrug of her shoulders.

"What are you driving at, Lunzie?" Varian asked.

"If we, too, make a significant contribution, the planet cannot be ceded entirely to the heavy-world colonists, even if their ship lands. We do that by continuing with the original intention of the landing party: a survey of the geological and xenobiological features. It would be better if we could prevent the colony ship's landing, any way we can. If we somehow validate the 'rescue' before the colony ship sets down, we could limit the settlers to that part they have worked."

"They'd do right well then," Triv said with a long sigh, "for the plateau is iron-rich. Aulia and I also found significant uranium traces along the upthrust of that long mountain chain the day they mutinied. Never did have a chance to tell you that, Kai."

"One wouldn't wish them to have nothing for their labors," Lunzie said with deep irony, before she turned to Varian. "There're also your pets, the giffs, Varian, who need to be permitted to evolve without interference. I'd go before the Supreme Council to defend their protection as a patently intelligent species."

"The whole planet should fall under that protection," Varian declared.

"Quite possibly," Lunzie said, "especially if Trizein's notion is correct about this planet's having somehow been populated with species from Earth's Mesozoic age. That could be the preemptive consideration."

"Not with a world as rich in transuranics as this," Kai said in a tone that brooked no contradiction.

"The two are not mutually exclusive," Lunzie remarked mildly. "But if the colony ship gets down . . ."

"And if we should be found?" Triv asked.

"Which is undoubtedly the first thing Aygar would instruct them to do," Varian said, remembering the fury in that young man's eyes, promising retribution.

"We could use Dimenon and Margit," Kai said thoughtfully into the silence that followed.

"And Trizein," Lunzie said.

"Why him?" Portegin asked. "He's only an analyst and he wouldn't have any facilities."

"He's our authority on the Mesozoic zoology," Lunzie said.

"Portegin, could you rig a jammer for the communications mast at the plateau?" Kai asked.

"That'd mean getting close to the settlement again." Portegin was making no secret of his disinclination.

"Not very close," Triv remarked blandly.

"They wouldn't be expecting a 'rescue' party to interfere," Kai said with a grin.

"Good point," Varian said, pleased and relieved that her coleader was reasserting himself. "And the sooner that is done, the better."

"Agreed!" Lunzie's single word was unexpectedly emphatic. "But, if doing that would use matrices required to reach the Ryxi . . ."

"No, I think enough are available," Portegin said, blithely unaware of the consternation on the faces of both Kai and Varian.

"Kai," and Lunzie turned almost brusquely from the technician, "how clearly do you recall the deposits of ore we'd already found?"

"Very clearly," Kai said in a tone that he hoped Lunzie would interpret.

"Excellent. When I go back to the shuttle, I'll run fiber through the synthesizer for writing material. Trizein never forgets anything he's analyzed, so he can rewrite his notes."

"Terilla could repeat those exquisite drawings of hers," Varian said.

"Children do not adapt well to the trauma of elapsed time," said Lunzie in a cool voice. "It's hard enough on adults to realize that most of their friends, and probably all their immediate family are aged or dead." The silence that greeted her remark caused her to glance at each of their faces. Her expression was kinder as she went on. "It's hard enough for us, but at least *we* have a task to which we can devote our energies." She paused again, looking about her. "I think we'd best get some sleep now. We've a lot to begin tomorrow."

8

ABOUT halfway through that restless night, Varian realized that with the possible exception of Lunzie, no one was finding sleep easy. She was divided between the desire to talk out the day's puzzles and the privacy of the night in which to sort out her muddled reactions.

The revelation that Lunzie had so subtly overlaid her consciousness with that of Rianav distressed Varian. Not because she minded assuming an alter ego but because, as Rianav, her reactions to the mutineers' descendants, and even toward Tanegli, had been sympathetic rather than vengeful. As Varian, she ought not to have any compassion for the man, considering that he and his fellows had robbed her of forty-three years of the companionship of her friends and relatives. Not to mention the minor fact that the mutiny had probably placed Varian's advancement in the Service in jeopardy. And the Service now constituted Varian's anchor. Her parents could be dead. Her brother and two sisters, all her friends, would be entering their seventh or eighth decades and their thoughts would be turned to whatever retirement activity they had earned during their productive years. They would hardly be likely to welcome a youthful Varian.

How many times had this experience happened to Lunzie? The question popped unexpectedly into Varian's drowsing mind and shook her out of the brief spate of self-pity. Lunzie had subtly altered since Varian awakened her. Or perhaps Varian, immersed in her xenobiology, had simply failed to take a proper measure of the medic. Lunzie had kept pretty much to herself and her duties before the mutiny. Lunzie's Service profile had indicated nothing unusual. Nor was it unusual for a medic to be Disciplined. Lunzie's posting to their expedition had all the elements of coincidence . . . but was it? She had revealed herself Adept, and showed a great deal of knowledge about the phenomenology of shipwreck, salvage legalities, and improper colonial takeovers. Had Lunzie been shipwrecked before?

Varian sighed, unable to correlate the nagging inconsistencies. She was deeply sorry for Kai. She'd seen his hands shaking and the occasional body spasms that everyone pretended not to notice. Would he regain his sense of touch and lose those disfiguring white patches from the fringe punctures? She wanted him whole, his old self, her friend and lover, as antidote to the attraction she felt for Aygar.

What were the fringes, for Krims' sake? Aygar said they were warmth seekers. But she and Triv had unearthed the sleds and not been attacked. Warmth? The Thek, Tor, would have radiated more warmth than forty humans while it was plowing back and forth across the old compound in search of the buried core. Tor, the family friend, had attracted the fringe, and left Kai to its embrace.

Varian thought that Lunzie was right not to rouse the children. Poor kids. And yet, they might still have living parents delighted to see them alive, even if their childhood friends would all now be in their middle decades. Wait a moment! Lunzie must be wrong. Children tended to adapt easily. Was Lunzie protecting the children for her own obscure reason? Varian could think of none, and Terilla would be an asset with her exquisite drawing. Bonnard had already proved his initiative and resourcefulness. However, Varian approved that Aulia would remain in cold sleep. No one had time to deal with hysterical temperament.

Varian told herself to stop running on in her mind and get some sleep. She was tired enough, wasn't she? And tomorrow would be stressful in other ways. Now, how could she make up for a forty-three-year gap in her xenobiological research? Some place in the middle of plotting her attempt, Varian drifted off to sleep.

Kai eased himself as quietly as possible into various positions but he couldn't achieve lasting comfort or sleep. Insomnia was a new sensation; he seemed to have spent most of his days lately either deeply asleep or drowsing.

Kai had not previously thought much of his personal appearance, or his body, which had been healthy as long as he could remember. But then, on a compound ship, one underwent periodical physicals as preventive measures. The *ARCT-10*'s medical department had diagnostic data from every system known to the FSP and could synthesize the rarest medicines and vaccines; ill health was quickly remedied. Varian might not want contact with the Ryxi, but if Lunzie was correct and the Ryxi had employed human mercenaries as ship crews, the crewmembers probably had access to treatment. Somewhere in the Federated Sentient Planets, a remedy for his condition could be found. Well, he could do nothing about it just then. He moved again, slowly, trying to make as little sound as possible though it occurred to him that sleepers normally move frequently and everyone else seemed motionless. Were they all awake with troublesome thoughts? And which thoughts?

He'd bet anything that Varian was worried about the Ryxi coming to Ireta and "investigating" her giffs. He could understand that in her. What he found harder to comprehend was her attitude toward the mutineers' descendants. Descendants? Survivors? Precolonists? Of course, that could just be a matter of shaking off the personality Lunzie had created as a protection for the ruse. But Varian was planet-bred and so she might sympathize with any successful implantation whereas he, ship-bred, had a more universal view. Or did he? Was he merely biased in another direction?

Kai had noticed that Triv, too, seemed ambivalent to the industrious settlers. Had it not been for the solidarity of the team behind Lunzie's suggestion to continue the geological and xenobiological surveys, Kai would have serious doubts about their loyalties.

Odd, too, that not one of them had mentioned the *ARCT-10* or expressed concern over the fate of its huge complement of sentient beings. Kai suppressed resentment. The *ARCT-10* had been his home but Triv, Portegin, Lunzie, and Varian were all contract specialists, gleaned from other star systems. The ship-bred of his detachment had been Gaber, now dead, Aulia, himself, and the three children, Terilla, Cleiti, and Bonnard. He was the only one awake who considered the *ARCT-10* home, so he ought not to fault his teammates.

What *had* happened to the *ARCT-10*? To the best of Kai's

recollection, no compound ship of her size had ever been destroyed. Units had been shattered or pierced, with loss of life, but an entire compound ship? The size of a small satellite? Kai really didn't care what happened to the heavy-worlders and their bid for Ireta. He would like to see even old Tanegli tried for mutiny. But other rich worlds lay ready for FSP to exploit—so long as his set of survivors profited. But he did want to know what had delayed the *ARCT-10*, where she'd been, what she'd done, why wasn't she here, if only to heal his distressing condition. He drifted off to sleep finally, trying to rationalize the nonappearance of his ship.

Triv lulled himself to sleep by repeating the coordinates of the finds made by the teams until he was sure he had the figures correct. At first, he had been annoyed to think that he'd be done out of the bonuses he'd anticipated from the expedition. He was much cheered to realize that something could be rescued to pay for lost time. Of course, his credit balances would have appreciated during cold sleep. As long as his whereabouts were uncertain, no credit organization could disperse his holdings. He amused himself by calculating the current balance at forty-three years' accumulated and compound interest. Having made few personal ties anywhere, Triv was not especially bothered by the elapsed decades. So long as his monies appreciated with interest, and he collected a just percentage of the wealth that was obviously to be mined on Ireta, he was satisfied.

He heard a soft scraping noise and turned his head slightly. Kai again. He experienced a fleeting sympathy for the man that only proved to Triv how right he was to avoid attachments of any kind. Pretty soon now, if the Iretan prospects lived up to his expectations and he could live off the interest of his credit balance, he'd find himself one of the less frequented planets, a soft leisurely world. He'd link up with some obliging person to attend his physical needs and then he'd do whatever he fancied, when he fancied it. Meanwhile,

a geologist with his ratings, a Disciple as well, never lacked
assignments.

Although Portegin was somewhat relieved that Aulia was
not going to be awakened, it irritated him, too. He knew her
faults, but they worked well as a team and they got on even
better as a pairing. He was beginning to miss her now he was
fully revived from the cold sleep. Then he brightened at a second thought: Aulia would be much more likely to contract
with him since they were contemporaries. She'd really have
difficulty forming a new relationship among those her subjective age.

Portegin was still irked by Lunzie's manipulations. He'd
never said she could tinker with his mind, no matter if she had
Kai's and Varian's consent. He was aware that Adepts never
misused their abilities, which was why so few were allowed
to attain that rank, but her interference rankled. In fact, the
only good to come out of the day had been the assurance that
they wouldn't lose out on mineral and ore bonuses. He wondered if Kai and Varian would go for stretching their subjective time a little, say, back three or four years; one got only
subsistence rate for being asleep on an assignment, no matter
the reason. He wished Kai would get settled, even though the
man was trying to be considerate, moving slowly. Too considerate, because his slow deliberate attempts to cut down noise
made the process longer. Lunzie hadn't so much as stirred
since she lay down.

Portegin had to admire the medic. Not for a single moment
had he suspected her of being more than just a healer. He
drifted into unconsciousness while calculating possible totals
to his bonuses.

Lunzie didn't move because her mind had commanded her
body to relax while she reviewed the day's achievements: satisfactory on many counts—though Varian's obvious attraction to the settler, Aygar, might become a problem. Distract
Varian with the giffs, put her on her professional mettle to

protect that species. Lunzie actually shared the girl's reluctance to have the Ryxi learn overmuch about the golden fliers. A most remarkable species, those giffs. It would be very interesting to discover how they, and the immense herbivores and grotesque predators of Mesozoic Terra, got to Ireta. All too pat, this planet so perfect for the continuation of a totally useless series of beings. The planet was rife with anomalies. Puzzles pleased Lunzie, especially if she solved them in advance of anyone else. This assignment was generating more riddles than she had ever encountered before. A routine assignment, huh? She ran through her probabilities again and decided that she had a better than average chance of pulling a hat trick. Then she chuckled silently at her unconscious use of such an anachronism. Space helmet trick? Well, she oughtn't to be greedy: that led to overconfidence, a state of mind which imperiled more than it aided. Two successes would mollify the Council of Adepts. However, if the two most important aspects of the assignment ended satisfactorily, it was logical to assume that the others would as well. Aware that she could juggle variations and probabilities all night and not fathom half the ramifications possible in this set of circumstances—and that without allowing for random factors—Lunzie initiated the hypnotic sequence that would end in sleep.

The next morning, after a potent breakfast stew, Lunzie took the four-man sled back to the giff cave. Varian went off with Portegin in one of the smaller sleds, combining both xenob and geological scouting. Triv went prospecting in an area where the radiation counter had begun chattering at the end of the previous day's swing.

Kai couldn't keep his eagerness to inspect the find out of his voice but in his weakened condition, he was more useful as duty officer. And he was kept busier than anticipated for the reason that they lacked materials on which to keep notes and mark coordinates. However, as the campsite contained a level area of packed dirt, Kai used a sharp stick to inscribe the figures as they were called in, plus whatever additional notes were relayed. On the other side of the path from his message board, he began working on as detailed a map of Ireta as he could call to mind. He started with his recollection of the basement rock area which was unlikely to have changed much in elapsed forty-three years. As he sketched, Kai grinned to himself. The others could fault Tor the Thek as much as they wished, but to him, the fact that the Thek had come to Ireta in search of the long-lost core of obvious Thek manufacture was a personal triumph. If the artifact had not been so significant to the Thek, Kai was certain that Tor would have remained. But why had it taken forty-three years to rouse the Thek to investigate?

Kai marked in the immense northeastern plain where the butte formations had caused them to place the secondary camp. He was tempted to place pebbles to signify the rocky outcroppings. He wasn't sure of the terrain leading to the settlement, but Triv said it was probably a raised sea bed of geologically recent upheaval. Quite likely, since it would have been beyond the "safer" basement area, at the edge of one set of the planet's restless tectonic plates. Volcanic disturbances had been recorded in the brief time the team had been there.

Kai had to leave the pole areas as *terra incognita*. Because of Ireta's peculiar formation and its very hot thermal core, the poles were hotter than the equator and considerably more active. Massive changes might have taken place there even in a brief four decade span.

Lunzie interrupted his cartographical labors to report her safe arrival at the cave, adding that she'd been escorted by three giffs. She had picked up sufficient vegetable fiber on her route to supply them with plenty of pulp paper, and while arousing the sleepers, she intended to make use of her spare time to experiment with juices that might make an ink. She favored the hadrasaur nut, for the shell left a stain on the fingers.

Kai could not help but feel chagrin when he returned to his map, but then he took heart—his map was three dimensional and much larger than any paper Lunzie could manufacture. He began to make mud mountains and simulate the giffs' inland sea, then he sited the three camps with flags made of twig and triangular purple leaves.

Varian reported in next, about the first pitchblende deposit, interrupting his construction of the terrain. She was tell-tagging great herds of beasts, varieties of hadrasaur she had not previously noted, and was nearly to the Great Rift where the carotene grass grew.

Kai returned to his work and gouged out the Rift. He was rather enjoying himself by then and was not too pleased to have his Rift-making interrupted by another summons to the comunit. It was Varian, highly excited. She'd flown across the smoking trail of recent lava flow and observed fringes large and small: some were hunting while others were folded, their thin envelopes swollen with prey.

"Some are even attached to the big beasts. Those stupids don't seem to know they're being eaten alive. And there's nothing I can do."

"Did you bring a stunner with you, Varian?" Kai asked.

"Kai, we don't have enough charges to waste . . ."

"Don't waste, Varian. Just see if the fringes are deterred by a stun charge."

"Point's taken," she replied in an odd tone. "I'll use it on some animal that has a chance." She signed off.

How much warmth would attract a fringe, Kai wondered as he watered dirt to make a mountain range beyond the Rift. Apparently Triv and Varian had not been warm enough to attract the one at the old compound. The current campsite, erected as temporary quarters for two geologists, was going to be cramped with seven. Was that over the critical warmth mass? If it was, would fringes be deterred by a force-screen? Kai rose from his map-making and prowled the perimeter. The ground sloped away from the ridge on which the dome rested. A barren rocky outcrop several meters beyond had defeated even Ireta's vegetation. They'd have visual warning of an attack by fringes.

The creatures' emergence as predators was another of Ireta's puzzles. There hadn't been much talk between himself and Varian. He'd been ill, of course, and she and Lunzie had done as they both saw to the advantage of the group. That was only logical. But he couldn't shake the notion that Varian was more distant. He tried not to relate that to her encounter with Aygar and the mutineers' descendants. He was wrong to call them that, perhaps, but the term sprang readily to mind. He must be imagining things: there was no change in Varian, merely the vestiges of the barriers that Lunzie had set for her protection.

The buzz of the comunit was a welcome interruption. Triv reported that he had detected a high ironstone reading along a vast ridge, but his sled had flushed an unusual number of large creatures from the thick vegetation covering the ridge.

"Not that landing for a sample would do us any good, but a sample of the rock makes a nice display until we have assay materials." The geologist snorted. "We should have been asking for supplies from Aygar's folk instead of offering them."

"They're an iron-age technology, Triv. We want to be in the transuranics. Forget the metals: watch that counter!"

Though Kai went back to his map, he had lost all enthusiasm for it. He had a wayward urge to trample it down into the soil from which he had raised it. He had in fact lifted one foot to obliterate the mountain when he caught sight of his bloodied fist. Startled, he examined the hand and then the other, and hastily returned to the dome to wash away the mud and examine the damage he hadn't felt. Fortunately it was no more than scrapes and minor cuts. He was still examining his hands when the first of the sleds returned. He almost resented the intrusion on his solitude.

No sooner had Triv parked his sled than the second, with Varian and Portegin, emerged from the evening haze. Varian halted Triv's entrance to the veil, saying she'd a lot of fruit and bean pods to bring in. No sooner were the three inside the screen than Triv saw the relief map and would have dropped his burden had not Varian shouted. Then she and Portegin stood, arms full, exclaiming over Kai's improvisation.

"I'd have to check scale," Kai said, disclaiming their fulsome compliments, "and, of course, we don't know how the polar region or the southern tip have changed with tectonic action . . ."

"Are you in there?" A harsh shout at the veil entrance distracted them.

"It's Lunzie," Varian cried, looking hastily about her for a spot to place her burdens.

"Come on, you three," the medic called, "this bunch isn't too steady on their feet yet. Kai, operate this damned veil."

In the excitement of welcoming Trizein, Margit, and Dimenon, Kai was relieved that Lunzie had no time to notice his hands, which he kept at his sides. Then Varian called him to help her unload the rest of her harvest while the newly awakened were made comfortable in the dome.

"If you'll just hold your arms out, Kai . . ." Varian stared down at the hands he obediently held upward for a load. She started to touch his scored fingers and then stopped, staring at his face. "That does it, Kai. We contact someone who can remedy this. Even a freighter will have medical files on its computer."

"Varian, if the Ryxi—"

"I've an override to protect my own species first, Kai." She exhaled, part in exasperation, part in anger until her eyes, avoiding his, fell on the map, its mountain mounds and the Rift outlined in the last of the westerly light. "And that's a contribution, too!"

She finished loading his extended arms, grinning conspiratorially at him as she artistically draped bean-pod leaves over his hands and then gave him an affectionate shove back to the dome.

Trizein provided an almost continuous monologue on the types, probable evolutionary steps, habit, temperament, and breeding methods of all the creatures he had seen on his way from the giff cave to theirs. According to Dimenon's amused aside, the chemist had nearly driven Lunzie to fury by his insistence that they divert the journey to follow this or that species until he had had a close enough look. He had also appropriated some of the pulp sheets Lunzie had extruded for Kai, insisting that his work would be far more important in the eyes of the FSP than any merely prodigious amount of transuranic elements. Why, the discovery of those beasts would settle for once and all an argument that had exercised centuries of paleontologists, biologists, and xenobiologists—the possibility of convergent biology, of similar life-forms evolving from cellular stews on different planets. He added, complete with wild gestures, that its happening with a third-generation sun was utterly improbable, incredible, and unlikely—as any zoologist of the lowest rating would tell you.

Trizein continued in this vein, occasionally stopping to admire one of his many sketches, apologizing for its rudeness and correcting a line or contour, until Lunzie announced that everyone had better eat something, then shoved Trizein's bowl under his nose.

The man's enthusiasm was so infectious that even Kai found himself smiling at the man's joy.

"You'll go out again, tomorrow, Trizein," Varian said, her voice bubbling with good humor. "I've the Rift grasses. Lunzie, do you need to synthesize—"

"More paper at the rate Trizein's using it up," the medic said with a sniff, but she'd a twinkle in her eye as well.

"Lunzie, what did the heavy-worlders do for vitamin A if it's so necessary to our diet?" asked Triv.

"This is a huge continent. If there is one such area of carotene-rich grass to supply these ancient beasties of Trizein's, undoubtedly there's another. Divisti would have known about the need for vitamin A or they'd all have poor vision—which I gather they haven't." Lunzie shot a glance at Varian.

"Portegin ought to go with you, Lunzie, and dismantle the beacon mast." Varian had everyone's stunned attention. "I've given the matter considerable thought and, if, as you suggested, the Ryxi have employed human mercenary ships and crew, that's who'd be sent to answer any call from us. I don't feel we can achieve enough without proper equipment. The heavy-worlders got what they wanted, and I refuse to see us deprived of more than time."

"More than time?" Dimenon demanded with considerable agitation.

"That's all so far," Margit said blandly. "The beacon does register *our* finds to our credit, doesn't it, Kai?" When Kai nodded, she went on, "So, our claims are valid—"

"Until that colony ship settles," Lunzie said. Her tenacity to that theme was beginning to puzzle Kai. She turned to Varian then and said, "I doubt that a Ryxi would answer a call from here. What's his feather—" and she wound her hand in the air as a memory aid, looking at Kai.

"Vrl," he supplied coldly.

"That Vrl's probably still alive. I doubt he cares."

"Ryxi have a long life span on low-gravity planets," Varian said, "but it's a chance we've got to risk. It's worth far more in terms of the supplies we must have to achieve our original objectives." She turned to Lunzie. "Tomorrow, Rianav and the helmsman from Cruiser *218-ZD-43* will make a second run to the plateau," and she inclined her head significantly. "We'll jam their beacon and then get a message off to the Ryxi."

"If a freighter is in," Kai added, "give them a course that'll fly past the mutineers' camp. That'll make them think twice about calling in their colony ship."

"Will there be someone to take me out tomorrow?" Trizein asked plaintively.

"I will," Triv replied.

"Then we can get on with surveying?" Margit asked hopefully.

"You'd better!" Kai said.

"I could stay in as coordinator, Kai," Lunzie said.

"Appreciated, Lunzie, but I've got to compose a message for the Ryxi . . ."

Varian's unrepentant grin, reminding him of previous occasions when he'd been left to communicate with the Ryxi, lifted Kai's spirits.

It was very early in the morning when Rianav roused her helmsman for an early start on their mission. A hastily prepared stew was simmering in the hearthpot when the medic awoke. Although Rianav knew that nothing could have penetrated the force-screen that surrounded the dome, it made her uneasy that no watch had been kept on what was, after all, a hostile planet. Still, the medic could close the screen after they had left. Which she did, with a silent wave of good luck as they departed in the two-man sled.

The gloom of cloudy night surrounded them, and Rianav was glad they had flown the course before and had some knowledge of the terrain. She kept the sled at a respectable altitude. The telltagger's infrequent spouting was the only noise to break the silence as they sped northeast.

They were an hour into their journey when the telltagger rattled hysterically.

"Krims! What was that?" Portegin demanded. "Something awful big, Lieutenant!"

"There's nothing airborne that is that big on this planet . . ."

"I hope!"

"Heat register's too high, anyhow." Rianav hauled the sled to starboard, her quick action preventing a collision. A massive object streaked across their previous line of flight. They could follow the bright yellow-white exhausts as the vessel flashed by on their portside.

"What under the seven suns was that?" Portegin asked, craning his neck to follow its course.

"A medium-light space vessel to judge by the propulsion configuration."

"From the heavies' camp?" Portegin's voice ran with understandable concern.

"I doubt it, helmsman. It came from due east, not northeast."

"Scouts?"

"Not that large a ship."

"Unless that colonist transport also carries military craft . . ." Portegin added grimly.

"Belay that, helmsman. We don't need to borrow trouble. We have our orders."

"So we do, sir." At the skepticism and near impudence in her subordinate's tone, Rianav grinned to herself. "Ma'am, shouldn't we inform base camp? And shouldn't we inform our cruiser of this violation of Ireta's air space?"

"Not if it also informs that intruder of the whereabouts of our base camp, helmsman. The cruiser would have observed the entry. I see no point in breaking comsilence and informing a listener of our presence. Especially as we are heading toward the plateau."

"But, if the heavy-world transport is down, we don't need to jam that beacon."

"First we get to the plateau, helmsman." Rianav spoke firmly enough to repress further suggestions.

The sullen Iretan dawn lightened the skies just as they reached the first of the falls below the plateau.

"Lieutenant, isn't that awfully bright for dawn?" asked Portegin, pointing slightly to starboard. A luminous bright yellow formed a curious circle under pendulous Iretan clouds.

"Damn funny!" Rianav piled on power and took the little sled up at a steep angle to get maximum height while still in the shelter of the hills surrounding the plateau.

Then several things happened at once.

"This is rescue mission! Is anyone on that beacon?" demanded an impatient voice. After a moment of silence, the voice spoke to someone in the background. "No luck on this frequency, sir . . . Roger. All frequencies at max power."

The telltagger began to hum. Not chatter or squawk but the hum which experience told Rianav was a large airborne object slowly approaching them from a height.

"A ship? Can you see it, Portegin?"

"No. Shouldn't I answer the rescue hail?"

"Not if they're homing in on this beacon. We say nothing. Oh Krims! and bollux!" Rianav swore fiercely and loudly, trying to deny what they saw.

"We've had it!" Portegin's resigned words came out in an awed whisper.

They had risen above the screening terrain, the hills from which the iron ore had been mined to cushion the vast bulk of the transport ship which was settling to earth. The light seen by Rianav and Portegin was radiating from its underside and from arc lights surrounding the landing site.

"That isn't what's making the telltagger talk," protested Portegin and looked over his shoulder. He opened his mouth to speak when a bolt spewed from the maw of the transport.

Rianav slowed the sled in a frantic effort to avoid the beam. That was all she remembered.

"Kai? Kai, are you awake?"

At the panicky tone in Dimenon's voice, Kai sprang awkwardly toward the comunit.

"I'm here."

"Kai, I'll swear it. We got Thek here. Thek all around. Big ones, little ones, like they were taking turns!"

"Where are you, Dim?"

"We're just over the pitchblende strike—"

Dimenon's words were cut off abruptly. Kai tried to re-establish contact. Not that Dimenon or Margit would be in any danger from the Thek, but he would prefer a little more detailed report. When he failed to raise the geologists, he switched to Lunzie.

"Whereabouts are *you*, Lunzie?"

"Nearly to the cave. Why?"

"Dimenon just reported there are Thek on the first strike. Then he went silent."

"Thek? Kai, I think we'd better raise Varian and abort that mission. If Thek are here . . ."

"THIS IS RESCUE MISSION. IS ANYONE ON THAT BEACON? THIS IS AN ALL-FREQUENCIES HAIL. WE ARE A RESCUE MISSION. WE ARE HOMING IN ON YOUR BEACON!"

The interruption stunned Kai and Lunzie.

"You are blasting our eardrums, rescue," Lunzie said. "What is your origin?"

"Ryxi."

"Maintain silence and home in on beacon." Lunzie interrupted in a tone that inspired compliance. "I'll get back to you, Base." Kai knew to maintain his silence.

Which beacon? he wanted to shout. And why were Thek appearing all over the landscape? Should he not attempt to warn Varian? Well, if the rescue ship was heading toward the heavy-worlders' beacon, Varian would abort on her own initiative.

His moment of panic subsided. The appearance of Thek meant that Tor had informed others. It was as likely that Tor had organized a rescue from Ryxi, and humans at that by the voice. Then Kai found another reason to be alarmed, since he seemed determined to be anxious: Tor would not know that Kai had roused other members of his team. Tor would know that the heavy-worlders were active on the planet. Surely a Thek could tell the difference between normal humans and heavy-worlders? Dimenon wouldn't panic when faced with a Thek, even a horde of them. And Dimenon would know to ask for Tor, wouldn't he?

Two anxious hours Kai waited.

"Kai, are you there?" Lunzie's voice had a buoyancy which Kai had never heard in it before.

"Yes, yes, I'm here! Where else?"

"At ease," Lunzie's voice had a lilt of laughter for his sarcasm. "All's well here at the cliff beacon. I'll have to apologize to Varian. Those giffs of hers are far more intelligent than we suspected."

"Why?"

"I'll swear they recognized the difference between my sled and the one Captain Godheir sent in. When I got here, the giffs were protecting the cave and our shuttle against *any* unauthorized intrusion . . ."

"Who's Godheir?"

"The captain of the Ryxi supply vessel, the *Mazer Star*. And I apologize to you, too. Your Thek, Tor, left orders with the Ryxi planet to mount a rescue mission for you. But the Ryxi vessel was away on a supply trip so it took them until now to respond. The vessel's medium-sized and had to land in the jungle. They sent in a sled and the giffs attacked it. They're formidable in the air. I arrived as the battle was in full swing. But Kai, when I approached, the giffs escorted me to the cave. And the captain will swear to it." Kai wasn't sure why Lunzie should sound so triumphant over that point. "So I've asked Captain Godheir to send a sled to collect you, and some men to guard the dome. And if his diagnostic unit doesn't have an answer, the cruiser's will. Godheir's trying to raise Dimenon but he's also agreed to send out a search party if you'll give me the coordinates." Kai quickly gave her the figures. "And Kai, I lodged an official charge of mutiny with Captain Godheir. You'll be asked to confirm."

Kai caught his breath because it was scarcely the function of a medical officer, even an Adept, to lodge such a complaint if either of the team's leaders were alive.

"You'll want it on record, Kai," and Lunzie's voice was not

the least apologetic for her usurpation of right, "because the colony ship's down and a cruiser is guarding it."

"Varian and Portegin?"

Lunzie's voice altered again, devoid of emotion. "Their sled received a bolt from the transport, but the cruiser was able to grapple it in time to break the full force of a crash. They're both alive and being conveyed to the cruiser. Just hang on there, Kai. We've got more help than we need."

"Any news on the *ARCT-10*?"

"No, but Godheir wouldn't necessarily know. The cruiser might. I'll ask when they've secured the transport. Take it easy now, Kai. No fretting. I'll see you soon."

Only then did Kai notice the blood running from his hands. He had been gripping the comunit so hard, he had lacerated his palms. He had no great hopes that either diagnostic unit could help him, but perhaps there'd be some skin-gloves and shin pads so he'd stop injuring himself. He thrust his hands into a basin of water, aware that he couldn't even sense the temperature. He salved the cuts and bandaged them.

So the colony ship had landed after all. Whether a cruiser was on its back or not now mattered little. Time had run out on their attempt to salvage something of this miscarried expedition. His first opportunity to prove his leadership ability had ended in disaster. Kai walked morosely around the relief map. With an air of finality, he picked up the discarded pods of hadrasaur nuts and placed the smallest one near the giffs' cave, the next largest on the edge of the heavy-worlders' plateau and the largest right in the midst of the grid. Then he sat, bandaged hands dangling between his legs while he waited for the rescue sled.

9

HANDS pulled urgently at Rianav, and she groaned. An ache encompassed her whole body.

"Lemmalone."

"Not when I have no choice but to retrieve you," a familiar voice said. Hands now reached under her armpits, lifting her strangely unresisting body out of the pilot's seat. "You're in one piece. Just relax, Lieutenant."

"Easy there, now," another voice called, its tone of command undiminished by distance.

"You're lighter than I'd thought," the familiar voice murmured.

Rianav forced her eyes open and gasped. Blood seemed to be dripping from her face. The arms that lifted her were heavily corded. She started to struggle.

"Don't," Aygar ordered impatiently. "I'm under surveillance, and I've no wish to be stunned again. You have nothing to fear from me. Or mine." His tone was bitter, but as he eased her from the damaged cockpit, his hands did not abuse his advantage.

"Cut the chatter," the other voice ordered. The voice came from below her. She couldn't make out her surroundings. "Just lift her out. Nice and easy. Medic!"

"I'll carry her down." Aygar has lost none of his arrogance, she thought. She relaxed as she felt him descending a steep and uneven way.

Despite blurred vision, partly due to the blood which streamed down her nose, Rianav looked about her as Aygar scrambled down a rocky incline. The sled had crumpled, nose first, into the side of a cliff and wedged in. Another sturdy young man was extracting Portegin's limp body from his side of the wrecked vehicle. On a much wider shelf about fifteen meters below were a pinnace and a cluster of uniformed personnel, some with drawn stunners, watching the rescue operation. Blinking to clear her eyes, Rianav looked beyond, to the vast plateau now inhabited by the immense squat bulk of a colony transport ship and the long sleekly dangerous form of a medium deep-space cruiser. As Rianav made out the designation, *218-ZD-43* on the stern fins, she experienced an unreasonable spurt of pure panic and clutched at Aygar's shoulders.

"I told you. I won't harm you. That bunch is just waiting for a chance to blast us out of existence." Aygar's bitterness was intense.

"Your transport shot us down."

"You and your phony rescue mission. All the time your cruiser was tracking the transport!"

Rianav flinched from his anger, aware of contradictory, nonsensical, and conflicting emotions. But the next moment Aygar had reached the ledge, and she was removed from his arms. She started to protest as she saw him pushed to one side by armed personnel. Then a medic was busy checking the pupils of her eyes and someone else applied an antiseptic pack to her bleeding forehead. She felt a spray go in one arm, a powerful restorative to judge by the flood of energy that surged through her body.

"You'll do," the medic muttered and stepped back, signaling his assistant to help Rianav clean the worst of the blood from her skin. The Iretan flies were buzzing in a cloud, attracted by the smell of blood.

"Lieutenant Rianav," and she turned to look at the officer who now confronted her. His face was totally unfamiliar to her. Even medium-size cruisers were not so huge that officers could remain unknown to one another. His expression was compounded of many elements: anticipation, curiosity, and a tinge of awe. "Commander Sassinak is waiting for your personal report."

To gain a moment to collect herself, Rianav looked over to where Portegin was being examined. "Is he all right?"

"He'll have a worse headache than you will, Lieutenant," the medic replied cheerfully then pointed to the long gash across Portegin's forehead. "Only a flesh wound. Here, you, let's get him out of this stinking air and away from those blood-sucking insects."

Aygar and his friend were summarily encouraged to lift Portegin and bring him into the pinnace.

"We used those two local lads to reach you," the officer was saying in an apologetic tone as he escorted Rianav to the pinnace. "They *said*," and he gave a skeptical snort, "they were on their way to rescue you anyhow." He dropped his voice to a confidential tone as they entered the little ship. "We haven't had a planetfall in months and we might have botched the climb. Couldn't let that happen. Sorry you landed so hard. We saw that transport zap you and the commander only managed to get a tractor beam on you long enough to cushion the fall— All secure back there?"

"Aye, aye, sir."

Rianav craned her head to see Portegin strapped into a seat, the medics on either side of him. Aygar and his companion were under the wary guard of four marines, two with drawn stunners.

"Why are those men under guard, Lieutenant?" Rianav asked as she fastened her seat belt.

"They're mutineers. Your people filed a charge of mutiny, you know. First thing your commander told mine."

There was something wrong with that statement, but Rianav could not fathom what, beyond the obvious error that her commander and his must be the same.

The young lieutenant leaned toward her, his voice low. "The other elements of your group have all reported in, Rianav. Don't worry about anything." He turned aside to order the helmsman to take the pinnace back to the *ZD-43*. Then he grinned complacently at Rianav. "The heavy-worlders' transport never even knew we were on their tails. Sassinak's a canny commander."

As the little pinnace took off, Rianav placed trembling fingers against her temples. That knock on her head had done more than visible damage for she was being afflicted with selective amnesia. She knew that there was to be a colony ship but not that her cruiser was chasing it. She knew she served on the *ZD-43* but she couldn't recognize any of the men on the pinnace, or conjure up the name of her commanding officer.

"That transport was being trailed?" She'd been so sure that her cruiser was in orbit above the planet, had had no intention of landing, and that she was part of a rescue mission, answering a distress call.

"Ever since the transport crossed into our patrol sector. Ships the size of that baby are leeched the moment the keel is laid. Part of the Federation's long-term plan to stop planet piracy. So the moment the leech activated our sensors, we checked Registry and knew we'd a live one." The lieutenant's grin broadened. "The transport was built in Voroshinsky, sold to Dopli—the heavy-world planet in Signi Sector—and it was heading in a very suspicious direction, there being very few systems open for colonization out this side. So we pursued it with the leech keeping it on a leash for us."

Rianav felt a gentle bump as the pinnace landed. Briskly the young lieutenant unfastened his seat belt and rose, ordering the medics to take Portegin to the sick bay, the marines to remove the prisoners and secure them in the settlement. He was turning, with more courtesy in his manner, to Rianav when the comunit on the pinnace console burbled a summons.

"Guarded message for Lieutenant Rianav, sir," the helmsman announced, rising from his place and gesturing for Rianav to take his seat. Then he and the officer discreetly left the pinnace.

"Lieutenant Rianav here," she said, depressing the screen toggle. Its tiny picture revealed a face which Rianav did recognize: her medic.

"Report, Varian."

As Lunzie's words dissipated the barrier, Varian-Rianav sank against the back of the contour chair, her mind reeling as one identity still impinged on the other.

"Slight miscalculation on our part, Varian. We now have more help than we can use. Are you okay?"

"A scratch on the scalp and a distinct feeling that I'd lost my memory. Portegin's still unconscious, but they say he'll be fine. Lunzie, did you know that this cruiser is the *ZD-43*?"

"So I'm told. Nice coincidence, isn't it? Did you pick up that all-frequencies hail on your way to the plateau?"

"Who was that?" Rianav–Varian remembered everything now.

"That was our friendly Ryxi rescue mission. No Ryxi, by the way." Lunzie chuckled. "Nearly blew Commander Sassinak's little surprise party. Kai's Tor gave the alert, but the Ryxi had to wait for the vessel to return from a supply run before they could dispatch it to our assistance. And Dimenon reported to Kai that the Thek have arrived in strength."

"In strength?"

"Dotting the landscape, thirty strong by the latest count. That's a lot of Thek."

"Any of them Tor?"

"Don't know. Dimenon fired in the report and then Kai lost the connection. Captain Godheir has sent a sled out after him and Margit. And I've got a lot to tell you about your precious giffs when you get back. After Commander Sassinak has had her chat with you. I didn't know about the cruiser when I filed a mutiny charge with Captain Godheir. I wanted that on record as soon as possible. Sassinak will want to have details from you. I'm reviving the rest of the sleepers now. Their reports are going to be needed, too. And they might as well wake up. We've got enough help now to complete the original mission."

"Lunzie, how's Kai?"

"In Godheir's sick tank. We can improve his condition. As I said, I didn't know about the cruiser. Its medical team can help if Godheir's doesn't come up with an answer."

Behind Varian, someone was noisily clearing his throat.

"I'll join you as soon as I can arrange transport, Lunzie. Just continue as you think best."

"Well, that gives me plenty of latitude."

"You don't need any more," Varian said in an ironic tone. Lunzie gave her a sardonic grin as she broke the connection. Then Varian rose to face the lieutenant.

"My wits have been rattled, Lieutenant, I don't know your name."

"Borander." He smiled. "Commander Sassinak is waiting for you." Borander now exuded an air of urgency. "You look a lot better now, you know. I was a bit worried about you for a while. You didn't seem yourself."

"You could say I wasn't."

Borander escorted her from the pinnace, which had landed near the cruiser by one of the open air locks. From her vantage point in the pinnace's lock, Varian had a good view of the heavy gunsleds in position around the massive hulk of the heavyworld transport. Cruisers were scarcely small, but the ZD-43 looked almost puny as it faced the colony ship. Only one of the transport's locks was open, but none of the heavyworld contingent was visible. Varian hoped that the cruiser's weaponry was trained on the transport. It looked so menacing, just sitting there, as if it meant to stay. She was only slightly reassured by the fact that most colonists were shipped in cold sleep to their new destinations.

"These guys built a proper strip, I'll give 'em that much," Borander said, gesturing to their right.

Aygar and his friend were squatting on their haunches beside the pinnace, and the friend scowled at her. Aygar was staring into the distance, indifferent to his surroundings and the marines' weapons.

"Borander, *why* are these men being guarded?"

"Why, because they're mutineers," Borander replied.

"These two men are *not* mutineers, Lieutenant Borander. They were born here on Ireta and they had nothing to do with the mutiny. There is no need to keep *them* under restraint."

"Now, look, your people registered a mutiny charge first with Captain Godheir and then with Commander Sassinak—"

"Which still has nothing to do with Aygar and anyone in his generation or even his parents'."

"And I suppose they didn't help build that grid to assist an illegal landing . . ." Borander switched from surprise to open scorn.

"I think the judicial will find that Aygar was acting on misinformation and could be excused from a conscious violation of EEC regulations."

Borander held himself stiffly. "That is not for me to decide. Now, Commander Sassinak is waiting for you."

"Then Aygar can accompany us, and I'll sort the matter out right now."

Aygar maintained his air of indifference, but his companion was staring at Varian, his jaw had dropped open and his face bore a surprised expression that put Varian in mind of Tardma.

"Why, I can't just walk into the commander's office with these two—"

"*I* can." Varian put the steel of Discipline into her voice. "I'll remind you, Lieutenant, that as coleader of an authorized expedition to Ireta, *I* have the rank of planetary governor *pro-tem*. Who outranks whom, Lieutenant?"

Borander swallowed, arching his back to attention. "You do . . . ma'am. But that doesn't mean the commander's going to *like* it."

Varian ignored that remark and turned to the Iretans. "Aygar, if you and your friend would be good enough to accompany us?" She stared pointedly from the marines to Borander who signaled them to sheathe their stunners. Aygar rose from his haunches with graceful ease.

"You'd be one of Tardma's grandchildren?" she asked the unknown Iretan.

"I'm Winral," the man replied in a surly voice, eyeing her with growing anxiety.

Borander stepped out quickly toward the cruiser's gangplank. Aygar fell in beside her while Winral tagged behind. Varian noticed but did not comment on the fact that Borander signaled the marines to bring up the rear.

"Lieutenant, would you know how much damage my sled sustained? I'll need transport to return to my base camp as soon as I've seen the commander."

"Apart from the crumpled nose, I'd say the bolt just drained your power pack," Borander replied in a formal tone. "I'll order it retrieved and repowered."

Varian received the distinct impression that Borander did not think she'd survive her interview with his commander. They were halfway to their destination when one of Ireta's sudden downpours caught them. It afforded Varian some amusement that she, Aygar, and Winral paid no attention to the rain though even the marines flinched.

"Let 'em have the place, I say," someone muttered behind Varian in a voice meant to be overheard. "I've smelled stinks—"

Borander whipped around, hoping to identify the speaker. His annoyance was increased as he noticed Aygar's sublime indifference to the elements.

Varian was not attached to any service unit, so the usual boarding salute to the flag was not required of her. Nevertheless, when she reached the top of the gangplank, she had to exert a conscious effort not to follow Borander's example.

The duty officer immediately stepped forward, objecting to the presence of Aygar and Winral.

"As planetary governor *pro-tem*, I wish to redress a wrong with Commander Sassinak. These men are here at my express invitation."

"Commander Sassinak has already interviewed the mutineers."

"Mutineer," and Varian laid firm stress on the singular. "These people cannot be held guilty of the transgressions of their grandparents. Have I made my position clear, Lieutenant?"

"Yes, ma'am."

"Now, if you will take me to your commander?" Varian turned to Borander.

The manner in which Borander escorted her revealed to Varian just how much the young man wished to be through with her. It had irritated her, or perhaps Rianav, to see Aygar held at stun-range. Rianav-Varian both could believe that Aygar had indeed been on his way to look for the sled's survivors. What his intentions would have been after the rescue, was moot. But she felt required to seek fair treatment for him.

As Varian, Aygar, and Winral followed Borander through the maze of passages into the cruiser's depths, she became aware of the almost palpable interest in these surroundings which Aygar could not suppress. This would be his first opportunity to view close-up the products of sophisticated science and empire. Quite likely he had been reared on tales of such marvels, as well as the heavy-worlder face-saving mendacities. Winral was clearly overwhelmed by everything, gawking about him and stumbling over the bulkheads. Aygar maintained his dignity and composure despite his obvious excitement and curiosity.

Then they were being ushered into the commander's office, a spacious apartment with computer terminals and viewscreens across the biggest wall. Seating units and serving counters made an informal grouping along the opposite wall, facing the screens. The commander was seated in a contour swivel chair before a console and wide desk. Varian made a rapid survey of the screens, one positioned on the settlement and the other eleven trained on various aspects of the bloated transport.

"Leader Varian, how pleased I am that you were unharmed," the commander said, rising and extending her hand. Sassinak was a tall woman of wiry build and the authority of many decades in a command position, though her short black hair was unsullied by gray and her supple figure gave an impression of limitless energy. She gave Aygar a careful nod. "We're in a bit of a muckle here. Your point about the . . . planet-born . . ." and she gestured courteously toward Aygar and Winral, "is well taken." She cleared her throat, tapping her lips with her left hand as she did so. Varian saw the humorous gleam in her eyes. "I assure you, it will be respected in all future dealings with the . . . ah . . . indigenes. Only one of the original mutineers is alive, you know. And, I fear, he is in very poor physical condition and could be termed senile."

"The charge of mutiny is a formality, Commander, necessary to protect *my* associates and to rectify the disposition of Ireta."

"I understand the situation, Leader Varian. A wise move, I assure you, since several entities appear to be interested in this planet. You have heard, have you not, that the Thek are represented by quite a concentration."

"Yes."

"You're as baffled as I, then. Good. I intensely dislike being uninformed."

"Commander, do *you* know where the *ARCT-10* is?" Varian asked urgently.

Commander Sassinak grinned ruefully. "That's another good question to which I have no answer. We have already inquired of the local Sector Command. You will appreciate that we have crossed several sectors in pursuit of the transport, and such information wouldn't necessarily be present in our banks. We'll let you know as soon as we have received an update. I have heard *nothing* about the loss of an EV ship and certainly *that* would have had a broad dissemination. Now that we are out of communication silence, we'll be able to ask for updates." Sassinak's attention was divided between Varian and the screens. Now her glance lingered on the stalwart figure of Aygar, sparing the briefest notice of Winral. "Now, sir, we must regularize your position. May I have your name?" She reached over to flip on a recorder.

"I am Aygar, son of Graila and Tetum, maternal grandson of Berru and Bakkun, paternal grandson of Paskutti and Divisti." There was pride and challenge in Aygar's tone.

"And you?"

"Winral, son of Aun and Mella, paternal grandson of Tardma and Paskutti, maternal grandson of Tanegli and Divisti." Winral was sullen.

"Yes, quite. With a small genetic pool, you would have to be careful of inbreeding, wouldn't you?" Sassinak tapped a few keys. "Born and raised on Ireta and your forefathers did, I suspect, have some sort of regulatory body. Your settlement seems very well organized." She looked inquiringly at Aygar.

"Paskutti was our leader until his death. Then the duty was assumed by Berru and from him fell to my father, Tetum."

Sassinak leaned back in her chair, steepling her fingers. "According to my understanding of planetary regulations, you are a citizen of Ireta, therefore an Iretan. My knowledge of your planet is limited to the reports, now forty-three years old, which we stripped from the beacon on our way in and suggests that there are no other sentient species . . ."

"There is a developing species," Varian said quickly, noting the surprise and puzzlement in Aygar's look and the surprise in Sassinak's.

"There was no mention of any in your beacon messages."

"Those were sent a long time ago—"

"I was informed that you were cryo until ten days ago?"

"My report mentioned an avian life-form, golden fliers—"

"Yes, it did. They're the developing species? Avians? And the Ryxi settled in the same system? They aren't going to like that."

"They haven't been told, have they?"

"Certainly not. I've been too preoccupied with this business to tend to yours, Leader Varian." Sassinak's voice took on an edge. "I'll deal with that if it becomes my business. However, Aygar, you are resident here. You are not, technically speaking, involved in the mutiny charge. Under Federated rules and regulations, your people of the two generations raised here have the right to whatever you have developed during your residence . . . including the landing grid, when put to authorized use." She signaled to the yeoman standing unobtrusively nearby. "I'll want it recorded and announced that the only person under the charge of mutiny is that Tanegli fellow. You are no longer under restraint, bind, or halt and may continue whatever employment and pursuits you choose."

"We have been preparing for a colonial supplement."

Sassinak chuckled. "I like you, young man. This world breeds sturdy people. However, *they*," and she flicked her hand at the screens showing the heavy-world transport ship, "are illegal immigrants on a world clearly designated as exploratory and uncleared for occupation. They can stay where they are until the tribunal can deal with the offense. It would be in *your* best interests," and her gesture included Winral and the settlement, "to have absolutely nothing to do with them for collusion will definitely jeopardize your current possessions and your future." She leaned across her console. "You have made a tremendous start here, Aygar. Consolidate those beginnings any way you can before the tribunal sits in judgment. Advice I also extend to you, Varian, although I understand you've already been doing just that since your awakening." She rose and walked around the console to stand looking up at Aygar. Sassinak was a tall, well-made woman, but Aygar's height and bulk dwarfed her. "You'd make a fine marine, young man, if you decide to quit this world."

Aygar looked down at her, his face and eyes expressionless. "This is my world, Commander. All of it—"

"No, Aygar, not all of it," and the steel was back in Sassinak's voice and manner, "only what you and the planet-born have cultivated. Do I make myself plain?" When he had nodded acknowledgment, she relaxed with a smile. "I would be greatly obliged if you would permit me to make a tour of your settlement and its installations. I like to know as much about the planets I visit as is possible." Sassinak offered her hand to Aygar.

For one moment, Varian was afraid that Aygar would ignore the gesture. Then, as his massive hand closed about the commander's slimmer one, Varian also hoped that he would make a vain show of his inherent strength. Why it should matter at all to her that Aygar should make a good impression on Sassinak, Varian didn't understand—since she was very well aware that she and Aygar held differing notions about Ireta's future. Varian might blame Rianav for her championing of Aygar, but it had been as Varian that she had insisted on the review of his status.

"There is much to be done now, Commander," Aygar said, releasing Sassinak's hand.

"I should imagine so," and Sassinak deftly indicated regret for being the agency which had occasioned such need.

"I believe I can speak for the rest of Ireta's citizens when I say that we would like to show you what we have wrested from a harsh and dangerous environment."

Sassinak nodded, smiling as she took up Aygar's meaning. Varian felt relief that Aygar had opted for a diplomatic approach where force was clearly inappropriate.

"Yes, I like your attitude, Aygar. I'll have my adjutant, Lieutenant Commander Fordeliton, call on you later today. You should listen to some disks, delineating your rights and privileges under FSP law, at your earliest convenience. Under shipwreck statutes, you may replace any items of equipment, bar weapons, which were issued to the original team. I'm prepared to make quite a lenient interpretation of that clause to help you consolidate your position." She gestured to the yeoman. "Del, escort Aygar back to the air lock, will you?"

Sassinak caught Varian's eye, aware that Varian would have preferred to leave with him. "We've some matters to discuss yet, Leader Varian," she said, resuming her seat at the console as Aygar left. "A rather remarkable specimen, that Aygar. Are there more like him here?" A ripple of sensuality in the commander's voice made Varian readjust, once more, her estimate of the woman.

"I've only encountered a few of his generation—"

"Yes, generation." Sassinak sighed. "You're now forty-three years behind your own. Will you need counseling? For yourself or the others?"

"I'll know when I get back to them," Varian replied dryly. "The phenomenon hasn't caught up with me yet. Commander, did you mean what you said about the *ARCT-10*?"

"Of course, I did. I've no orders to dissemble, though by the gods, this situation becomes more complex with every hour. A displaced expeditionary force, a mutiny charge, a missing EV, a population of off-worlders, an indigenous sentient species and Thek popping up in unexpected strength. Fifty of the blighted things by latest count. Yes?" she said, turning to acknowledge the discreet reappearance of her yeoman.

"Leader Varian's sled has been repaired and is available to her."

"Yes, I expect you're anxious to return to your group. I shall want a comprehensive report from every member of the survivors—especially your youngest members. I shall want them tomorrow. And you'd best update your mission's accounts. Are the supplies aboard Varian's sled?"

"Yes, Commander."

"You've been very generous, Commander."

"You don't even know what the supplies are, Varian," and Sassinak's right eyebrow quirked with amusement. "Records, for one thing, tamperproof. And your medic sent in some urgent requests. The Ryxi vessel doesn't have all she requires. Not surprising. As planetary governor *pro-tem*," and Sassinak mocked Varian gently, "you have only to requisition whatever you require from Fordeliton, my executive officer. Your medic's name *is* Lunzie, isn't it?" Sassinak leaned toward Varian again, in a confidential attitude, her eyes sparkling with humor. When Varian nodded, she grinned. "It was inevitable that one of us encountered her. A celebration is in order. Will you convey my deepest respects to Lunzie? And my invitation to a proper dinner at the first opportunity? I expect that the *Zaid-Dayan* will be here a while—at least until the tribunal arrives—but one never knows in the service. I cannot miss the chance to meet Lunzie. It isn't often one gets the chance to entertain one's great-great-great-grandmother. Del, do escort Leader Varian to her sled?"

Slightly dazed by Sassinak's totally unexpected parting remark, Varian was halfway to the air lock before she recalled Portegin. Del was quite willing to detour by way of the sick bay.

"We don't get a skull fracture report from the diagnostic scan, Leader Varian," Mayerd, the chief medical officer explained, "but he's clearly disoriented."

"You mean he has trouble believing this is the *ZD-43*?" asked Varian, appreciating Portegin's confusion.

"How did you know?"

Then they were in the infirmary, Portegin its only occupant.

"Krims! but I'm glad to see you, Lieutenant," he said, urgently beckoning her to approach his bunk. In an anxious whisper he added, "There's something peculiar going on here, Lieutenant. I don't recognize anyone. How could they switch crews midtour, unless the heavies—"

"Report, Portegin," Varian said, mimicking Lunzie's clipped accents.

"Huh? Oh, Krims!" Portegin fell back against the bolster, tension easing from his face and body as blocked memories flowed back. "I thought something was wrong with me!"

Varian squeezed his shoulder in sympathy. "Me, too."

"Hey, then everything is all right?" Portegin caught her arm with urgent fingers. "I mean, that heavy-world transport zapped us, and I wake up on a cruiser. Was that rescue mission from the *ARCT-10*? How're the others? How come we thought we were from *this* cruiser?"

Varian gave him what answers she had and then called Mayerd over, indicating Portegin's improvement and asking to have him released. Mayerd reluctantly agreed, extracting from Varian a promise that Portegin would undertake no strenuous activities for a day or two.

"Nothing more strenuous than juggling matrices and wielding a soldering iron," Portegin assured her, slipping into the new ship suit he was given.

Once aboard their crumple-nosed sled, Varian filled Portegin in on some of the details while he elatedly sorted through the supplies, exclaiming over the variety of matrices, tool replacements, and packed food-stuffs.

"Hey, we got us a bottle of Sverulan brandy—Ah, fardles! It's got Lunzie's name on it. Compliments of Commander Sassinak? A friend of hers?"

"You might say so," Varian replied, discretion overcoming her wish to confound. It occurred to her that Lunzie might not wish to claim a relationship so far removed in time.

"Fardles! That stuff goes down a treat. Real smooth." Portegin carefully replaced the brandy and resumed his seat beside Varian. "Hey, we got our escort back. How did they *know* it's us with so many other aircraft zipping around?"

"I'll remember to inquire. Lunzie says they can tell the difference between one of our sleds and those of the *Mazer Star*."

"No? Well, every motor has a distinctive sound to it, I'm told, even if they were manufactured in the same place, of identical components, but the signature usually only shows up on sophisticated monitors."

"Brains are still the ultimate in sophisticated computers. We got some on wings, that's all. Say, did you happen to notice if they tracked us up from the base camp?"

"It was dark when we left there, Varian, and we were kinda occupied . . . besides using different brains. I don't know what they think they're doing for us out there, but I kinda like seeing 'em."

"So do I. And I'll be seeing a lot more of them in the next few days if I have my way."

Circumstances combined to thwart Varian's plans. Just as they reached the cliffs of the golden fliers, a squall broke over them and Varian had all she could do to wrestle the sled safely inside the cave. That put the skids on an immediate study of the giffs. Considerable progress had already been made to improve the amenities in the cave, including partitioned sleeping quarters at the back, tables, comfortable loungers and lighting near the hearth which had been augmented by cooking, cooling, and disposal units. Bug-screens kept the insects at bay. Mindful of Sassinak's requirement, Varian forced a cassette on Portegin before he disappeared into the shuttle's pilot compartment to restore the console. When she asked Lunzie the whereabouts of the rest of the team, she received another check. As soon as Kai had finished his session with the diagnostic unit on board Captain Godheir's *Mazer Star*, he had drafted the assistance of a crewmember who professed to be an amateur geologist and went off to seek Dimenon, Margit, and Tor.

"In that order," Lunzie said. "If the Thek let them land, considering their fascination with Iretan mineral deposits. Dimenon says they're just squatting and gorging themselves. He swore six ways to Sunday that he can see the Thek growing."

"Then the diagnostic unit has a cure for Kai?"

"No, but it's much healthier for him to immerse himself in matters geological than sit about fretting and making mud maps," Lunzie replied crisply. "He's in a padded suit with skin-gloves. I've threatened Perens, that's Godheir's navigator, with grievous bodily harm if there's so much as one new welt on Kai's hide when they return. You ought to be glad that Kai's got a second wind."

"I am. I am. Where're Triv and Trizein?" She could snag the geologists later for their reports.

"They're off, too, in the four-man sled. Triv did promise Trizein to go beast-hunting with him, you know. Now that he's 'fifty-eight,' Bonnard insists he's old enough to be a full team member so he went off with them. Terilla wanted to be their scribe, so I let her go, too. Don't wish to stretch Godheir's hospitality with fretful kids."

"Cleiti?"

"She's in the *Mazer Star*, helping Obir construct bunkbeds for our sleeping quarters." Lunzie waved to the back of the cave. "Godheir is determined to arrange for as many comforts of home as possible. Everyone's the better for doing some light work to get muscles working again."

"Aulia?"

Lunzie's expression altered. "She . . ." and Lunzie wiggled one hand in a derisive gesture, "is recuperating from the shock of discovering herself time-stranded. I did point out that, when we got back to the *ARCT-10*, she'd look four decades younger than her contemporaries."

"Did that cheer her?"

"Not as much as Triv's reminder that all her bonus money has been collecting interest for forty-three years. She was demanding a transfer to the sanctuary of the cruiser until I mentioned that they were guarding the heavy-world transport. Sure cured *that* notion. Now, I expect you'll want to be off stalking your bird friends. I'm going to catalog the local edi-

bles and Divisti's pharmacopia in case they've other useful
medical applications." Lunzie triumphantly hoisted the microscope loaned by the cruiser's science officer.

"Not until you've reported your version of our mutiny,"
and Varian stayed Lunzie's departure until she had tucked a
disk in her chest pocket. "By the way," and Varian considered
it only fair that she had a revelation to spring on Lunzie,
"Commander Sassinak says she's your great-great-great-
granddaughter."

As a series of emotions crossed the medic's usually well-
schooled face, Varian wished she had a recorder handy. Shock,
surprise, denial, consternation, and finally resignation marched
across the woman's face. Then Lunzie blinked and displayed
her usual composure.

"She could be, I suppose. My family tends to the services,
and wandering."

"Did you know she was commander of the *ZD-43*?"

"No. How could I? She couldn't've been when we went to
sleep forty-three years ago. The cruiser was only just commissioned. I'd seen the announcement on the *ARCT-10* which
is why the designation fell so easily from my tongue when
needed."

"She's invited us to dinner at the earliest opportunity."

"What sort of person is she?"

"Well . . ." and Varian maliciously delayed her assessment,
"I think there's a distinct family resemblance . . . in manner."

Lunzie gave Varian a long shrewd look. "As Fleet com-
manders generally spread a good meal, and I'm getting bored
with stews and simple Iretan fare, I accept."

"She sent this with her compliments." Varian handed over
the square Sverulan brandy bottle.

"A discerning relative. I expect good things at her table."

"Lunzie!" Varian pointed at the tape in the medic's pocket.

"Yes, yes, I'll do that first. We'll broach the bottle tonight!"
Then Lunzie, juggling microscope, bottle, and a tray of other

supplies, made her way to the compartment that had been, two weeks ago, Trizein's laboratory.

Just as Varian dutifully sat down to dictate her own report, a sled entered the cave. A short, chesty man with a round face wreathed in an expression of constant, surprised good humor, waved cheerily to her.

It was Captain Godheir, arriving to present his apologies in person.

"I could have dropped down here any time the last fifteen years if I'd had any idea of your situation. When we got that Thek summons, I checked the computer banks, right then. Your last contact with Vrl was logged all right enough, but the Ryxi didn't attempt to raise your camp for another five months. The entry indicated no response, so it was assumed you'd been recovered by the *ARCT-10*."

"Have you heard anything about the EV?"

"No, but that's nothing," Godheir assured her with a smile. "EVs don't have much cause to tell mercenary captains like me this, that, or twaddle. But," and he waggled a finger at her, his expression sincere, "that might be all to the good. I sure would have heard if an EV got itself lost. Mullah! They're still bitching about the *LSTC-8* that tangled with that gas cloud last century. No news *is* good news, you know. And that cruiser'll get an update. Meanwhile, anything me and my crew can do . . . including a spot of bird-watching. Did their net act this morning—now that's a sight to see!"

"You didn't happen to record it, did you?"

"I sure did record it! Furthermore," and Godheir grinned broadly, "we got their attack on us, Lunzie's arrival, and all that to-do on a high-resolution tape. One of my crew's an amateur naturalist. You should see his tapes of the Ryxi—"

"Captain Godheir, your contract doesn't oblige you to disclose all activities to the Ryxi, does it?"

Godheir gave her the broadest possible wink. "We don't exactly converse with 'em at all, which you will understand if you know the Ryxi—which I suspect you do or you wouldn't worry about 'em—so don't worry about me or any of my crew babbling. Those Ryxi pay well, or you may be sure we wouldn't keep renewing the contract." He leaned across the table and patted Varian's shoulder reassuringly. "Now, you need anything me or my men can cobble up for you to get settled in? I got a few more items Lunzie requested. That nice little girl Cleiti's been helping us. Too bad she's so long separated from her folks."

"Cleiti's here?" Varian reached for another cassette.

"She's out in the cave, setting up the bunks."

Varian went out, followed by Godheir who assured her that Cleiti was only supervising as Obir was under strict orders to prevent her doing anything strenuous. And, to be sure, Cleiti was perched on a stool of recent manufacture, listening to the comments of the garrulous jack of all trades. She rose when Varian appeared, with a brave, sad, little smile more poignant than tears would have been. Varian repressed a self-indulgent urge to hug Cleiti. Instead she explained the necessity for the report.

"I can do it while Obir's busy," Cleiti said, holding the cassette with curious awkwardness. "I'll have no trouble remembering everything exactly as it happened. After all, for me, it was only the week before last."

Varian managed to murmur something appropriate, catching Godheir's amused wink, as she turned away. Rain still lashed down and the screen of vine waved with erratic vitality in the squally winds. The vine should be cut down now, she thought. The screen's purpose had been accomplished. She wished hers could be, and Ireta's weather was frustrating. So . . . she'd work on that blasted report until the rain abated.

"You've probably got a lot to do, lassie," Godheir said, hearing her sigh of exasperation. He took a bulbous object from his thigh pocket and a small pouch from another. "I'll just blow a cloud of my own." Varian recognized the artifact as a tobacco pipe. "Not that I could smell anything in this atmosphere. Nor will I be polluting it!" He chuckled as he settled himself on another stool. "Half the pleasure of smoking a pipe is the smell of the tobacco."

"What's the other half?"

"The pure relaxation of fussing with a pipe."

Varian watched the process for a moment. "It looks complicated." Then she thanked him once again for all his courtesies. "Would you give me a shout when the rain stops, Captain."

"My pleasure!"

It could have been imagination, but Varian did think, as she returned to the shuttle, that she could smell the aroma which rose from the captain's pipe.

As Varian organized her recollections of the events leading up to the mutiny, she envied Cleiti her innocence of the "week before last." Varian made copious notes, additions, and changes until she was sure she had events in order. She made no comments, such as her initial suspicions about the heavy-worlders' unsavory activities of that fateful rest day, for the mutiny was an undeniable fact, emphatically substantiated by the time gap between the two groups. She listened carefully to the replay of her report, aware that she could not erase now. She added a few brief explanations to her remarks. Then she strode to the shuttle iris and looked out toward the cave entrance.

Cleiti, Godheir, and Obir were seated in a companionable group about the fire, the captain's pipe still sending gray-blue plumes of smoke to waft about in vagrant puffs of wine. No question of it, Varian thought. She *could* smell the tobacco above the usual pungencies. When she saw Varian, Cleiti brought over her cassette.

"Captain Godheir seems to know all about the mutiny, Varian," she said in a low voice, her eyes round with surprise. "Is it all right to talk about what happened? Or are details classified?"

"You can talk about it all you want, Cleiti," Varian replied, hoping discussion might restore the unnaturally subdued child to her former ebullience. Damn Paskutti and Tardma for the shock they had given the child: a shock undiminished in Cleiti's memories of the "week before last."

"Captain Godheir said he's never talked with a person who'd been mutinied before."

"It's not something that happens frequently, Cleiti. He's had our official report, but I think he might be interested in your reactions. But don't talk about it if you don't *want* to."

Cleiti considered pensively. Then, with a slightly less strained smile, added, "Yes, I think I'd like to tell the captain and Obir. They both listen so politely. They *say*," and the smile betrayed a touch of Cleiti's old impishness, "that it's because I'm older than they are." She rejoined the men at the fire.

Varian was still muttering imprecations against the heavy-worlders when Lunzie appeared with her record cassette.

"Isn't Cleiti abnormally quiet, Lunzie?"

"All elements considered, not too much so. Part of it's due to the restoration, and part to delayed reaction. That's why I want to keep everyone as busy as possible. Gives 'em less time to worry and think."

"Aulia?"

Lunzie snorted with derision. "Oh, she's busy, too. Feeling sorry for herself. She can make that into a full-time occupation. I expect Portegin will change her mind—if he ever surfaces from the shuttle's control panel. Varian, do you think you could get a specimen of the fringes from the giffs' eating rock?"

"D'you mean, would I oblige you or would I be *able* to? Because the giffs like me and someone else tried and failed?"

Lunzie twitched her nose.

"Well, he might have succeeded if he'd waited until the catch had been distributed. But they do know you. An analysis of fringe toxins would be invaluable in healing Kai's condition."

"I'll have to wait until this squall blows over."

"I was thinking that the squall would keep the giffs in their caves and this would be the safest time to collect fringe. Take the stairs to the surface."

"Stairs?" Varian stared in surprise.

"I told you Godheir was making us very comfortable." Lunzie pointed to the right side of the cave. "It's only a cage pole with foot rests, but you can't get blown out of it and it gets you right to the top. Rather an improvement on swinging down vines, isn't it?" she added as she followed Varian to the new access way. "Godheir's drive mechanic, a man named Kenley, does amateur photography and bird-watching. He's also got a long-handled gripper, protective gloves, and a container for fringe samples. Topside!" Lunzie gestured with her thumb and grinned at Varian. "You *are* our resident expert on giffology."

"Never give a sucker an even break, huh?"

"Never. You need to be kept busy, too. And active."

"I'm just fine when I'm allowed to do what I came here for." Varian gave Lunzie a grin and then nimbly climbed the ladder, grateful for the cage as the wind still had some strength in it.

Kenley was waiting for her on the cliff top, lounging against his sled. He was parked not too far from the spot where Varian had first rested her sled that long-ago rest day. Kenley's force-screen blocked most of the light rain and all the reemerging insects. He was slender, dark-skinned, dark-haired, and brown-eyed, with even, undistinguished features and a placid disposition. She shortly discovered in him a staunch advocate of the golden fliers.

"Were you the bold one who tried for the fringes the first time?" she asked, as she took the sample-collecting tools from him.

"Yep. Forgot the first rule of animal psychology. Never bother one that's eating. Fortunately I had my lift-belt and

I pelted for the cave mighty fast. They were most annoyed with me."

Varian grinned as she noted that he had his belt on; his recording equipment was slung from a second belt. They had reached a spot just below the feeding rocks.

"You don't have to follow me, but I'd appreciate it if you could record any giffs who drop by to investigate."

Kenley nodded as Varian arrayed the implements so as not to impede her climbing.

"I'm going to ascend as far to the right of the feeding rock as I can, away from any edible food. The fringes get flipped to the far edge or into the chasm."

Both Varian and Kenley looked toward the giff cave, visible now that the rain had let up. There wasn't a giff in sight. Varian began to climb quickly, Kenley just behind her.

"Krims! Here they come!" Kenley warned her, and she heard the whirr of his recorder. "They got some perception. What do they use? Sonar? Radar? What?"

"I hope to find out. You're getting all that?" Varian said, keeping her eyes on the giffs winging through the drizzle.

They landed on the sea edge of the feeding rock just as Varian reached the top. Several fringe carcasses, dried to brittle outlines, were inches from her boot. A meter away, two more feebly wavered. One was closed over, the other open.

"Hello!" Varian said in her most cheerful tone, holding her hands out to the giffs as she edged closer to her target. "I ought to have brought you some Rift grasses, but we haven't been there lately and I didn't think about it until just this moment. Actually, since what I want is something you have no use for, I don't want to get you into the bad habit of expecting presents everytime we meet. Is it all right if I just take one of these?" She had donned the gloves and opened the container as she spoke. Very slowly then, without taking her eyes from the giffs, she extended the long-handled grippers toward one of the semimoribund fringes.

"Watch out!" Kenley's cry seemed to lend her impetus.

With considerable dexterity, she had managed to secure both fringes in the clasp of the gripper, whirling to hide her actions from the giffs as she beat a hasty retreat before their charge. "Did you get one? Krims! What are they doing now? Say, I don't think they were after you . . ."

Safe on the rocks below the feeding area, Varian paused long enough to thrust the fringes into the container while holding her breath against the stench of the things, before she looked to see what was exciting Kenley so much. Methodically the giffs were flicking every evidence of the fringes off into the chasm, as if deliberately clearing away a menace which they were not going to permit their visitors to handle.

"*I* got two!"

"I got it all down," cried Kenley. "They are quick! In the air or on the ground. Though I think you'd have to say they were semiairborne when they came after you. You know, I think they were trying to keep me away from the fringes this morning—not away from the edible food."

Just then Varian and Kenley flinched away from the rock wall for the two giffs loomed above them, stern and chittering nonharmoniously. They spread their wings, flapping them as if to emphasize their remarks, then extended their heads down toward the two humans. The distance was too great for contact but Varian and Kenley ducked.

"Like kids to avoid a well-deserved slap," Kenley said, grinning at Varian.

"Then let's pretend we're suitably punished and get the hell out of here."

Once back in their cave, the sample container turned over to Lunzie, Kenley regaled Varian with the spectacular record he had made of the giff attack on the *Mazer Star*'s sled and the astonishing withdrawal as Lunzie's sled made its appearance and was escorted safely past the intruder. Unfortunately his footage of the feeding was marred by drizzle and haze. He hadn't thought to change tape or use an appropriate filter.

"I'll redo that record. Maybe with you, I can get in closer."

"Better yet, we'll both follow the fishers tomorrow on their daily round. That's a sight to take. Fardles!" Varian snapped her fingers as she recalled that Sassinak awaited the reports. "Well, with any luck, I'll give the commander what she needs and be back in time to take you fishing. I want to show their high level of basic intelligence in that sort of a joint enterprise." She was recounting to the entranced Kenley the incident with the Three Giffs and her surmises when Kai returned with Dimenon and Margit.

Kai had not been able to locate Tor, nor indeed engage any of the Thek—large, small, or medium—in conversation.

"The silence of the Thek is profound," Kai remarked. He seemed more like his old self. "Maybe in a year or two, one will remember to forward my message."

"Kai would go up to a Thek, rap on the shell and say in a loud clear voice, 'Speak?' " Dimenon was also in good spirits. He dangled both hands at chest level and then uttered a series of short barks, grinning with no apology for his whimsical behavior, " 'Require Tor response.' "

The geologists had little time for further conversation because Triv returned with Trizein, Bonnard, and Terilla. Trizein was so ecstatic about each and every new species that their expedition had sighted that he would break off describing one to cite the more fascinating specimen they had next encountered. Bonnard pretended to be weighted down by the film clips. Terilla waved a sheaf of drawings while Triv made for the hearth and some food. Varian waited until the first exuberances had been expended before she explained the need for Sassinak's reports.

"But they're all dead, aren't they?" Terilla's expression mirrored her sudden fright and her voice held an unsteady quaver. Bonnard stepped to her side and put an arm about her.

"Tanegli's alive but he's very old and senile," Varian told Terilla with a reassuring smile.

"I wouldn't have thought the mutiny was the major issue now," Triv said, surprised at the disclaimers. "Well, how can it be? With a colony ship illegally landing—"

"Mutiny is always an issue," Kai said angrily.

"Planetary piracy is more serious."

"That's because there's been more of that than mutiny," Portegin said, half-joking.

"Far too much," Lunzie said, not at all amused. "Generally the Federation doesn't know of a takeover unless dissidents among the pirates inform. Then it's too late."

"When is 'too late' too late to punish criminal activity?" Kai demanded, obviously referring to the mutiny, not the piracy.

"The tribunal will decide that, Kai," Lunzie said more kindly. "The ramifications are far too complex for my understanding of the laws. But, Kai, wouldn't you say that senility and the knowledge of the futile outcome of forty-three years' hard work constitute a punishment?" When she saw the obstinate set of Kai's features, she shrugged. "What about consoling yourself with the knowledge that you've been instrumental in preventing the illegal occupation?"

"Say, are there Federation rewards for hindering pirates?" Triv asked.

Despite a spate of cheering at this suggestion, no one had an answer.

"What sort of reward could buy back the time we've lost," Kai asked stiffly, "or the health?"

10

AFTER a dinner made lavish by the generosity of Commander Sassinak, Varian received a message from the cruiser, couched in the politest terms but nevertheless a firm request that Kai and Varian attend an important meeting on the cruiser at 0900. Kai was already asleep.

"Sleep he needs," Lunzie said quietly. "He expended a good deal of energy today which he didn't have, trying to find his Thek." She beckoned Varian down the corridor to her quarters, away from the partitioned section where Kai lay sleeping. "C'mon. Let's broach that brandy my discerning relative sent. This day has been a whozzer! Brandy'd go down a treat."

Varian was quite willing to indulge and followed Lunzie to her compartment, which was now quite comfortable. The microscope held the place of honor on the wide working desk, where neat piles of notes and slides testified to the good use Lunzie had made of her afternoon. A cot, more shelves, a recorder, a viewer, and two comfortable chairs completed the furnishings.

The brandy uncorked with a satisfactory *schewack*, and Lunzie muttered admiringly under her breath as the amber liquid gurgled into the glasses. She passed one to Varian, inhaling the bouquet from hers and then, with a rare smile on her face, settled into the other chair. She lifted her beaker to clink against Varian's.

"Here's to the gods that grew!"

"And here's to the soil that fed."

The brandy went down smoothly until it hit the bottom of her throat. Then Varian found herself gulping cooler air, her eyes about to pop her skull. Tears formed and then dispersed as the fine aftertaste began to spread throughout her mouth and throat. Varian swore she could feel the nerves at the base of her spine untwist.

"That's some skull-pop!" Her voice was a respectful whisper.

"Indeed!" Lunzie seemed not to feel the same effect, sipping again while Varian regarded her portion with considerable respect. The warmth and relaxation continued to diffuse. Varian took another small mouthful, expecting the fiery result. Somehow the brandy was mellower. Or her throat was numb. "Sverulan as a planet," Lunzie went on, "has very little to recommend it other than the raw vegetable material that ferments into this brandy." She gestured toward her notes on the table. "I'm hoping that Divisti found something equally good. I can't imagine that the heavy-worlders could have existed long on this place without some sort of a stimulant." She lifted her glass again.

"Lunzie?"

"Hmmm?"

"Do you know something you haven't told us?"

Lunzie's eyes met Varian's without hesitation or guile. "About Ireta? No. And certainly nothing about a planned piratical takeover. That was completely fortuitous. If you refer to the opportune appearance of the *ZD-43* . . . Well, just as all elements of the Fleet have standing orders to pursue a leech when it appears on their sensors, so people like myself, on routine assignments," and Lunzie accorded Varian a droll grin, "have been primed to obstruct attempts at planet theft whenever and however possible. Don't know what more *we* could have done for Ireta than we did but . . ." Lunzie glanced reassuringly again at Varian, "I was not planted with this expedition any more than *we* were planted. And we weren't! I would have said Ireta was the least likely takeover property. The heavy-worlders must have been fairly desperate to stake a claim on a world that stinks as much as Ireta."

"The stink of transuranic riches must have smelled better."

"It's not like you to be cynical, Varian. Restore your faith in mankind by a close study of your giffs. They're worth the trouble it takes to preserve them. Remember, if this planet is thrown open, the Ryxi are just a short hop away—"

"Why would the planet be thrown open?" Apprehension overwhelmed Varian as she thought of the pompous, intolerant Ryxi.

"It's rich, that's why. There is already an established settlement with an immense grid to facilitate the landing of the heaviest ore freighters. Those heavy-worlders in their transport will be given short shrift and tossed back into space. But the tribunal might throw the rest of the planet open to competitive explorations, just to keep Aygar's group in order— that is, if the Thek are willing to forgo their obvious prior claim to Ireta's wealth, staked with those old cores Kai has dug up. There is, however, a statute of limitations on how long an unworked claim remains the property of the original discoverers. That herd of Thek might well be the vanguard of Thek exploiters. However, as xenobiologist, you'd do well to investigate the fringes. Two emerging species are better than one, even against a superior claim lodged by the Thek."

Varian felt a shudder of distaste and revulsion.

"Don't discount them," Lunzie said. "Predators can display intelligence, too, you know. Look at *us*! I grant you that the fringes don't have the intrinsic appeal of your giffs, but the more weight you can pump into your investigations, the more chance you have of protecting the giffs. If only by default." Lunzie took another sip of the brandy. "By the way, I accepted an invitation to dine with Sassinak tomorrow evening. You and Kai are included." Lunzie's expression turned serious again. "I'm hoping that Mayerd's more sophisticated diagnostic unit can analyze that fringe toxin and come up with a purge to flush the toxin out of Kai's system. *And* a nerve regenerator. Oh, the toxin will dissipate in time . . . but he's needed now, in proper working condition." To that Varian solemnly lifted her glass and drank. "I figure you'll just about make it to your bed before that brandy immobilizes you."

Lunzie proved correct, and the sound night's sleep improved Varian's outlook. Her mind was clear, and she felt able to combat—well, fang-faces, if necessary. Kai had more color in his face when he and Portegin joined her for breakfast, discussing priorities for Portegin's skills: the new core screen or completing repairs to the shuttle's damaged console.

"We've communications capability, and I can rig up a remote outside here," Portegin was saying. "It won't take me that much longer," then he turned with an apologetic grin to Varian, "though I do need a few more matrices and more weld-wire, two number-four—"

"Put it on a list!" Varian said with a mock resignation.

"I did," and there was nothing sheepish about the speed with which Portegin handed over his "few" requirements, "and then we can communicate directly with the *ARCT-10* when, as, and if it makes its long overdue appearance."

"Dimenon and I want to know if the Thek really are squatting on the sites of the old cores. He remembers some of the coordinates, but what we sank were so near to some of the older ones, we can't be sure unless we have a screen."

"Why would they go after theirs? It's more logical to go after ours, isn't it?" Portegin asked with some exasperation.

"Thek logic remains obscure to us poor mortals," Lunzie said, "but I'd prefer to be in communication with as many entities as possible . . . the ones that have the courtesy to answer."

Kai turned to Lunzie in considerable annoyance. "Can't you *see*, Lunzie, how important it might be for me to be *here* today? What can the cruiser's diagnostic unit do for me that Godheir's can't discuss with it?"

"Because we now have a sample of fringe to serve into the diagnostic unit, and Mayerd's a specialist in planetary exotic toxins, and the sooner we get the poison flushed out of your system, the sooner you can get out of that padded suit and operate on normal channels! Do I make myself plain? Besides," and she tossed her hand up, "Sassinak wants you there this morning at 0900. It won't take you that much longer to go through a diagnosis again, now will it?"

To that, Kai had to agree.

"Then let's go. Kai, will you be recorder for me?" Varian asked briskly as she looped the bag containing all the reports over her shoulder. "Then I can make use of the journey time." A little reminder to Kai that he wasn't the only one to have his plans altered might help. "If you could get our usual escort on tape," she said as they settled themselves in the battered two-man sled, "I really must see if the nose can be repaired."

With cautious and studied movements, Kai got into the sled and strapped himself in. His padded jumpsuit was of a softer than regulation fabric, padded on shin, thigh, calf, elbow and forearm, with skin-gloves to prevent inadvertent injury. Then he pulled the recorder toward him to check its load and sighted for focus and available light. As he completed these preparations, Varian noticed that his eyes were deeply shadowed, a strange contrast to the white flesh about the puncture marks.

"Ready when you are!" he said.

Varian nodded and took the sled out of the cave into the still misty morning. The passage of the sled swirled the yellowish fog about, and she used instruments rather than visual guidance in such a pea soup.

"So much for an outbound record," she said in disgust. "Nothing will filter that."

The telltagger sputtered. "Well, life-forms are coming in at seven o'clock," Kai said with a semblance of a grin. "You've got your escort."

"*How* do they see through this murk?"

"Why don't you ask them?"

"Funny fellow! When do I have the opportunity?"

"I know the feeling!"

Whatever tension had existed between them dissipated at this exchange. They traveled on in the murk, Kai silent in deference to the concentration Varian required to fly in such conditions. They had been airborne for over an hour when the mist began to disperse.

"Kai, why *wouldn't* Tor be here?"

"That has puzzled me. Especially since Tor took the trouble to rouse the Ryxi and get Godheir down here to help us."

"Isn't it unusual for so many Thek to gather?"

"Highly. I've never heard of it before. I wonder if Commander Sassinak would give me a little time on the cruiser's memory banks."

Varian grinned to herself. "She seems to wish to cooperate in any way she can. Oh, turn that thing off," Varian added, for they were having to raise their voices to be heard above the telltagger. Kai flicked it off mid-blip.

Just then they emerged from the mist into a brilliantly clear sunlit band, over tree-dotted plains, not too far from their original site. Varian craned her neck and saw the three escort giffs emerge from the fog, the sun gilding their fur.

"Why would Sassinak want us at a meeting?"

"I could think of half a hundred reasons."

"Maybe she's had a report about the *ARCT-10* that she won't commit to a broadcast?"

Varian shot her companion a quick look, but his face gave away no internal emotions. The fate of the *ARCT-10* would be of primary importance to Kai: his family had been ship-bred for generations. The *ARCT-10* was his home far more than any planet had ever been hers.

"Could be," she replied noncommittally. To dismiss the idea out of hand would be unkind, no matter how she wished to reassure Kai. "Sassinak's not the sort to sugar-coat a pill—"

"And she'd be aware of the morale factor for most of us."

"Kai, how long does an update take to reach a cruiser this far from a sector headquarters?"

Kai's breath hissed as he inhaled, and then he gave her a slightly sheepish grin. "Not by this morning if the first asking was yesterday."

"And as Captain Godheir said, he'd've heard something if the *ARCT-10* was known to be lost."

"Hmmmm."

"Scant reassurances, I know, but this is a time when no news can be good news. Say, I haven't had a chance to tell you, but Sassinak is Lunzie's great-great-great-granddaughter!"

"No!"

"That was Sassinak's parting remark to me yesterday. Took me the entire flight back to get over the shock. To cushion the shock she sent Lunzie a bottle of Sverulan brandy." Varian gave Kai a very gentle nudge in the ribs. "Now, I know you don't appreciate planetary brews, but this stuff is gorgeous. Get on Lunzie's good side and she might just give you a sip— if she hasn't already finished the bottle on the sly. No, she couldn't have—no one could drink that much Sverulan brandy and function the next day!"

"I just can't imagine Lunzie as a mother."

"I can. She mothers us in her fashion. It's the ancestor part that stuns me. That original child is probably long since dead, and the next four generations as well, and here is Lunzie, motoring along in fine shape. And younger than Sassinak."

"Ship-breds like me don't usually run into this sort of anomaly."

"Ireta's full of *them*! All kinds, why not a human paradox! I wonder if Lunzie will ever tell us how long she's cold slept. One thing, it hasn't affected her wits at all."

The patch of clear sky abruptly gave way to a fast-moving heavy squall and managing the sled took all Varian's attention. They rode it out, and the weather cleared to lowering clouds scudding across the sky just as they reached the plateau, so Kai had a good view of the area. Varian came in above the grid so that Kai got the full effect of the two space vehicles, the smaller one, lean and dangerous, the other gross and brooding. From that vantage, Kai could also see the settlement, the foundry, and the unoccupied length of the grid.

"They meant to have more than one transport land here, didn't they?"

"It would appear so," she replied. "Krims! Aygar took Sassinak at her word." She pointed to the three sleds parked at the edge of the settlement and the people busy loading them. "They aren't wasting any time. I wonder where they're going."

Kai scowled. "They've been given transport?"

"They're just as entitled to replacement equipment as we are—"

"Mutineers may not profit—"

"Only Tanegli qualifies as a mutineer—"

"Those people *are* accessories to a conspiracy against FSP." Kai pointed agitatedly at the transport vessel.

"Yes, *they* are. *They* are the real criminals, Kai, not Aygar and his group."

"I don't understand your reasoning, Varian." Kai's face was strained. "How can you possibly take their side?"

"I'm not taking their side, Kai, but I can't help respecting people who've managed to survive Ireta and achieve that grid!" She banked the sled to land it close to the open port of the *Zaid-Dayan*. "If only the *ARCT* had stripped the beacon, or kept its schedule with us."

" 'If,' " Kai said contemptuously.

"I'd cheerfully settle for a lousy 'when,' when we get you operational again. When we find out what the Thek are doing. When we find out what the tribunal thinks of all this . . ."

They landed, and very cautiously Kai eased himself out of the sled. Varian made a show of checking the records in her shoulder bag. She couldn't watch the once agile, active young man reduced to the slow motion of the invalid. Then she picked up the container with the fringe samples Lunzie had frozen.

They were met at the portal by a very dark-skinned officer, lean and bouncy. This one wore the rank device of a lieutenant commander and the fourragère of an adjutant. He gave them a white-toothed smile before gesturing urgently over his shoulder for someone to hurry up. "Fordeliton, Leaders Varian, Kai. Very pleased to meet you and at your service. We saw your sled approaching. And here is Mayerd."

The chief medic came bustling up, her eyes narrowing as she greeted Kai. Then she turned to Varian. "How's Portegin?"

"Constructing a core screen from that wealth of space matrices and units the commander supplied us with," Varian said. "I've a fringe sample for you."

"Just what I need." She took the sample case from Varian. "Kai, you go on with Fordeliton. I'll collect you when we've analyzed this information." Mayerd hurried off down the corridor.

"If you'll come with me," and Fordeliton gestured in the appropriate direction. "Portside at the next corridor junction, Varian. And that second door . . ."

Varian halted at the door which bore Fordeliton's nameplate. "I thought we were to see Commander Sassinak."

"In a manner of speaking, you will. I don't think we will have missed anything. They'd only just been escorted in when I went to collect you," he said cryptically as he thumbed the catch on his door and motioned for Varian and Kai to precede him.

For a cruiser his quarters were unusually spacious. One wall contained terminal, displays, and auxiliary controls. The main viewscreen was operational and, to Varian's surprise, tuned to the commander's office and the meeting that was in progress.

"No, she's checking their papers. The commander said she would spin that out indefinitely until I had you here. If you'll be seated—" and he leaned over to touch a button. "There, she knows you're here. Yesterday we arrested them for landing illegally on an unopened planet. They protested that they had responded to an emergency distress call and merely homed on the beacon. Sassinak suggested this morning's meeting to discuss the irregularity. She wanted you both here for obvious reasons."

Eyes on the screen, Varian felt for the offered chair with fumbling hands. "She's not in there alone with them, is she?" she asked Fordeliton in a hushed voice, reacting unconsciously to the menace presented by the five heavy-worlders perched implacably in front of Sassinak.

"That's a stun-wand the commander is handling so casually." Fordeliton wore an amused expression. "And there's a group of Wefts in marine uniform just beyond our view plus, of course, the usual sort of escort personnel."

"Wefts?" Kai was surprised. Wefts were enigmatic shape-changing morphs of unusual abilities. No humanoid of any variety had ever emerged victorious from combat against a Weft.

"Yes, as luck would have it, we've six groups with us this tour! The others are inside the transport, strategically deployed. In their own flesh."

Varian and Kai were both impressed and reassured. Varian released the arms of her chair and glanced quickly at Kai to see that he had cautiously splayed his fingers on his thighs, then she devoted her entire attention to Sassinak's performance on the screen.

As the commander read through the transport ship's documentation, she tapped the wand through her fingers repeatedly, mimicking a nervous habit.

Just beyond her desk sat the five heavy-worlders, three men and two women with the massive physiques and broad, almost brutish features of their mutation. They wore soiled ship suits and the wide kidney belts that were the fashion of their kind. The clips and buckles were empty of the usual weaponry and tools. Varian tried to tell herself that the facial expressions were not hostile; it was simply that heavy-worlders were not given to needless gestures or expressions even on planets with considerably less gravity than their own. Unfortunately, she could more clearly remember Paskutti and Tardma deliberately and enjoyably injuring her and Kai and needlessly terrorizing two young girls. She could not muster impartiality or neutral detachment.

"Yes, yes, Captain Cruss," Sassinak was saying, her voice velvety smooth, and almost unctuous, "your papers do seem to be in order, and one cannot fault your chivalry in diverting to investigate a distress call."

"It was not a distress call," Cruss said in a heavy, almost hollow voice. "It was a message sent by homing capsule to the *ARCT-10*. As I told you when your ship challenged me yesterday, we found the capsule drifting in space. It had been damaged beyond repair. We were able to playback the message. It was sent by Paskutti. The voice pattern matched that of one of our planetary explorers on contract assignment with the *ARCT-10*. We verified that he had not been heard of in over forty-three years. Naturally it was our duty to investigate."

"What disaster had overcome this Paskutti?"

"His base camp had been overrun by stampeding herbivores of unusual size. He and five others had escaped with only their lives. Most of their equipment had been damaged beyond repair. A homing capsule is sturdy, and so it survived. He sent a message, but the *ARCT-10* did not receive the capsule for it was damaged just outside this solar system, where we found it. I have brought it to show you."

With that Captain Cruss deposited a battered shell of metal on her desk with a courtesy that bordered on insolence. The homing capsule had long since lost its propulsion unit and the power pack so that it looked truncated as well as bent. The message core remained, scored and dinged. Sassinak wisely refrained from handling the heavy object.

"How under the seven suns did they manage to mess up a homing capsule like that?" Kai demanded under his breath.

"Heavy-world equipment for heavy-world purposes," Fordeliton remarked cheerfully.

"And the message, of course, has been recorded in your computer banks," Sassinak stated.

"*Can* that be done, Kai?" asked Varian.

"Not easily," Fordeliton replied. "It would depend on how the message was recorded. If our suspicion is correct and there is a broad conspiracy among all the heavy-worlders to take whatever opportunities present themselves, then Paskutti would have constructed the message so that anyone could extract it. Sssh."

"You are welcome to extract that message from our computer, Commander," Cruss replied.

"Providential that such a capsule was available to this Paskutti. Possibly the battering it received during the stampede caused its subsequent malfunction.

"You have acted properly, as FSP expects a civilian ship to do when a distress message appears out of the black. However, Captain Cruss, that act of charity does not detract from the fact that this planet is clearly cataloged as unexplored in my computer banks and, as such, not released even for limited colonization. You must understand that I am bound to adhere to FSP strictures in such an instance by standing orders. I have sent a direct signal to Sector Headquarters and no doubt I shall receive orders shortly. Since this is an exceedingly hostile and dangerous world," and Sassinak permitted herself a delicate shudder, "I must require you, your officers, and any passengers not in cryogenic suspension to remain aboard your vessel—"

Captain Cruss rose from his chair. So did his companions. Sassinak neither flinched nor quivered as the heavy-worlders dwarfed her at her desk.

"Actually," she continued in her conversational tone of voice, "the shipwrecked personnel seem to have done extremely well in adapting to the hostile environment, even to the commendable work of engineering a grid for their eventual rescue by a passing friendly ship. Most ingenious of them. However, I understand that they would be willing to supply you with fresh vegetable protein and fruit if you desire a change from long-voyage rations. In return, of course, for the usual items of barter." She smiled. "I hope your water supplies are adequate. The local water is foul-tasting and smells." With a surly growl and a dismissive flick of his vast hand, Captain Cruss indicated he needed no replenishments. "Very well, then. I'm positive you will wish to continue on your way as soon as we have received clearance for you. The indigenes will have all the help we can give them. You may be sure of that." Sassinak rose then, to signify the end of the interview.

Varian noticed that she held the wand in her right hand, tapping it carelessly against the palm of the left. When Cruss made a motion to reclaim the capsule, she lowered the wand to forestall the attempt, not quite touching his wrist.

"I think that had better remain. Sector will wish to discover why it did not reach its intended destination. Can't have our emergency devices malfunctioning."

What Cruss might have done, Varian didn't know, but abruptly Wefts appeared, one by each of the heavy-worlders. Varian noted with pleasure that the usual heavy-worlder sneers quickly altered to alarm. Cruss wheeled and stamped out. The others followed and the escort closed in behind them.

As soon as the door had slid shut, Sassinak swiveled her chair and looked directly at them. Fordeliton made an adjustment on the console and Sassinak smiled.

"Did you two catch the entire act?" She raised one hand to massage her neck muscles.

"Your timing was as usual superb, Commander," Fordeliton said.

"They had the contingencies covered, all right enough, including documentation to that heavy-worlder colony two systems down. Unless I am mistaken, and I want you to check it out, Ford, that world has reached its colonial quota. Varian, were all your records destroyed?"

"If you mean, do we have the homing capsule serial number on file, yes, it's probably in the shuttle's memory banks. We can retrieve it once Portegin has the shuttle's console fully operational. But *that* capsule was stolen from our stores *before* the stampede . . ."

"Did you mention that fact in the report I hope you have for me?"

"*I* did—" Varian glanced at Kai for his answer.

"I did, too. Commander?"

"Yes?"

"Do you believe that they detoured here to answer a shipwreck message?"

"I would have had no reason to doubt it, would I, if you weren't alive to give a conflicting account. They have, I do believe," and Sassinak's smile was smugly malicious, "hoisted themselves on their own petards in this case since you can prove the complicity. They don't know that you lived—"

"Aygar does." Kai's voice was harsh.

"Do you think we've allowed Aygar and his friends to communicate with the colonists? Come, come, Leader Kai. I shall permit no intercourse between the two groups, and the surviving mutineer is in maximum security on this vessel. Would he recognize you?"

Varian answered. "When I encountered Tanegli, at first he thought I was from the colony ship. When I told him that I was part of a rescue team, he couldn't wait to get rid of me. On the other hand, he wouldn't be expecting to see Varian. For him a long time has elapsed."

"Yes, so it has," Sassinak mused, a slight smile on her face. "It really doesn't do for the heavy-worlders to get so arrogant and presumptuous with us light-weights, does it?" Sassinak leaned forward, her expression sad. "The irony of these instances is that those who struggled to pave a way would have found themselves discarded by such as Cruss, castaway entirely, once their purpose had been served—I wonder if Tanegli and his fellow mutineers ever considered that possibility. Of course," and a complacent smile bowed the commander's mouth, "your survival is as unexpected as my arrival. Not to mention the interest the Thek are evincing in Ireta—can you explain that for me, Kai?"

"No, Commander. I haven't been able to get any of them to speak to me. My personal contact, the one called Tor, is not among them. May I have access to your computer on the subject of Thek? I want to check other occurrences of such numbers descending on a planet. They seem to be settling on the points where we discovered existing cores."

"Existing cores?" Sassinak was surprised. "According to Fleet records, this planet has never been explored."

"That was our understanding, too, Commander," Kai's tone was dry. "Nevertheless, my geology team found cores of extreme antiquity in place."

"Fascinating. I can only hope that we shall be enlightened in due course."

"Commander Sassinak," Kai began more formally, "does your presence here constitute the relief of the *ARCT-10* expeditionary team?"

"How could it, my dear Kai?" Sassinak grinned. "I didn't know you existed. My jurisdiction begins and ends with that transport out there. You were, and still are, an authorized exploration team to Ireta. As Varian has reminded me, that makes you both governors *pro-tem* on Ireta. Since your EV has not collected you in the time allotted for your explorations, in FSP law that makes you shipwrecked—stranded, if you prefer. And it is standard Fleet procedure to give all aid and assistance to stranded personnel. Have I made my position plain?"

"Indeed, you have."

"Will I see you both at dinner this evening?"

"You will, Commander, and our thanks for the invitation."

"It isn't often that representatives of two generations four times removed get a chance to meet, is it? Even in this crazy universe!" Sassinak was smiling as she broke the connection.

"Do you need any supplies urgently, Governors?" Fordeliton asked with a grin. Kai and Varian tendered their lists. "Good, then, I can escort Kai to Mayerd's clutches and take Varian on to the quartermaster. Mayerd's very good, you know," Fordeliton went on easily as he preceded them through the confusing maze of corridors. "Loves nothing better than a medical puzzle. So much space medicine is fairly cut and dried—if you'll forgive the puns. She's always writing obscure essays for the *Space Medical Journal*. This is our first planetfall in four months. Too bad the planet stinks so. We could use shore leave."

"The first forty years are the hardest," Kai remarked.

Fordeliton paused before the sick-bay entrance, and Kai, with a grimace, waved them a jaunty farewell.

11

VARIAN and Fordeliton had swung down the corridor toward the quartermaster section when Aygar and two of the group from the camp meeting came down another access hall. Aygar gave Varian only a brief nod of acknowledgment. All three wore the brief Iretan costume adopted by the native-born, now enhanced by forcebelts, stunners, and clips. Varian decided the Iretans were really much more attractive as human derivatives than the heavy-world adaptations.

After she had filled her list, with the exception of the nose plugs which the quartermaster felt would be her most pressing need, Varian was asking for help to convey her booty to the sled, when Fordeliton's caller sounded.

"A moment, Varian, this concerns you, too. Commander Sassinak's compliments, and can we join her immediately? Crewman, secure those supplies in Governor Varian's sled."

Varian was surprised to find Kai, the medic Mayerd, and Florasse, Tanegli's daughter—whom she had met when barriered as Rianav. While she was being introduced, Aygar was admitted.

Then the commander activated the main screen. "This report has just arrived from the southwest, from the geologist Dimenon. He thought we should know about this development."

"That's the site of Dimenon's last strike," Kai said when he recognized the terrain.

"And the current habitat of twenty-three small Thek if my

tally is correct," Sassinak added with wayward amusement.
"Now watch the edges of the picture."

Even as she spoke, Kai let out an inadvertent gasp of horror and revulsion. He held both hands out in front of him as the fringes advanced in their inimitable close-stretch propulsion, heading directly toward the sedentary Thek.

"Those critters are in for a big surprise, Governor," Sassinak remarked.

Nonetheless, Kai sucked in his breath and arched his body backward, as the first fringe spread to envelop a Thek. Varian was not the only one more interested in Kai's reactions than what was occurring on the screen. Mayerd was discreetly watching him. The fringe had been attracted by a lethal entity, for its sides began to melt and, before the creature could desist, it had been reduced to its crumpled cartilaginous framework. The other fringes met the same fate. Then, as the fascinated observers watched, fringes that had not deployed on their intended victims began to slow their advance, and came to fluttering halts.

"Varian, have you done much investigation of these—what did you call them, Aygar?" Sassinak asked.

"Fringes." Aygar's single word broke Kai's transfixed gaze from the screen to the Iretan's presence.

"Young Terilla named them that," Kai said in a flat cold voice, turning away from Aygar.

The big Iretan made no comment, inclining his head briefly. "Whatever those black pyramids are—"

"Thek!" Kai was almost surly.

"The fringes have met their match, then, in these Thek. Do they generate much heat?"

"Yes."

"What was it you told me, Kai?" Mayerd said into the awkward pause after Kai's response. "The Thek are gorging themselves on raw Iretan energy?"

Kai nodded curtly.

"Were we told about Thek, Florasse?" Aygar asked.

The woman shook her head slowly, her eyes never leaving the screen. "They are not of this world, Aygar, so why would *we* have needed to know?" Florasse's voice held overtones of betrayed trust and disillusionment, enough to make Kai regard her with surprise.

"What interest do the Thek have on my world?" Aygar asked, his glance sliding from Kai's closed expression to Varian.

"We would feel easier, Aygar," Sassinak answered him, "if we ourselves knew. The Thek are a long-lived race who keep their own counsel, vouchsafing to us poor ephemerals only such information as they consider us worthy to receive."

"They are your supreme rulers?"

"By no means! They are, however, a vital force in the Federated Sentient Planets. One does not—as you just saw—meddle with a Thek with impunity. What is germane to us right now is the question, what do you native Iretans know about the fringes?"

"To stay away from them." Aygar's glance flicked to Kai.

"And?" Sassinak prompted him.

"They are attracted by body heat and envelop their prey, clasping the digits midsection to secure it. Then they consume their victim with a digestive juice. The ship suit you were wearing saved your life," Aygar remarked to Kai. "Fringes have trouble digesting synthetic fibers."

"What weapon do you use to protect yourselves against the creatures?" Sassinak asked.

"We run"—and Varian was certain now that the powerful young man was possessed by a fine sense of humor—"as we possess no effective weapons against the fringes. A few Thek posted about would be ideal deterrents."

Fordeliton coughed aloud and even Sassinak looked a trifle surprised at Aygar's irreverent suggestion.

"Is fire effective?"

Aygar shrugged. "I've never seen them melt before, nor have we had any liquid flame to use. So far they have not penetrated to this plateau."

Sassinak turned back to the final frame on the screen: the fringes retreating from the Thek.

"We observed aquatic fringes before we went cryo," Varian said, "but no evidence at all of communication between the species. Perhaps the land fringes are further along in evolution." She shuddered. "I don't like even to think what they could do in cooperation. The aquatic ones are considerably smaller. Oh, and the golden fliers keep well away from them, too."

"Fringes in the sea?" Aygar swung toward Varian, with a puzzled frown.

"Yes, our chemist ran some tests on fringe tissue. They're one of the many anomalies this planet presented us. A life-form with a cellular development completely different from that of the dinosaurs—"

"Dinosaurs?" Fordeliton erupted in surprise.

"Yes, it's all in my report," Varian said. "Tyrannosaurus rex—I called him fang-face—hadrasaurs of all varieties, crested, helmeted, hyracotherium, pteranodons which I call golden fliers, or giffs—"

"But that's preposterous," Fordeliton began.

"That's what Trizein said. He's an amateur Mesozoic naturalist—"

"Do you have dinosaurs on this plateau?" Fordeliton eagerly demanded of Aygar.

"No. We picked the plateau as our settlement because it is mercifully devoid of the large life-forms," Aygar said. "We avoid the dinosaurs as we do the fringes. Especially the golden fliers." He glanced at Varian.

"The giffs are harmless," Varian said stoutly.

Aygar's eyebrows lifted slightly in an expression of doubt, a doubt which Florasse seconded.

"There's obviously a great deal of information to be shared," Sassinak said, firmly regaining control of the meeting. "And considerable reason for you all," and her gesture made one group of them, "to cooperate. I estimate you have a week, two weeks at the outside before I receive orders, either from my Sector or the tribunal. As I have mentioned before, any ship of the Fleet encountering shipwrecked survivors is required to render whatever reasonable assistance is requested. We'll ignore that—" and she jerked her thumb in the direction of the heavy-worlder transport, "complication for the nonce. My ship has been on tour for four months and my crew could use some shore leave, even on a planet that smells as bad as this one. Many of them have technical avocations—geology, botany, metallurgy, agronomy. There are analysts of all persuasions." She extended one printout sheet to Kai and one to Aygar. "I'm sure that we can arrange duty rosters for anyone you think would be helpful, Governor. My people would make up in enthusiasm what they might lack in expertise." Kai took the sheet from her, but Aygar remained stolidly regarding Sassinak. With a hint of testiness, she rattled the sheet at him. "You have a perfect right to be suspicious of gratuitous offers of assistance, young man, but do not be stupid. You have as much to lose or gain as these people. You may not realize it, but my profession is to protect life in all its myriad and mysterious forms. Not destroy it."

Florasse stirred restlessly, her hand twitching, but just then Aygar stepped forward and took the list with another of his stiff nods.

"For *my* information, I would very much appreciate a report from you Iretans on the life-forms you have encountered. Thank you for your attention." She rose, signifying an end to the meeting, her glance indicating that Varian and Kai should remain. "Now," she said when the door had slid shut again, "any luck with your investigations, Mayerd?"

"Too soon to tell."

"What? Your pet diagnostic let you down?"

"My *unit* has a great deal to chuckle over, but it has confirmed the interim medication that the *Mazer Star* recommended. We'll soon have a more exhaustive report." She sounded confident.

"Can I get back to my team, then?" Kai's expression was unusually set.

"Only if you'll take Fordeliton with you. He's a devoted dinosaur buff."

"There *must* be some mistake," Fordeliton said, his words bursting forth.

"Not according to Trizein. Our chemist is also a dinosaur buff," Varian replied. "Geologically, this planet is stuck in the Mesozoic."

"There is no way, my dear Varian, that Ireta could evolve creatures similar to the monsters that roamed the planet Earth millions of years ago."

"We're well aware of that improbability, Commander," Varian assured her with a rueful grin, "but that's what we've got and Trizein verifies it. It's all in our reports."

"I can see that I'm going to have to pay those reports considerable attention. I was going to have Ford do it for me," Sassinak's face made a moue of resignation, "but I can't in conscience keep him cooling his heels here if those beasties really are out there. Don't we have other naturalists on the list, Ford?"

"Yes, ma'am—Maxnil, Crilsoff, and Pendelman. Anstel as well, but he's on watch."

"They're not essential crew, are they? No. Would you care for some passengers back to that eyrie of yours, Governors?" When she received an eager affirmative from Varian, she nodded to Fordeliton. "See to it, will you, Ford. You may have transport, and you'd best take supplies. Keep in touch. Now, all, shake a leg out of here." She picked up the first of the report cassettes and slid it into the replay slot on her console. "*I've* got a lot of reading to do." She flicked her hand at them.

Almost like children released from a tiresome class, they left. Fordeliton's excitement was palpable.

"Look, I'll get Maxnil, Crilsoff, and Pendelman, raid the galley and the recorder stores, and follow. Okay?"

"Would you have time and the space to take one or two of the geology people?" Kai asked.

"Sure, sure." Fordeliton craned his neck to see the list in Kai's hand. "Baker, Bullo, and Macud are good, and they work hard. They're off-duty right now so they'll be bored and easily persuaded to accompany me." Fordeliton grinned. "No problem. Don't want to inundate you, but you've no idea what a treat this is."

By this time, they had reached the air lock. Varian had a clear view of the sky and saw the departure of three sleds from the Iretans' settlement, heading southeast. She wondered if they were going to consolidate their position on the first campsite that they had abandoned. She looked quickly to see if Kai had noticed the sleds, but he was discussing supplies with Fordeliton.

"If you have any telltaggers in your stores, you might want to mount one on your sled," Varian suggested to Fordeliton.

"We have. I will, I'll follow as soon as I assemble the men."

12

FORTUNATELY Fordeliton gave them a few minutes advance warning of his arrival, which allowed Varian just enough time to become airborne and prevent the cruiser's sled from being attacked. Fordeliton was tremendously excited by the variety of creatures he had seen on his way to the giff cliffs. When Varian guided him into the cave, he was enraptured by the giffs themselves and his companions—Maxnil, Crilsoff, and Pendelman—were equally thrilled.

"Now that I have you here, I'm not quite sure what to do with you," Varian said truthfully. "Trizein is out with young Bonnard and Terilla—"

"Could we join them?" Fordeliton was all eagerness.

"There's not much point in duplicating effort. What sort of speed and range does your sled have?" Varian asked as she rummaged for a sketch map of the main continent of Ireta which Kai had made the previous evening.

"Fleet standard, supersonic."

"Really? You wouldn't mind working up in the polar region, would you? We hadn't penetrated that far. Your sled could function in high temperatures?"

"Of course!"

"Well, now." Varian pointed to the northern polar area. "I'd rather like to know if there are variations of these critters that have adapted to the intense heat."

"I'll just put this map through the scan, and we'll be off to do a reconnaissance."

No sooner had she sent him on his way than a second sled penetrated giff territory. They had not thought to announce their arrival so that Varian had a chance to witness the giff attack mode. The resultant commotion brought Lunzie from her lair.

"You'll have to go up yourself and escort them in," the medic told Varian.

"I think we've got too much of a good thing," Varian said under her breath as she went to the rescue.

This time it was a second shift from the *Zaid-Dayan*, the geology buffs, Baker, Bullo, and Macud. Kai contacted Dimenon and arranged an unexplored sector for the cruiser's men to assess. They went off in high spirits.

"We can't keep alarming the giffs like this," Varian said, "even if we *do* need help to accomplish our mission."

"Why not return to our original site, then?" Lunzie suggested. When she noticed Kai's stiff posture, she shrugged. "Well, it was just an idea."

Kai took a deep breath. "Not a bad one, actually, Lunzie. In fact, a very sensible solution. I'd like to see if a force-screen would keep out fringes. They couldn't have developed from aquatic to land beasts in just forty-three years, could they? Well, then," and he swallowed, took a deep breath, "it was Tor who attracted the fringe to the site. We'll just try to make sure that we keep our Thek visitors to a minimum. Okay? Then let's plan to reestablish our original camp. It makes sense in a number of ways, not just protecting the giffs. It's where *ARCT-10* will look for us. And since the *Zaid-Dayan*'s sleds all have long-range capabilities, then we won't have to establish secondary camps. And you can stay on here, Varian, and observe the giffs without all this coming and going."

"I like it, Kai," Lunzie said, thoroughly approving. "But we need a lot of equipment—"

"We'll make up a list. Sassinak did say that she's supposed to replenish any lost equipment."

"Isn't replacing a whole basecamp asking a bit much?"

"I'll lean on my relation this evening," Lunzie said. "Blood is thicker than water and a few odd pieces of standard Fleet issue."

The giff alarm was heard yet again and, cursing with a fervor and an inventiveness that made her listeners grin, Varian went out to give escort. Mayerd arrived just as Varian had maneuvered her slower vehicle out. Mayerd opened the canopy of her sleek one-man craft as Varian returned, and gave her a cheery, apologetic wave. She stepped out of the little ship, turning to gather three large parcels and one small before she moved toward Kai and Lunzie.

"My diagnostic unit chuckled to itself for a good two hours after you left, Kai, but it came up with medication and a few tentative conclusions. It rarely makes definitive statements. You are Lunzie, aren't you?" Mayerd asked, juggling her parcels so that she had a free hand to extend to Lunzie.

"I am and I surmise that you are Lieutenant Commander Mayerd."

"Mayerd'll do." Then she turned again to Kai, grinning. "Not only did that fringe digestive juice poison you, Kai, but you are allergic to the poison. My DU not only came up with tablets to help flush the poison out of your system and counteract the allergy but also a salve to anoint the punctures and reduce that desensitivity. And DU highly recommended the new nerve regenerative." She turned expectantly to Lunzie. "The Crimjenetic: the regenerative we had to use to combat the Persean paralysis." When Lunzie's expression remained polite but otherwise unresponsive, Mayerd blinked. "Ah, but you wouldn't have known about that. It happened twenty years ago . . ."

"During a nap I took," Lunzie commented.

Mayerd smiled. "You'll want to read up on this Crimjenetic then. It has proved remarkably effective on all kinds of bizarre nerve poisonings. And I've some disks on the latest

Federated Medical Review I can lend you, as well, to make up for that naptime. Remind me this evening. Which brings me to these . . ." She handed out the parcels. "I thought green for you, Lunzie. Medical research has proved that our profession choses green as their favorite color nine to one. I hope you're not the odd one out."

"I generally am, but green is a flattering color, and you were very thoughtful to fill the need."

"I got the notion that dress clothes might not have been on your most needed list and, after I saw the preparations going on in the officers' mess, I decided I'd better play costumer for you. Blue for you, Kai, and this garnet red should be most becoming, Varian. Sorry about arriving unannounced. Those pteranodons of yours are magnificent."

"So are these," Lunzie said, one blunt-fingered hand stroking the deep green fabric. "Just how big are the *Zaid-Dayan*'s stores?"

"Pretty damned all-inclusive," Mayerd said with pride. "We're only four months into this tour so our supplies are basically untouched. Maybe not esoteric. Why? What do you need?"

"A few odd domes, some heavy duty force-screens . . ."

"Capable of frying fringes?" Mayerd asked with a sympathetic chuckle.

"You got it in one!"

"Just hand me your list. Clever of you to be related to the commander, isn't it?"

"Providential!"

"We haven't actually written up a list yet," Varian said. "We only just decided to leave here before the giffs lose their fur in fright."

"A cavern did seem an odd place to set up as a major campsite," Mayerd remarked.

"It was a good port in a . . ." Varian broke off her sentence because one of Ireta's sudden boisterous squalls erupted, blowing the vines inward, rain and debris falling just short of the little group.

"Not that the heaviest duty force-screen would keep off that sort of storm," Mayerd said, establishing herself beyond the storm wrack on a hearth stool. She took a pad and scripter out of her thigh pocket and looked about her expectantly. "Now, how many domes? How large a force-screen? Furnishings? Supplies? Old lamps for new?"

By the time Mayerd had left, she had prompted a far more exhaustive list of requirements from them than they would ever have listed without her encouragement. When Varian suggested that they might be overdoing it, Mayerd dismissed the notion immediately.

"Sassinak has given orders that you are to be given any reasonable quantity of supplies—"

"I wouldn't call *that* exactly reasonable," Varian said, indicating the filled pad.

Mayerd regarded her with eyebrows raised in polite surprise.

"When Sassinak sees domes, force-screens—"

"Sassinak," and Mayerd paused briefly to emphasize her commander's name, "won't *see* a trivial list like this. She's got one very big problem in a transport, occupying her waking hours. This," and Mayerd waved the pad, "goes directly into QM, and I'll see that it's delivered to the site tomorrow morning." She moved lightly to the little one-man craft, slid back the canopy, and seated herself. "That is, assuming any of us are capable tomorrow morning. Let me check the coordinates of that campsite now, while I'm able." Kai glanced at the notation and confirmed it. "See you later."

Varian couldn't resist the temptation to swing out on one of the vines and see what the giffs made of the speed of Mayerd's craft. Some younger fliers took off in pursuit, but it was immediately obvious that they could never catch the speedy sled, so they began to make lazy swirls in the clearing sky, first to the left and then to the right. Almost, Varian thought, as if they made the tip of first one wing and then the other the pivot of a private circle of sky.

"I wish you wouldn't take risks like that," Kai said, frowning anxiously as she reached the safety inside the cave and released the vine.

"It's exhilarating, for one thing. For another, I had to move fast or miss the sight, and the ladder was too far away. Kai," and Varian held out one hand, meaning to clasp his arm to transmit understanding. The gesture was not completed because she remembered his handicap and wasn't sure just how light a touch might harm. She dropped her hand. "Kai, I just wanted to say that I think you're perfectly splendid to shift camps to protect the giffs from unnecessary interference."

Kai shrugged. "Being here would make your job impossible if you wanted to catch the giffs going about their regular routine. If they have one. And anyhow," he grinned ruefully, "I think it would lay a lot of ghosts to rest to go back there. D'you want to keep the shuttle as your base?"

Varian looked about her, at the amenities which Captain Godheir and Obir had so thoughtfully arranged.

"I'd be very comfortable here, without the shuttle. And then there's the matter of the giffs' reaction to the departure of the shuttle. That'll be interesting to observe." She grinned.

"D'you think they've wondered if it will sprout wings when it's big enough? Or hatch?"

"They've been that road once, when Tor paid you the visit."

They grinned, once again in harmony with each other. Then Kai gave her arm an affectionate squeeze.

"C'mon. Once again we've got some organizing to do."

13

Kai, Lunzie and Varian arrived at the *Zaid-Dayan* as the brief Iretan twilight fell over the edge into night. Lights winked on in the settlement, a huge spotlight illuminating the large clearing around which the individual residences were grouped. Red nightlights went on around the looming mass of the heavy-worlder transport, making the great ship seem more ominous than ever. Twinkling here and there, patrol vehicles flitted on seemingly random courses like fireflies. The patrol carts were little more than powered platforms for the two men seated on them, but they were effective mobile sentry units. The gangway was clearly lit, and as Varian landed the sled, she was surprised to see men trotting out to form an honor guard from the gangway to their sled.

"Why is it that you never have *human* escorts when you really need them?" Lunzie murmured. The usual three giffs had guided them to the plateau.

"Have they gone?" Varian asked. Far above them hung a layer of thick black clouds, under which the visibility was unusually lucid in the twilight, which was punctuated now and then with lightning.

"Now that they've delivered us safely to the *big* eggs." Lunzie was in good spirits, and Kai wondered if she could continue that way all evening. It could be a dinner to be remembered for many reasons.

A sudden shrill whistle greeted them as they emerged from the sled.

"Muhlah! She's thrown the whole ceremony at us," Kai exclaimed, forgetting to watch his movements and catching his hand on the canopy frame. Neither Varian nor Lunzie noticed as their attention was on the naval honors being accorded them. He glanced quickly down at his gloved hand but saw no damage. He quickly fell in step behind the women, as complimented by the courtesies as they.

"Blessings on Mayerd for her parcels," Varian said quickly to Kai.

"Well, now look what we have here!" Lunzie cried, holding her arms wide apart.

In the companionway Fordeliton stood in the silver, black, and blue dress uniform of the Fleet, complete with all his honors—and there were many—on his breast. Slightly to one side waited Mayerd, equally splendid, with the Medical sash crossing her chest. Neither were a patch on Sassinak, however, who also awaited her guests. The commander wore a flowing black gown, its full skirts decorated with tiny stars while the close fitting bodice was goffered with blue. Tiny jeweled formal-dress honors adorned her left breast while the rank emblems were jeweled shoulder ornaments. Kai did not remember ever seeing the *ARCT*'s officers in full-dress regalia, but perhaps EVs followed customs different from those of the Fleet.

"Lunzie, it is indeed a privilege and a pleasure to meet you!" Sassinak stood very straight and saluted crisply.

"It is a unique occasion, certainly," Lunzie replied in a drawl, but there was no diffidence in her firm handshake.

The two women stood for a long moment, then Sassinak grinned, cocking her head slightly to one side in a mannerism so like Lunzie that Kai and Varian exchanged startled looks.

"You have been exceedingly generous to a stranded relative, Commander Sassinak. That brandy went down very smoothly."

"Sassinak, please," and the commander indicated the direction they should take. "Surely one must mark the chance encounter with an ancestor."

"This is going to be some evening," Mayerd murmured as she took Kai by the arm.

"Stand down the honor guard, Besler," Fordeliton ordered the duty officer with a salute. "This way, Governor Varian . . ."

It was indeed an evening long remembered by the participants. Fordeliton abandoned any pretext of composure after Lunzie's fourth outrageous pun. Varian had no compunction and howled with laughter. Kai grinned so broadly he wondered if he was doing his face an injury. Mayerd had few inhibitions anyway and was respectful but unawed by her commander. The stewards managed to keep their expressions under reasonable control, but several times Varian was certain that she had heard bursts of laughter erupting from the serving alcove. And the food was superb! Varian watched Kai sample the unfamiliar portions with a tact born of the desire not to embarrass Lunzie. Varian found the dishes so utterly delicious, unusual, and much tastier than their recent fare that she felt Kai ought to have eaten with greater gusto. Each subtle taste was balanced by the next and none of the portions was too large, each was enough merely to tempt the palate to the next course. Their glasses were changed with each new course, and the wines were perfect.

When they conferred together on the point later, Varian and Kai were both disappointed not to learn more about Lunzie's early career or her planet of origin. Not even the name of the child who had produced this latter-day descendant, Sassinak. That the two were actually bloodkin was obvious in a dozen small resemblances, in mannerisms or expressions, a gesture, a tilt of the head, a quirk of the eyebrow, and a shared humor that certainly bridged the generation gap.

All but the tiny cups of *cha* and elegant afterdinner liqueur glasses had been cleared when Sassinak turned to Kai.

"I understand that you are shifting back to your original camp site, Kai. Wasn't that where the fringe attacked you?"

"Yes, but I feel only because Tor's warmth had attracted it.

We exude a fraction of the body heat of a Thek. Forty years ago we didn't see any land fringes though we had a full complement in the camp. The campsite has not lost the advantages which led us to choose it in the first place."

"I believe I can offer you an even greater security, at least while we're still in the vicinity. Fordeliton, don't you think we should give the globes a test run in this unusual situation?"

"Yes, indeed, I do, Commander. They haven't yet been tested by such diverse life-forms. Thek, human, dinosaur, the avian golden fliers, and fringes! This environment will be a very good test of globe capability."

"Globes are an early warning device that have recently been released for Fleet use. I can't go into specifics, but with a properly programmed globe hanging over your encampment, Kai, you'll be safe from such predators as the fringes and the bigger dinosaurs. Now tell me, just how did you escape from the dome and avoid the stampede?"

"It's in my report," Kai said, surprised.

"Your report, and I quote, says, 'We exited from the rear of the dome and reached the safety of the shuttle just as the vanguard of the stampeding hadrasaurs breached the force-screen.'" Sassinak stared hard at Kai for a long moment and then turned to Varian. "You were even less forthcoming. 'We escaped from the dome and reached the shuttle.' Period. So how exactly did you escape to the shuttle?"

"Triv and I called on Discipline and parted the dome at the seam."

"At the seam?" Fordeliton was impressed and glanced at his commander, who merely nodded.

"The young man, Bonnard, had not been apprehended by the heavy-worlders?"

"No, Bonnard was at large," Kai said, with a wry grin. "He'd the great good sense to hide the power packs—"

"Rendering the sleds inoperative. Good strategy. I would suggest that the mutineers made the usual classic mistake— they underestimated their opponents. A lesson Naval Tactics always emphasizes, does it not, Ford?" Sassinak raised one eyebrow and regarded her aide with a tolerant smile.

"Indeed, yes." Fordeliton dabbed at his mouth with his napkin and looked anywhere but at Sassinak.

"Leaping ahead in your story, then, Kai and Varian, the golden fliers must be discriminating indeed if they protect you, and yet are aggressive to the Iretans, a hostility I infer from Aygar's remark this morning."

"The giffs had thresholds for their behavior, one of which was stimulated—and this is surmise—by the mutineers who probably searched near enough to the giff caves to provoke attack. They would repel anyone approaching our refuge from the ravine side. They also seem to be able to distinguish among sled engines."

"What more have you observed about the giffs?"

"Not as much as I would like. To date, my observations have mainly dealt with their reactions to us, not interactions among themselves. That's what I'd like to explore."

"Excellent! Excellent! That's just what you should do."

"What interested me most," Mayerd said, hitching forward in her chair, "was the fact that those creatures knew a specific remedy for the fringe poison. And realized that you needed it. I'd say that places their intelligence level well above primitive norms."

"What establishes them above primitive norms is . . ." Sassinak broke off, aware of a shadow hovering anxiously just out of sight in the corridor. "Yes, what is it?"

Borander stepped into view, every inch of him reluctant to interrupt the gathering.

"You ordered that you be informed of any attempt at communication between the transport and the Iretans, Commander."

"Indeed. Who's trying to get in touch with whom?" Sassinak shed her party manner in that instant.

"A transmission from the transport has been monitored, directed at the Iretan settlement and requesting it to open communications."

"And?"

"There has been no reply from the settlement."

"How could the Iretans reply?" Lunzie asked. "They haven't any comunits!"

"They don't?" Now Fordeliton registered amazement.

"It isn't likely that the original units have survived forty-three years in this climate," Varian said. "Unless the Iretans were issued replacements."

Fordeliton shook his head. "We were surprised, but Aygar said that he didn't have much need for that sort of equipment. Nor did they request any power units suitable for a comunit of any current type."

"On what frequency was Cruss broadcasting?" Kai asked suddenly. Sassinak raised her eyebrows with approval. When Borander gave the frequency, Kai smiled with satisfaction. "That was the frequency the expedition used, Commander."

"Very interesting, indeed. Now how would our innocent Captain Cruss have learned that from the 'message' in the damaged homing capsule? I've read and reread the text. The frequencies were not included. He has well and truly used enough rope."

Lunzie chuckled. "I wonder why Cruss is trying to contact people who don't wish contact with him."

"Could Aygar be playing a deep game?" Sassinak asked.

"I wouldn't say he was playing any game," Varian said, watching the frown on Kai's face deepen at her remark. "He has stated his position quite clearly—this is his planet and he intends to remain on it."

"More power to him if he can," Sassinak replied. "Borander, my compliments to Lieutenant Commander Dupaynil. I think this is a matter for his skills." As Borander went off on his errand, Sassinak turned to her guests. "Dupaynil's Naval Intelligence. Varian, do the Iretans have any particular accent or provincial dialect? . . ." And when Varian reassured her, she continued, "My friends, too many attempts at planetary piracy have been successful, too many well-organized expeditions have appeared on planets which were not scheduled to be colonized for a half century. And—to be candid—generally not by groups which are amenable to observing Federated Charter obligations as regards ecology, minority, and nonaggression. The *unusual* circumstances of the *spontaneous* settlement are all reasonably explained—always after the fact, when the Federation is powerless to disband a by-then established, productive colony. The more we can discover about the *modus operandi*, the quicker we can squash the whole movement."

"Are the heavy-worlders always the pirates?" Kai asked.

"By no means," Sassinak replied, twirling her liqueur glass gently around on the damask table-covering. "But they have been the most successful at the game, usurping planets that were destined for other minorities. Ireta is a good case in point. Gravity is normal here."

"That's about the only thing that is," Lunzie muttered under her breath.

"Be that as it may," and Sassinak shot her relative a sympathetic glance, "Ireta is too rich a plum to be plucked by the fardling heavy-worlders! Let them find high-gravity worlds where their mutation is useful."

"It would be quite valuable, then, to discover if a group has been organizing these piratical ventures?" Lunzie asked.

"Invaluable, my dear great-great-great-grandmother Lunzie, invaluable. Have you any ideas?"

"One which I see no point in discussing prematurely. It's just that something you said is twitching a memory." Lunzie flung up one hand in disgust at her inability to recall it. "I'd like to assist this Intelligence man of yours, if I may . . ." and her glance took in Varian and Kai as well as the commander.

Varian shrugged and looked to Kai.

"It would afford me considerable pleasure," he said, "if we could thwart the planetary pirates."

A discreet rap on the door was immediately acknowledged by Sassinak and a slim, swarthy man eased into the wardroom. After one quick glance around the table, he gave all his attention to his commander.

"Dupaynil, how would you like to pose as an Iretan, eager to admit the heavy-worlders to this planet?"

"The very thing to while away my tedium, Commander."

"I apologize for the abrupt end to this exceedingly pleasant evening, ladies, gentlemen," Sassinak said as she rose, her manner brusque, no longer suited to the elegant gown that swirled about her legs. "Lunzie, may we avail you of your offer? Ford, see our guests to their transport."

"You will keep us informed of developments, Sassinak?" Kai asked, rising slowly and carefully.

"Indeed, she will," Lunzie said with a little smile. "I'm a firm believer in ancestor worship."

14

THE next morning Varian and Kai called together all the survivors to explain their move back to the original campsite. The only one to protest was Aulia, and she did so at the top of her lungs, hysterically proclaiming that they were being transferred to their deaths where those hideous animals were ready to charge at them again, not to mention the things that had eaten Kai. At that point, even the insensitive Aulia became aware of the disapproval from all sides. Her monologue subsided into a rebellious mutter.

"Commander Sassinak has equipped us with attack-repulse force-screens," Kai said, "and a device which is new to us but infallible in detecting aggression from any source. I think we can return in good heart. That site is, after all, where *ARCT-10* will search for us."

"Kai, *ARCT-10,* you can't honestly think we'll ever see *them* again, do you?" Aulia's voice was quite shrill.

The three youngsters tensed and looked intently at Kai, waiting for his response.

"Yes, I can honestly believe that the *ARCT-10* will return for us. This is an instance where no news can be construed as good news. Neither Captain Godheir nor Commander Sassinak found anything in their data banks about the loss of an EV. And such a loss would have been news galaxywide. Commander Sassinak has requested a Sector update with specific references to a position report on the *ARCT-10.*"

"In forty-three years the *ARCT-10* could be in another galaxy. Maybe that's why no one has heard of it."

"By the same token," Lunzie called in a dry taunting voice, "it could have taken forty-three years to maneuver out of that cosmic storm."

Eager to continue the attack, Aulia took a deep breath which she exhaled on a gasp as Portegin pinched her upper arm. Rubbing it, she turned to Triv. When she saw the set of his jaw and the irritation in his expression, she subsided into a petulant sulk.

"Now, we'd best organize the removal. The *Zaid-Dayan* people will be meeting us at the campsite at 0900. Let's get cracking."

Lunzie pointed a very stern forefinger at Kai. "You will be executive director of the proceedings. Seated here!" Her forefinger then indicated the stool by the hearth.

Kai grinned at her and made a show of assuming his command position.

It did not, in fact, take much time to secure the sparse furnishings in the shuttle, nor to pack oddments in the sleds.

Varian was going to retain a two-man sled for her own use and keep a few basic necessities in the cave, to allow her to continue her observations, if weather and circumstances ever permitted. Kenley then arrived with other crew members from the *Mazer Star* to assist in the removal.

Triv was to pilot the shuttle, and firmly grasping the unrepentant Aulia by the elbow, propelled her into the shuttle. Lunzie followed "to deal with her, if necessary," the medic said in an angry aside to Varian. Portegin brought up the rear, looking as glum as Aulia but for a different reason. Dimenon was to take Trizein, Terilla, and Cleiti in the four-man sled, along with Trizein's accoutrements. Trizein was full of directions to the girls on what should be recorded on their outward trip, while Portegin would take one of the smaller sleds, giving Bonnard a driving lesson which, Bonnard allowed vehemently, was long overdue for a man fifty-eight years old. Margit and Kai were taking the other small sled, packed with whatever was left over.

When all were ready to take off, Kenley went up the ladder to the top of the cliff, determined to film the exodus and giff reaction to it. Weather permitting, he sourly amended. A black squall line was making its way across the inland sea. Varian, and another recorder, would remain in the cave. She was rather hoping that the Elder Three Giffs would enter the cavern, once the "big egg" had flown away. The shuttle's take-off could pose quite a cultural shock to the giffs, but its removal couldn't be helped. The shuttle was an essential unit for the main campsite. Its departure would certainly give insights to giff intelligence and perception, parameters which Varian was eager to establish despite the considerable shock it would occasion the giffs.

The smaller sleds went first, buffeted a bit by the squall winds but flying quickly away from the turbulence. The heavier shuttle had to be turned, a maneuver Triv accomplished deftly, then it moved majestically from the cave, and rose with great dignity above the cliff. Varian grinned to herself: there was an element of unexpected theatricality in old Triv. She thought she heard a muted cry of astonishment from Kenley, but the wind had got up and she couldn't be sure.

With the sleds and shuttle gone, the cave seemed barren, her small alcove an intrusion. She settled lightly on the stool, shifting the weight of the recorder to her shoulder. The vines billowed in, and a splatter of the morning rain reached her, misting across her face and hands, making the small hearth fire hiss. She was positive she heard giff cries, shrill and excited. Why hadn't she thought to equip Kenley with a wrist unit so he could tell her what was happening. Yes, she did hear what could only be a whoop, and a completely human emission. Patiently she waited.

She was rewarded. Suddenly the vines were shoved aside as three large golden fliers glided in, coming to a halt a respectful distance from where the shuttle had nested so long. Varian grinned at her use of terminology as she recorded them. All Three Giffs stared at the empty space, their wings still half-extended. The end giffs turned their heads inquiringly toward Middle Giff who gave the equivalent of a shrug and neatly laid his wings to his back in a gesture that might be rendered as resignation to an unpleasant truth.

Then each of the giffs appeared sunk down on its legs, pulling its wings tighter to its body and retracting its neck slightly. Varian perceived an aura of sadness and disappointment about the giffs. A small sound, just at the audible level, came to her ears. It had to be emanating from the giffs for it was not a squall or wind noise: a sad and sorrowing note. So sad that Varian felt the short hairs on the back of her neck begin to rise and decided it was time to make a move.

She had just shifted the recorder when Kenley unexpectedly slid down the ladder pole. The giffs extended their wings, hissing and exclaiming so loudly that Varian was alarmed.

"Kenley, stand still! Spread out your arms! You're peaceful!"

"I'll say I am!" Kenley complied with her instructions but backed against the ladder as the nearest means of escape from the winged creatures obviously bent on attacking him.

To give him full credit, Kenley stood his ground while Varian dashed around the advancing giffs and jumped between them and Kenley.

"Don't hurt him!" Varian cried, arms spread wide in front of the giffs to impede their progress. "You know me! You must know me."

"What if they don't remember you?" Kenley had grabbed the first rungs of the ladder.

"I'm friendly! You know me." It took a tremendous effort for Varian to keep her voice friendly. The giffs were so close to her that she could smell the aroma of fish and spice that they exuded. Their long pointed beaks had raised slightly, and she was being regarded by very keen, hostile eyes. The mid-wing digits were flexing as if to seize her.

"I'm sorry I still don't have any of the Rift grasses for you. Now is really not the time to appear before you empty-handed, but I didn't expect Kenley to come flying down here before I'd had a chance to talk with you. Not that you could understand more than the tone of voice, but you do see that I'm trying to be pleasant and friendly. Don't you?"

Middle Giff was towering over her, digits working, its head cocked slightly as it kept its right eye fixed on her.

"Krims, Varian, I don't even have a stunner on my belt! What're you going to do?"

"I'm going to keep talking," she said, smiling so broadly she felt her cheeks might crack. "And you're not going to move a muscle unless they dive on me. Then you better move it up that ladder." Her tone was lightly cheerful despite her ominous words, and when Kenley groaned, she added, "Don't do that to me, friend. You be as cheerful as I am. They understand tone, and that wasn't a good one. Okay?"

"I gotcha."

Varian had to grin at the intensity of his rejoinder. Then very slowly she extended her hand.

"Now, let's see if we can make the first overtures of what I hope will be a lasting friendship." She watched Middle Giff's body, flicking her glance to his wings briefly, but it was as curious about her next move as she was about the giff's reaction to it. Moving with great precision, Varian touched the wing claw of the giff. It twitched but the giff did not retreat. Varian let her fingers drift from the claw to the wing surface. "Hey, you feel almost oily. It's not like fur at all."

"That thing has fur? I thought birds always had feathers."

"There's a point in evolution when fur was feathers or the other way round. Giffs are furred."

Varian withdrew her hand from Middle Giff who had been regarding her with unblinking eyes. Now suddenly it blinked several times, for all the world like a small child which had steeled itself for an unknown experience and had received a pleasant surprise.

"There! That wasn't so terrible now, was it?" she said, grinning in an honest reaction to its manner.

She turned her body toward the smaller giff and, allowing it time to withdraw, touched its wing claw lightly. It endured the contact but immediately took a small backward step.

"Okay, I get the message." She looked at the other small giff and as if it sensed her intention, it, too, stepped back. "I receive you loud and clear." She looked back at Middle Giff. "You're the courageous one, are you?"

Something like a croon could be heard from Middle Giff. Its throat was vibrating.

"Oh, you agree with me, huh?" Slowly, once again, she extended her hand for the wing claw, its three digits lying loose. She took one between her thumb and forefinger and pressed very gently. "An Iretan handshake. First contact between species."

"You got guts!" Kenley breathed behind her.

"Just don't move, Kenley."

"Not a hair. I'll leave it all up to you."

She maintained the light grasp, and her wide smile, aware of the intense scrutiny of Middle Giff. Then, tentatively, the claw lightly closed about her fingers. It felt warm and dry, and she wondered what impression the giff had of its contact with her flesh. The claw released her fingers, and she drew back her hand.

"Ordinarily, one says, hello, how are you today?" Varian inclined her body in a slight bow and gurgled with triumph as the giff rocked forward slightly toward her.

"I should have had that recorded, Varian. I really should. That's what I'm here to do, isn't it?" Kenley sounded aggrieved, and Varian had to contain her ire.

"If you hadn't clattered down that ladder like the Galormis were after you." Varian had to keep her voice pleasant, but she was annoyed with Kenley for his entrance.

"I wouldn't have," he replied with exasperation, "if I'd known you had this trio here. But I didn't. How did they get here?"

"They flew."

"Sorry. I guess I was in a hurry. Hey, I've got to get this recorded."

"Just move slowly is all I ask, Kenley." Varian held the gaze of Middle Giff.

It had made a slight noise, deep in its chest, and the other two giffs had begun to back away from Varian. Then, as if this were a much rehearsed courtesy, the Middle Giff began to back up, an awkward movement for one of its size. Then, with a second comment, the three giffs waddled with a certain stately dignity to the mouth of the cave and dropped off. Kenley raced to the edge, recorder trained on their exit.

"Wow! I got that recorded!" Kenley ignored the fact that it was his behavior that had caused him to lose the more impressive scene of the first contact.

Varian let out a sigh of intense relief. Sweat was standing out on her forehead, and she wiped it away on her sleeve as reaction weakened her knees. She moved back to her stool and sat down heavily.

"Rule number one in recording animals of unknown habits and custom—approach cautiously from any direction."

"Hey, Varian, the three who were here have gone to roost, but there's a whole flotilla of 'em disappearing southeast, down the sea."

Nervous reaction forgotten, Varian sprinted to the entrance, hanging onto a vine to swing out past the lip, craning her head upward. The earlier squall had departed, and in misty sky she could see the golden fliers on their daily rounds, fish nets trailing from their feet.

"Hope you have plenty of footage left, Kenley, because we're going fishing! C'mon!" He joined her in the sled. Thanks be to Krims, but it great to be doing what she'd been yearning to do ever since she woke up.

15

WHEN Kai's group reached the campsite, they found four vehicles of various sizes from the *Zaid-Dayan* already awaiting them. A work party was already tearing out the old force-screen posts. The replacements, thicker by half again, lay to one side alongside the control mechanisms.

As Kai glided in to land by the vehicles, Fordeliton emerged from the largest and waved to him. Then both men turned to watch Triv bring the shuttle down in a deft landing on the exact spot it had occupied forty-three years earlier. Experiencing *déjà vu*, Kai found that he had to turn away from the spectacle and so engaged Fordeliton in conversation.

"I think you'll find that everything you ordered through Mayerd is here," Ford said, waving expansively at the three sleds and the sleek pinnace. "A few incidentals were added by our commander."

"A bottle of the Sverulan brandy I've heard so much about?" Kai asked, with a grin.

"*That* would surprise me. She guards the vintage like the destruct codes. However, she was looking quite pleased with herself, and there hasn't been a hair seen of the hide of that Dupaynil. Lunzie have anything to say for herself?"

"I haven't had time to ask her," Kai said, having forgotten all about that aspect of the previous evening's events. "Lunzie never makes gratuitous admissions."

"Takes after her great-great-great then." Fordeliton compressed his lips in exasperation. "However," and he changed moods, "let us not prod imponderables. I have here the little device which Commander Sassinak mentioned. I have coded it with information from our various tapes and files about this planet. Even fed it that tape from Dimenon about the fringes. So it only needs to be set in place." He beckoned Kai after him to the pinnace, where he laid hands on a small black plastic traveling case. Kneeling, he opened it and lifted out an opaque globe. He rose, displaying the object to Kai, a big grin on his face. "This is quite a device." Opening a small compartment, he made a few minute adjustments and closed it. "Now, we just let it sail."

"Sail?"

"Well, we give it a bit of upward impetus," Fordeliton amended, beckoning Kai to follow him out of the pinnace. He spotted and then walked quickly to a small cairn of stones. "This was adjudged the exact center of the area enclosed by the force-screen. So," and flexing his knees, Fordeliton gave a leap, heaving the globe upward at the top of his jump. The globe continued up and then paused, spinning in a leisurely fashion, a pale light coruscating from it. Fordeliton dusted his hands together. "Now, nothing small, large, medium, programed or unrecognizable can approach this site without *you* knowing and the intruder, if on the unwanted list, being stunned senseless. Feel safer?"

"If you say so."

"I do." Fordeliton gripped Kai's shoulder in a firm but understanding grasp. "Now, what else can we do for you?"

Just then the force-screen came on, and a cheer went up from the survivors as well as the volunteers from the *Zaid-Dayan*.

"Now we can get back to the business interrupted forty-three years ago."

"Once the domes are up," Ford amended. Kai nodded agreement.

This time, Trizein elected to have a dome instead of quarters in the shuttle. He also volunteered to supervise the three youngsters so one of the larger units was erected, providing him with a large working area and four small sleeping sections. Dimenon and Margit elected to return to their secondary camp. Portegin, Aulia in tow, settled on a site for their dome. Triv took a single, as did Kai. Then a place for the largest dome, meeting room *cum* mess hall, was chosen. As the supply of domes had been generous, two more were placed, one for Varian and another for such visitors as might care to stay over. As Kai once again surveyed the natural amphitheater, its force-screen spitting as it demolished unwary insects, he could not fail to notice that none of the newly erected domes had been sited where those of the first encampment had been. An understandable phenomenon.

Among the volunteers were two stewards from the *Zaid-Dayan* and they supplied a midday meal utilizing some of the Iretan fruits and greens.

"Surprised me, it did," the man said, "considering how this planet stinks. Wouldn't have thought anything would taste halfway edible. And it does!"

"I think we can't taste right, is what I think," the second steward said, "with all that smell messing up our tasters and smellers."

"Just goes to show, doesn't it," Margit allowed, "that neither looks nor smells is everything. So, Kai, shall Dim and I get back to our bailiwick?"

An ear-piercing whistle interrupted any answer Kai would have made. As he glanced upwards, thinking the globe was alerting them, he saw Ford depressing a knob on his wrist comunit. A momentary flash of disappointment crossed the officer's face but was quickly erased. He turned to Kai with a rueful smile, nodding to his men who had been alerted by the noise.

"I'm sorry, Kai, that's recall. We've been on yellow alert since we landed. It's now red." He rose to his feet, making a broad sweeping gesture with his arm. "All right now, crew. Recall."

Disappointed mutters and groans could be heard but the crew members moved quickly toward the door.

"Don't like to eat and run. Me mammy said it was bad manners," the older steward said, grinning apologetically at the disarray in the catering area.

"We'll save 'em for you to come back to," Margit called in a good-natured taunt as she followed the crew out.

"If I can, I'll let you know what's up," Fordeliton said as Kai jogged with him to the pinnace. "I don't think *you* need worry about anything with the globe up there."

"Good luck," was all Kai could think to say.

Triv opened the veil of the force-screen to permit the sleds and pinnace to exit, then closed it and walked purposefully back to Kai.

"Does their emergency mean we're stuck in here?"

"Ford didn't mention any restrictions on us."

"Then shall we indeed pick up where we left off?"

"Portegin, is the new core screen working?"

Portegin raised his eyebrows, a knowing expression on his face. "It is indeed, and it has a very interesting tale to tell us."

"How so?" Kai asked as they all climbed the rise to the shuttle.

"You'll see," Portegin replied confidently.

His meaning was as plain as the blips lighting the screen in the shuttle's main cabin. Where once the duality of core lights had confused the geologists, only single clear lights formed a network.

"The Thek have recovered *all* the old cores?"

"That's what it looks like. Did they eat 'em, d'you think, Kai?" Portegin asked. "Dimenon thinks they do."

"I wouldn't put it past them," Triv said.

"How long have the faint cores been gone from the screen?"

"There were still fifty or more yesterday when I was setting the screen up and testing it," Portegin replied. "I didn't have it on today until we'd finished setting the domes up. I had a look at it just before they rang the chow gong. There were only a few left," Portegin indicated the edges of the screen, "and now, not an unblessed one of 'em. They *must* eat 'em. Cores will register through anything."

"Except a Thek," Margit said.

Triv smiled. "Cores should register even through the silicon of a Thek."

"Then they did eat 'em." Portegin would not be dissuaded from that opinion. "And digested every last morsel."

Kai looked at the screen for a long moment, not seeing its display. "We're here. We have equipment again. We still haven't finished our original mission. It's better to be busy than sit around idly speculating on what we can't change and better not interfere with. Margit and Dimenon, you two get back to your camp and continue the survey. At least we don't have outside interference to upset Portegin's screen. Triv, what's your option?"

"I'd like to strike north, past the last point we surveyed. There's quite a volcanic chain north and east that might be very interesting geologically."

"Good. Will you take Bonnard along as your partner?"

"Be delighted."

"Lunzie," Kai turned to the medic, "have you plans for the rest of the day?"

She shook her head.

"Would you pilot Trizein?"

"You'll be base manager? That's perhaps a good idea."

"I rather thought you'd approve." He grinned at her.

"Well, you look a shade better, but I wouldn't like to see you overextend yourself without a damned good reason." She strode out of the shuttle.

16

WITH a great deal of good-natured bustle and confusion, the teams departed on their diverse errands.

"In case you've wondered, Kai," Lunzie found time to tell him quietly, "Dupaynil and I had a few interesting words with Cruss by com." A mirthless smile crossed her lips. "Dupaynil has assumed a Paskutti-Tardma grandson identity, and I opted for Bakkun-Berru. Cruss's present objective is to smuggle a few of his people off the transport and onto this world. He hints at great connections and substantial rewards for cooperation. Dupaynil is playing coy, and I'm plainly suspicious. I'll keep you informed."

The prospect of heavy-worlders' enjoying even the most tenuous occupancy on Ireta was unsettling to Kai. He had never been a vindictive person, being basically fair-minded and tolerant, but he found himself contemplating Cruss's subversive tactics with an emotion bordering on fury. He wished he had gone with Dupaynil to bait the trap, but his anger would have betrayed him. He also took a profound pleasure in the knowledge that Cruss was incriminating himself further.

Kai tried to tell himself that such negative emotions were unDisciplined, and he should purge them from his system. Then he realized, and laughed at the realization, that, however unsocial hatred was, it stirred the blood as well as the imagination. He was certain that he had felt his fingertips that morning when he had applied the salve. More likely the progress was due to the efficacy of the new medication, rather than regeneration due to indignant wrath. He flexed his fingers inside the skin-gloves, which he could not yet feel against his skin. In one sense that was to the good, for he could use his hands in normal fashion.

As Kai made his way across the amphitheater to the shuttle, he found the unpopulated campsite eerie. On the other hand, he would have few distractions while he organized the information on the finds Dimenon and Margit had made the previous day—a rich source of metals as well as transuranics the heavy-worlders would have acquired had their takeover not been challenged!

No sooner had he reached the shuttle's iris air lock than he heard the frantic buzz of the comunit. He raced to the pilot's compartment and slammed on the transmit toggle so hard he could feel it jar his hand.

"*Zaid-Dayan* to EV Base!" the signal flashed. Then the screen displayed the control deck of the *Zaid-Dayan*, and

Commander Sassinak. "I was beginning to think that you'd all left the compound. Kai, have you transport? We have a large Thek convoy approaching and requesting landing permission. Their message was first directed toward the giff cave beacon."

"Ah," Kai said, recalling a significant oversight, "we forgot to dismantle Portegin's beacon from the giff cave."

"No real harm done." But Sassinak's grin suggested that Varian had been quite surprised to have had to communicate with laconic Thek.

"Is Tor among the incoming?"

"They have not identified themselves."

"I've no transport here."

"The pinnace is on its way."

Kai had recorded messages on the comunit for anyone calling in to base and checked the perimeter of the encampment for gaps in the screen before he heard the supersonic bang of the pinnace's arrival. The globe brightened momentarily, then resumed its normal color. Ford was the pilot.

"I've brought our stewards back. They really hated to leave the mess hall in such a state," Ford said. Kai grinned farewell as the first man reinstalled the force-screen veil. Then Kai entered the pinnace.

Ford gestured for him to take a seat and belt up.

"I've never seen such a concentration of our friendly allies before. Our science officer has been monitoring the ones on Dimenon's site and he swears they've enlarged considerably."

"Dimenon thinks they've been gorging themselves. And they have apparently consumed every trace of the ancient cores which were ghosting our core screen."

Fordeliton swung the pinnace about, almost on its tail fins, and before Kai had a chance to grab a breath, had jammed on the power. Even with the advanced design of the pinnace, the g-forces of supersonic speed were uncomfortable.

"How many have been sighted?" Kai managed to ask through lips pressed against his face bones. Abruptly the pressure eased.

"Nine, three of them nearly as big as the transport. Or so they appear on our sensors."

Kai was surprised at the magnitude of the visitors. "Any small units?" If only Tor was among them. . . .

"There are three Great-Big Bears, three Medium-Size Bears, and three Teeny-Tiny Bears." Fordeliton gave Kai a totally unrepentant grin. "Don't worry. One of Sassinak's specialities is Thek conversation." Then he grinned with a definite hint of malice. "Though I wonder if the good commander will be able to cope with such a concentration of our noble allies."

The speedy pinnace accomplished the journey in ten minutes. Ford was deftly dropping their forward speed when an urgent signal was beamed from the *Zaid-Dayan*, giving alternative landing coordinates.

"They want us down by the settlement," Ford said, glancing at the area map, and veered in the appropriate direction as he flipped on the forward screen for a visual check of their arrival. "And I can see why!"

Leaning forward against the seat belts, unwilling to lose a single detail of the extraordinary sight before them, Kai gasped in astonishment.

Fordeliton's whimsical reference to the awesome Thek caused Kai to grin with a wayward appreciation of that irreverence. His grin broadened as he watched three Teeny-Tiny Bears, which were likely to be taller than his nearly two meters, settling down by the main air lock of the *Zaid-Dayan*, where sailors were quick-marching into the ceremonial formation. One of the Medium-Size Bears was slowly descending behind the three. The other two Medium-Size Bears could be seen positioning themselves to either side of the massive prow of the heavy-worlder transport. In one quick glance Kai took in that deployment and then turned his incredulous gaze toward the three immense Great-Big Bears which were sedately lowering themselves onto the grid beyond the transport.

"It is extremely lucky, isn't it," Fordeliton remarked, "that the Iretans made such a *big* landing grid. Otherwise those big brutes wouldn't have risked a landing here. Whooops! Spoke too soon."

Fordeliton was hovering above the appointed landing site, maintaining the pinnace at an altitude which gave them a superb view of the event. With great dignity and no visible means of propulsion, the three Great-Big Bears lowered their bulks onto the grid. And continued their downward movement while the grid began to smoke, melt, and bubble. Molten iron began to ooze out around the three Great-Big Theks. Fordeliton roared with such infectious laughter that Kai joined in. Suddenly the continued decline of the Theks ceased, the molten metal about their bases went from red to dull cold metal in an instant, solidifying.

"That was close, wasn't it?" Fordeliton flung out his arms, giving Kai a buffet on the chest for which he instantly apologized. "I just hope someone got it on tape. That's one to save for posterity. What if they had just kept on melting down, down, *down*?"

"No chance of that, I'm afraid. The grid was built here because there's a rock shelf under that plateau that would stop even the Thek." Kai grinned at Fordeliton. "But I doubt the heavy-worlders meant to accommodate Thek. Have you ever seen any that big before?"

"I thought that they stayed put at that size. Kai, what have you got on this forsaken planet to wrench them out of their comfortable niches? Do Thek inhabit niches? Or mountaintops? Never mind."

Fordeliton landed the pinnace. He and Kai quickly made their way toward the *Zaid-Dayan*, where Sassinak and a contingent of her officers were advancing to where the Theks were squatting. Fordeliton and Kai joined the group. Sassinak noted their arrival with a nod of her head.

Suddenly a sound stopped everyone, and one of the not so Teeny-Tiny Bears moved forward.

"Kaaaaaiiiieeee!" The sound was both command and recognition.

Kai looked inquiringly at Sassinak.

"That does sound like your name, Kai. It's all yours." The commander gestured him forward. To his astonishment, she winked as he passed.

"Tor?" he asked, coming to a halt in front of the Thek, for surely it had to be his acquaintance from the *ARCT-10*. No other Thek could have recognized one human among so many. "Tor?" It was awesome enough to be faced by four Thek, overheard by five more; it would be slightly less daunting if he spoke through a Thek he knew.

"Tor responds."

Kai breathed a sigh of relief, and then realized that Tor was answering an unasked question. Or rather the question Kai had fruitlessly posed of the Thek removal squad.

With a speed that blurred movement, a Thek pseudopod extended a core to Kai. When he reached out to take it, the core was withdrawn beyond his grasp, and he thrust his hands behind him, feeling more like a small miscreant than ever in this Thek presence.

"Toooo hotttt. Eggsamine."

Hands still behind him, Kai leaned forward and peered obediently at the core. It looked like the same type of ancient device which Tor had recovered from their abandoned campsite.

"Is it Thek design?"

Thunder rumbled underfoot. Although the cruiser contingent glanced warily skyward where Ireta's clouds rolled across a silent sky, Kai reckoned that the thunder was a Thek exchange of conversation and that it emanated from one of the immense Thek whose crowns were just visible over the bulk of the transport.

"Where found?"

Kai was startled by such a mundane question, but the coordinates of that find came quickly to mind and he recited them.

Then thunder rumbled again and was answered by a lesser

noise which Kai decided was Tor's rejoinder for the Thek's upper third rippled slightly, as if courteously turning in the direction of the questioner.

"Kai, ask it if this planet is claimed by the Thek?" Sassinak requested, leaning forward to murmur in Kai's ear.

"Verifying!" To everyone's astonishment, the Thek answered her, and then compounded the surprise by a second gratuitous command. "Dismiss. Will contact." Tor's outline assumed a rigidity which Kai knew meant it would answer no further question or summonses.

He turned around to Sassinak.

"Dismissed, are we?" She was more amused than offended by Thek abruptness. "They'll get back to us when they've had a good old think about all this?"

"I'd say that's a fair analysis of the exchange," Kai said, and he was once again put in mind of Fordeliton's impudent analogy of the old children's tale and the categories of the Thek. The Thek so rarely generated anything approaching amusement, yet Kai now found it difficult to control his laughter. He glanced quickly at Fordeliton who turned an expression of bland and utter innocence on him.

"Ford, the men can stand down. Secure from red alert. Just the sort of thing that Thek complain about. Lack of proper attention to detail. Shall we adjourn to my quarters, gentlemen? Can you spare us a few moments, Kai?"

He nodded and Sassinak swiftly led the way back into the cruiser and to her quarters. Fordeliton and a tall gaunt man with a lean aesthetic face and exceedingly sharp eyes entered the commander's cabin along with Kai.

"I don't believe you've met our science officer before, Kai. Governor, this is Captain Anstel."

"My pleasure, Governor," Anstel said in an unusually deep bass. "I have read your reports. Fascinating! Completely engrossing. Not only the dinosaurs—and that is indisputably what they are—but also the fringes. I did a complete analysis of their chemistry. Totally new, although there are two points of resemblance between these fringes and the plastic Wahks of Lesser Delibes planet . . . Ah, yes, sorry about that, Commander." Anstel subsided, his gaunt face losing its animation as he folded his long body into a chair.

"If your duties permit, Captain Anstel, I'm sure that Trizein would enjoy exchanging information with you," Kai said.

"I should like nothing better. It has always amazed me how much fascination those prehistoric creatures have for us, who are such insubstantial creatures in the scale of time."

Deciding that business must be done, Sassinak took charge of the conversation. "Kai, what do you make of this latest development?"

"Can Thek be worried?" Kai asked, glancing around.

"Is that your interpretation of thunder rumbling underfoot?" Sassinak grinned. "As is only proper for an ephermeral, I have great respect and admiration for our silicon allies. But such a—" she paused to find the appropriate word "—convocation on an otherwise undistinguished world must surely be unique. That must suggest interest of a high degree. Mountainous, I might say."

"And who is cast as Mohammed?" the irrepressible Fordeliton asked quietly.

Kai suppressed another laugh and noticed Sassinak's brief acknowledgment of her adjutant's wit.

"I don't really see our pirates cast in such an auspicious role, Ford. Nor have I yet seen anything *that* spectacular about this noxious planet of yours, Kai. *Was* that the same core which brought Tor to your rescue, Kai?" When he nodded, she continued, "And all those little Thek concentrated on gobbling up the remaining old cores—when they weren't frying fringes. Kai, it appears to me that your revival and the providential arrival of the *Zaid-Dayan* in pursuit of the heavy-worlder transport are incidental to a vastly more important problem. Therefore, since the records of both your EV and my Sector Headquarters list Ireta as unexplored, though Thek artifacts have unquestionably been discovered here, I will venture the perhaps bizarre opinion that there may have been a missing link in the famous Thek chain of information. And it broke here on Ireta. Do you agree?"

A grin might not be the diplomatic response to Sassinak's astute opinion, but with Fordeliton's irreverent analogy still tingeing his once dutiful respect, Kai found it possible to entertain the possibility of Thek fallibility. If the Thek were the Bear entities of the old folktale, who was the parallel for . . . ah, yes, Goldilocks? Surely not the pirates who were finding the planet far too hot for them. Suddenly the analogy lost its appeal. Kai was not at all certain that he wanted the Thek to lose their reputation for infallibility.

"The old core was definitely of Thek manufacture," he finally admitted. "And unquestionably it has generated Thek interest. But I can't see *why* it or this planet should evoke such an unprecedented response."

"No more than can I," Sassinak admitted, picking up her wand and playing it through her fingers. "I scanned your initial reports again . . ." She shrugged. "Ireta is rich in transuranics, some of the exotic earths and metals, but . . . Or perhaps, the Thek must establish to their own satisfaction why this planet is so miscataloged. And I confess, I'm probably as curious as they are to know how such a break occurred. None of us wishes to cast aspersions on the infallibility of the Thek. No one *likes* his anchors to come adrift." She smiled at Kai as if she fully appreciated and shared his ambivalence.

"When our screen first showed the ghost cores, they went as far as the area of basement rock. No farther," Kai said tentatively.

"Which would suggest that the cores were planted—" Anstel paused, stunned by the immensity of the elapsed time.

"Several million years ago," Kai finished for him, "considering the geological activity of this planet."

"And the Thek have rendered all of the old cores, completely denying us the chance to date the artifacts," Anstel said, his eyes flashing with indignation. Then he fixed Kai with a hopeful stare. "You didn't by any chance? . . ."

"No, we didn't have any dating equipment, since our mission was supposed to be the first."

"Eons ago the Thek cored this planet?" Sassinak asked.

"If not the Thek then some other—"

"Not the Others again!" Sassinak humorously negated that possibility. "I don't wish to lose god and nemesis in the same day."

"Couldn't have been the Others," Kai said, shaking his head vigorously. "That old core was of Thek manufacture. Undeniably. We're using recent cores of the exact same design. Until today I never appreciated just how good the design was. The screen blips were faint, but they were *there*!"

"Are we not forgetting that planets visited by the Others are invariably lifeless, reduced to barren rock? Stripped. Lifeless!" Anstel spoke with the distaste of one who values life in all its forms.

"Then why have we been visited by this Thek delegation?" Sassinak asked.

"Someone forgot that this planet *had been* explored and classified," Fordeliton suggested, "and they intend to repair that oversight. Your friend Tor did say 'verifying' in its distinctive fashion."

"How will they verify that," Anstel asked, "when Thek have disposed of the evidence of the old cores?"

"Perhaps," and there was a wicked gleam in Sassinak's sparkling eyes, "they had to digest them to find out?" She leaned forward and tapped instructions into her console. Immediately the screens came to life: the Great-Big Bears had not moved, nor had the Medium-Size ones. The three small ones had disappeared. The fourth screen showed the site on which the Thek had been attacked by the fringes. It was unoccupied. Just then a buzzer alerted Commander Sassinak. "Yes?

Oh, really?" She made another adjustment, and Kai half rose from his seat in astonishment. A myriad of Thek forms inhabited the plain below the campsite.

"Muhlah! Every fringe on Ireta will be homing in on us."

"I doubt it. Nor would they pose *you* a problem if they did. Between Thek and the globe, you couldn't be better protected."

"But what are they doing there? I'm here. Tor knows that. Muhlah!" Kai's startled reaction was shared by everyone in the room. For the Thek were spinning off in all directions, nearly thirty small Thek pyramids were hurtling skyward and disappearing with astounding speed. "Now what?"

"Now what, indeed?" Sassinak's expression sparkled with amusement and speculation.

17

SASSINAK adjourned the discussion to the wardroom where off-duty officers were enjoying a noon meal. When Sassinak apologized that the lunch was made of processed foods, Kai, mindful of his praise for the previous night's dinner, forbore to mention that he was better suited to it. But after his first mouthful of the protein, he wondered if his eating preferences had been undermined by circumstance. While the cruiser's mess was appetizing and well served, Kai for the first time recognized the faint aftertaste that Varian had always complained of.

"I suppose you were too busy with the geological aspects of the mission," Anstel was saying, his gaunt face animated as he addressed Kai across the table, "to have much time for the dinosaurs?"

"Unfortunately, I was," Kai said as he belatedly caught the end of Anstel's comments and realized that some response was due. "We did have an orphan hyracotherium for a pet—" Kai broke off, then finished as if his pause had been to swallow, "but that was before we went cryo."

"A hyracotherium?" Anstel's eyes bulged with excitement. "Really? You're certain? Why, that creature evolved into the equine species on Old Terra. Did you know that?"

Feeling unequal to a lecture on the matter, Kai tried a diversion. "We also have furred avian creatures. . . ."

"Furred?" Anstel was entranced.

"Actually," Fordeliton began with so bland an expression that those who knew his ways become alert, "Varian, whom you must concede is a reliable source, said that most of the dinosaurs *she* observed suffered from overweight, bad nutrition, parasites of remarkable tenacity and variety, and were not affectionate by nature."

"One does not expect dinosaurs to be lovable," Anstel said with quiet dignity. "They fascinate by their size and majesty. In their diverse species, they dominated the Mesozoic era of Old Terra for several million years before a shift in the magnetic fields of the planet traumatically changed their environment."

"Nonsense! A cosmic cloud obscuring the sun caused the climatic change," Pendelman corrected firmly.

"My dear Pendelman, there is absolutely no *proof* of that theory whatsoever—"

"Oh, indeed there is, Anstel. Indeed there is! Bothemann of the New Smithsonian of Tyrconia has documentation, both—"

"Bothemann's hypothesis is shaky at the very best since the geological area in Old Terran Italia that allegedly supported the contention, was engulfed in the mid-European plate shift in the early twenty-first century—"

"Ah, but records from the Central Repository, made by that Californian group, are—"

"As suspect as many other theories from that neck of the woods—"

"Gentlemen, how or why Old Terran dinosaurs met their end is not pertinent," Sassinak declared. "What is germane is that dinosaurlike creatures are alive and in relatively good health on Ireta. Enjoy that reality for however long you are able to indulge your fascination. Save the great debates for the long watches of the night!"

A yeoman caught her attention. She beckoned him over and listened to his message. Turning to smile at Kai, she murmured a quick answer. The yeoman speedily retraced his steps.

"Varian has arrived. She'll join us here."

"Would she remember where you found the hyracotherium, Kai?" Anstel asked.

"Yes, but I must remind you that that would have been forty-three years ago."

"Surely, it was not an isolated example of the species?" Clearly Anstel would not rest until he had seen one.

"She's concentrating on a study of the golden fliers who could well be an emerging species," Kai said, to give Varian room to maneuver if she didn't wish to get involved with Anstel.

"I must look up my reference disks. Hyracotheriums I recall in perfect clarity, but I'm not certain about . . ."

"Trizein has identified the golden fliers as the pteranodon."

"Pteranodon!" Once again Anstel's eyes widened in shock.

"Yes, my dear fellow, exactly like pteranodons," Pendelman said, delighted to contribute to Anstel's confusion. "I saw a whole flock of them rise from the cliffs and soar. Quite a feat, I assure you, on a storm-tossed planet like Ireta."

At that point the yeoman returned with Varian who greeted Kai with undisguised relief.

"Sorry it took me so long to get here," she said to Sassinak. "I see the Thek found you?"

"It was Kai they wished to find and addressed in their inimitably succinct fashion."

"So, what has happened? Or . . ." Varian glanced around her, mindful of discretion. Only a few officers remained, most chatting quietly at a wall table on the far side of the mess hall.

A gesture of Sassinak's hand gave Varian immediate reassurance, and the commander's glance gave Kai the office to explain.

"Tor has returned."

"With company to ward off our great big beasties?"

Kai grinned. "Tor has returned. It and the other Thek are in the process of verifying."

"Verifying what?"

"They did not specify." Sassinak's dry tone put Kai and Varian strongly in mind of Lunzie.

"Oh."

"They dismissed us, in a word," Sassinak went on, "and 'will contact.' "

"They do have a way with them, don't they?" Varian turned to Kai. "Not one of us thought to dismantle that old distress beacon Portegin rigged. Kenley has it down now. I'd rather not subject the giffs to further invasions, especially ones conducted by the Thek. I didn't know there *were* that many of the critters. And thanks be to Krims, they didn't attempt to land on my cliff, considering what they've done to Aygar's landing grid." Varian giggled then.

"It's entirely possible," Fordeliton said into the thoughtful pause that followed, "that the Thek have made a mistake."

"Thek? Making mistakes? How refreshing!"

Kai felt compelled to set the problem out properly in simple justice to the Thek, who were so very seldom mistaken in their dealings with other planets and sentient species. "Now, Varian, that old core *is* of Thek design. It's got them in a scramble. You know how Thek transmit knowledge, from generation to generation—"

"And there's been a generation gap?" Varian asked, her voice bubbling with a laughter shared by the others at the table.

"Evidently. Though the Thek way is supposed to prevent the total loss of knowledge in any line."

"Well, Ireta would be the right place for that, wouldn't it?" Varian quipped, then became thoughtful. "Though, I can't see why that would call for the presence of so *many* heavy-duty Thek. I mean, Ireta is extremely rich in the transuranics but . . . Or have they been monitoring planet piracy, too?"

Sassinak cleared her throat. "Not that we know of."

"Then why are the big Thek squatting about the transport like they mean business?"

"The biggest Thek landed beyond the transport because of the grid."

"Grid didn't do much for 'em, did it?" Varian said with another malicious grin. "Now what?"

"My precise words," Sassinak said. She gave a deep sigh. "However, since the Thek are here and the Fleet enjoins its officers to cooperate with those entities, I suppose we must be dismissed until such time as we are recalled to notice. How many years did it take them to answer your distress call, Kai?"

"Forty-three."

"But only three days to answer your query about Tor's whereabouts," Sassinak added. "A noticeable improvement."

"Look what it brought us, though," Ford said, waving his hand aft toward the Great-Big Bears.

"Commander, I am not on the duty roster and I did request permission to join a shore-leave party," Anstel began, rising from his chair and putting it back under the tale in the habit of a person inherently tidy. When Sassinak inclined her head, granting permission, he executed a slight bow in Varian's direction. "Kai mentioned that you had found a hyracotherium

before you went cryo. Is there any chance that your travels today will take you near their habitat? I would dearly like to
observe those creatures alive. We dinosaur buffs, I've discovered, all have a favorite species. The equine types are mine."

"I don't see why not," Varian said with a wide, encouraging
smile. She rose. "Kenley and I got some superb footage of the
giffs fishing. The aquatic life performed some acrobatics—
scared Kenley out of his wits when some fringes nearly
reached us." She paused. "The aquatic fringes are a great deal
smaller than the land ones. I should get some more records of
them, I suppose."

"I'd consider it a privilege to help you in any research,
Governor."

Varian smiled up at him, for the man was considerably
taller. "Well, then, time's a'wasting. And Ireta's giving us a
relatively squall-free day. Grab your gear, and I'll meet you at
my sled." She turned to Kai. "Shall I drop you off back at the
camp or are you staying on here, in case"—her grin became
mischievous—"the Thek come to a quick decision?"

Kai rose. "No, I'd better get back." He turned to Sassinak
to thank her.

"If there's no objection, Commander, I'll just retrieve the
men I left guarding the camp. Quicker in the pinnace, anyway." Fordeliton got to his feet.

"And I'll follow protocol and inform Sector Headquarters
of the Thek arrival," Sassinak said.

They left the mess hall, separating in the corridor. Fordeliton walked with Kai and Varian to the access air lock. Fordeliton peered with exaggerated caution toward the transport
and the triangular tops visible above the looming carcass.

"Still there?" Varian asked.

"In residence!"

"They're impressive, aren't they? Oh-ho, and I wonder
what he thinks about them?" Varian pointed.

The two men followed her finger and watched as a sled approached the Medium-Size Thek.

"That would be one of the Iretans, I think," Fordeliton said. "We gave them a sled with that registration."

"Aygar," Varian said. "What have they been doing, d'you know?"

"I haven't had time to catch up on their activities, so much has been going on in your camps. I believe they have already smashed one sled. Takes a while to get used to modern conveniences."

However, Aygar landed his sled deftly, emerged, and walked around the Thek. It made rather an interesting contrast, Varian thought, a fine specimen of a man, wearing little in the way of modern clothes or weapons, striding arrogantly about one of the oldest living creatures in the galaxy: each entity very certain of its position in that galaxy, even if Aygar was willing to limit himself to one planet. Having finished his circuit, Aygar noticed the observers and paced stolidly toward them.

"What are those things?"

"Thek," Varian replied, grinning.

"What are they doing here?"

"Verifying."

Aygar swiveled his upper body to look at the silent and rigid Thek. "Verifying what?"

"They didn't say."

"Do they always mess up landing grids like that? Must make them unpopular visitors."

"When you get that big, no one has the nerve to complain."

"That commander woman said they're allies?" When Varian nodded, he went on. "Allies of whom? Your lot," and his gesture included the cruiser, "or them?" And he indicated the transport.

"Who are you allied with?" Fordeliton asked in a suspiciously bland tone. "Them or us?"

Aygar grinned back, the first time Varian had seen genuine amusement on the young Iretan's face. "You'll know when I have decided. If I do."

With that he swung about on one heel and marched back to his sled, moving with an unexpectedly graceful economy of motion. In a single fluid movement, he climbed into the sled, closed its canopy, and took off.

"Varian?" Anstel's call was breathless. "Oh, I was afraid that you'd taken off. I just needed a few things."

Varian choked on her laughter. Anstel had festooned himself with a variety of equipment, some of which she could not identify."

"Well, I'm ready when you are," Varian said. "Keep me informed, will you, Ford? Kai? It's as well to let the giffs settle down to normal this afternoon so, Anstel, this quest of yours is most welcome. Shall we go?"

18

THE two men left at the campsite were still goggle-eyed about the appearance of so many Thek.

"More than I've ever seen, thassa fact," said the older steward, "and I been around this galaxy, so I have. Seen a lot of them, you know, only sort of one here and then another there, but so many at once?" He scrubbed at his stubbly pate, dragging his hand down his face, and then mimed the wiping off of an expression. "Quite a sight, really! Something to swap for drinks."

"Did any address you?"

The steward's mouth dropped in amazement. "Address me?" he cocked his thumb and jabbed it against his chest.

"Me? I told 'em to locate the cruiser," and he paused to wink broadly, " 'cause I know they can find anything anywhere."

Kai and Fordeliton exchanged amused glances.

"They found you." He exhaled a hissing breath. "Never seen anything like it, though, all those Thek," and he planed their angle of arrival with his left hand, "just flowing in—if silicon triangles *can* flow—just sort of gliding in and never losing their formation, just all of a sudden *down* on the ground."

"Thek can be impressive," Fordeliton agreed urbanely and then gestured for the men to board the pinnace.

"Governor, we left some dinner on the hob like. Had some time to kill," the older steward said, and the younger one began to grin, well pleased with himself. "I like messing with real foodstuffs. Only this time, someone else gets the KP."

Kai nodded, grinning. "That's fair enough. Believe me, your efforts will be much appreciated by everyone."

"Least we could do, you guys having had such a rough time and all."

As the pinnace took off with a high-speed *whush*, the globe's glow caught his eye, brightening momentarily before regaining its regular coloration. Then the silence in the amphitheater was broken only by the faint hiss of the force-screen as it disintegrated insects, a comforting noise. Kai took in a deep breath, inordinately relieved to be alone, to have a few hours before the others trooped back in. He strolled over to the mess hall, sniffing at the odor of simmering stew.

He realized suddenly that he had never had the chance to delve into the *Zaid-Dayan*'s memory banks, to check whether there had been any similar mass movements of Thek. Not that his original question held any pertinence in view of the day's development. Surely the presence of—and Kai grinned—the Great-Big Bears was exceptional. He'd swap a few drinks on that account himself when he got back to the *ARCT-10*. Kai inhaled sharply. "When," he'd said. Another matter he'd forgotten to ascertain, though surely Sassinak would have mentioned any communication about the *ARCT-10*! Better to assimilate the day's startling events than deal with . . . with unknowns.

So, the Thek *had* been here and no living Thek had retained a record of the event, despite the much praised memory of the species. Kai knew that when each new Thek was created—and some wits insisted that propagation occurred when two Thek bumped into each other with sufficient force to chip off fragments—it immediately acquired the race memory as well as the working memories of every Thek in its direct line. No reliable figures about the exact numbers of Thek were available. Once again, the humorists' theories filled a vacuum. They maintained that old Thek never died, they became planets.

A sudden thought, more fanciful than Fordeliton's, erupted into Kai's mind: could Ireta, itself, be a Thek? The notion had a certain appeal, if no plausible scientific basis. But was it possible that somewhere in the areas his team had not yet penetrated, there *was* a Thek mountain? Kai ran from the mess hall, and then, because his curiosity was intense, he increased speed, pelting up the slope, mindful though not to catch his shoulder on the iris as he entered the shuttle. He did bang his hip against the narrower door into the pilot's compartment. Then he tapped out the file designation of the probe survey maps, hoping that time or some unforeseen wipe had not yanked those records from the shuttle's memory banks.

To his relief, his request was implemented and the screen showed the probe's journey as the vehicle zoomed in on the planet. As usual, clouds covered most of Ireta's face but the probe's filters very quickly produced a clear view of the nearing planet. All right, now, what does an ancient Thek resemble? A pyramidal form might be the most common, but was it the most enduring, the most effective long-term configuration? Surely a silicon mountain would be unusual enough for a probe to register? Catching his underlip on his upper teeth,

Kai watched as the probe changed orbit to overfly a new portion of the planet's main continent. Unless—Kai tapped for a magnification of the island chains, but the shattered formations were almost uniformly, and easily identified as, volcanic atolls. Theks had great patience and never "blew their stacks."

If there had been a Thek, where was the most logical place for it to have positioned itself on Ireta? Basement rock! Kai called back the map of the main continent and peered over the area, sighing as he realized that the teams had traversed most of the shield rock and had not sighted any unusual mountains. But then, had they been *looking* for a Thek mountain? No, but wouldn't Tor have noticed, or been contacted by such an elderly Thek? When did a Thek stop emitting conscious thought to its peers? And would it not have propagated to continue its existence? To perpetuate its memories? Or had *that* search been the one conducted near Dimenon's site, when forty Thek had landed? Were the old cores merely incidental to that vastly more important search?

"Verifying," Tor had said. Verifying not that the old cores had been Thek manufacture or that the planet had been claimed by the Thek, but verifying the whereabouts of that incredibly ancient Thek which had *not* been linked with any current generation of its kind.

And, if the Thek did claim Ireta for their own, how would that effect Kai and his team? A long sad sigh escaped his lips. Just when they thought they had a chance to snatch some profit from the debacle, a prior claim appears. All they'd end up with after forty-three lost years would be their base pay and a kindly handshake from the Exploration and Evaluation Corps. At least, he thought to cheer himself from the depression that now engulfed him, Varian might be able to rescue something positive.

He heard the bleep of the globe, a friendly warning of arrivals. Wearily and with considerable effort, Kai rose from the pilot's seat. He dismissed the data he had retrieved and went to see who was returning. It was with a sense of reprieve that he recognized the big sled with Trizein's group coming in to land in the vehicle park. But he realized that he must warn his team of his reflections, if only to cushion a subsequent shock. And if he had put the facts in the wrong configuration, one of the others might refute his conclusion or suggest an alternative operation so that they could rescue some gains.

"Oh, I am glad you're here, Kai," Trizein said, his face suffused with excitement as he jogged up to the veil opening in the force-screen. Behind him Bonnard was laden with record disks, his face wreathed with a smug smile. Terilla and Cleiti followed, chatting animatedly. "We have had the most incredible encounter with the Thek. They are here in the most incredible numbers."

"A horde, Kai, a real horde of them!" Bonnard confirmed.

"What were they doing?" Kai tried to keep his voice even but his level of depression increased in direct proportion to their enthusiasm.

"Looking!" Bonnard said triumphantly.

"No, my dear boy, they must have been surveying."

"No, they were looking because they were keeping an awfully close line to what *I* think is the shield rock area." Bonnard looked to Kai to support him. "We can use the shuttle's data banks again, can't we? I'll show you what I mean because I took coordinates of the positions and angles of flight of the Thek to back up my observations." He gave a decisive nod of his head in Kai's direction, again seeking reassurance.

"Let's check then," Kai said with a heartiness he did not feel. He did manage to keep his voice calm and maintain a composed expression, despite a sensation bordering nausea for this crushing disappointment. Thus does Muhlah reward the doubter! he thought as he retraced his steps back to the shuttle.

Once Kai had called up the required maps, he had little to do, for Bonnard, cheerfully but firmly arguing with Trizein, proved his coordinates, and his theory, that the Thek were searching the edge of the shield rock.

"And it was a search pattern, Kai," Bonnard said firmly. "I mean, they were hovering ground level," and Bonnard showed the distance with his hands, "and scouring, back and forth and back and forth. I thought they'd been sitting on old cores, or something. What could they be looking for now?"

"An ancient Thek," Kai said.

"An ancient Thek?" Trizein turned to frown at Kai, concern and surprise on his seamed face. "Our telltagger has never registered that sort of heat mass, now has it, Bonnard?"

"Nope," replied the boy cheerfully.

The globe's cheerful *bleep* penetrated to the shuttle's interior and Kai gratefully used it as an excuse to escape Trizein's saurian enthusiasms and Bonnard's innocent confidence in Thek infallibility.

"Kai!" Bonnard came after him. "Kai."

Reluctantly Kai paused, turned, saw the boy removing an antiseptic wipe from his first-aid pouch. Bonnard extended it to him with a bashful grin.

"You've got a trickle of blood on your chin. I don't think it would do to let Varian or Lunzie see that." Bonnard turned on his heel and ran back into the shuttle.

Dabbing at his lower lip, Kai felt a warmth suffuse the tight knot of despair that had taken up residence in his chest. Then he continued to the veil.

<u>19</u>

IF Varian had come back to the main camp that evening; *if* Triv, Aulia, and Portegin had arrived back for the evening meal; *if* Dimenon and Margit had, for any reason, visited the camp, Kai might have felt obligated to air his pessimistic speculations about Thek and Ireta. Instead the dinosaur buffs from the *Zaid-Dayan* and the *Mazer Star* convened an informal enthusiasm session, matching unusual specimens with Trizein and the three children. Kai was torn between the social obligations of raising his spirits to the level of the others and the need to worry privately about his new anxieties. He was apparently dissembling well enough so that not even Lunzie noticed. The medic was examining Terilla's detailed sketches, pinning the more colorful ones on the walls of the dome, "to brighten things."

More out of a wish to distract himself, Kai approached Perens, the *Mazer Star*'s navigator. "Why do dinosaurs fascinate you and these others so much? They are smelly animals, crawling with vermin, not very intelligent, and I can't give them any marks for beauty. To me they are nothing but mammoth walking appetites. If Ireta wasn't also blessed with a vegetation explosion, they'd've died out long ago of starvation."

Perens, a dapper little man with a pencil-thin moustache, which he stroked lovingly, grinned at Kai. "Didn't you get the capsule history of Old Terra in your tutorials?" When Kai nodded, Perens continued. "Well, the only thing I remember

about it in any detail was the chapter on prehistory. The rest
was sort of wars and power struggles, no different from what
we have today in the Federated Planets, only more intense because it was limited to the one small planet and, generally, to
one or two continents. But I remembered the dinosaurs and
the Mesozoic age. I remembered because they had lasted, as a
viable life-form, for more millions of years than *we* have!"
Perens smoothed his moustache absently. "I've always wondered what kept the dinosaurs going for so long on Old Terra,
when *Homo sapiens*, operating in a much shorter time scale,
came so close to pulling the plug on itself." Then he shrugged
and grinned ingenuously at Kai. "Dinosaurs are big, they're
ugly, and they're fascinating. Raw power, a force of nature,
majestic!"

Just then, Lunzie appeared beside them, in her hand a tray
with glasses filled with her special Iretan brew. Nothing could
have been more welcome. "Muhlah! You've been well occupied, Lunzie." He turned to grin encouragingly at Perens.
"Hope you're a drinking man because this stuff may be a local brew but it's good!"

Lunzie raised her eyebrows in mock surprise. "But it's
planet-brewed, Kai, not processed."

"I'm learning chapter and verse like a good Disciple," he
said, toasting her with his glass. He had the touch of the
liqueur on his lips when he stayed his hand. "It won't react
with Mayerd's medicine, will it?"

"If it might, I wouldn't have served you."

"In that case—" and Kai knocked back the entire glass,
holding it out for a refill.

"Hmm. My, how the pure have been corrupted!" But she
complied before she moved on.

Perens was cautious. He merely wet his lips, then judiciously ran his tongue over them. Then he took a tiny sip,
washing the liquid about his mouth. Kai watched him with a
certain respect, for the spiritous beverage had a bite to it. Finally Perens condescended to drink.

"Not bad at all. I wonder what she uses. If you'll excuse me," and Perens slipped away in pursuit of the medic.

Kai wandered over to Trizein, who was lecturing Maxnil and Crilsoff on the evolution of the families of hadrasaur, noting that one had traded a keen sense of smell for improved vision. The two officers were listening with every outward show of interest, but Kai noticed that they were sipping the liquor in hefty swallows. Maxnil caught Lunzie's attention, miming the need for a refill. As Lunzie apparently had few qualms about serving her beverage to the group, the evening shortly assumed a rosier aspect for Kai, and by the end of the evening the cruiser contingent had to be issued bedding for none of them could have been trusted to pilot the others back to the *Zaid-Dayan*.

A variety of claxons eventually roused them all. Recalls became shriller summonses as the polite first request was ignored by sound sleepers. The comunit became equally insistent in Kai's dome. With groggy fingers he opened the toggle and grunted acknowledgment.

"Governor Kai, Commander Sassinak's compliments, and she is sending the pinnace to collect you for an important meeting here. And, sir," the polite voice of the communications duty officer added, "would there be any chance that Lieutenant Pendelman, Chief Petty Officer Maxnil, and . . ."

"They're in the main dome. I'll kick 'em out. For that matter I can hitch a ride with them."

"No, sir, their boat isn't fast enough. 'Scuse me, Governor, they just came on line."

Important meeting? Kai felt conflicting emotions of relief and fearful anticipation. He really should have spoken to his team last night, if only to prepare them. Then he berated himself for borrowing trouble where it might not exist. Any number of things could account for Sassinak's meeting: the arrival of the tribunal, a report from Sector Headquarters that she didn't care to broadcast, even a report from Dupaynil.

Kai was outside his dome now and aware that, by way of a special blessing, Ireta had produced a glowing sunrise of spectacular brilliance. Mouth agape, he admired the eastern sky, clear blue in a band above the distant mountains. Above that, clouds were a blood red, tinged with orange and yellow, vivid primaries to startle the eye. The vaster bowl of deeper-gray night clouds began to spread with a deep purple, rolling back from the clear morning sky. Thunder rumbled in the distance and a cool sweet-scented breeze wafted gently through a force-screen which would have rebuked stiffer winds. Such a spectacular dawn could only be the harbinger of great things, Kai thought. But he was not prone to believe in presentiments and frowned at the whimsy.

"For once, this blighted planet is pretty," Lunzie said as she quietly joined him.

Kai smiled at her, pleased to share the dawn's magnificence with someone else.

"What's the commotion? Every signal in the camp's sounding." Lunzie rubbed her eyes, sleepily.

"Sassinak's sent for me."

"My presence has been requested as well. Varian, too?"

"I'd expect so. And I'm just on my way to rouse the officers."

"I'll help." Lunzie's smile had a touch of malice for the men of the *Zaid-Dayan* had imbibed mass quantities of her brew. Lunzie could take an unkindly delight in the discomforts caused others by overindulgence.

They had roused the deep sleepers when the globe bleeped cheerfully. As Lunzie and Kai emerged from the dome, dawn light reflected from the side of the pinnace. Kai was opening the veil when the vessel's sonic boom cracked.

"They wasted no time, did they?" Lunzie said.

Fordeliton was the pilot. "We're to collect Varian as well," he said, gesturing for them to belt up in their seats. "Sector HQ sent an update, and Kai," he turned to give the geologist a broad grin, "the *ARCT-10* is okay. In fact their message only just reached Sector."

"What happened to it? Have you any details?" Kai strained against his seat belt, leaning toward the pilot in his excitement.

"If you'll shut up," Fordeliton replied good-naturedly. "That cosmic storm they went off to investigate was considerably more powerful than even the wildest estimates. Sector has sent down The Word that that sort of space hazard is to be 'avoided, repeat, avoided' in the future. Your ship lost one whole drive pod and the main communications frames, with severe damage to the other three drive units. Some of the living compounds were riddled by debris, but there was no great loss of life. The names of casualties were not included in the message. At any rate, your EV had to limp to the nearest system on auxiliary power. Which took forty-three years. Sector sent them a signal about your safety and well-being. So you should soon have a status report." Ford grinned over his shoulder at Kai, delighted to be the bearer of good tidings.

"That sunrise was a good augury," Lunzie remarked with an air of pleased surprise.

Kai squirmed against the restraint of the seat belts, sensible of a relief so intense that it left an ache at the base of his skull.

"I never have understood why the EVs consider themselves invulnerable to the hazards of space," Lunzie said. "One reason I opted for your mission when it came up, Kai. I figured I'd be a lot safer on a planet than tagging a cosmic storm." She gave him a wry grin. "Of course, I have been safer."

"What? With mutineers, cold sleep, fringes, and now pirates?" Fordeliton demanded, astonished.

"At least my feet were on solid ground and there's plenty of oxygen in Ireta's air."

Fordeliton made a deprecating sound and pinched his nostrils. Then leaned forward over his console as the pinnace began its descent to collect Varian. She was standing on the cliff top as the pinnace slid to a landing.

"The *ARCT*'s okay, Varian," Kai cried as soon as she entered. Her jubilation had to be cut short as Ford ordered her belted up for the run to the plateau. Kai repeated as much as he knew about the status of the *ARCT-10*, reliving his own immense relief in Varian's expressions of joy.

"But if the *ARCT* isn't even on its way to us, why this early morning call from Sassinak?" Varian asked.

"Thek," Ford replied succinctly.

"They've verified?" Lunzie asked.

"That's Sassinak's assumption, but the word arrived in typical Thek language. No details."

"Very interesting," Lunzie said. A note in her voice made both Kai and Varian stare at her. "Were Thek in evidence?"

"No change in the Bears," Ford said. "I take that back," he went on, suddenly alert. "They've moved!"

He flipped on the main screen in the pinnace, and they could all see the plateau. The cruiser and the transport had not moved, but Medium-Size Thek was gone from its sentry position near the cruiser's gangway, and the three Great-Big Thek were no longer just beyond the squat hulk of the transport. They were at the far end of the landing grid. The comunit buzzed.

"Fordeliton here. Yes, Commander. We just noticed the redisposition. Yes? Aye, aye, ma'am." He made a slight deviation in approach path. "I'm to deliver you there. Muhlah!" he cried as all the proximity alarms went off.

"Don't deviate!" Lunzie's cry was so authoritative Ford did not correct his flight path. But the pinnace shook as incoming Thek brushed past, speeding to join the others at the far end of the grid.

"What was that?" Varian demanded, aware of the near collision.

"Bonnard's horde of Thek," Kai replied, with considerable

irritation. Even Thek, or especially Thek, should follow ordinary flight safety procedures.

"What did they think they were doing just then?" Varian demanded, expressing a similar outrage.

"Preparing for a conference," Lunzie replied, and once again her tone was strained. Abruptly, she divested herself of the seat belts. "Can you slow down, Ford? Just Kai and Varian are called to this meeting?"

"No, the commander is, too, and," Ford now pointed to the viewscreen, "it looks like someone from the settlement *and* the transport have received invitations." Captain Cruss was plodding across the grid, and the two sleds, one from the cruiser and the other from the settlement, each with a single passenger, headed toward the Thek. "*Now* what are they doing?" Ford demanded in a perplexed tone.

He flipped up the magnification on the forward screen for a better view of the activity. The smaller Thek horde had not landed by the bigger ones. While some hovered, others began to attach themselves to the Great-Big Bears, defying gravity by creating an overhang. Suddenly the three Medium-Size Bears appeared. Two of them hovered as well, turning tapered ends down to fit themselves into the gaps between the biggest Thek.

"Yes, I was right," Lunzie said softly. "I've heard of this configuration, but I never thought to see one. It's a Thek conference!" Awe and amazement tinged the medic's voice. "Kai, Varian, if you're to remember more than just what they want you to know, I'd better buffer you."

"I don't understand," Kai said, glancing from the edifice the Thek were constructing to Lunzie's stern expression.

"Do you trust me?"

"Of course, and I trust the Thek, too. They've never done our species any harm."

Lunzie's mouth twitched in a wry smile. "You do know the opinion they have of us ephemerals, though? They subscribe to the 'need to know' school of information transmission. Frankly, I'd rather know all there is to know about what has been happening on Ireta that has broken out so many Thek. Wouldn't you?"

Kai had to concur with that.

"Well, then, I know three things about a Thek conference. One, they don't happen frequently—maybe once a century. Two, there is no way to elude complete disclosure during one. I don't even know how Thek delve into alien minds, but there is absolutely no doubt that they do." Lunzie's stern expression relaxed to the point of a reassuring nod. "You have nothing to fear, Kai. Your clear consciences and pure hearts will stand you in good stead now. The third point is that, considering the time generally spent within that Thek enclosure, the reports of participants confirm the fact that they remember relatively little of what actually occurred during the conference. In fact, only what concerned them in particular. I don't know if a mind buffer will help, but I think it's worth a try in these circumstances. Don't you?" She cocked her head, regarding Kai steadily.

"Lunzie has made three valid points," Ford said with a quiet earnestness that held a note of urgency. "And I'm going to have to land soon."

"I'm game," Varian said, straightening her shoulders and pointedly not looking at Kai.

"This conference is something you will *want* to remember, Kai, *in toto*," Lunzie added gently. "Once in a while, we ephemerals need a break. It's no disloyalty to the Thek, you know."

With a sharp nod of his head, Kai agreed, despite some lingering reluctance. He couldn't have said why he resisted what was eminently a sensible precaution because he most emphatically wanted to know exactly what had been happening on Ireta. Especially if the *ARCT-10* had reported in and could very well be on its way to retrieve the expedition.

"Relax," Lunzie said, "clear your mind of thought, breathe slowly and deeply, ready to enter trance."

Unlike a barrier situation, Lunzie merely reinforced commands originally implanted during the training Varian and Kai had received as Disciples, intended to prevent post-hypnotic suggestions. She finished the buffering just as Fordeliton brought the pinnace down, a slight distance from the towering Thek edifice. A narrow aisle remained between two of the Great-Big Thek while the Medium-Size Thek hovered. The smallest Thek which had not fit into the roof of the building had locked themselves against the sides like flying buttresses. A cathedral! Yes, Kai decided—that's what the structure resembles, and a suitable reverence suffused him.

Sassinak and Aygar descended from their sleds, the young Iretan looking at the Thek structure with outright suspicion. "Why have they done that?" he asked Varian, then looked almost accusingly at Kai. "What's going on? Why was I compelled to come?"

"The Thek are about to tell you," Sassinak replied.

"Then why don't they get on with it? Why do they need to build a monument?" He made a derisive gesture toward the edifice.

"You've been accorded a unique honor, young man," Lunzie said, aware of Kai's growing antagonism.

"Lately, I seem to be the recipient of many I could well do without." Aygar's supercilious glance swept them all, resting finally on the massive figure of Captain Cruss. "What's the matter with him? He shouldn't have trouble walking on this planet."

His comment caused the others to turn and look at the heavy-worlder whose gait was, indeed, curious. He seemed to be leaning slightly backward and his legs moved only from the knee in an oddly constricted gait.

"I don't think he approves of this meeting any more than you do, Aygar." Lunzie smiled mirthlessly. "But he's attending it, will he or won't he."

Captain Cruss was near enough now for the expression on his face to be visible: one of furious indignation and resistance. It could also be seen that he wasn't walking, he was being transported just above ground level and all the time trying to reach the ground to dig in his heels.

"A little help from a friendly Thek would have saved *us* a lot of trouble, wouldn't it?" Lunzie remarked to Sassinak, her eyes sparkling with delight at the heavy-worlder's predicament. "Will you be able to remember the proceedings?" she asked the commander.

"My memory will be clear, I assure you. Come, we are all here now. It would be impolite to keep our hosts waiting."

With a grin, Sassinak took Aygar by the arm and strode boldly into the Thek monument. The unwilling Captain Cruss brought up the rear. The instant he passed the portal, it closed with a soft thunk.

"Cathedral" is quite appropriate, Kai thought, appraising his bizarre surroundings. The illumination of the interior enhanced that choice.

"Is Tor here?" Varian asked Kai in a subdued voice.

"I hope so," Kai murmured, scanning the individual triangles of Thek making up the ceiling. Thin lines of light defining the various parts of the whole abruptly closed. Yet there was no appreciable darkening.

"I think they located their ancient Thek," Sassinak said, also speaking in a low voice. She pointed to the far side. Kai now distinguished the outline of an object lying on the ground. It seemed to be a collection of porous shards, a dull, dark, charcoal gray rather than the usual Thek obsidian. "And if that is indeed a very ancient Thek, we ephemerals will have to revise some favorite theories . . . and some jokes."

Kai wasn't sure her levity was appropriate; nevertheless he felt oddly reassured by her comment.

"Commander, I demand an explanation of the outrageous treatment to which I have been subjected," Captain Cruss cried, his heavy voice reverberating so loudly that the others winced.

"Don't be stupid, Cruss." Sassinak pivoted on her heel to face the huge man. "You know perfectly well the Thek are a law unto themselves. And you are now subject to that law, and about to sample its justice."

It occurred to Kai that they had inadvertently fallen into a triangular pattern themselves: Cruss at one apex, Aygar at another, himself and Varian at the third while Sassinak was at the center. That was the last observation he had time to make for the Thek began to speak.

"We have verified." The statement was a shock to Kai, not for its content for he had assumed that was why this extraordinary meeting had been convened, but because the statement was a full sentence, and because the sound which provided the sentence seemed to move about the inner walls in syllables. "Ireta is for Thek as it has been for hundreds of millions of years. It will remain Thek. For these reasons . . ."

A curious note sounded in Kai's mind at that point, but he had control enough only to notice that Varian was similarly affected and then conscious thought was impossible as a white sound enveloped them all.

20

A GROAN restored Kai to his surroundings, a groan he echoed for his skull pounded with an intensity that surpassed any previous affliction. He was aware of other discomforts, a suffocating heat, of being drenched with sweat and unable to focus his eyes. These discomforts were understandable for the sun was directly over their heads. It had rained heavily and recently to judge by the fetid humidity and the rusty mud surrounding the depressed triangle of dry ground on which they reeled. Varian was clinging to Kai, blinking to focus her eyes, and Sassinak was leaning against Aygar. On the ground crouched Cruss in an attitude of such dejection that Kai felt a detached pity for the heavy-worlder.

"Commander Sassinak!" Fordeliton's glad cry roused them from their stupor. "Commander!" He rushed toward them, Lunzie and Florasse right behind him. "You're all right? You've been in that conference for four-and-a-half hours!"

"Conference?" Sassinak frowned.

"Don't expect sense from them now, Ford!" Lunzie paused to look in each face before she took Varian and Kai by the arm and gestured Ford to assist his commander. "Let's just get them out of this sun."

"What did those Thek do?" Florasse demanded. She was looking not at Aygar but at the pathetically crumbled transport captain.

"Exactly what he deserved, I suspect," Lunzie replied.

"Aygar?" Florasse turned the Iretan by the arm, giving him a little shake. "He's in shock."

"Quite likely. Get him in out of the sun. He could probably use a stimulant, but he'll be himself in an hour or two."

"But what's happened to them?" Florasse stared with growing anxiety at the bowed Captain Cruss.

"They've been in a Thek conference, an unusual experience. Aygar will tell you what's pertinent when he recovers. Now, get him out of the sun, woman. C'mon, Ford!" Lunzie led the way to the pinnace.

In the relief provided by the relatively cool darkness of the little ship, the three people visibly relaxed.

"Shouldn't you give them something?" Fordeliton asked anxiously as he swung the pinnace toward the cruiser.

"I will when we get back to the ship. Some of that Sverulan brandy would go down a treat, I'm sure."

"Did your buffering work?"

"I don't want to put it to the test just yet."

Taking her hint, Ford lifted the pinnace for the short flight back to the cruiser. By the time he had landed, Sassinak thanked him, rose and calmly walked out of the pinnace and up the gangway to the cruiser. With equal calm and slight smiles on their faces, Kai and Varian followed her. Fordeliton hastened after them while Lunzie, able to smile now that her friends were recovering, brought up the rear. With no hesitation, Sassinak led the way to her quarters. There she made straight to her desk, taking her seat and swiveling in a fluid motion to her console.

"Pendelman? Recall the Wefts from the heavy-world transport. Secure all patrols. That ship will be taking off shortly."

Then Sassinak swung about, blinking uncertainly. With an exclamation of impatience, Lunzie looked at Fordeliton.

"Where does she keep her liquor?"

Fordeliton opened a cabinet near him, brought out a bottle and glasses. Lunzie poured hefty shots and handed them around. Then she motioned for Ford to pour drinks for them.

"We could use a jolt, too, after all this excitement." Then she lifted her glass. "To the survivors!"

Responding automatically, Sassinak, Varian, and Kai drank, emptying their glasses. The stimulant took immediate effect. Color came back into their faces and their expressions regained their old liveliness.

"Well, now, my friends, what have you to *report*?" Lunzie asked, heavily stressing the last word.

Sassinak frowned slightly, looking with surprise at the glass in her hand, at the others seated opposite her. Kai sank deeply into his chair, almost dropping his brandy glass while Varian, recognizing what she had in her hand, took a healthy swig, looked to Fordeliton for a refill. He quickly passed the

bottle about. Then they all began to talk at once, abruptly recalled their manners, and fell silent until Sassinak chuckled.

"Can I assume from your reactions that the buffering
worked?" Lunzie asked.

"It did, indeed, respected ancestor," Sassinak said. "I did
recall the patrols and the Wefts, didn't I, Ford? Good, that
was, I believe, my first order. Did Cruss survive?"

"Barely!"

Sassinak chuckled. "He took quite a beating." Her fingers
gingerly touched her temples. "We all did."

"Despite our clear consciences and pure hearts," Varian
added with a sly grin at Lunzie.

Sassinak depressed the comunit button. "Pendelman, request Lieutenant Commander Dupaynil to join us. And didn't
we just get exactly the information we needed. Cruss spilled
his guts. Not that I blame him."

"Then you know who's behind the piracy?"

"Oh yes." Sassinak smiled beatifically. "I'll wait until Dupaynil gets here. Kai and Varian have been covered with
glory, too. Which is only fair."

"Yes, apparently we rescued Ger in the nick of time." Kai
took up the account, grinning broadly. "Ger was the Thek left
here as a guardian—"

"This planet's a zoo, Lunzie. A sanctuary for the dinosaurs.
The Thek have been stocking it for millennia—even before
the cataclysm," Varian broke in excitedly. "Trizein, and all the
other buffs were right, the critters are from Mesozoic Terra."

"Ger was caught in a massive earthquake," Kai said, "and
buried so deeply that it was unable to summon help. It had
all but exhausted its substance when the Thek started looking
for it."

"You see," Varian went on, "the Thek surveyed Old Terra
eons ago and were entranced by the dinosaurs. Long before
the animals were threatened with extinction by a climatic cataclysm, they had imported them to Ireta which they knew

would permanently provide the proper environment. The Thek even *brought* the Rift grasses for the dinosaurs since Ireta has no natural vitamin A. Dinosaurs are Thek pets."

"Suitable combination, I expect," remarked Lunzie. "Both have insatiable appetites."

"Dimenon was exactly right when he said the Thek were gorging themselves. They were!" Varian said with a crow of laughter.

"Originally Ireta was slated to be a Thek feeding ground," Kai said, taking up the tale again, "because of all that raw energy being released after every good earthquake or tectonic shift. That's why those old cores had been put down. Ger was in the process of digging them up. By the strangest coincidence, the old core we first uncovered was actually close to Ger when the *quake* trapped it. There's a Thek dating device on those cores, and when the Thek ingested them, that's what they were looking for. But the searchers were having a free meal at the same time. Young Thek, especially, have to be closely supervised or they'll strip a planet!"

"What!" Lunzie half rose from her chair while the three who had endured the Thek conference favored her with smug expressions. "You can't possibly imply that? . . ."

"That's my interpretation, Lunzie," Sassinak agreed. "We got *comprehensive*, *Thekian* explanations though what we were supposed to remember related only to our personal involvement in this adventure. Part of the explanation was a large wedge of Thek history." She gave Fordeliton a stern look. "Which, if you value your rank and role as a Disciple, Lieutenant Commander, had best remain locked in your head. In their youth as a species, the Thek were driven into space by their insatiable appetites to discover planets which would supply their need for raw energy. They find the transuranics especially succulent. Even then, fortunately, they had a regard for developing species. Otherwise, a planet with no emerging life-forms would be reduced to bare rock by Thek hungers."

"The Thek are the *Others*," Lunzie gasped.

"That is the inescapable conclusion," Sassinak agreed. "Thek are nothing if not logical. It became apparent in a millennium that, if they couldn't curtail their appetites, they ran the risk of eating themselves out of the galaxy."

"No wonder they have an affinity for dinosaurs," Fordeliton exclaimed with a whoop of laughter.

"We may all be grateful that the dinosaurs did not evolve into space travelers," Sassinak replied.

"And grateful, too, that the Thek have preserved them. But what will happen now?"

Varian beamed. "Because we are ephemerals, short-lived and vulnerable, we would not make the mistake the Thek did, in leaving only one guardian . . ."

"You mean, zoo keeper," Kai said.

"So I have the option to stay on Ireta," and Varian's expression was tinged with awe, "as a planetary protector. I can study the giffs, all the dinosaurs, and even the fringes if I feel like it. I may have as much staff as I require." She turned to Kai expectantly, her eyes twinkling. "Tell 'em your good news, Kai."

Kai grinned shyly. "Ireta is restricted, of course, as far as the transuranics go, but I, and my 'ilk,' as they put it, have the right to mine anything up to the transuranics for . . . is it as long as *we* live? I'm not sure if the limit is just *my* lifetime."

"No," said Lunzie. "By ilk, the Thek probably mean the *ARCT-10* for as long as it survives. You deserve it, Kai. You really do."

"Curiously enough," Sassinak said into the respectful pause that followed, "the Thek did appreciate the fact that you all have lost irreplaceable time. In doing so, of course, you set up the circumstances which retrieved the lost Ger and the forgotten planet. Thek justice is unusual."

"What about Aygar and the other Iretans?"

Varian shot a quick glance at Kai, whose expression was of

resigned disapproval. "The Thek lumped all humans in one group as survivors. In a sense, that's correct. Aygar plans to stay."

"He made that plain, Thek or not." Kai's tone held grudging respect.

"And the Thek will permit a limited support group for us and however many of Aygar's Iretans plan to remain."

"I wonder if some of them might consider enlisting in the Fleet," Sassinak mused. "Wefts are excellent guards, but Ireta produced some superb physical types. Ford, do see if we can recruit a few."

"Tanegli?" Lunzie asked.

"Mutiny cannot be excused, nor the mutineer exonerated," Sassinak answered, her expression stern. "He is to be taken back to Sector Headquarters to stand trial. The Thek were as adamant on that score as I am."

"And Cruss is being sent back?" asked Ford.

Sassinak steepled her fingers, a satisfied smile playing at the corners of her mouth. "Not only sent back but earthed for good. Neither he, nor his crew, nor even any of the cryo passengers will ever leave their planet. Nor will their transport lift again."

"The Thek do nothing by halves, do they?"

"They have been exercised—if you can imagine a Thek agitated," Sassinak went on, "about the planetary pirates and patiently waiting for *us* to do something constructive about the problem. The intended rape of Ireta has forced them, with deep regret, to interfere." A polite rap on the door interrupted her. At her response, Dupaynil opened the door, surveying the group quickly. "On cue, for I have good news for you, Commander. Names, only one of which was familiar to me." She beckoned the Intelligence officer to take a seat as she leaned forward to type information on the terminal. "Parchandri is so conveniently placed for this sort of operation . . ."

"Inspector General Parchandri?" Fordeliton exclaimed, his expression shocked.

"The same."

Lunzie chuckled cynically. "It makes sense to have a conspirator placed high in Exploratory, Evaluation, and Colonization. He'd know exactly which planetary plums were ready to be plucked."

Kai and Varian regarded her with stunned expressions.

"Who else, Sassinak?" Lunzie asked.

The commander looked up from the visual display with a smug smile. "The Sek of Fomalhaut is a Federation Councillor of Internal Affairs. One now understands just how his private fortune was accrued. Lutpostig appears to be the Governor of Diplo, a heavy-worlder planet. How convenient! Paraden, it will not surprise you to discover, owns the *company* which supplied the grounded transport ship."

"Doubtless others in his fleet will meet the same fate," Lunzie said.

"We could never have counted on uncovering duplicity at that level, Commander," was Dupaynil's quiet assessment. He frowned slightly. "It strikes me as highly unusual for a man at Cruss's level to know such names."

"He didn't," Sassinak replied equably. "He was only vaguely aware that Commissioner Paraden was involved. The Thek extrapolated from what he could tell them of recruitment procedures, suppliers, and what they evidently extracted from the transport's data banks."

"And how can we use the information they obtained?"

"With great caution, equal duplicity and superior cunning, Dupaynil, and undoubtedly some long and ardent discussions with the Sector Intelligence Bureau. Fortunately, for my hypersuspicious nature, I've known Admiral Coromell for years and trust him implicitly. However, knowing where to look for one's culprits is more than half the battle, even those so highly placed."

"You will keep us informed of your progress, won't you?" Lunzie asked wistfully.

"By reliable homing capsule," Sassinak replied, but her grin quickly faded into regret. "I have been given sailing orders, too. So, Fordeliton, brush up on your eloquence and see whom you can recruit from among the Iretans. Kai, Varian, Lunzie, if you need any more supplies to tide you over until the *ARCT-10* arrives, it will be my pleasure to oblige. Just have them loaded into the pinnace. I'll have Borander deliver you back to your camp. Just one more thing—" Sassinak swiveled her chair about, fingering the digital lock on a cabinet behind her. She extracted first one, then with a shrug of her shoulders, two more of the distinctive square bottles of Sverulan brandy. "Clean glasses, please, Ford, for I've a toast to propose."

Glasses were found, generously filled with brandy. Sassinak rose to her feet, the others followed suit.

"To the brave, ingenious, and honored survivors of this planet! Including the dinosaurs!"

Don't miss this exciting new
novel from **Anne McCaffrey**
and her son **Todd McCaffrey**

DRAGON'S KIN
A New Novel of Pern

Young Kindan has no expectations other
than joining his father in the mines of
Camp Natalon, a coal-mining settlement
far from safety and civilization. Then disaster strikes and in one terrible instant,
Kindan loses his family and the camp
loses its watch-wher, a creature uniquely
suited to specialized work in the dark,
cold mineshafts.

Grieving, Kindan finds a measure of
solace in a new friendship with Nuella, a
mysterious girl no one seems to know
exists. It is Nuella who assists Kindan
when he is selected to hatch and train a
new watch-wher, a job that forces him to
give up his dream of becoming a Harper;
and it is Nuella who helps him give new
meaning to his life.

Published by Del Rey
Available wherever books are sold

Don't miss this wonderful new omnibus edition from **Anne McCaffrey**

ON DRAGONWINGS

Three thrilling Pern novels in one beautiful new volume!

Perfect for long-time fans as well as readers discovering McCaffrey for the first time, this dazzling new volume features three classic novels from the early years of Pern—Dragonsdawn, Dragonseye, and Moreta.

"Few are better [than McCaffrey] at mixing elements of high fantasy and hard science fiction."
—*The New York Times Book Review*

Published by Del Rey Books
www.delreydigital.com
Available wherever books are sold

Visit www.delreydigital.com— the portal to all the information and resources available from Del Rey Online.

• Read sample chapters of every new book, special features on selected authors and books, news and announcements, readers' reviews, browse Del Rey's complete online catalog, and more.

• Sign up for the Del Rey Internet Newsletter (DRIN), a free monthly publication e-mailed to subscribers, featuring descriptions of new and upcoming books, essays and interviews with authors and editors, announcements and news, special promotional offers, signing/convention calendar for our authors and editors, and much more.

To subscribe to the DRIN: send a blank e-mail to join-ibd-dist@list.randomhouse.com or sign up at www.delreydigital.com

The DRIN is also available at no charge for your PDA devices—go to www.randomhouse.com/partners/avantgo for more information, or visit www.avantgo.com and search for the Books@Random channel.

 www.delreydigital.com